CW00349328

Strictly Between Us

JANE FALLON

PENGUIN BOOKS

PENGUIN BOOKS

UK | USA | Canada | Ireland | Australia
India | New Zealand | South Africa

Penguin Books is part of the Penguin Random House group of companies
whose addresses can be found at global.penguinrandomhouse.com.

First published 2016

018

Copyright © Jane Fallon, 2016

The moral right of the author has been asserted

Set in 12.75/14.5pt Garamond MT
Typeset by Palimpsest Book Production Limited,
Falkirk, Stirlingshire
Printed in Great Britain by Clays Ltd, St Ives plc

A CIP catalogue record for this book is available from the British Library

PAPERBACK ISBN : 978–1–405–91767–4
OM PAPERBACK ISBN : 978–1–405–91771–1

www.greenpenguin.co.uk

PART ONE

I

'I should get going,' Patrick says. I'm hardly going to argue.

I pull my red hoody on. Zip it up. Cross my arms to form a barrier.

Patrick is adjusting his clothing too. We are both looking everywhere but at each other. To be honest I can't get him out of the flat fast enough. He's fumbling about with his shoes and I have to stop myself from leaning over and helping him tie his laces. Keeping my distance is probably a good idea at this point.

'Michelle . . .' He stops himself, but the word hangs there like a flag fluttering in the breeze.

'Of course.'

I should explain. Michelle is my best friend. Has been for twenty-odd years. More even. Twenty-five. Patrick is her husband.

And what just happened was a terrible mistake.

For the sake of my own sanity I have decided I am going to make a Bill Clinton-esque distinction. 'I did not have sex with that man.' Yes, there were tongues and hands and heavy breathing involved. Clothing rearranged. Sound effects worthy of a cheap porno. OK, so I had sex with him. But, thankfully we stopped short. Came to our senses before we – technically – went all the way. It's not much of a consolation, but at the moment it's all I've got.

Pretty much the worst thing I could ever do, I think you'll agree.

But it's not how it sounds. Actually, if you look at the bare facts I suppose it is. Strictly speaking it happened. It's just that it wasn't meant to. I didn't set out to do it and, I'm fairly certain, neither did he. There was no big seduction, no making eyes across their distressed oak kitchen table the last time I spent the evening round at theirs and Michelle turned away to pour us both another glass of wine.

It's not like I've ever even thought about it. Never had a guilty fantasy that left me unable to look Michelle in the eye the next day. Not since before they met anyway. It simply didn't occur to me to view Patrick in that way. He was – is – my best friend's husband, end of story. And yet here we are, at a quarter past seven on a mundane workday Tuesday evening, entwined on my cream sofa with bits of my clothing where they shouldn't be, and I'm trying to make sense of what just occurred. But my mind is fogged by the wine I've drunk and the enormity of what just happened.

'Shit,' I say.

'I know,' Patrick mutters. Who says the art of conversation is dead?

I feel as if I should say something profound, but I can't find the words that would be adequate for the momentousness of the occasion. I want to tell him this isn't like me, I'm not the kind of person who would ever do what we have just done, but apparently that's exactly who I am now. I'm that woman. So I keep quiet. Wait. Maybe he can make some sense of it.

4

On the scale of how meaningful things are, this rates higher than the day I set up my own production company. Or when I first got Ron, my rescue fox terrier/Jack Russell/something-hairy cross (who I now notice is sitting in a corner of the room staring at me judgementally, his big sad eyes letting me know that I've let him down in a hundred more ways than even I can imagine). Or the time one of the shows my company makes got nominated for an award. OK, so it was for Best Sound Editing, which is hardly prestigious, and the awards were the Television Technical Awards, which no one has ever heard of, and in the end it didn't even win, but still, that was a good day in the office.

Today will not go down in history as such a good day.

I feel the need to explain myself. To go back to the beginning and try to put into words how I ended up here. I know I started out with good intentions – which is the story of my life, by the way. I meant well. Michelle needed my help and I have never not been there to help her. At least I thought she needed my help. Maybe that was my first mistake. Lesson One: leave well alone. You really don't need to interfere, to take over and try to sort out someone else's life for them.

But that's the way it's always been. I'm the decisive one, the doer. Michelle is more easy-going. She's happy for me to take charge.

I'm completely aware that my need to create order in other people's lives is some kind of diversion from the fact that my own personal life is chaotic, to say the least. It's the waving handkerchief that's meant to ensure you don't notice the magician is palming your card. I've left a string of disastrous relationships in my wake. Sometimes it's me, sometimes it's them. Actually, technically, it's always me because I could avoid the bad ones if I wanted to, but convincing me of the merits of that would be like trying to persuade a heroin addict that he would be better off having a nice cup of tea.

Nothing I have ever done comes close to this though. I've never been a husband-stealer. Not my worst enemy's, let alone my best friend's.

'You won't tell her, will you?' I turn back to Patrick who half raises an eyebrow at me.

'No. Of course not,' he says and I breathe a small sigh of relief, although I didn't really think he was going to suggest Face Timing her right now and staging a re-enactment.

Anyway, back to my attempt to justify the unjustifiable. Here goes.

Give me a chance.

At least hear me out.

2

Let me fill in the basics first. Don't worry, I'm not going to bore you with my whole life history or the long drawn-out story of my immediate family (happy, nuclear, youngest of three, just in case you're interested). I'll stick to the essentials. My name is Tamsin Elizabeth Fordham, I'm a thirty-eight-year-old executive producer and co-founder of a small and not particularly glamorous TV company, mortgage-holder of a two-bedroom flat in Belsize Park, owner of a small dog, all my own teeth.

Castle Productions specializes in afternoon property shows. Long-running series where people buy houses. We produce various versions: about-to-be-divorcees having to look for two homes for the price of their one; newly-weds wanting their first nest; one where we help find both a house and a job for would-be relocators. It's basically the same programme with a slight tweak here and there. They're very popular and extremely cheap to make. Consequently we are doing well. Financially that is. We're hardly setting the arts world alight.

In context you can see why we were all so excited about the Best Sound Editing nomination. Some companies have an award shelf in their meeting room. A shrine to their success. We don't even have a meeting room. Usually we all cram into one of our offices. If there are more than six people involved we go to the pub next door.

There are two of us who run the place. Me and my partner Ian. Ian used to be my boss, and we set up together about four years ago. It works. We get on well, but not so well that we feel the need to intertwine our lives too much outside of the office. Ian is married with five kids, and he and his wife Fiona always invite me to the big events but, thankfully, are completely understanding whenever I decline. I'm not very good with all that happy-families stuff.

Then there's Anne Marie, who looks after the business side of things – the contracts and the accounts, all the fun bits. She's a bit older, early sixties, and she takes care of us all whether we like it or not. She's a big baker (I blame Paul Hollywood) and most days she brings in trays of biscuits or cupcakes that she's rustled up the night before. Which is very sweet. No one ever eats them, though. Not because we're all watching our weight, but because they're usually rock hard and taste of little more than burnt sugar. I've wondered before if she has a side business as a dentist and she's just trying to drum up trade.

There are three assistants. Lucy, who works for Ian, is a bit of a stroppy cow but he likes her efficiency. Watching her organize paper clips on her desk I always feel she would have made a great Nazi officer. There's Ashley, who sits at the reception desk but also does all the general stuff – answers the phones and does admin for Anne Marie. She's . . . I don't know, she's one of the few people in the world I have absolutely no opinion of. She's not been with us long, seems to be doing OK. She hasn't done anything to piss me off yet, anyway.

And then there's my right-hand woman, Bea. I love

Bea. I have absolutely no idea what I would do without Bea. I would marry Bea if she were a man. Actually, I'd marry her anyway if she'd have me.

And that's it. That's our little work family.

Our headquarters in trendy but cheap West London oasis Brook Green consist of two floors above a shop selling vintage home furnishings. Reception, where Ashley sits behind a desk opposite a sofa and two chairs, a smaller room housing Bea and Lucy, and the kitchen on the first floor. An office each for Ian, Anne Marie and myself on the second. Loo on the landing.

We are small but perfectly formed.

Outside of work it's just me and Ron – through choice I should add. The day that I realized I was earning enough to be able to kick my lodger out of the spare room was right up there with nomination day. I am what they call 'selectively single' at the moment. Every now and then I stick a toe back in the water, sign up for some dating site or other and spend a few miserable nights out before deciding I am better off as I am.

One of these days I guess I'd like to meet someone and settle down, get a house and a girlfriend for Ron. But I'm not in any rush. I'm definitely not going to plump for any old person just for the sake of having a partner. And as for kids, forget it. They have never been on my radar.

Michelle, on the other hand, has been struck down with a serious case of broody-itis for years. When she and Patrick got married she could hardly wait to get pregnant (doing it the other way round would have been as alien to Michelle as putting her socks on over her shoes). But

9

Patrick wanted to wait. They had all the time in the world, he said. They should focus on their careers for a few years, give themselves a solid foundation.

'What's the point of having kids and not being able to provide for them?' he said when the subject came up at dinner one night.

'Or you can provide for them but you never see them because you're working all hours to try and get yourself established at work?'

Michelle shrugged. 'We'd work it out.'

I tried to stay neutral. Patrick was having none of that, though.

'Tamsin knows I'm making sense. Don't you?' He turned to me and I muttered incoherently into my forkful of mashed potato.

'I just don't want to leave it too late, that's all,' Michelle said.

'You're thirty-six!' Patrick said exasperatedly. This was a couple of years ago. 'Women are having babies when they're fifty now.'

I snorted into my drink and even Michelle laughed. 'Name me one woman who's had a baby at fifty.'

'What do you mean, name one? Of course I can't name one. But I've read about it.'

'Ah!' I said, relieved the conversation was about to take a lighter tone. 'Patrick's been reading the *Sport* again. MIRACLE BABY BORN TO POST-MENOPAUSAL WOMAN.'

'WOMAN GIVES BIRTH TO OWN GRANDCHILD,' Michelle said, and we both dissolved into fits.

'OK, OK. Point taken. Maybe not fifty.'

'I just don't want to leave it late and then find out it's

not straightforward, that's all,' Michelle said, serious again as she spooned more broccoli onto my plate despite my holding up a hand to say I didn't want it. 'What if it takes me ages to get pregnant once we start trying . . .'

Patrick put a hand over hers. 'We won't leave it too late, I promise. Just not quite yet.'

Now, though, Michelle's broodiness has reached critical mass. She feels as if the clock is ticking fast. Mostly because she wants to have at least three. Patrick is blissfully unaware of this fact.

Michelle and I met on the bus home from school. I'd seen her around, of course. We were in the same year but different forms, so we only crossed over in Maths, where we both languished in the lowest but one stream. We'd never spoken, though. In retrospect I realized she was shy. At the time I think I thought she was a bit of a goody-goody so I just didn't bother.

Anyway, I was on the bus home one afternoon. Michelle was sitting a few seats in front of me, head in a book as always. A couple of girls from the year above were sat behind her, messing about, being loud. I recognized them and, if I'm being totally honest, I was a bit scared of one of them – Lisa – because she was known to be something of a psycho. So I kept my head down, pretended to be engrossed in my geography homework.

After a couple of minutes they went a bit quiet and that made me look up. Psycho Lisa was wielding a pair of nail scissors and she had hold of one of Michelle's blonde plaits. She was sawing through it doggedly. At first I thought Michelle hadn't noticed so, I'm ashamed to admit,

I decided the best thing to do was to pretend it wasn't happening. But then I noticed a red flush creeping up the back of her neck. She knew exactly what they were doing, she was just too scared to say anything.

I'd love to say I stormed over, confronted Lisa and her henchman and they broke down and said sorry, promising never to bully anyone ever again. Of course I didn't, I was as frightened of them as Michelle clearly was, and I didn't want them turning their attentions on to me. Instead I got up, rang the bell, breezed up the bus as nonchalantly as I could, gurning a big smile, and slapped Michelle on the shoulder matily.

'Hey!'

The sawing stopped – I was sure only momentarily – and I could feel Lisa's mad-cow eyes boring into me, but I kept my gaze firmly on the prize and didn't even acknowledge that I'd seen her.

'I'm getting off here and going into town, want to come? There's a sale at Warehouse apparently.'

I practically hauled her out of her seat and along the aisle to the stairs before she could say anything like, 'Who the hell are you?' To be fair, I kind of knew that, given the choice between getting off the bus and pursuing her prey – which would have meant walking – or being dropped off at the stop right in front of her house, Lisa was always going to go for the option of least exertion. She wasn't known (only behind her back, of course) as Lumpy Lisa for nothing.

'You saved my life.' Michelle gave me a look that I imagine a puppy might give you when you've pulled it up from the depths of a deep dark well, where it has been quietly starving for a week. I think I became instantly addicted to that look, I won't lie. It was like the crack of the looks world.

'They're just stupid,' I said, embarrassed at being elevated to hero status so quickly. 'You don't have to come to Warehouse with me, by the way. I don't even know if there really is a sale on . . .'

But Michelle had already linked her arm through mine. 'Let's go and have a look anyway. I'll buy you a Coke to say thanks.'

And the rest, as they say, is history.

3

After Bus-gate Michelle and I were inseparable through school. We even lived together after we left college, until we each bought our own tiny places in a fit of would-be-grown-up, late-twenty-something angst. We had both landed in our chosen careers young – me in television, Michelle in marketing – so by this point we were starting to earn enough to crawl onto the bottom of the property ladder with the help of 100 per cent mortgages, postage-stamp-size properties and areas where people weren't only scared to go out, they were scared to stay in.

The reason I ended up in the TV industry is down to her by the way. Or, really, her dad. I always thought it was the most glamorous thing ever that Mr Franklin – Julian as he eventually forced me to call him, even though I resisted as long as I could – worked for the BBC when we were growing up. I used to imagine his days filled with glamorous encounters with stars, long lunches and glasses of champagne. Of course, I know better now – apart from the long lunches that is. You try raising anyone at the BBC on the phone between midday and three thirty.

Anyway, to cut a long story short, by the time we were about to graduate he had moved to Channel 4. Michelle steadfastly refused the foot on the bottom rung that he offered her. She wanted to do something on her own, she said. She didn't want people to say she had only been offered a job because of who her dad was. I, on the other hand, didn't even think twice. It was hard enough to get a job as it was, let alone in an industry you would have killed to enter. Let them say I was nepotized. I couldn't have cared less.

'I'll do it,' I said.

Julian had looked a little taken aback.

'Oh. Would you like to?'

'I'd bite your arm off,' I said. 'Figuratively, of course.'

Miriam – Michelle's mum – had laughed. 'I should hope so.'

'All I can do is open the door,' Julian said. 'What you do after that will be up to you.'

'That's all I need. I won't let you down, honestly.'

So, I started as a gopher and, eventually and with Julian's blessing, worked my way up, moving on to bigger and better things. If he was disappointed that it was me and not his daughter who was his protégé he managed not to show it. Years later, when I told him I was setting up Castle, I saw his eyes go a little misty and I knew that he was proud of me.

Anyhow, the point of me telling you all this is that this is how I met Patrick. He works in TV, too, but as a commissioner. That means he sits in an office and decides who to give the company's money to. He's like one of the millionaires off *Dragon's Den*, but it's not even his own fortune he's playing with. These days he's the big boss at the Home Improvement Channel – a humungous fish in an extremely tiny unloved, slightly smelly pond – but when we met he was the deputy deputy assistant something or other at Channel 5 and I had gone in to pitch him an idea for a new series. I forget what it was now. He didn't go for it. He didn't even like it enough to pass it up to his bosses actually.

I have to confess that for a brief moment when we first met I fancied him. He fits my ideal physical profile. Tallish. Angular. Icy blue eyes. He's stupidly good looking. Stupidly in the sense that when you get over the initial impact it becomes very apparent very quickly that he's not in the least bit attractive. He's way too aware of his looks, of the power they have. He's a classic mirror watcher.

The tiny crush I had completely withered and died the day I went in for a second meeting with him a while later. I'd been looking forward to it. I was planning on batting my eyelashes at him across his desk. The office runner – a timid girl who was probably being paid expenses only for the privilege of the experience – had brought us coffee. Patrick took one sip of his and practically spat it out.

'God, that's disgusting,' he said, scowling.

The runner – who no doubt had a crush on him herself – looked crestfallen.

'Do you want me to make you another one?'

'Well, obviously,' he said imperiously. 'I'm not going to drink this shit.'

I was embarrassed, didn't know where to look. The runner went to pick up my mug, too, but I put my hand out to stop her.

'Mine's fine, thanks.'

Patrick snorted. 'Let her get you a new one. It's what she's for.'

No way was it possible to have a crush on that man after that.

When I saw him hone in on Michelle at an industry party – I had taken her as my plus one – I'd tried to warn her that he was a bit of an arsehole, but she was smitten in an instant. And to be fair, so was he. I had bumped into him with a series of perfect tiny blonde girlfriends by this point, so I should have known she'd be his ideal type. I bit my tongue. Rule number one of any good friendship: never criticize their choice of partner. They might end up marrying them. And, unfortunately, she did.

I've always thought she could have done better in all honesty. OK, so he's good looking, he's successful, he loves her. But he's a bit of – actually make that a lot of – a knob. I've seen that Little Prince side of him many times over the years. With waiters or shop assistants or cleaners. People he clearly thinks are beneath him. It's ugly but I suppose I've got used to it. God knows what that says about me. As for Michelle, she doesn't even seem to notice. Even five years on she's blinded by love.

Oh, and the reason Patrick ended up as one of the Home Improvement Channel's head honchos by the way? Michelle's dad, Julian. He's now the Chairman of a company that owns a whole slate of cable channels. He's Rupert Murdoch without the millions or the scandal. And who better to entrust one of those channels to than his beloved son-in-law? And why not? It's the next best thing to Michelle taking an interest. He knows he can rely on him. Knows he'll do a good job.

I still don't much like Patrick if I'm being honest ('Really?' I hear you shout. 'You've just had sex with him, haven't you?'). But he can be good company. He's funny. He's smart. He can just be a bit entitled. More than a little pleased with himself. He makes Michelle happy, though, and that's the main thing. And I've never questioned whether or not he loves her. Until recently that is. Recently I've started to have my doubts about him. Suspicions even.

And that's where this all started. Somehow my suspecting that he might be up to no good has led to him being up to no good. With me.

Fucked-up doesn't even come close.

So, Michelle and Patrick, happily married, blah blah blah. A couple of months ago, though, I picked up an odd whisper at work. Someone I was talking to about a new show idea that we were going to try and sell to the Home Improvement Channel made a joke about how we should send Lucy in to pitch it (Lucy is tall, thin, pretty and only twenty-six. Maybe this is the reason I dislike her so much).

'Patrick Mitchell'd probably commission it on the spot,' she said.

'What do you mean?' I asked, genuinely confused.

'He likes them young and pretty, apparently.'

I was so taken aback I didn't say anything at first and then, annoyingly, Ian rushed in saying, 'I'm sure that's not true, he's married to Tamsin's closest friend,' so I never got the chance to get to the bottom of it.

I dismissed it then because our business is full of rumour and gossip and you have to listen to every piece of news you're given through a hundred denier bullshit filter. Especially if it's about the commissioners. It's like any other line of work. People love to have a go at the bosses. I do it myself and then I have to remember that in my own small world I'm also a boss, so I try to curb myself.

Then it happened again. Different person, same sort of comment. And again. It started to become hard to ignore. I tried asking around, but everyone would clam up the moment they remembered that Patrick was my friend's husband. They would change the subject and start savaging another unsuspecting target. Someone I had no vested interest in. So, for a while I did nothing. To be honest I couldn't really believe it was true. Admittedly Patrick could be a bit of a flirt, but if you sentenced everyone on that basis then the cheaters' prison would be full to overflowing. Plus I always thought it came with the job. Networking, schmoozing, flirting, what's the difference really? It's all just a way of getting what you want.

So I tried to convince myself it was just idle speculation; there was no hard evidence to back any of it up. And besides, it was none of my business. Unfortunately that last argument really didn't resonate with me, but I kept repeating it to myself anyway. I put up a sign in my mind: KEEP OUT. Every time I got the urge to say something to Patrick or, God forbid, Michelle about what I'd heard I would try to visualize it. Sometimes with a little man hammering it into the ground.

I confided in Bea quite a lot at this time. Have I already told you how much I love Bea? She's hands down the best assistant I have ever had, and I've had a few. With a couple of them I ended up being way too matey, so in the end I could hardly bring myself to ask them to photocopy a document because I was so worried it would come across as demeaning. A couple of others brought out the cold, hard *Devil Wears Prada* ice queen in me. I have no idea why. One I was downright petrified of. The first few times I asked her to do something she pulled an expression that implied I'd suggested she clean the toilet with her bare hands, and after that I could barely get up the courage to talk to her. God knows what she did all day but it wasn't anything to do with me. She didn't last long. Of course I was too scared to fire her, so I bigged her up around the industry and eventually, mercifully, someone poached her. Good assistants are like gold dust.

With Bea, somehow, everything has fallen into place. Right from the moment she walked into the interview I knew we'd be a good fit. She didn't say 'Totes amazeballs' for a start, like the girl who was in before her. Nor did she announce that really she was just filling in time before she got a 'proper job'.

'Tried that,' she'd said, smiling expansively. 'I spent six years working in banking, comparing myself to my contemporaries, worrying about how quickly I could work my way up, and then I realized I hated everything about it. Now I just want to do something I think I'll enjoy and not even think about where it might lead later.'

'So why TV?' I had asked. One of my standard questions.

'It's creative. There's a product coming out at the end, not just another row of numbers. I like the idea of being part of a team all trying to achieve the same thing – even if I'm only a tiny part. I think it would be satisfying.'

It was a done deal before she even left the room. I actually chased her out to the lift and offered her the job on the spot after Anne Marie and I had quickly agreed we were never going to find anyone better.

The thing about Bea is that she's a grown-up. Yes, she's smart and could probably handle a more senior position, but she has the sense and maturity to realize that she doesn't have the experience yet. She's happy to do her time. Unlike a lot of the younger PAs I've had (Bea is thirty-one, the others ranged from twenty-three to twenty-eight, and I think those few years make all the difference) she understands that this isn't a race.

I don't even let myself think about what will happen when she decides to move on. I've asked her to let me know well in advance so that I can bring someone new in early and she can train them to be her clone. It's not going to happen for a while yet. When she started she told me she was happy to do what she was doing for three years and she's only just had her first anniversary. I'm already scheming about what position I could create that would make her stay and move up the ladder with us. For all I care she could have my job and I'd stay and work for her, that's how much I rate her.

I've always felt that I can ask her to do anything. At the beginning I kept it strictly to office business, but as we got to know each other better and she made it clear she was happy to look after every aspect of my life if I needed her to, I started to feel OK with her collecting my dry cleaning, making bikini-waxing appointments, once nipping round to my old flat to take Ron for a walk when I had to work late. When I went on a rare date a while ago she even went to Westfield and bought Spanx for me. Nothing is too much trouble. She never complains, never does that slight eye-roll thing that Lucy has down to a T whenever Ian asks her to go the extra mile. Her whole ethic is about making sure I'm supported and that any pressure that can be taken off me is taken off, leaving me to get on with my job.

Plus, we've become friends. We're allies. We often take twenty minutes out to have a coffee or a walk round Brook Green and chat about whatever's going on. She's become a great sounding board and I'd like to think I'm the same for her. She's very discreet. I never feel like I have to bite my tongue in case something I say ends up in the wrong hands. Like I said before, she's a grown-up.

So, it was inevitable that I would find myself confiding my fears about Patrick to her. She's never met him, but she knows his name, of course. There are only a handful of commissioners that we deal with – basically each of the broadcasters has one person who commissions all their factual entertainment programmes, and during their tenure they become the most important people for programme-makers like me to suck up to. Then they leave and go back to being one of us in an instant. Worse off often, if they've pissed off a lot of people during their reign. Instant karma.

We were huffing around Brook Green. My latest half-arsed attempt to get fit. This was my third day of bringing my trainers into work and attempting to 'power walk' for half an hour at lunchtime. Previous form dictated that after two more sessions I would forget I'd ever started. Bea had agreed to accompany me and was barely breaking a sweat while I was already regretting the fact that I hadn't brought a clean top to change into later.

'Don't listen to gossip' was the first thing that came out of her mouth.

'I don't. Not usually. It's hard to ignore when it's about a friend of yours, though.'

'Have you noticed how people almost always gossip upwards. Because they're jealous. Or they're bitter that they're still doing a shitty little job while someone else has done well for themselves.'

'I know. It's just that it's all on a similar theme. It feels like too much of a coincidence. Slow down a bit.'

She ignored my request. 'That's because every time someone passes on a piece of gossip they big it up. It makes them feel important. So then it spreads like a virus.'

I stopped. Seemingly for dramatic effect, but really so I could catch my breath. Trust me to start exercising when it was eighty degrees out.

'Shit. I wish I knew if there was any substance at all behind it.'

'Ignore it and it'll go away, that's my advice.'

'Just do me a favour and keep your ears open, will you? Everyone clams up when they realize he's married to my best friend.'

'OK,' Bea said, setting off again. I fell in beside her. 'But I still say you shouldn't listen to any of it.'

'I know. I won't. I just want to know what "it" is.'

Since then she's reluctantly reported back the odd thing but, of course, none of it's substantiated. All along the same lines: Patrick Mitchell can't resist an attractive woman.

Meanwhile, I couldn't help but look at him a bit differently. I'd notice a flirty gesture. It started to bother me how often Michelle would suggest I come over or we go out, because Patrick was at some do or other. I know there's a certain amount of socializing that comes with his job, but I got it into my head that he was making up excuses to go out without Michelle tagging along. See, this is the problem with gossip and conjecture: it makes you misinterpret every little gesture. Patrick wasn't being any different to usual but suddenly everything had a significance. And I got a little bit obsessed, I won't lie. I felt as if I had to protect Michelle like I've always protected her. I couldn't be myself when I saw them together any more.

I know it's not easy to see how I got from this state of righteous indignation to having sex with him myself. Of course it isn't. It makes no sense to me either. But the next thing that happened was what galvanized me into action.

Bea and I were eating lunch in my office, chatting idly about nothing much in particular.

'You didn't get a chance to ask around about Patrick Mitchell, did you?' I asked when we'd exhausted our other conversation. I hadn't wanted to put Bea on the spot, but I'd been dying to find out if there was any fresh news.

Bea was quiet.

'What?' I said. 'What's happened?'

'It's probably not true,' Bea said, taking a big bite out of her brie and cranberry baguette. That woman never seems to need to watch what she eats.

I felt my throat go dry. 'Tell me.'

Bea sighed. 'I asked around a bit like you told me, which was probably a stupid thing to do.'

'Oh shit,' I said. I knew whatever was coming wasn't going to be good.

'There's some story about him and a woman who works in HR. How they had a thing for a while . . .'

'How does everyone supposedly know this, that's what I don't understand?'

'She told people apparently. So the story goes he didn't behave very well.'

'And it's over now?' I said, clutching at straws that maybe – if it was even true – Patrick had just had a quick mid-life crisis and then immediately seen sense.

'I think so, but . . . sorry . . . I don't get the impression she was the first, though.'

I felt my heart pound on the inside of my ears, as if it was trying to escape. 'If I find out he's cheating on her . . . honestly, I'll fucking kill him.'

Bea gave me an exasperated look. 'Yes, that'd help.'

'You know what I mean.'

'So, let's think about the worst-case scenario.' Bea is ever the pragmatist. 'Michelle finally gets pregnant. It's all true. Patrick runs off with whoever and she ends up a single mother.'

'Oh God,' I said, putting my tuna and salad sandwich down. I couldn't even think about eating it now.

'So are millions of women . . .'

'This is Michelle, though. For her it's all part of the fairy tale. I can guarantee she has never factored in for a second that she might bring her kids up on her own.'

'Well . . . what if Patrick died? Or, I don't know, got run over on the way home or something. Then she'd have to.'

'It's not the same,' I said, although it was hard to explain why.

25

'It's 2015,' Bea said, as if that made a world of difference.

'You don't know her. She doesn't just want to have a baby for the sake of having a baby. She wants a perfect family. A mum, a dad, three kids, a dog.'

Bea shrugged. 'Then maybe Patrick Mitchell's not the person she should have settled down with. Because it doesn't seem to me like he wants any of those things.'

I picked up my tuna and salad again. Took a large bite. 'Exactly.'

4

A couple of days after my conversation with Bea, Michelle and I were sitting in a hot tub, swimsuits on, trying to block out the chatter of the rest of the women around us. Trying to relax. I've never really understood hot tubs. For me it's a bit like lying in a giant bowl of dirty soup, some of which is getting a bit agitated and slamming up against your spine. It always takes all my concentration to maintain a vaguely upright position, and to stop my legs drifting off and starting up random and inappropriate games of footsie with whoever's sitting opposite. Plus, where are you meant to look? Doesn't everyone else in there think it's a bit weird that we're all effectively in the bath together and we haven't even exchanged first names?

Anyway, the reason we were there was that Michelle loves a spa more than anything. She's a bit like a cat in that respect. One hint of pampering and she's anybody's. Tickle her under the chin and within an instant she's flat on her back, offering you her belly. So, for her birthday present I had bought us vouchers for a whole day at Syon Park. Treatments included. Full use of the facilities. It had been a good choice. She looked blissful lying there, head back, bubbles up around her jaw, blonde hair fanned around her like a mermaid.

'What's Patrick up to today?' I asked, trying not to make my question sound loaded.

27

'God knows,' she said lightly. 'I told him he has to pick up the dry cleaning at some point, but other than that the day's his own. He's probably watching kids' TV in his PJs.'

'Nice.'

'He needs a day doing nothing,' she said, repositioning herself in front of one of the jets. 'He's knackered at the moment.'

'Really?' I said, ears pricked up like a dog who can hear its owner's Volvo coming up the road from half a mile away. 'Why?'

Michelle shrugged. 'Work. Stress.'

'Yes, it must be exhausting sitting in your office deciding who lives and who dies.' I planted a smile on my face as I said this, so she knew I was just teasing. It's always been one of my favourite things to do to Patrick, to compare him to a Roman Emperor giving a thumbs-up or thumbs-down to the poor peasants like me.

'It's a lot of pressure, you know that.'

I desperately tried to think of an in to the conversation I really wanted to have. I knew I had to tread carefully. I couldn't just blunder in with something like 'So, there are rumours that Patrick's putting it about a bit. Thoughts?' Equally I didn't want to let this opportunity slip. I decided on a 'be vague and hope she says something enlightening' tactic.

'No worse than usual, though?'

'No. Same old . . . you know.'

I waited, hoping she might offer something else up. Maybe she had something heavy weighing on her chest, a worry about Patrick, an unconfirmed unease. That would certainly have made my task easier. She said nothing. Uttered a small groan that I assumed meant the jet of

28

water was working its magic on her lower back. I decided to push it a little.

'It feels like he's been away a lot recently. That must be stressful.'

'Mmmm . . .'

Clearly, if Patrick was up to anything Michelle was yet to notice.

'Does that ever bother you? Him having to go to all these events and set visits and stuff?'

'Of course not. It comes with the job.'

'Shall we get out for a bit?' My fingers were starting to feel spongy.

'Oh, that reminds me,' Michelle said, standing up and clambering out. 'I just remembered. What are you doing on Tuesday night? Patrick's got to go up to Manchester. There's some problem with that renovation show they're doing – they're massively behind and they've already gone over budget apparently – and he wants to take the producers out to dinner.'

I felt my heart sink. 'That'll teach them.'

'He needs to get to the bottom of what's going on, I suppose. I guess that's easier over a bottle of wine.'

And maybe provide himself with an excuse to stay out all night?

'Right. Sure. Lovely.'

'Great. I'll get something in. What do you fancy? Salmon? Sea Bass?'

I hardly heard her, though, because my mind had started whirring. I was relieved when someone came to call her away for her facial.

* * *

29

'What if she recognizes my voice?'

Bea was not happy, I could tell. She has this thing where her left eye starts to twitch in the corner when she's panicking and I could see the flicker starting to happen now. I knew she'd agree in the end, though.

'She won't, why would she?'

'Because I speak to her all the time.'

'She speaks to hundreds of people every day probably, and anyway, even if she thinks, That woman sounds like Bea from Castle, why would she doubt what you were saying? Honestly. Trust me.'

What I was asking Bea to do wasn't actually that onerous in the grander scheme of things. I thought it might be an idea to check whether Patrick's 'date' with the producers of *Old House, New Look* was real, so I'd suggested she call his assistant, pretending to be from the production to confirm the details. There was no one else I could trust.

Bea sighed and I knew I'd got her.

'I'll put on an accent,' she said. 'Can I shut myself in your office?'

I let her, of course. A couple of minutes later she opened the door again and beckoned me to come in.

'Well?'

'She didn't rumble me. I did Scottish – want to hear?'

Bea started talking in some kind of cod Glaswegian gibberish that sounded something like 'Heyloo ma naieem ish Morag.' I had no patience for it.

'What did she say? About Patrick I mean?'

'They're having dinner at his hotel at seven thirty. And the producers are both men, by the way. I googled it.'

For some reason I felt deflated. I'd thought I was being so clever.

'That's good, isn't it?' Bea said when I didn't respond.

'What if he's meeting someone up there afterwards? He has dinner, it's the perfect cover and then he's off out somewhere after ... or he has someone stashed in his room, I don't know.'

'Shit. He could phone an escort service,' Bea said, suddenly wide-eyed. 'Or go to one of those dodgy massage parlours. They're everywhere.'

'No,' I said. 'We're getting carried away. This is Patrick we're talking about here. I can't believe he'd stoop that low.'

'What do you want to do?'

'Nothing,' I said decisively. 'I'm being ridiculous. Let's just forget about it.'

I meant to take my own advice, I really did. But I've never been a good listener.

5

I was in Michelle's kitchen, chopping tomatoes for a salad a week or so later. I've always been so at home there that I often find myself starting to prepare food if it's anywhere close to a meal time.

'How was Patrick's trip to Manchester?' I asked as nonchalantly as I could.

Michelle looked up from the pine nuts she was weighing out for pesto. No ready-made jars in this household. 'Oh, fine, I think. He didn't say much about it.'

'Right.'

I couldn't think of anything else to say.

I feel as if I should have a go at describing us all here so you can get the full picture, but I'm not sure I can do much more than the basics. I'll have a go, though. Just to give you an idea.

Michelle, as you know, is blonde. She's average height, slim, blue eyes. Yes, I know I've just described about a fifth of the female population, but I'm not sure what else to say. She's definitely pretty. She was always slighter and more graceful than me. But she's completely unaware of it. It's almost as if she's defying it to last. I've never met anyone with such a complete lack of the need for grooming. There is no adornment with Michelle. She was just granted good genes and the rest is down to chance. I'll try to think of a comparison. She's a bit like Naomi Watts if she was playing an accountant. By which I mean Michelle has a conformist streak that governs how she styles her hair and her dress sense, too. Plus she wears glasses for reading pretty much anything. You know who she looks like? She looks like that secretary character who you don't even notice until she takes off her specs and messes up her hair and then you realize she's lovely, you just haven't seen it before.

Patrick is always rough shaven. He likes that perma-stubble look. His hair is . . . well, it's sort of bog standard man's hair. What can I say? Shorter on the sides than the top. He also has blue eyes, as you know, so their kids are pretty much destined to be full on Hitler Youth. Only his are a piercing icy blue. They're paler than you'd expect and it still sometimes takes me by surprise. He's a jeans and retro band T-shirt kind of man outside of work.

As for me, here are a few of my good points: big eyes (brown), good hair (thick, brown with chestnutty high-lights), taller than your average bear (five foot eight). Good enough figure when clothed. Take them off and it's apparent in a second that I've rarely done a day's exercise in my life. One of these days I'll start, I really will. Before it all begins to go south.

Bad points: big mouth. BIIIG. I'm not talking Julia Roberts here, more wide-mouth frog. When I laugh it must be like staring into the depths of the Grand Canyon. Short legs. Not on the global scale of things but propor-tionately. Short for my height. No skinny jeans for me. I'm a classic pear, a size bigger on the bottom than the top, with a tendency to put on weight around my hips, no doubt due to my unwillingness to go for a run. I spend a large part of my life thinking of ways to shift a few stubborn pounds. It's a hobby.

Put all those attributes together like an e-fit and I imagine you'd come up with a picture of an orangutan. It kind of works OK for the most part, though. Mustn't complain, as my mum always says. Mind you, she also says, 'Cheer up, it'll never happen,' quite a lot, so I make a point of not listening to her.

So, now you can visualize us all sitting round the table: secretary Naomi Watts, Clint Eastwood's younger, more ordinary brother and his simian mate Clyde.

Michelle and Patrick's house is GROWN UP. They have a coffee machine and a dedicated lemon zester. The art on their walls is actually art and not posters or old holiday photos they've had framed. They get a paper delivered every day (the *Independent*) and an organic food box once a fortnight. I realize this might make them sound like a pair of tossers to a few of you, but I am in awe. My own place – now a two-bedroom flat in an impressive red-brick terrace, with a beautiful bay window in the living room – is a master class in disorganization. I have a lot of lovely things, they're just in the wrong places or buried under a topsoil of clutter. Going round to Michelle and Patrick's is like a sanctuary for me.

Not so much on this day, though, because, however hard I tried to ignore them, my mind was still whirring with the whispers I'd been hearing. Bea had managed to glean a few more bits of – alleged – information. Patrick, as far as the stories went, was a serial womanizer. He simply could not resist a pretty face. There was no one woman, more a series of discarded dalliances, a litany of it-meant-nothings. It seemed, she said, as if we were the only people not to know about this. Common knowledge, that was the phrase she used.

'Are you going to the Lifestyle Cable Choice Awards?' Michelle said out of nowhere. We were all still working our way through the pasta mountain Michelle had knocked up to go with the salad I'd made. Patrick was on dessert duty, which meant he would put some ice cream in a bowl and squirt all manner of gooey stuff on top of it. We called them our Heart Attack Saturdays.

I had been doing – I thought – a pretty good job of acting normally around the two of them. By which I mean I was drinking too much and making stupid jokes as per usual. Patrick's and my friendship only exists on a very surface level. A piss-taking, teasing level. We can make each other laugh, but we never go deeper than that. It works for the most part too. It has to.

'God, no. We don't have anything nominated and those dos are so deathly dull if there's not at least the possibility that your name might get read out.'

'Pad's going, aren't you?' Michelle said and reached out a hand to stroke Patrick's head, as if in sympathy.

My head whipped round like the kid in *The Exorcist*.

'Are you? Has one of your shows been nominated then?'

'No, but I think it's good to show your face at these things sometimes.'

'Really? I can't imagine anything worse . . .'

Patrick smiled a disarming smile. He has a range of disarming smiles. One for every occasion. I'm pretty much immune to them these days. Or at least, I thought I was. 'Me, too, to be honest.'

'You should make Michelle go with you. At least then you might have a laugh.'

Did I imagine it? Did he look a little shifty, a tad nervous for a second?

'It's work. I'll have to network my arse off. You know how it is.'

I did, of course. It really wasn't done to take your partner unless you were there because you'd personally received a nomination. I understood that. But I still couldn't understand why he was going at all. As far as awards ceremonies went the Lifestyle Cable Choice Awards was right down there with the Technicals. I couldn't really imagine someone in Patrick's position making invaluable contacts over the lamb cutlets. But it was a great excuse if he wanted a night out with no possibility his wife would want to tag along. Which was hardly a hanging offence in itself but, given the latest intel I'd been given, it suddenly felt dangerously convenient.

My heart hiccupped a little. A tiny missed beat.

'Well, rather you than me,' I said, turning my attention to my pasta and pesto. But my appetite had left the building.

6

Bea was filing things in my office. Or, to be more precise, she was clearing the detritus of a hundred lunches and mid-afternoon snacks off my desk so that she could locate some papers that needed to be filed. Every time I eat at my computer I wonder whether we should think about doing a show around work station cleanliness. A sort of *How Clean Is Your House*, but with forensic experts tracking all the germs left by the crumbs of old egg mayonnaise sandwiches and slices of Anne Marie's homemade cakes. I read somewhere once that your computer keyboard is five times dirtier than your toilet. Who discovered this and why I couldn't tell you. Some people have way too much time on their hands.

Anyway, she was tutting in a kind of jokey way, armed with an antibacterial wipe and a black bin bag, gingerly shuffling bits of paper around and occasionally picking one up and examining it.

'This?'

'What is it?'

'Post-production schedule for *House Wars*. Didn't that go out on air already?'

'Yes. Bin it.'

She peered at another scrap. 'Some kind of shopping list?'

'Let me see.'

She handed it over.

'It looks like groceries.'

I lobbed it straight in the bin without looking. Bea dabbed at the space that had been created on the desk. Tiny lethal microorganisms spluttered and died.

'He's going to the Lifestyle Cable Choice Awards. Don't you think that's a bit odd?'

She looked at me quizzically. Obviously Patrick and his possible lack of fidelity weren't at the forefront of her mind like they were mine.

'Patrick.'

'Oh. Well, that's work isn't it? You can hardly read anything into that.'

'He's going all the way up to Birmingham to go to an awards ceremony where his network doesn't have a single nomination and where there will be absolutely no one of any note that he doesn't already have a working relationship with.'

Bea nervously picked up a paper coffee cup, looked inside, sniffed it. 'Oh, come on! Maybe he just fancies a night out. Are you trying to grow some kind of biological weapon here?'

I took the cup from her. Inside was a furry green forest. 'Eeew. Sorry.' I added it to her bin bag.

'I know. But if that was the case wouldn't he just go to the pub with his mates?'

Bea shrugged. 'I don't think it's that big a deal. I mean, if I hadn't told you what I'd heard would you even think twice about it?'

I thought hard. Of course I wouldn't. Going to dull events was a legitimate part of Patrick's job.

'No.'

'Well then.'

'But you did tell me. That's the difference.'

'Do you want me to pick this up at lunchtime?' Bea said, holding up a dry-cleaning ticket that I thought I'd lost weeks ago.

'What? Oh, yes. Brilliant. Thanks. And could you get me a salad from Chopped? Mixed leaves, tomatoes, avocado . . .'

'Radishes, spring onions, cheddar cheese and chick peas. Yes, I know. Pecan brownie? Skinny latte?'

'Have I ever told you I love you, Bea?' I said, laughing. 'I mean in an appropriate boss/assistant kind of way.'

'Many many times, but you can say it again.'

'Oh, and maybe pick up the new *Broadcast* and get me a copy of *Glamour*? And see if those shoes you took in to get the heel fixed are ready.'

'Sure.'

She carried on sifting through the debris. The pile she had earmarked for filing was starting to look like the leaning tower of Pisa. I brooded some more.

'It's the fact that it's up in Birmingham. I can't help wondering if he just wants an excuse to stay away for the night.'

Bea stopped what she was doing for a second. Looked up. 'He's staying the night?'

'Apparently.'

'But . . . what? You think he's just hoping to get lucky?'

'That's exactly what I think.'

'Seems a bit random.'

'Big fish, small pond. Some ambitious third assistant

working on *Britain's Smartest Caravan* will be flattered by his attentions. I don't know . . .'

'You know what I think?' she said. 'I think you can read anything into anything. If you started scrutinizing anyone's behaviour it would probably be open to all sorts of interpretation.'

'You're right. I need to do some work, take my mind off things.'

'I'll get out of your way,' she said, tying up the now straining black bag. 'What time do you want lunch?'

'Oh, whenever. One?'

I knew she was right, knew I was probably fabricating a whole snowy mountain range out of a tiny bump in the grass, but that didn't stop me going over and over it in my head while I tried to read through the contents of my inbox. I was relieved when Ashley stuck her head round the door and asked if I wanted a slice of Anne Marie's Battenburg cake. Ever since the previous week's episode of *Bake Off* I'd known the Battenburg was an inevitability. It was only a question of when.

'Just a small one, thanks. Tiny.'

Ashley laughed. 'Oh no, you don't get away with it that easily.'

'How much does it weigh?'

'It's like a collapsed star.'

'Perfect.'

She hovered in the doorway. 'Is there anything else you need while Bea's out?'

'Nothing. Thanks.'

In actual fact I did need someone to photocopy a

budget I'd been sent to approve, but for some reason, even though Ashley works for all of us equally, I always save all my jobs for Bea. I feel more comfortable that way. I know they'll get done properly.

Ashley smiled. 'I'll be back with the cake. I'll be the one wearing a back brace.'

How can I describe my work mates so that you can adequately picture them? I know, I'll see if I can ascribe them each a few key words or phrases to give you a short-hand. Just enough to allow you to create a sketch in your head.

Ian: forty-four. Prematurely greying. Prematurely bald-ing. Glasses wearing. Fit, though – in the athletic sense of the word only. He runs marathons for fun.

Anne Marie: sixty-three. Short. Blondish bob with a fringe (in my opinion the new default blue rinse and set for the older woman. I have already decided to resist that hairdo till the day I die). She has the build of a small wiry terrier. I imagine she could have won a bar fight in her day.

Bea: thirty-one, as you know. Tall, slim, long brown mane, striking features (i.e., a bit of a big nose). The one on *Next Top Model* that they would describe as 'editorial'.

Lucy: twenty-six. Also tall, also slim, also brunette. Chocolate-box pretty. The one on *Next Top Model* they would describe as 'commercial'.

Ashley: twentysomething. The one who wouldn't even get on *Next Top Model*. Normal height. Normal-looking girl. Hair. Eyes. Arms. Legs. All present and correct.

By the time Bea got back, my salad, magazines, dry clean-ing and reheeled shoes in tow, I'd had time to think. I had

A PLAN. It had popped into my head out of nowhere. I had examined it. Dismissed it as crazy. Thought it through again. Weighed up the pros and cons and gone over the many ways in which it might go wrong. On balance I had decided it was worth it. It was all I had anyway. I just had to get Bea to agree.

'Sit down a sec,' I said when she'd finished counting out the change from the thirty quid I had given her before she left.

'Everything all right?'

'Just hear me out. Don't say anything till I've told you the whole thing.'

'Oh God,' Bea said, moving an old Costa carrier bag with the remains of breakfast inside out of the way so she could perch on the arm of the sofa. Crumbs fluttered onto the carpet and she leaned down to pick them up.

'This doesn't sound good. What have you done?'

Her nervousness made me laugh. It was so unlike her. 'Nothing. Not yet anyway. And actually, even then, it won't be *me* doing anything.'

I took a deep breath. Braced myself.

'It'll be you.'

Bea looked at me, eyes wide.

'No Tamsin. Whatever it is, no.'

7

'You're talking about a honey trap.'

'Technically, yes, I suppose so.'

Bea and I were still locked in fevered debate. I had laid out the details of my idea and she had laid out every objection she could come up with. I have to say I was starting to lose my resolve the more she pointed out the pitfalls.

She sat back and folded her arms. 'There's no "technically" about it. That's what it is.'

The scheme I had come up with was this. Patrick apparently could not resist a pretty face. Bea definitely had one of those. He was going to be at the Lifestyle Cable Choice Awards without his wife, and with an empty hotel room waiting for him upstairs. Surely, if the rumours were true, then if an attractive young woman basically offered herself up on a plate he would find it hard to say no? Bingo. Caught in the act. I would have the proof I needed to understand exactly what kind of a man my best friend's husband had turned out to be and then . . . Well, I didn't quite know what would happen then to be honest. I hadn't got that far.

Some of Bea's counterarguments had included:

'What if he already has a woman lined up? Then you'd be none the wiser.'

'What if he just doesn't fancy me? However bad he is he can't fancy everyone, right?

'What if he works out who I am somehow?'

I tried to bat each one away. Even if he did already have an assignation set up, she might be able to spot who it was with, note some inappropriate behaviour on his part. She was gorgeous, what red-blooded man would be able to resist? (Well, that would prove nothing then, Bea snapped back. If any old man would go for it then Patrick would be no worse than the rest of mankind.) They had never met, never even spoken on the phone, why on earth would he rumble her?

'What am I supposed to do if he goes for it? Are you asking me to *sleep* with him?' She looked straight at me, nostrils flared. I knew I wasn't handling this very well. If indeed there ever could be a good way to handle it.

'No! God, no. What's that phrase they use in the papers – you could just make your excuses and leave. But then we'd know. We'd have him.'

'Honestly, Tamsin, you know I'd do anything for you. But this is too much. I'm sure it must be illegal or something.'

'What? Propositioning a man at a party?'

'I don't know.' She put her head in her hands. 'Please don't ask me to do this.'

I felt bad for her, I truly did. I knew I had overstepped a line in boss/assistant protocol. But I also knew – if I'm being really honest – that she would struggle to say no to me.

'You don't have to. Of course you don't. It's just . . . I have no idea what else to do.'

Bea laughed a nervous laugh. It didn't sound very convincing. 'How about nothing?'

'What if it's true, though?'

'Why does it have to be me? Lucy's hot . . .'

That one was easy. 'You're the only person I can trust.'

Bea let out a dramatic sigh. 'I'm not sure I can pull it off.'

I saw a chink in the armour. 'Of course you can. Wear that red bodycon dress you've got.'

'I haven't got a ticket. It might be sold out.' I couldn't help but notice the tiny glimmer of hope in her voice.

I had already addressed the ticket situation. Before I spoke to Bea I had called and enquired and been told that there were indeed tickets left. I'd got the feeling the man on the other end had wanted to say 'loads' or 'hundreds' or something like that. He'd certainly sounded disappointed when I'd said I didn't need a plus one.

'I doubt they're sold out,' I said now. 'Let me call them. And I'll pay, obviously. And for any expenses. Your fare and room and stuff.'

'I don't want to have to stay up there,' she said, and I knew I'd got her.

'It might be better. That way you can get ready in the hotel. Otherwise you'll have to negotiate the train in your full slap and killer heels. At rush hour, too.'

We sat there in silence for a moment. I knew I had to wait for Bea to speak.

'Shit.' Pause. Silence. Nothing but the white noise from the overhead light. I held my nerve.

'OK.'

I couldn't quite believe it. 'Oh my God. You're an absolute star. I owe you.'

'You need to tell me exactly what you want me to do. I

mean, I don't even know what he looks like for a start.'

'You've got a few days. We'll go over and over it, work out anything that could possibly go wrong and a way to handle it.'

'And the point is to get him to make a pass at me. Invite me up to his room, something like that? I don't have to do anything?'

'God, no! Of course not. Just act like you're up for it and see how he behaves.'

'This is going to go so wrong.'

She was right, of course. My master plan had the potential to veer off course in a million different ways. I couldn't even begin to factor in the variables that might mean we didn't get a true reading.

'It's my only option,' I said.

For the next couple of days pretty much all Bea and I spoke about was THE PLAN. We worked out a whole cover story for who she was and why she was there (a development person at a fictitious new independent company called Kismet, for some reason. Bea had wanted to call it Honey Trap Productions but I had vetoed that idea pretty swiftly), I had assured her there was bound to be a seating plan somewhere, so she could track down her prey, and I'd forced her to look at a hundred happy snaps of Patrick that I'd taken over the years.

'She looks nice' had been her response when the first one of him and Michelle together had popped up.

'She is,' I said. 'She's a sweetheart.' I had spent the previous evening poring over the photos myself as I decided which ones to show to Bea. Michelle looked blissfully happy in all the pictures of the two of them together. I vowed to punish Patrick in a hundred different ways if I found out he'd cheated on her.

We had conceived endless scenarios in which Bea might introduce herself to Patrick: a spilt drink ('Oh, I'm so sorry, let me get a cloth and wipe you down'); a case of mistaken identity ('You look just like my friend Tom. I really thought you were him for a second there. Maybe you're related?'); an all-out head-on assault ('Can I sit down? You're the only person here who looks half-way interesting'). Understandably, Bea had baulked at the latter.

'Just imagine you really have seen someone you like the look of. What would you do?'

She pushed her sunglasses up her nose. We were sitting outside the frozen yoghurt shop during the pre-lunch lull. Cars chucked their toxic fumes at us as they idled at the lights.

'I don't know. Lurk about and hope they approached me I suppose.'

'You might have to be more proactive on this occasion. Tell him you want to pitch him an idea, or ask if he likes cats or . . . ballroom dancing.'

'Is he gay?'

'Of course not. I'm just using examples. If all else fails, fall over in front of him. Or, even better, on top of him.'

'Tell me things he's into so I've at least got half a chance.'

'Good idea,' I said. 'He's a big retro fiend. Anything from the seventies and eighties.'

'I could wear a ra-ra skirt. Or short tartan trousers,' Bea

said sarcastically. 'Or, I know . . . carry a placard about the miners.'

'Very funny. Just flutter your eyelashes at him. If he's up there on the lookout it's not going to take much.'

'If I wind up getting arrested for soliciting it's on you.'

She stabbed her plastic spoon into what was left of her Peanut Butter and Banana, then pulled it out and waved it at me. I wasn't entirely convinced my bribe of a half-hour skive and a free frozen treat had won her over.

'You'll be fine. It will all be fine.'

'That's easy for you to say.'

'Honestly, Bea, you have no idea how grateful I am. This is above and beyond and all those things. I'll make it up to you somehow, I promise.'

'Maybe this is where I should ask for a pay rise.' Bea laughed to let me know she was joking.

'If it was just up to me I'd give you one, too. You can have the whole of Friday off, how's that?'

Maybe I should stop for a moment and explain why Michelle's happiness means so much to me. Why I would go to such ridiculous lengths to secure it. The fact is that I would do anything for Michelle. She might think I saved her that day on the bus, but the truth is she has saved me many times over.

I'm not just talking about the little things. The late-night phone calls, sympathetic ears or just simply being theres. I'm talking about the big stuff. The time when we got caught shoplifting (my idea. I wanted a pair of earrings from Top Shop really badly but I had no money) and she took the rap for it because my parents were a hundred times more strict than hers, or the time she got out of bed at three in the morning and drove halfway across London to pick me up after I'd lost my bag on a night out and had no way of getting home. Or the time she came to the clinic with me when I'd found out I was accidentally pregnant and I knew I couldn't – shouldn't – go through with it. She was the only person I told and, even though she already wanted a baby more than anything in the world, she never once tried to talk me out of it.

When we were fifteen my dad got a job in Sheffield. My two brothers had already left home, so it made no difference to them. I was presented with a fait accompli. A school had been chosen that would take me. We would move in the summer holidays. Telling a fifteen-year-old girl that she has to up and leave all her friends and move hundreds of miles away is not unlike telling a fifteen-year-old boy that he is never allowed to lock his bedroom door again. It's like delivering a death sentence. I cried, I shouted, I sulked. My mum and dad were immoveable. And then Julian and Miriam stepped in and suggested that I could live with them in term-time if my parents were agreeable. I moved into their house – and into Michelle's room – for the next three years. If we had been close before we were inseparable then. I became a part of their family. I would do anything for her.

So, you see, she's more than a friend, she's like a sister. But the good kind. The kind that wants the best for you, not the kind who only phones you up to tell you that you're a shit daughter and you should go and visit your parents more often.

I simply don't know what I would do without her. I

love my brothers, I love my mum and dad, but Michelle is the first person I call when anything happens to me. She's the only person who knows everything about me. Until now, that is – obviously.

I let Bea leave a couple of hours early on the Thursday so she had time to get to the station before the after-work crowds would be too overwhelming. I wanted to make sure she had lots of time to get herself ready. It was important she looked her seductive best. All the rooms at the hotel where the function was being held had turned out to be taken, so I'd booked her into the Premier Inn five minutes up the road.

'Get a taxi, won't you?' I said, like a worried parent. 'I don't want you walking home late at night.'

'I have no intention of still being there when it's late.' Bea was checking through her overnight bag in my office, making sure she had everything she needed. 'As soon as I've accomplished my mission I'm leaving. I'd rather eat room service and watch *Newsnight* than hang out with a load of people I don't know who are sad enough to think the Lifestyle Cable Choice Awards are a fun night out.'

'Ring me, won't you? Make sure you charge your phone in the hotel before you leave.'

'Yes, Mum.'

'If for some reason we don't talk tonight, call me first thing. What train are you getting back?'

'No idea. I'll call you. Try not to worry.'

'Good luck,' I said, hugging her tightly as if she was off to Helmand Province and I might never see her again. 'Just . . . try your best.'

'Will do. Right, I'd better go . . .'

'Bea,' I said as she was about to open the door to leave my office. 'Is this a really stupid idea?'

'It sucks. But, like you said, what's the worst that can happen?'

The minute she left it crashed down on me exactly what I was doing. Sending my hapless assistant on a wild goose chase to try to seduce my best friend's husband. Or, at least, to allow him to try to seduce her. It was never going to work. And if it did, what kind of a person did that make me? By the time I left for home – having bitten one of my fingernails down to the quick, a habit it had taken me years and many bottles of poisonous-tasting nail polish to grow out of – I had decided I was no better than a madam. A pimp. I was like Fagin taking advantage of poor old Bea's good nature, sending her off to do my dirty work. I nearly called her and told her to turn back and forget all about it. I didn't, of course. I wish I had now. Then maybe I would never have done what I've just done.

8

I decided I needed a distraction for the evening. Something to take my mind off whatever was happening in Birmingham. Ian and Fiona had been pestering me forever to go on a date with one of their single friends.

'He's perfect for you,' Fiona had said, words guaranteed to strike fear into the heart of any unattached woman.

Meeting who your friends think is your ideal match is like seeing yourself through their eyes. That unattractive/dull/stupid man makes them think of you. You're so alike. Unless the man in question turns out to be drop-dead gorgeous and a member of Mensa it's an insult. So I usually avoid any attempts to set me up. But desperate times called for desperate measures. I phoned a slightly surprised-sounding Adam and asked him if he wanted to meet for a drink. A one-night-only offer.

As soon as I arrived at Galvin's at the top of the Hilton on Park Lane, pushing my way through the hordes of suited after-work cocktail drinkers, I knew that this was never going to be the greatest love story ever told. I recognized Adam from a snap Fiona had shown me. That was a good thing. I've met up with so many potential suitors who look nothing like their pictures. More like the older, sadder, heavier brother. The bad thing was that I already knew I didn't fancy Adam. He stood up to greet me. If he felt any disappointment it didn't show on his face. I am an expert at spotting the subtle eye flicks and shifts in body language that give away when someone is unimpressed by what they see. He gave me a big smile – the smile he wore in his picture – and it exuded friendliness and warmth. Without it, though, his face was, well, a bit potatoey. A bit undefined.

The bottom line is that I like sharp and pointy and Adam was soft and doughy. I'm not shallow enough to think that looks are everything, but they are something, and a quite significant something at that. It's not that I want all my dates to be good looking. I've fancied men in the past who would scare off crows if they stood in a field long enough. But they had something about them that appealed to me. And Adam didn't.

I told myself I was here for a reason. Operation Take My Mind Off Patrick and Bea. I would just have a few drinks, make idle chit chat and leave having managed to kill the best part of the evening. Adam stuck out a hand to shake mine.

'I've always wanted to know what Ian and Fiona thought of me. Now I'm not so sure.'

Ordinarily this would have made me laugh, but I had too much on my mind.

It turned out he was a teacher at one of Ian and Fiona's kids' schools and he tried his best to keep me entertained with stories from the playground. He was funny, too, I just wasn't in the mood. I did feel a bit guilty about how distracted I was, but I couldn't stop myself from checking my phone every couple of minutes. I hadn't heard a thing from Bea since a text when she'd first arrived at the venue that said, *'The eagle has landed ha ha,'*

53

and my mind was racing with the possibilities of what might be happening.

'Expecting something important?' Adam said as I picked up my mobile for the tenth time.

'Oh, no, sorry. That is, yes. My mum's ill . . .' I have no idea why I said this. It just seemed like the excuse that would garner me the most leeway to keep checking my messages.

'Oh, I'm so sorry,' Adam said. 'Not bad, I hope.'

I blathered through some half-baked story about diabetes and a fall. Adam was all sympathy. I answered his questions in monosyllables. He ploughed on valiantly, asking me about myself and my world. I knew I should be reciprocating, but it hardly seemed worth it. Eventually he pretty much gave up and sat gazing out of the floor-to-ceiling windows at the whole of London spread out below us.

At about half ten, just as I was wondering whether I could make my excuses and leave, my mobile rang. I stood up abruptly, gesturing to Adam that I had to take this. I answered it before I even checked who was calling, but thankfully it was Bea because my opening words were:

'What the fucking fuck is going on? I've been getting really worried.'

I heard Bea laugh. 'Jesus. I told you I might not be able to call. And by the way, nothing is going on. They only just finished giving out the awards. This thing is INTERMINABLE.'

I walked away from the table and stood by the windows. On any other night the view would have taken my breath away.

'Oh God, really? Have you spotted him yet?'

'Yes. Don't worry. I'm about to go over. I was just calling because I knew you'd be sitting by your phone like a lovesick fourteen-year-old. Now go to bed. I'll call you when I get up.'

'Try me later.'

'I'll ring when I can. It might be a while, though. I can hardly go off to make a phone call in the middle of trying to impress him. Don't panic if I don't get you, that's what I'm saying. It's all taking longer than I'd hoped. Now I need to try and grab him before he leaves. If he's got any sense he'll be out of here like a shot.'

I resisted the urge to ask her a million questions about whether Patrick was on his own or if she'd seen him acting flirtatious with anyone. I would have to wait.

'OK. Go get him.'

'Wish me luck.'

There was no reason to hang around any longer. I probably wouldn't hear from Bea for hours, if at all, so I might as well head home and try to get some sleep.

'I have to go,' I said to Adam, pulling on my jacket. I dug my purse out of my bag and put down a couple of tens.

'Hopefully that'll cover my half.'

'Is your mum worse?' he said with a slight raise of his eyebrows that I knew meant he wasn't buying any of it.

'Something like that. Thanks for a lovely evening. I enjoyed it.'

'Yes,' he said. 'I could tell.'

I started to apologize but then I realized there was no point. I was never going to see him again.

* * *

55

Back home I took Ron down the front steps to his bathroom on the kerb, waited while he just stood there and looked at me, convinced that if he hung on long enough I would give in and take him for a walk – despite the proliferation of late-night muggers that had hit the area recently he always lived in hope – played that game where I pretended to give up and be about to lead him back inside and he panicked and lifted a leg on next door's recycling boxes, and then got into bed with a book and my phone on the pillow beside me. I thought there was no chance I would drop off any time soon, but the next thing I knew my alarm was buzzing and it was time to get up. I always sleep well. I can – and frequently do – sleep anywhere and everywhere. One ex used to call me 'The Dormouse' because of my love of napping. He didn't last long, obviously.

I dragged myself out of bed just as my phone beeped to tell me I had a message. Bea.

'I have good news but bad reception. Call you when I get somewhere better. But all good!'

Good news. That must be, well, good, right? She wouldn't have told me that, given me that piece of hope, unless she was sure. Patrick must have come out of it well, been tried and proved himself innocent. I felt a weight lift off me, as if I were loosening a tight corset, peeling off my control underwear at the end of a long night out. My breath rushed in, flooding my lungs, making me feel light-headed.

Of course I couldn't help but try to ring Bea back. Over and over again. I wanted to be sure that the moment a conversation was possible we were having it. I was starting to regret giving her the whole day off when I had still heard nothing by ten past eleven.

In Bea's absence Ashley was supposed to step in and assist me, but I refused all offers of help except for sending her to Caffè Nero for a skinny latte. Everything else could wait for Bea's return on Monday. Somehow even the coffee she bought me didn't taste as good as it does when Bea gets it. It was weak and watery. I drank it anyway, marvelling at how she could have managed to screw up something so simple, and then headed to the kitchen to make myself a cup of instant.

Ian was already in there, fussing about with the kettle.

'How was last night?' he said, and it took me a moment to remember what it was he was talking about.

'Oh. Adam. Yes. Nice man.'

'Ah! Damned with faint praise,' he said. 'Oh well, I'll break it to Fiona that she's not going to be bridesmaid just yet.'

'Sorry,' I said. 'We just didn't ... you know.' I hoped Adam hadn't reported back that I'd had all the manners of a surly teenager. Now it seemed Bea had good news for me I was feeling a touch guilty about that.

'Can't win them all,' he said, pouring water into two mugs he'd already spooned coffee into. I assumed he had tried to ask Lucy for one and then bottled it and offered to make one for her instead.

'Want a cup?' he said and I nodded yes. I found another mug in the cupboard and handed it to him.

'Thanks, though,' I said unconvincingly. 'For setting me up.'

Reluctantly I went into a budget meeting with the

producers of one of our shows, although I could scarcely concentrate. My sole contribution was to offer up that the catering allowance looked a bit high. By the time I came out there it was. A missed call from Bea. I shut myself in my office and phoned her straight back.

'So?' I said before she even had a chance to say hello. 'What? What happened?'

'Well . . .' Bea said, prolonging the suspense. 'Either he just found me repulsive or he's really not the player you think he is.'

'He didn't bite?'

'Not even a flicker.'

'Oh my God, Bea. So . . . you went over . . .' I needed to hear all the evidence.

'In the end it was getting so late that I just went over; plonked myself down next to him and started chatting.'

'And . . .'

'And he was perfectly nice. Polite. I flirted my ass off, I'm not even joking. I even started telling him where I was staying and how he should come and see my room because it was so amazing – it wasn't by the way, it was basic to say the least . . .'

'Sorry.'

'But he didn't even indulge me by flirting back. In fact, he mentioned Michelle within the first two minutes.'

'Really?' I felt so happy I could have burst into song.

'It was pretty obviously his way of trying to stop me in my tracks.'

'So what then?'

'Oh God, Tamsin, I feel sick when I think of some of the things I said. I thought I'd better have one last push just to make sure he wasn't merely being cautious. So I basically propositioned him right there.'

'Shit! What did you say?'

'I can't bring myself to tell you. But he knew that it was all his on a plate if he was up for it.'

'And he said no.'

'He didn't just say no, he pretty much got away as quickly as he could. Said it wasn't his style. He wasn't the kind of man who would do that to his wife. And then he left not long after. On his own, I hasten to add. I didn't even see him speak to any woman for more than about two minutes.'

'So what about all the stories then?'

'Malicious gossip, I reckon. Chinese whispers.'

'You can't believe how happy I am. I'm so grateful, Bea. I know it was an awful thing to ask you to do.'

'I'm never going to let you forget it,' she said, laughing.

'OK, go and have a nice day off. I'll find some way to make it up to you.'

The relief was overwhelming. Although it was tinged with a fairly large dose of embarrassment, it has to be said. I felt like a bit of an idiot for having allowed my suspicions to escalate to such a fever pitch, and for roping Bea into my crazy plan. Thank God she was the only one who knew about it. I knew I could trust her to keep it to herself.

The good feelings won out pretty swiftly. It gave me a warm fuzzy feeling that Patrick had talked about Michelle to ward off an overzealous flirt. She was on his mind. He wanted the world to know he had no intention of betraying her.

All was right with my world.

I know, I know.

9

I'm never very good when the doorbell rings and I'm not expecting anyone. Half the time I just ignore it and hope whoever it is will go away. I hate surprises and that includes unannounced visitors. Plus when I am at home I'm never in a fit state to see anyone. I'm in my pyjamas about five minutes after I walk through the door, showered, scrubbed and dressed for bed with a large glass of Sauvignon Blanc in my hand.

For once, though, I was dressed and looking halfway presentable because I had decided to spend my precious Saturday doing exciting stuff like food shopping and going to the dry cleaners.

I recognized Patrick's voice on the intercom straight-away. Although it was unusual for him to drop round alone, it wasn't unheard of. There had been odd times when Michelle had sent him round on some errand or other. That was about it, though. He and I had never had an independent friendship. Of course, he and Michelle together had spent countless evenings sitting in my living room or eating in my kitchen. But anyway, the point is that I didn't immediately think, What's happened? Or, Who's died? I just invited him in and asked if he'd like a cup of tea.

'You on your own?' he said by way of an answer, look-ing round as if he thought I might have picked up some man the night before, and he was about to emerge from my bedroom dressed in nothing but one of my nighties (for the record I don't own any nighties. I am strictly a pyjama and T-shirt girl).

Ron, who is getting on a bit and whose reactions are not what they were, finally realized we had a visitor and barrelled out of the bedroom, throwing his whole weight at Patrick's legs. Patrick leaned down and ruffled his wiry head.

'Hey, boy.'

There was something not right about him. Patrick that is, not Ron. Something a bit on edge. The good feeling that had carried me through the past twenty-four hours started to dissipate.

'Is everything OK?'

'Can I talk to you about something?' Patrick said, words that no one ever wants to hear. Why was he here on his own and on a Saturday? I jumped to the worst conclusion.

'Is Michelle OK?'

'God, yes. I didn't mean to worry you . . .'

'Julian and Miriam?'

'Yes. They're fine. Everyone's fine. At least, I think so. That's why . . . shit, Tamsin, I don't really know where to start . . .'

'Let's sit down,' I said, feeling suddenly as if I might keel over if I didn't. Ron was still bounding about, doing his best comic turn for attention. No doubt he was remembering the time his favourite Uncle Patrick gave him a beef-flavoured rubber bone and hoping there might be another on the way. It seemed unlikely at this point.

'Sit, Ron. Stay.' I couldn't bear to watch his unrequited

efforts. His joy was too hopeful and pure for him to understand why it wasn't being reciprocated. He did as he was asked. Of course he did. He's a dog, he can't help himself.

Was this it? Was this the point where Patrick told me he had other women on the side and that he needed my help to break it to Michelle? Not after what Bea had reported back surely? I couldn't bear the suspense.

'So . . .'

Patrick let out a long breath. I had to stop myself from going over and shaking him, demanding that he spit it out – whatever 'it' was – right now.

'I think . . . I think Michelle . . . this is going to sound so ridiculous . . .'

'Patrick, just say it, for God's sake.'

'I don't think she trusts me.'

He sat back and looked at me as if to say, 'There, now do you see?' I didn't.

'What?'

'I think she's got it into her head that I'm a cheater or something.'

Ah . . .

'Why would you think that?'

'Something weird happened at the awards the other night.'

Oh God.

'What do you mean weird? And what's this got to do with Michelle?'

'OK, so this woman came over to me, out of nowhere, and started chatting me up . . .'

'Right.'

'I didn't think anything of it at first, I just tried to get rid of her.'

I sat there. Breath baited.

'But she was really persistent. And then she said a couple of things that made me think she knew Michelle.'

For fuck's sake, Bea. I should have known it all sounded too good to be true. I tried not to feel irritated with her. It had been unfair of me to put her in that position and expect she might be able to carry it off after all.

'What kinds of things?'

'I can't remember the exact words, but she came over like she didn't know who I was and then when I mentioned my wife – because she was really coming on strong – she said something like, "Oh, Michelle?" and I said, "Do you know her?" and she got all flustered.'

Oh God. Please. Do. Not. Let. Him. Be. Able. To. Trace. This. Back. To. Me.

'So who was she?'

'I have no idea. Her name was Cheryl. I didn't get her surname. I don't know any Cheryls and neither does Michelle, as far as I know.'

OK, so I could let out a small sigh of relief.

'But was that all? I mean, there's bound to be a rational explanation. She'd probably overheard you saying something . . . or something.'

I crossed my fingers that he would buy what I was saying, felt myself attempting to cross my toes.

'No. I asked her that because it seemed so odd, and she just stood up and said, "Do you want to come to my room or not?"'

I tried to feign a laugh. Acting is not my strong point.

63

'She sounds a bit crazy to me. Are you sure someone hadn't put her up to it? For a joke or something?'

'No, I think they had, that's the point. But not for a joke.'

Shit. Fuck. Bollocks.

'I think Michelle did. I think Michelle suspects I'm playing around and so she set this woman up to try and catch me out.'

Breathe.

'That's preposterous! As if—'

He interrupted me.

'I thought she might have told you—'

'What? No! Not that I believe it for a second by the way, but no.'

'Has she said anything to you, though? About not trusting me?'

For once I could tell the truth. 'Never.'

'I couldn't bear it if she didn't. I'd never . . . I mean, you know, don't you? That I'd never cheat on her.'

'Of course.'

Oh shit. He was really taking this hard. I pushed all thoughts of the many ways I wanted to punish Bea for giving the game away out of my head and concentrated on Patrick. He looked close to tears. What the fuck had I started?

'I refuse to believe Michelle would do something like this.'

'Who else would, though? It can only be her.'

'I'm not saying you were imagining it, but do you think you might have read something into it that wasn't there? We all have cloudy judgement after a couple of drinks.'

'I wasn't drinking. It was a work function. And, no, I

don't think I was overreacting. Some woman comes up, out of the blue, basically asks if I want to sleep with her, accidentally drops Michelle's name and then gets very flustered trying to cover it up. Come on, Tam. What other explanation could there be?'

I picked at a fingernail, avoiding his eye. Worried it into splitting. Tore the top part off. 'Michelle's just not the suspicious type.'

'Because she's never had anything to be suspicious about. Maybe now, for some reason, she thinks she does.'

'I still can't imagine her doing this though? It's so . . . extreme. Apart from anything there's all the organization. You know that's not her strong point. And where would she find the woman?'

'I don't know. Aren't there companies where you can go? You hire someone for the night to hit on your spouse?'

Are there? I wish I'd thought of that. 'I have no idea.'

'To be honest, that's why I thought she must have got you involved. You're so much better at practical stuff than her.'

'Absolutely not.'

His face crumpled. He sat forward in his chair, elbows on his knees. 'I don't know what to do. I thought we were so happy.'

'You were. You are. This is clearly all a big misunderstanding.'

'Will you talk to her, though? Try to find out what's going on? She'll tell you, right?'

'If there's anything to tell then, yes, I'm sure she will. But there won't be. You have to stop worrying.'

His eyes had teared up. I have never seen Patrick cry.

Never. He'd come close at their wedding. He'd done that wobbly-lip thing that unreconstructed men do when they're trying to hold it all in. But he'd caught himself just in time. Now I could see a watery would-be escapee at the corner of his eye. He tried to wipe it away and it plopped down onto his cheek. He swiped at it again. I looked away. It seemed like such an intimate gesture.

I can't even begin to tell you how bad I felt. I had created this whole thing. Nothing had been wrong with their marriage. Nothing. And now – because of me, because of my stupid willingness to believe rumours that clearly had no basis – there actually might be.

Patrick sniffed. Got out a tissue and dabbed at his eyes clumsily. I felt sick with guilt.

'It'll all be something and nothing. All I know is that Michelle adores you. And she has never even hinted to me that she thinks anything is wrong.'

I tried to imagine how I would have reacted if I hadn't in fact known that Patrick was right about his suspicions. Would I have laughed? Got angry on Michelle's behalf? I was finding it impossible to act naturally.

'How can I ever feel the same about her knowing she would do something like that?'

'You're overreacting. You're imagining things . . . she wouldn't . . .'

I had no idea what else I could say to get him off this track.

'I couldn't deal with it if anything happened . . . I just couldn't.'

A second plump tear landed on his cheek and negotiated its way through the stubble. This time he didn't even

66

try to mop it up. He looked such a mess. This was so unlike the cocky over-confident Patrick I knew. I couldn't help myself. I stood up and walked over, plonking myself down on the sofa next to him. I put an arm round him and he leaned into my shoulder while I stroked his back, like I did to Ron whenever he was under the weather.

Can you see where this is leading yet?

IO

It didn't happen then.

We sat where we were for maybe five minutes. Him crying and holding on to me like his life depended on it. Me stroking his back. I looked over and saw that Ron was still sitting rooted to the spot, as I had told him he should who knew how long ago. He looked confused. Worried that he didn't recognize this behaviour in two of his favourite people. I patted my knee – the universal sign for 'come here' to a dog – and he trotted over, laying his head on my leg in sympathy. It struck me briefly that we must look like some kind of alternative nativity scene, and I almost laughed. Out of nerves more than anything else.

Eventually Patrick sat up and we shuffled apart. I think we were both feeling slightly self-conscious, not sure how we should behave. I don't think we'd ever been in such close physical proximity before.

'Sorry,' he said, a small embarrassed smile appearing on his face.

'Don't be. I completely understand. It *will* all be OK, though. I promise you.'

'Will you try and talk to her?'

'Of course.'

'Thanks. And I'm sorry for getting you involved.'

'Stop apologizing.'

'Sorry.'

Thankfully, he laughed as he said this and that eased the atmosphere a bit. I stood up. I couldn't wait to get him out of there, to be honest. Luckily he took the hint.

'I should go. Mich thinks I'm only going to get a paper.'

'I'm braving Budgens,' I said, standing too.

He leaned over and hugged me, patted Ron on the head. 'Will you call me if . . . you know, if she says anything . . .'

'Of course. And stop worrying.'

'I feel much better just for having said it out loud.' He didn't look it, to be fair. He looked awful.

'Any time,' I said, not meaning it in the slightest.

I showed him out. Went back to the living room and slumped on the sofa. I hadn't got a clue what to do next.

That was last Saturday. Today is Tuesday.

Of course I called Bea straightaway and told her what had just happened and she was abject. I felt guilty for ruining her weekend, but I wanted to hear just how bad the damage really was, whether she had given away more than Patrick had let on. She eventually admitted to having accidentally mentioned Michelle by name, but she insisted that she had covered well and that Patrick couldn't really have deduced anything concrete from her mistake. So I tried to cling to the hope that the whole thing might be a massive overreaction on his part. That somehow it might all blow over and go away of its own volition.

And, of course there was nothing for me to talk to Michelle about given I already knew all the answers. I did make a show of calling her on Saturday night, though, and asking her if she fancied meeting me for a potter round Spitalfields Market the next day. I was hoping Patrick would think this was a ruse so that I could quiz her about her suspicions, and would decline to come along. Then I could tell him that we'd had 'the conversation' and that everything was fine, Michelle had no worries, she thought their marriage was perfect, and 'Cheryl' was clearly some kind of psychic mad woman who he should just forget all about. Job done.

He clearly picked up the signals because it was only Michelle waiting for me by the stinky cheese shop, our agreed rendezvous.

'You on your own?' I said, trying to keep the hopeful note out of my voice. Maybe Patrick had just popped inside to try some Montgomery Cheddar.

Michelle rolled her eyes in a jokey way. 'He said much as he loves you he didn't want to spend his Sunday morning admiring vintage ladies' clothes. He's gone for a run.'

'Good,' I said, matching her tone. 'His loss.'

We wandered amiably up and down the rows of stalls, tried on clothes in Collectif – or, at least, I did and Michelle watched – and flopped on sofas we would never be able to afford in One Deko. It didn't feel like we were quite our usual selves, though – from my point of view at least. I couldn't shake the picture of Patrick crying from my mind. Or the sense of guilt that I felt about the atmosphere I must have created between them. I struggled to find our usual effortless common ground.

'Is something up?' Michelle said eventually, once we had sat down inside Canteen for a sinful brunch. 'You seem a bit quiet.'

'No. I'm fine. Just knackered.' I hoped I sounded even halfway convincing. I was tired actually. I had hardly slept the night before. That's how much Patrick's state of mind had unsettled me.

'You work too hard.'

'We all do.'

'Well, yes, there is that. You look a bit down, though, I don't know.'

'Honestly I'm fine. Now, my mum's birthday. You have to help me . . .'

Michelle took the bait.

'Oh God, yes. I should get her something, too.'

'Let's have another walk round once we've eaten, there's bound to be something.'

Michelle picked out a 1950s tea set that I knew my mum would absolutely love. I kicked myself for not having thought of it first. Although my mum's the sort of person who, if it came from me, would look it over carefully for about three painful minutes and then say something like, 'What's this?' whereas if Michelle gave it to her she'd declare her love for retro chic in general and fifties china in particular.

At one point we stopped at a stall selling handmade baby outfits that would have reduced Cruella de Vil to a broody mess. Brightly coloured animal appliqués adorned tiny onesies in a variety of dazzling colours. I tried to edge on past them casually. Move along. Nothing to see here. Michelle, however, had other ideas.

'Oh my God!' she squealed. 'Look at these.'

'Cute,' I said, and shuffled towards the next stall, which

wasn't as easy as it sounds. It gets busy there on a Sunday.

'Hold on,' Michelle said and I turned to see she was holding a babygro in neutral orange with a – I have to admit – stupidly cute giraffe character on the front.

'Do you think it's a jinx if I buy it?'

I raised my eyebrow at her in what I hoped was a sceptical fashion. Michelle knows what I think about jinxes and fate and all that other nonsense.

'OK, so then I'm buying it.' She held it out to the woman running the stall. And then noticed a sign saying you could get two for ten pounds rather than pay seven pounds just for one.

'Choose one,' she said to me, her face lit up with happy anticipation. This was not a woman who would ever suspect her husband was playing around. Or whose husband should ever have worried that she did. I cursed myself for my stupidity again. I poked around among the piles of tiny outfits, found one that was green with a darker green crocodile.

'This one.'

'Perfect. I'm dying to get pregnant,' she said to the woman as she proffered her ten pound note. 'I just have to convince my husband that it's the right time.'

I grimaced. 'Too much information.'

The woman smiled, ignoring my comment. I suppose her business thrives on hopeful parents-to-be. 'How lovely. Good luck.'

By half past twelve we were both ready to call it a day.

'I'm going to have to eat lunch now, too,' Michelle groaned as we got into a taxi, her heading for Highgate, me for Belsize Park. 'I think Pad's hoping for a roast at

The Angel. I don't know how I'm going to fit it in.'

She hugged me as the cab pulled up to drop her off. If she thought her husband had been behaving oddly since Friday she certainly didn't give anything away.

That afternoon I'd arranged to go to the cinema with Anne Marie. We do this about once a month, when there's something on at The Everyman that we both want to see. We flop in our comfy seats, have a glass of wine, watch the film and then stuff in a pizza across the road at Pizza Express, while putting the world to rights.

I've already decided I would like to be Anne Marie when I grow up. She lives on her own – through choice, she has been proposed to many times – but she has a social life to rival Kim Kardashian's. She's always seen every film, play, art exhibition worth seeing. She was married once, years ago, but it was miserable and in the end she walked out one night with nothing but a tiny suitcase, and she vowed never again. Now she does exactly what she wants to do whenever she wants to do it. I doubt she's ever lonely, she doesn't have the time.

We sat through a slightly worthy new version of an old classic. It's a book I love and know well, so it didn't really matter that my mind wouldn't stay focused.

'Ashley seems to be settling in nicely,' Anne Marie said afterwards, as we ordered an American Hot for me and a Fiorentina for her.

I shrugged. I had no opinion. Anne Marie took that as a sign that I didn't really want to talk about work, so she asked me if I was thinking about going away this summer and we chatted about Italy versus Greece and villas versus hotels for a pleasant twenty minutes or so. I was only half present, though. Conversation by numbers. If she noticed, she was polite enough not to say as much.

Bea arrived on Monday morning bearing muffins from the little bakery round the corner, so I knew she was feeling guilty. I had already decided not to bring it up again. Although it was tempting. She launched into another apology as soon as she walked through the door and shut it behind her, though.

'I've been going over and over it in my mind ever since you called me. I just can't believe he worked it out. Even though I said her name. God, I am so sorry about that, I was really nervous and it came out before I could stop it . . .'

She was rambling, something Bea always does when she's under pressure. The telltale eye twitch was present. I stepped in to put her out of her misery.

'It's OK. It's fine. I just have to convince him that Michelle doesn't, and hasn't ever, suspected him of cheating – which shouldn't be too hard because she doesn't and she hasn't – and then hopefully things'll go back to normal.'

'At least now you've got your answer, I suppose.'

'I know. And I feel like an absolute idiot. Remind me never to listen to idle gossip again.'

'And Patrick'll forget about it soon enough, once he realizes Michelle isn't behaving any differently towards him.'

'God, I hope so.'

'You were looking out for your friend, that was all,' Bea

74

said. 'I don't think anyone could fault you for that. And if I hadn't . . .'

I laughed. 'OK, stop, let's just agree we both feel bad. Beating ourselves up is not going to help.'

'What can I do to make it up to you? Coffee to go with the muffin? More muffins? Coffee-flavoured muffin? Muffin-flavoured coffee?'

'How about some work? I left a stack of crew CVs on your desk. Could you sort through them and send any that look interesting over to the *Downsize Divas* production office? They need to be Manchester-based.'

'Done.'

'And yes, coffee to go with the muffin. Thank you.'

'And done.'

I had learned a big lesson. I did not always need to be Michelle's protector. She did not always need to be protected. Sometimes it was better just to leave things well alone.

By the time I got home from work today I had started feeling a little better. Things would calm down. Everything would go back to normal with a bit of time. I changed out of my work clothes, showered and dressed again in my black and white gingham pyjama bottoms and a vest top. I put my Juicy Couture red hoody over the top, tied my hair up in a ponytail and wandered into the kitchen to start planning what I was going to eat.

Tonight the fridge was looking especially bare because Patrick's disturbing visit on Saturday had made me lose my appetite for Budgens. I decided to phone out for a takeaway, but then I couldn't decide what I wanted so I poured myself a large glass of red instead.

I had just sat down in front of the Channel 4 news when the doorbell rang. My first instinct was to keep quiet and pretend no one was home, but curiosity got the better of me and I couldn't resist answering. With any luck it would be the front door equivalent of a wrong number.

Of course, it wasn't.

When I let Patrick in he didn't look any better than he had on Saturday. He smiled when he saw my get-up, though.

'Well, I'm glad you made an effort.'

'I wasn't expecting anyone,' I said, self-consciously pulling the zip on my top up a little higher.

'Really? All dressed up and nowhere to go?'

'You're very funny.'

He followed me into the living room. I was trying to swallow the anxiety his unexpected arrival had triggered in me.

'What are you doing here anyway?'

'I can't stop thinking about it. I know you said Michelle seemed like her normal self but I just wanted to hear exactly what made you think that . . .'

I had called Patrick yesterday – Monday – when I knew he would be safely at work and out of Michelle's earshot, to tell him that I was convinced he had imagined the whole honey-trap scenario. I'd had to pretend to be on my way into a meeting and therefore unable to talk for more than a few brief seconds. I couldn't get off the phone quickly enough. I'm not, and never have been, a very confident liar.

'Well . . .' I said, thinking on my feet. 'It's just that I gave her lots of opportunities to tell me if she had anything on her mind. And we talked about you lots. Not specifically that . . . obviously . . .'

'And?'

'And she didn't say anything. She seemed really happy. Talked about your weekend away coming up, as if she was really looking forward to it, that kind of thing. Honestly, I'd be absolutely gobsmacked if she had even considered setting some woman up to test you.'

Patrick sat down on the nearest armchair.

'OK. Thank God.'

'Do you want a cup of tea?' I said, although I felt as if I could do with a stiff brandy myself. I was hoping he would say no, he had to get back, and then I could pour myself a plus-sized glass to enjoy on my own.

'A drink would be better.'

'Aren't you driving?'

He nodded. 'One'll be OK.'

'Great. Red or white?'

'White.'

I opened the bottle (screw cap, thank God. I didn't want to have to waste time fannying about with a corkscrew) and poured him the smallest glass I thought I could get away with without appearing rude. I didn't feel up to facing the third degree. I wasn't sure I would pass the test. I topped up my own glass with the red while I was about it.

'Is Mich not expecting you?' I said, clutching at straws.

'She's gone over to her mum and dad's.'

'Right.'

'The thing is, it's not like I've never had the opportunity. I mean, I'm sure she has as well. I just would never . . .'

'I know.'

He looked like he was on the verge of tears again. I sat there, not knowing what to do with myself. This was not a side of him I had ever seen before and it made me feel uneasy. Maybe I'd misjudged him all these years and he was really just a big softy.

'I think you have to put it out of your mind. Whatever happened it was just some weird coincidence.'

'You weren't there. Do you mind if I get another?'

He had drunk his wine in record time (well, I had only given him about three mouthfuls) and was holding out his empty glass.

'Should you?'

Patrick shrugged. 'I can get a cab if I have to.'

I didn't really know how I could say no. I hardly looked as if I was on my way out for the night.

'OK.'

I poured us both another – much larger this time. Sod it.

Then I offered up the first even vaguely plausible scenario I could come up with, in the hope that I could shut the conversation down. 'You know what I think? I bet someone there put her up to it, this Cheryl. Someone who knows you and thought it would be funny.'

He didn't look convinced. 'And they told her Michelle's name?'

'It's hardly a state secret. They were probably talking about you, said something about you having a wife called Michelle and then said, "Wouldn't it be funny if you went and threw yourself at him just to see how he'd react." I don't know, something like that.'

'Why, though?'

'God knows. Because they have a warped sense of humour.'

'And what was she going to do if I'd said yes, I'd love to come to your room?'

'Probably shout gotcha and run away. I'm sure that's what it was, a stupid joke. It was probably someone whose show you'd turned down, or who you sacked off something once, and they thought it would be fun to make you feel like an idiot.'

Patrick dragged his hand through his hair. 'I don't know, Tamsin.'

'I can't believe you've let it affect you like this.'

'It's frightened the life out of me – the idea that something might be wrong . . .'

And there it was, another fat tear exploded onto his cheek. I felt overwhelmed with pity. He was obviously feeling wretched. I couldn't believe I had been so wrong about him.

I drained the last of my drink, refilled both our glasses to the brim and crossed over to where he was sitting, plonking myself down on the arm of the sofa. Instinctively I put my arm around his shoulders again. I was an old hand at this now. He leaned into me. I felt slightly lightheaded. I knew that I'd drunk my wine too quickly. So I did what I always do under those circumstances. I drank some more.

'It'll be OK,' I said to the top of Patrick's head.

'I hope so.'

He reached his arm up and draped it over my leg, pulling me closer to him. This is the point when I should have stood up, patted him on the back like a friend would, insisted that we have a coffee to clear our heads. I didn't, of course. Although it was a strange sensation, us sat there with our arms around each other, this was Patrick, my best friend's husband. I still had no conception that it would turn into anything else. And – if I'm going to be really honest, and I might as well be – it felt nice. Comforting.

We sat there like that for a minute or so, and then I became aware that his hand was moving. Just slightly. Just the barest hint of his fingers stroking my thigh. I knew that wasn't quite right. Me rubbing his back in a soothing motion was one thing, but this felt altogether more intimate. Still, I put it down to his fragile state of mind and the Sauvignon Blanc. I eased back a tiny bit. Carefully. I didn't want him to realize what I was doing and feel embarrassed.

And then he was looking at me and I was looking back at him, seemingly unable to tear my eyes away, even though I knew I should. He was reaching out to sweep his fingers across my cheek and I was letting him. We were kissing. Full on. All out. As if we had been waiting to do this for the past five years.

I could have pulled away. I could have stopped it before it went too far, tried to laugh it off as a tipsy misunderstanding. We would have got over it eventually. But his hand had started creeping up the inside of my top, pushing my resolve out ahead of it as it went. I let it. I didn't want it to stop.

And then it all goes a bit blank.

I 2

I can't even tell you what I was thinking. I wasn't thinking. Let alone that what we were doing was about the worst thing we could ever do, short of me murdering him and leaving him dead on Michelle's doorstep with a fetching ribbon tied around his neck in a bow and a note saying, 'Ha ha.'

After a few minutes (I've decided to say fifteen, the prosecution may say twenty-five) it was as if I came to my senses, like I'd been given a shot of adrenalin to counteract the overdose. Drunk to sober in sixty seconds. His fingers were now inside my underwear. Inside me. I pushed him away.

'We can't do this.'

Patrick put his hand out to pull me back towards him. I shuffled backwards to make it clear that whatever had just happened was over.

'No. This is crazy. We can't.'

It was as if he suddenly realized what we were doing too. He dropped his hand, looked down at it as if it had a mind of its own. Did up his flies (his flies were undone!).

'Fuck. No. Of course we can't. Shit.'

Once there was a gulf between us, Patrick sat looking in my direction while not actually looking at me at all. He kept his gaze fixed on the ground like a dog caught standing by the breakfast table with a Pop Tart in his mouth.

'Shit,' I said. And then, 'I'm getting up.'

'I should get going . . .'

I readjusted my clothing. Zipped up my hoody over my still undone bra.

'Michelle . . .'

'Of course.'

'I don't know what to say,' he somehow forced his eyes up to almost meet mine as he said this.

'Me neither.'

'I didn't mean for that to happen.'

'Me neither. Jesus. We just need to forget it ever did. Like . . .'

'Right.'

'We've just had too much to drink. Me anyway . . .'

'Me too . . .'

'Perhaps I shouldn't come over for a bit . . .'

'No. I don't want you to feel you have to stay away . . . Just . . . I don't know.'

Both of us seemed incapable of actually finishing a coherent thought.

'Anyway,' he said, making a vague gesture towards the door. 'I should go . . .'

I nodded, hands firmly in my pockets.

'Bye then.'

'Are we . . .' he said. 'I mean, is it going to be OK?'

'It has to be.'

He turned and opened the door, waving a low hand at me as he went. Once he'd shut it again I double-locked it behind him.

That was half an hour ago. All I've done since is sit and stare at the walls, a creeping feeling of self-loathing and fear threatening to engulf me. What the fuck have I done?

This time there's no one to confide in. My two usual sounding boards, Michelle and Bea, are out of the question obviously, and I'm clearly not about to divulge what's happened to my brothers or my mum. We rarely get deeper than 'How's work?' or 'What are you having for your tea tonight?' and I don't think me telling them I've just had a fumble with Michelle's husband would be the way to change that. My family love Michelle. I think my parents have entertained the thought that she's really the daughter they should have had. So have I for that matter.

I decide to get changed again, now that I'm sure he's not about to come back. I shove all my clothing into the washing machine and set it to high. I don't care if everything shrinks. I can feel a hangover kicking in already. I force myself to drink a vat of water, take Ron out for a quick bathroom break, and by half past nine I'm curled up under my duvet, wishing the world would go away.

The worst part is that there's nothing I can do now to change what's happened. It's going to be there forever. It's on my record now, written in indelible marker. No chance of parole. We might not have 'had sex' but we HAD SEX.

I know I'm not going to get any sleep. But I know I don't want to get up either. I don't want to risk catching sight of my face in a mirror.

Somehow I am out cold when my alarm goes off, though. Sprawled across the width of the bed in a semi-circle around my half-conscious dog. My first thought is, Oh shit, is it time to get up already? My second thought is just, Oh shit. I'm tempted to call in sick. I'm the boss, who's going to question it? I'm not sure I can face people. I don't know how I'm ever going to be able to act normally again. But the thought of spending all day at the scene of the crime is worse.

The first order of the day is our development meeting. We have these every other Wednesday and they generally consist of a quick rush through our slate with everyone contributing any news they have on any of the projects, followed by a twenty-minute gossip drinking coffee and eating biscuits. Everyone except Ashley attends. Lucy and Bea take it in turns to make notes that they later transcribe and distribute to Ian, myself and Anne Marie. I doubt any of us ever refers to them again. It's the only time we formally all get together, though, so we cling on to the tradition regardless.

We always gather in Ian's office – the largest of the upstairs rooms. It was easy for us to decide who would be where when we first moved in. He cared about size, I cared about view. Ian is sitting on his desk chair but, as usual, he's pulled it to the side so as to appear less formal, Anne Marie and I occupy the two-person sofa and Bea and Lucy perch on chairs they've wheeled through from the other rooms. It's a scorching hot day so we have the little window open as wide as it will go (no aircon here in our mid-Victorian terrace) and consequently have to shout above the invading street noise.

I have nothing to contribute. Nothing. My head is

completely elsewhere. I'm feeling exposed, as if the others might be able to sense what I've done. The way some dogs can sniff out cancer or spot an epileptic fit before it happens. Even though I spent an extra ten minutes in the shower this morning scrubbing and exfoliating till my skin was pink, to try to erase all traces of Patrick, I feel as though I can still smell him on me. As if he got under the epidermis and now I'm sweating him out, bit by bit.

I explain my fragile state to Bea – who notices everything – as a hangover, plain and simple. At least I don't need to act that part. There's a small toffee hammer knocking on my temples every few seconds and someone seems to have put my brain in a vice. My stomach hurts, but whether it's from genuine or guilt-induced nausea I can't tell. She laughs sympathetically and produces an ancient Resolve from her bag, mixes it with a glass of water and hands it to me.

When we get to any of my projects I just say 'nothing much to report' and let Bea fill them in with whatever she's managed to glean from my emails and phone calls. Because she's Bea, this means she pretty much knows everything about everything, so no one really notices the fact that I am mentally absent.

'Are you OK?' she hisses as we head back to my room once the meeting is over.

'I'm fine,' I snap. And then immediately feel bad. 'I'm never drinking again,' I say, attempting a joke.

'Where did you go last night?'

My brain won't even function well enough to make a proper excuse. 'I don't want to think about it. Suffice to say me and my friends are too old for clubs.'

'Ha!' Bea says. She knows I despise nightclubs. 'You went to a club? Which one?'

'Shit. I can't remember the name. It was in Notting Hill somewhere.'

'Mode?' she says. 'Or Peacock? Although that's more of a bar.'

'I need to sit down,' I say and it isn't really a lie.

'Of course, sorry, I'll shut up.' She stops in the doorway to my office. 'Do you need anything?'

I adopt a gentler tone of voice. Even though I'm fighting the urge to say, 'This is all your fault,' I know it isn't. It's mine. 'No, thanks. I'm just going to get on with some stuff.'

I go in and shut the door behind me, something I rarely do. Then I sit at my desk, elbows on the table, and put my head in my hands.

13

After about half an hour of pointless introspection and self-flagellation I have decided what I have to do next. In the short term anyway. The very short term. I need to speak to Patrick to make sure we are on the same page about this having been an unfortunate one-off incident brought on by alcohol and emotion, and never to be repeated or indeed spoken of ever again. And I need him to guarantee me that he won't get caught up in a fit of guilt and confess all to Michelle.

This is obviously the opposite of the advice I have given in the past to friends who have slipped up. 'Honesty is the best policy,' I have always trilled blithely, as if I'm some kind of expert. 'What kind of relationship are you going to have if you can't tell him/her everything?' I can hear myself saying, 'It's not as if technically you had full-on sex with them, you're all grown-ups, just come clean and it'll all work out for the best.' I want to punch that smug know-it-all now.

In this case honesty is definitely not the best policy. The best policy would actually be some kind of time travel where I could go back and do everything differently, but as that seems unlikely to happen, at least in the next few days, then the kindest, least hurtful path would be to agree that Michelle never needs to know the way in which the two people she cares about most in the world – parents aside possibly, although that's not a given – have betrayed her. We can't change it. We can't undo what's done, how-ever much we regret it now, so all we can do is try to forget it ever happened. It's not as if there's ever going to be a repeat performance.

It suddenly becomes urgent that I make him understand how crucial this is. I don't want to risk calling him from the office. Even though my closed door might as well have 'Do not enter' written on it, there is still the slim chance that someone might interrupt me. Or even overhear what I'm saying. So I grab my mobile and head down the stairs.

'I'm going out for a bit,' I shout to Ashley, without stopping long enough for her to ask me any questions. 'Can you tell Bea?'

'OK,' she calls back. 'Shall I take messages or put every-one through to her?'

'To her,' I shout up the stairs. 'I won't be long.'

I walk up the road to Brook Green. It's only half eleven but it's hot, so it's already full of people lying prone on the grass like so many rows of the wounded. Offices every-where must be empty. Calls going straight to voicemail. There's a bench in the shade that's unoccupied, so I park myself there and scroll through looking for Patrick's mobile number.

It rings once, then his voice cuts in. 'Hi. This is Patrick Mitchell. Leave me a message and I'll call you back.' Short and to the point. Damn. I hadn't even considered that he might be busy. On the spur of the moment I decide to leave a message. I know that Michelle's the last person in the world who would snoop through her husband's phone. Oh the irony. Nevertheless, I try to keep my voice neutral 'Hi. It's me. Tamsin. I need to talk to you. Give me a call.'

I sit there for a few minutes, willing my mobile to ring, and then I realize he might not get back to me for hours. On the way back to the office I buy myself a carton of coconut water at the little shop on the corner. My alibi.

Five minutes later my direct line rings. I dive for it, thinking he might have phoned me in the office if he was having trouble getting through on the mobile.

'Hello,' I say in a loud whisper. I look up and check the door is closed.

'Tamsin,' a woman's voice says loudly. 'It's Fi.'

Fiona. Ian's wife. I'm very fond of Fiona but I have no desire to talk to her at the moment.

'How are you? Is this an OK time?'

'Um. I'm a bit—'

Fiona is one of those people who never wait for you to finish your sentence before they start their next one. Consequently any conversation becomes a battleground of who is talking when.

'It's just I wanted to ask how you got on with Adam. Ian said you weren't that taken but I thought I'd put a word in for him anyway. He's a thoroughly nice bloke.'

God, really? This is why she's called me?

'I'm sure he is. We just weren't a good—'

'Match? He's Becca's favourite teacher. At least he was, she doesn't have him this year.'

'I don't think we had anything—'

I pick up my mobile. Check for missed calls. Nothing.

'I haven't had the chance to ask him what he thought, but I will if you want.'

'No! No, thank you. Listen Fiona, I have to—'

'Because I'll almost certainly run into him at Parents' Evening.'

'I've got another call coming thr—'

She starts to say something else, but I clatter the phone down. I hope she doesn't think I'm being rude. Chances are she doesn't. Fiona doesn't really need anyone else on the other end of the line to have a conversation.

'So,' Bea says when she gets me on my own, having first established that I am feeling a little better. 'How are things with Patrick Mitchell and his wife?'

There's only one reply I can give. 'They're fine. I think it's all blown over already.'

She plonks herself down on the armchair in my room, long legs hooked over the side, wedge-heeled sandals dangling. 'Oh thank God. Can I stop feeling guilty now?'

I force a laugh that wouldn't be out of place in a bad am dram production of *Charley's Aunt*. I think I actually say the words, 'Ha ha.'

'Totally. I should never have made you feel bad in the first place.'

'Completely understandable. So, guess what? Lucy flat-out refused to type up the notes this morning. Even though I did it last time.'

How difficult and self-aggrandizing Lucy can be is one of Bea's and my favourite topics. I don't want to play today, though.

'Actually, Bea, I need to watch the rough cut of episode three of *Space Seekers*. I promised them I'd—'

Bea jumps up before I can finish.

'Sorry, of course. You get on. I'll bring you in a coffee in a bit.'

'Do you want to watch?' I like to hear Bea's thoughts on our shows. I am often too quick to judge. One shaky edit or cheesy reaction shot can have me tutting and rolling my eyes about the incompetence and lack of taste of everyone involved so violently that my concentration is shot. However much I try to remind myself that first cuts are always – and I mean always – awful, I can't help myself. Every niggle and irritation I have had about the production team since day one rises up to greet me. I told them not to do that, I said that if they took the shot from there it would look ugly. I knew that presenter would come across as patronizing if they didn't keep reminding him to adopt a warmer tone every take.

Of course, my rational self knows that there are a hundred different versions of each programme within the same footage, just waiting to be brought out. The editing process is like watching a miracle unfold. And rough cuts are just what they say. Rough. Templates for discussion. No one is suggesting that this be the finished product. It doesn't stop me despairing, though. Even after all these years.

Bea, on the other hand, being one step removed and an altogether calmer human being and less prone to knee-jerk reactions, tends to see the bigger picture. She often has helpful suggestions, too. I have been known – only when under extreme time pressure I should add – to get her to view an edit for me and to pass her notes off as my own.

'I've already seen it,' she says and pulls a face that I take to mean I'm going to hate it.

'That bad?'

'Doable. Just take deep breaths. Keep calm.' She laughs.

She shuts the door behind her so I can concentrate, which leaves me free to stare at my mobile for another ten minutes, willing Patrick to return my call.

Eventually I force myself to give up. I watch the *Space Seekers* first cut and go through my usual range of emotions – irritation, outright anger, resignation – before calming myself down by making copious notes about ways in which it could be improved. As always, once I've thought it through rationally I emerge the other side, optimistic that the programme will be good with some careful re-editing. All the material is there, it's just in the wrong order.

Bea's suggestions tally with mine. Although I'm confident about my own opinion, I won't deny it's sometimes nice to have it seconded. Especially because the producer of *Space Seekers* is notoriously tricky and seems to view every note as an affront. I get him on the phone, argue the finer points of cutting a scene – where the presenter patronizes the home owner by explaining at length how louvre doors work – or just tightening it up, for way too long. I get my way in the end and he promises me the offending footage will go straight into the digital bin. In return I agree that he can keep a toe-curling exchange between the same presenter and one of the handymen in its cringy entirety. I send an email to Ian, copying Bea in, to remind me to replace the front man if the series ever gets re-commissioned.

I've managed to kill another hour. My phone is still stubbornly silent. I do that thing where I pick it up and press a few buttons as if to make sure it's working properly and there isn't a return message from Patrick hidden away in there somewhere. Not that I would have missed him if he called, I have the ringer turned up to full volume and every five seconds or so I stare reproachfully at the handset in case I miss something.

I start sweating, thinking that maybe he's confessed all to Michelle already. I imagine his guilt is on a par with mine. He's bound to be beating himself up, going through agonies of self-loathing alternated with fear of discovery. If he'd told Michelle everything, though, she would have called me. Turned up at my office with Ron in one hand and an axe in the other probably. I need to reassure him quickly, though. Let him know that I will never divulge what has happened. Never. Who would it benefit?

I briefly consider calling him on his work number, or even going over there, but I know that would only draw attention to myself. He'll call me as soon as he's able. This is as important for him as for me.

I can't just leave it all to fate, though, so I decide to send him a text. I agonize over what to say, and in the end I conclude that being to the point is best.

'Still can't believe we did that last night. Too much wine, ha ha. I'm feeling horribly guilty and I'm sure you are too. Def right that we never tell Michelle. It would only upset her even though it meant nothing. T.'

I add a kiss, like I always do, take it off, put it on again, then take it off for good. Too soon.

I need a distraction, so I head downstairs to Bea and Lucy's shared office.

'Lucy, have you done the minutes from this morning yet? It's your turn to do them, isn't it? I need to check something.'

94

In so far as I know no one has ever been interested in reading the general meeting minutes before. She looks trapped, like a rabbit in some very bright headlights.

'Um . . . I haven't got round to it yet. I'll do them now. What did you want to check? I can look in my notes.'

'No. Just do them as soon as you can, if you don't mind. Thanks.'

I turn to leave. Bea smirks at me and I give her a hammy wink as I go.

14

By home time I am a nervous wreck. Why is Patrick not returning my calls? I know that I can't try him again now that there's a possibility he might be at home and in the same room as Michelle. Even I'm not that stupid.

On the way to the tube station Michelle herself phones and I lose my bottle and can't answer in case she starts screaming that I am a home-wrecking bitch and she hates me. When I listen to the message she left it's almost worse – she's her normal, jokey, friendly self, just calling for a catch-up. I don't call her back – I have no idea how I can pretend that everything is as it should be.

I can't even be bothered to change out of my work clothes. I head straight for the fridge, gag when I see some wine, and pour myself a glass of cranberry juice the size of a small lake. I flop down on the sofa, gulping it back. Thankfully Sharon the dog walker has been in and will have taken Ron for a romp on Primrose Hill, as she does every afternoon, so he's flat out on the wooden floor, probably dreaming about having her for an owner instead of me. My plan is to retire to bed before it even gets dark and take a Nytol. I appreciate this is no good as a long-term strategy, but for tonight it's all I have.

The sound of my phone nearly makes me jump out of my skin. I grab it before whoever it is can decide to ring off. Patrick.

'I've been waiting for you to call me all day,' I say as an opener.

'Sorry, sorry. We had our big strategy meeting. I was with people all the time . . .'

'Where are you now?'

'Walking home from the tube. Are you good?'

'Yes. No. Are you?'

'Not really.'

There's a long uncomfortable, weighty silence.

'So?' Patrick asks eventually.

'We were drunk, obviously . . .'

'Obviously. I have a terrible hangover by the way. Do you?'

'Awful. But that's no excuse . . .'

'Exactly.'

'I'm sorry,' he says. 'Really sorry. I have no idea what came over me.'

You'll be relieved to know I resist the obvious response.

'God, me too. Don't blame all this on yourself.'

'It's hard not to. I was the one who was all needy and emotional. Now I'm exactly the person Michelle was worried I am.'

'You're not. What we did was wrong. Awful. But it could have been much worse. I mean, it doesn't bear thinking about . . .'

'OK, steady on,' he says. 'Don't go mad.'

I can't help but smile. 'You know what I mean. But it was a mistake. A drunken, stupid mistake. It never would have happened otherwise. It's not like we set out to do it.'

'No! Of course not.'

97

'So you're not that person. We fucked up but you're not that person.'

'I've never lied to her before. I don't know if I can . . .' he says and I feel my heart jump a beat.

'You have to. We both have to. It's the only way things'll ever be OK. It's not as if it's ever going to happen again.'

'Maybe she'd understand. If she knew we were drunk and I was all over the place . . .'

'No. God. She'd never feel happy about us seeing each other again. Imagine thinking you couldn't trust your best mate and your husband to be on their own together.'

He sighs. 'Shit. And if she is worried about whether she can trust me at the moment this'll just make things ten times worse. You're right. It just feels so wrong.'

'I know. But promise me you won't say anything. Please, Patrick.'

'Of course not. We agreed.'

'I know but I needed to hear it again. The thought of Michelle—'

'You don't have to tell me, I'm married to her, remember.'

I still feel the need to hammer the point home.

'Whatever happens you never tell her. If you have a fight or . . . I don't know . . . something happens between you one day . . . please.'

'Jesus, Tamsin. Nothing is going to happen between us. I adore Michelle. And if it makes you feel better I promise that even if she has some kind of personality transplant and runs off with Jim from next door I swear to you I will never say a word. Never. OK?'

I know I can't push him any more, even though my

instinct is to stay on the phone all evening making him repeat his words over and over again.

'And the same goes for you too, obviously?'

That's easy. I know I've already locked away this particular secret and thrown out the key.

'God . . . yes, I swear. I don't think we should ever even talk about it again between ourselves. And you'll delete that text I sent you, won't you? Just in case.'

'Agreed. And already done.'

'Was everything . . . she didn't think anything was up when you got home?'

He exhales loudly. 'No, thank God. She'd never suspect . . . not us . . .'

'What a mess.'

'Shit. What were we thinking?'

There's not even a little bit of me that minds that he's viewing me as a ghastly mistake. I'm glad. I feel exactly the same.

'I have no idea.'

'You do know this is the only time . . . I mean I've never . . . with anyone. I was being truthful with you before.'

I don't doubt him for a second. It's clear he's feeling as bad, as confused, as I am. 'I know. OK, so everything back to how it was. Like it never happened.'

'Who are you again?' he says and that makes me laugh. It's such a stupid Patrick joke.

'I might see you at the weekend. I don't know.'

'Yes. Come over. Otherwise Mich is going to worry about what's up with you. It'll be OK.'

'If we pretend everything's normal then it will be, I suppose.'

'Exactly. At least I hope so. We can't change what happened. I wish we could.'

Now I know why they talk like they do in the soaps. Sometimes a cliché is all you've got.

I feel as if I want to apologize for getting us in this mess in the first place but, of course, he doesn't know the half of it, so I just keep my mouth shut.

'I'm pretty much home, I should go.'

'I feel a lot better,' I say, and I do if I ignore the big black shadow that's lurking just out of my vision.

'Good. Things will be OK.'

'They will. I just have to get over my self-loathing first.'

'Me too.'

'Night, Patrick.'

Just carry on as normal I tell myself. Eventually you might feel as if it is. And then I remember that I've promised to have an early drink with Michelle tomorrow. I don't know how I could have forgotten. We arranged it last week when she decided we hadn't been seeing enough of each other because she'd been under pressure at work. We even jokingly typed the date into our calendars, promising only to renege in the event of death or serious illness.

I look around wondering if there's some kind of 'accident' that could befall me, resulting in a one-night-only hospital stay and no ill after-effects, but I'm way too much of a baby. The sight of needles makes the world sway and the floor disappear from under me. Anyway, the bottom line is, short of a miracle, I will be in the office as per usual tomorrow and available for drinks after. I toy with the idea of making up a work crisis, but

Michelle knows I'm having a quiet time. She would be able to tell I was making excuses. Carry on as usual, that's what Patrick and I promised we would do. Drinks with Michelle it is then.

15

She's already there when I arrive. She always is. I am pretty punctual by nature but for Michelle it's almost a psychosis. She's so afraid of being late that she actually arrives everywhere a minimum of fifteen minutes early. Once I arrived bang on time and she was looking at her watch and drumming her fingers on the table impatiently. She laughed when I pointed it out.

I stop in the doorway for a moment, taking her in. She's leaning forward, looking at something on her phone. Smiling. Her blonde hair hangs forward over her face and she reaches up to hook it behind her ear. She's way prettier than I could ever hope to be. Not that it's ever bothered me. I haven't even really thought about it since we were teenagers and that kind of thing seemed to matter. Now it strikes me as being of huge significance. She's much more even-tempered than me, probably smarter, clearly a nicer person. What was Patrick thinking? What was *I* thinking, more to the point? Why would either of us risk losing her?

I have been asking myself if a tiny bit of me feels flattered by the fact that – even if only for a brief moment – Patrick must have fancied me. I'm so nothing like the perfect pretty girls he has always gone for. I don't want to admit it, even to myself, but I'm afraid there might be an element of truth in there somewhere. I really don't want to have to acknowledge that I'm that shallow.

I almost lose my resolve and turn round and walk away again. The little restaurant cum bar where we always meet has huge windows, though, and it would be just my luck that Michelle would look up from whatever she's doing and see me just as I was sending a text saying I'd been run over by a taxi. And right on cue she does, and a wide smile takes over her whole face and I feel like the shittiest, most disloyal, worst friend ever.

Michelle stands up to hug me. She smells of citrusy shampoo and CK1, the perfume she's worn for at least the last twenty years. I can't catch a whiff of it anywhere without thinking of her. There is already a large glass of white wine – presumably Sauvignon Blanc, my white of choice only because it's one of the few I can name – sitting on the table in front of the empty chair. Despite my post-Patrick resolution never to get drunk in company again I pick it up and throw back a mouthful guaranteed to knock out a smaller mammal before I even sit down.

'Thirsty?' Michelle says with a hint of a smirk on her face.

I force myself to put the glass back on the table. 'Mmm. It's hot out there.'

'Should we get some water?' She looks around, trying to catch the waitress's attention.

'Just tap,' I say, glad of the distraction. On our post-work-drink catch-up evenings we always leave to go home by half seven at the latest and anything that fills the time between now and then that isn't Michelle and I talking about our personal lives is fine by me.

'Is that new?' I say, indicating her businesslike summer shirt. This is the kind of insightful, deep conversation you can look forward to if you're best mates with me, obviously.

'It is. Warehouse. I had to find something quick because I burned a hole in my other one so I actually went to a shop all by myself and picked it out without you to help me. Impressed?'

'Lovely.'

There's nothing much else I can say. It's a mass-produced functional shirt. I'm a little obsessive about patronizing the small independent clothes shops in our respective areas to try and stave off the inevitable big chain takeover myself. Not that I seem to be making much of a difference. It soothes my conscience, though. Or at least it did when the biggest things troubling it were where I bought my shoes and whether the fish I ate was ethically sourced. The epitome of first world problems.

Now I wouldn't care if the whole of Belsize Park was flattened to become a superstore with its own sweatshop out the back so long as it meant I could rewrite the events of the past few days.

'I have no summer things.' If I keep going at this scintillating rate we could talk about nothing but clothes shopping for the next hour. Michelle's not having it, though.

'Did you get anything for your mum yet?'

I see an in and I start to drone on about various gift options I have considered and the reasons I have rejected them, desperate to fill the hour with idle chat. I'm boring myself, but I persevere. When Mich looks away for a second I surreptitiously look at the time on my phone. Six forty-five. Only three quarters of an hour to go before I can make my excuses and leave. I gulp back the remains of my second large glass of wine, ignoring the fact that I know I should keep my head clear.

'Shall we have one more?' Michelle says. She's only just finishing her first – single – vodka and tonic.

'Sure. I'm not in a rush.' I can say this safe in the knowledge that she will have arranged a time to sit down and eat with Patrick. On catch-up evenings he always cooks and has dinner ready for when she gets home.

By the time the drinks arrive I have steered the conversation on to work-related things. I know Michelle has been knee-deep in coordinating a campaign for a new app that's being launched – something to do with price comparisons on beauty products in high-street stores, I don't really understand – so I quiz her about how it's going.

After that, out of politeness if nothing else, she has to ask me about my work, so I bore for England about a couple of shows that are in different stages of production and then, thankfully, it's time to go. We haven't actually talked about anything beyond the polite conversation of acquaintances. Perfect.

Michelle, it transpires, has arranged to meet Patrick at a restaurant in Soho for dinner. I wonder if it was his idea. If this is his way of trying to prove what a good husband he is.

'Why don't you come?' she says as I flap my arm about to stop a taxi.

'No!' I say far too quickly. 'No. I'm not going to intrude on your date night.'

Michelle laughs. 'It's not like that. He just had a screening to go to so I said I'd meet him after.'

'Honestly? I'm knackered.'

I managed to shove her into the cab, relieved that we're not going the same way. Three drinks in and I really don't feel like going home and sitting in my empty flat thinking about what a fuck-up I am though. I want to go out and get wasted. All my other friends will be tucked up at home with their partners and/or their children. I don't know anyone who goes out drinking on a week night any more. Actually, scrub that, I do.

Bea answers almost immediately. I can hear noise in the background that tells me she's in a pub or a restaurant.

'Is everything OK?' she says before I can even say hello.

'Yes. Sorry to call in the evening. I just wondered what you were up to – whether you fancied a drink.'

'Sure . . .' she sounds hesitant. This is a request without precedent. Like I said, despite how well we get on we tend to keep our social lives separate beyond an after-work quick one in the local. 'I'm in the pub on the corner of my road with Ali.'

Ali is Bea's flat mate. One of them. She has two, I think, Ali and Sarah, and there is usually a drama unfolding. Bea seems to be in charge – she has kicked a couple of them out in the time that I've known her.

'Oh. Well . . . I don't want to muscle in . . .'

'It's fine. It means Ali will have to stop going on about her ex, which'll be a relief, to be honest.'

I hear Ali object in the background, laughing shrilly.

'Are you OK?' Bea continues.

'I just feel like some company, that's all.'

'Get over here then.'

She reminds me of her address. It's only five minutes

from Angel tube but I get a cab anyway. I'm not even half-way there when I start to regret it. I'd be far better off holed up in solitude in my little flat. I'm a loose cannon. It's good that Ali's going to be there. We can keep the conversation general, have a few drinks. Numb my brain enough so I can sleep.

Don't make an idiot of yourself, I remind myself as the taxi pulls up. You're a bit tipsy. A lot emotional. And you're still Bea's boss when it all comes down to it. Don't have one too many and fall flat on your face in the middle of the pub. Order a Diet Coke, some part of me says, but the rest of me just laughs in its face.

The pub is like something you might see in a Guy Ritchie film just before a major gun battle breaks out, killing everyone except the biggest name actor. It's very man heavy. I assume the wives and girlfriends are all gathered somewhere pink, necking back vodkas and moaning about their men-folk. There is a pool game going on and I can't help thinking how much the cues look like weapons. I edge my way through to the overcrowded patio out back. Bea is sitting at a corner table with a woman I assume must be Ali. She's about Bea's age. Short hair. Big glasses. Angry expression. Looks like one of Chumbawumba.

'Hey,' Bea says when she sees me. 'Welcome to my local. Very retro, don't you think?'

'Are you here ironically?' I ask, only half joking.

Ali turns her furious-wasp face to me. 'It's authentic.'

Great, this is going to be a fun evening. 'Oh . . .' I stammer. 'Of course.'

Ali glares at me and then her face creases up in a huge smile. 'I was joking. It's a shit hole.'

Bea is laughing heartily. 'But it's our shit hole.'

'OK, who wants a drink?'

Bea indicates their mostly full glasses. 'We only got here just before you called so we're OK.'

I head back inside to jostle my way to the bar. One of the advantages of being in such a testosterone-fuelled establishment that clearly still thinks it's the 1970s is that they all make way for 'the lady' and I get served in record time.

On the way back with my vodka and Coke I stumble rather attractively over the leg of a chair. The three glasses of wine I sank earlier have caught up with me.

'Are you pissed again?' Bea says, incredulous.

'No! A little bit. I was out with Michelle before.'

'Ah,' she says knowingly. 'And how are things there?'

'All fine,' I say, not wanting to talk about it. 'All blown over.'

'Well that's a relief.'

For a minute I'm worried that she's going to fill Ali in on the details, even though I swore her to secrecy about the honey-trap plot on about a hundred different occasions. She doesn't, of course, because she's Bea, which is shorthand for reliable and trustworthy.

'Tamsin's friend has been having a few problems,' she says to Ali by way of an explanation. 'Nothing major thankfully.'

She turns back to me, a mischievous glint in her eye. 'Ali was just telling me how she bumped into Stuart, her ex, with his new girlfriend, in M&S Food yesterday.' She raises an eyebrow at me and I know she's saying, 'Go on, I dare you.'

I remember that Ali is the over-sharer. Bea once warned me that if I ever met her I should avoid asking her anything personal. 'You'll never get away. I have to feign emergencies to shut her up.'

'That must have been tricky,' I say, taking the bait. 'When did you split up?'

Ali's owlish eyes widen and I feel a bit bad. Eleven minutes later, when I've heard the whole history of Ali and Stuart's relationship – in intimate detail I should add – this sympathy has largely dissipated. I know now that Ali and Stuart met at a singles night for people who are into techy things; that the first time they had sex she asked that they turn the lights off because she was worried about her puffy legs, but Stuart had insisted they turn them on and he hadn't seemed put off at all; that she had always wondered if she might be gay, but being with Stuart had convinced her otherwise, and that eventually, just as she had started dreaming about a small but intimate wedding in Greece, he had announced he wasn't in love with her after all, and two weeks later he had shacked up with Tara from his work, who Ali had been worried about all along if she was being honest.

After a while I start to find her prattling on quite soothing. Once I realize I'm not expected to contribute beyond the occasional 'really?' and 'ooh' in seemingly random places I switch off completely, apart from the odd shared raised eyebrow with Bea. I don't think about anything except the warm night and the passing traffic. It's cathartic.

'How about you, Tamsin?' I suddenly hear Ali's voice penetrate my fog. 'What's going on with your love life?'

'Oh . . . nothing,' I say, looking at the table, my drink,

the honeysuckle growing up the trellis. Anywhere but at Bea. I feel as if she would read the lie on my face in a second.

'Tamsin is selectively single,' Bea says, smiling at us both in turn. 'That's why she's so rational and sane. No drama.'

'That's what I aspire to,' Ali says.

Bea takes a long sip of her drink. 'I don't think it's possible to have a life with no drama in it. There's always something.'

She looks at me quizzically, and for a split second I actually consider it – telling Bea, and by default Ali – what happened. Purging it all and then asking her to tell me what to do, absolve me. It would almost be a relief. She would probably give me the standard 'what's the big deal, you were pissed and you didn't actually go all the way' pep talk and I would decide she was right and immediately feel better.

'Here's to drama,' Ali says, sweeping up our now empty glasses and standing up. 'Same again?'

I suddenly feel like I should get a grip. Head home before more alcohol loosens my tongue and I turn into a confessional mess. 'Actually, I should make a move. I don't want to feel like shit in the morning.'

Bea jumps up and gives me a hug. 'Do you want me to help you find a taxi?' she asks, ever concerned about my welfare.

'I'll be fine. I'll get the tube, it's still early. See you tomorrow. Nice to meet you, Ali.'

I wave as I pick my way through the crowd.

16

Everything is back to normal. Or at least, the new version of normal. Normal with a hidden hint of dysfunction that only Patrick and I know about. Normal on the surface but a bit fucked-up underneath.

It's been just over six weeks. Six long weeks since that evening. Gradually I have forced myself to spend more and more time with Michelle until I am almost back at pre you-know-what levels. At first it was painful. I tried to stick to meeting up with her on her own, or timing my visits to theirs when I thought it was most likely Patrick wouldn't be there. The first time I got it wrong and he suddenly stepped into their kitchen as Mich and I chatted over a cup of tea. I don't know who looked more horrified, me or him.

It had been sixteen days. Michelle had told me that Patrick was doing a set visit to Nottingham on a Thursday evening, because some show he'd commissioned was doing night shoots using some kind of new low-light vision technology or something, which meant you could show off a revamped garden in the dark without having to floodlight the place. He was keen to see how it worked, she said. If it did it could save them a fortune in hours wasted setting up lamps. She'd invited me over to keep her company and, as I had just about got back to the stage where I could act normally around her again – after a couple of encounters when I couldn't even remember what our regular conversation was, let alone make it, to the extent where she'd ended up asking me if I was OK, and I'd had to lie about problems at work and an argument with one of my brothers – I'd agreed. I missed her.

I had finally stopped obsessing about what I'd done. It was still there, don't get me wrong. A few days after the event I had forced myself to confront the full horror of what had happened and there it was in glorious technicolour: tops pushed up, trousers unzipped, hands and mouths everywhere. We had got a lot done in fifteen (OK, twenty-five) minutes. I'd made myself consider, for the first time, whether I actually did have feelings for Patrick. Whether I had been harbouring my old secret crush for years, just waiting for my opportunity. I honestly didn't believe I had.

After that I had tried to park the whole incident at the back of my brain and dump a couple of skips full of bland, inoffensive rubble in front of it. I know that doesn't really work as a metaphor, but you get the picture. Out of sight, out of mind.

I think it helped that I hadn't been able to discuss what had happened with anyone. I hadn't seen or spoken to Patrick since that initial phone call, of course. I had mercifully resisted the urge to confide in Bea. I could almost make myself believe it had never happened.

So, anyway, Michelle and I were sitting at the kitchen table, mugs of tea in front of us – we were both attempting a no-alcohol month, that is, I was attempting it and she was accomplishing it with ease – talking about, if I remember rightly, the fact that she had bumped into one of our friends from school on the tube, when suddenly I heard a noise and there was Patrick standing in the door-way wearing nothing but a towel.

I jumped. He jumped. Michelle laughed, thinking our discomfort was down to surprise, not guilt.

'I thought you were out,' I said and it came out more accusatory than I meant it to. I tried not to notice his unclothed upper body. Felt myself blush red.

'I just popped home for a shower,' he said, clutching the top of the towel.

Michelle was still finding our over-the-top reaction hysterical. 'Sorry, I thought I'd said.' She laughed, waving her arm at me. 'Your face!'

'I was just startled, that's all,' I said, trying to force myself to laugh along.

'You both look like you've seen a ghost.'

'I didn't think you'd be here yet,' Patrick said, which to my ears also sounded like an accusation. 'Or I'd have got ready earlier.'

'God, she's seen it all before,' Michelle chipped in. I looked at the floor.

Thankfully he turned on his heels, muttered something about being late and went upstairs to get dressed. Five minutes later he stuck his head back around the door, leaning in just enough to kiss the top of Michelle's head.

'Won't be late,' he said, and he was gone before I could even say goodbye.

I decided I needed to start dating again. I didn't want my last encounter with a man to be with Patrick. I needed something to wash the taste out of my mouth, as it were. OK. That ended up sounding way more graphic than I meant it to, but you know what I mean. So a week or so later I re-registered at Other Half, my dating site of choice. Tried to convince myself that all sorts of unlikely looking people might prove to be my soul mate.

I spent an age working on my profile. I know my good points. Or, at least, I know what my good points were before I was forced to revise my opinion of myself. Loyal, honest, reliable, hard working.

I realize this sounds like a for-sale ad for a carthorse.

Funny. Supportive. Good fetlocks.

OK, I made that last one up. But I do have quite sturdy calves. I tried to say something funny to show off my GSOH. Failed. In the end I settled for factual. I mentioned Ron (Must love dogs) and a bit about my job.

Obviously I left out all my negatives: I'm unforgiving, critical, a looks fascist where men are concerned (which is ludicrous given said calves), pessimistic, occasionally overbearing and controlling. Untrustworthy.

The end result was a biography so bland I wouldn't want to date any man who might think I was a good catch. Like Groucho Marx said, I wouldn't want to join any club that would have me as a member.

I forced myself to press send. Tried to forget all about it.

The first date was fine. Just that. Fine. His name was Mario. That was the most colourful thing about him. He was a nice-looking man with a nice personality and an unchallenging job in a recruitment agency. We made nice conversation over a nice meal and then we said goodnight, both knowing that there was no reason for us to ever see each other again. Or, at least, so I thought. Turned out Mario thought we'd had a 'spark' and persisted in emailing me for a couple of days, asking when we could meet up again, until eventually I had to spell out that there really was no chance of us going anywhere.

His reaction was, well, to be nice. Of course it was. I just wished I could have liked him more.

My second attempt was more eventful. Owen was as attractive as his picture promised. Dark-haired and light-eyed – a fatal combination in my book. Tall, slim, muscular. He oozed pheromones. I couldn't quite believe he had singled me out. Turned out I possessed the one thing he found irresistible: a vagina. We met in a pub in Bloomsbury, with the intention of going on for a meal if we hit it off. He was in full-on seduction mode from the first moment and, even though I found it cheesy beyond words, I found myself going along with it. In the end we skipped the food part, went back to mine, had what I thought was fantastic sex and then, the minute it was over, he grabbed his stuff and left. He didn't even pretend to make a promise to call. To be honest I didn't care. I would never usually do something so reckless with a person I had known for a full hour and a half, but it almost felt like an exorcism. I had no interest in trying to pursue a relationship with him. His conversation had mostly been about himself and his gym routine. As he left I had to stop myself from shouting, 'I've just used you as much as you've used me,' after him.

Tonight Michelle, Patrick and I are celebrating. Michelle has landed some big new account at work. Something virtual, God knows. Anyway, she announced that she wanted to toast her success with a glass of bubbly. It's the first proper evening the three of us have spent together since . . . well, since.

We've all met up at the Charlotte Street Hotel after work and somehow, miraculously, managed to bag a spot out on the street. The credit needs to go to me for that one, really. I am skilled in the art of standing and staring resentfully until someone feels bad (or intimidated, I don't much care which), and decides to call it a night and vacate their table.

Patrick clicks his fingers to get the waiter's attention. I look away. I hate the finger-clicking. Whatever happened to a good old-fashioned 'Excuse me?'

'Pad!' Michelle says. It's as far as she ever gets to acknowledging his bad behaviour.

We all raise our glasses. 'Here's to your swanky new campaign,' I say. I clink her flute and then, of course, have to clink Patrick's too.

'Hear hear,' he says. 'Let's hope it pays you a fortune and I can retire and live off your hard-earned cash.'

'Actually, it's not really that big of a deal. I just wanted an excuse to get together with my two favourite people in the world. I feel as if we hardly spend any time together any more, the three of us.'

If I said there was an awkward silence I would be doing it a disservice. It's deafening it's so quiet.

'Well, this is nice,' is the best I can come up with. I'm finding it hard to look at Patrick. I'm still scared I'll give myself away.

'Oh,' Patrick says, as Michelle tops up our glasses. 'I bought these today, look.' I realize he's trying to force a conversation and I'm grateful.

He digs around in his bag. Comes up with a pair of sunglasses. 'Good, huh?'

He pops them on. They're brown and a bit retro-looking. By retro I mean they're like those giant monstrosities you used to get in the seventies.

I can't help myself. I laugh. 'You look like an ant.'

Patrick feigns a hurt expression. 'I got them from that vintage shop in Endell Street.'

'Just because they're vintage doesn't mean they're stylish,' Michelle says laughing. 'They're very . . . Roy Orbison.'

'They're Gucci,' he says huffily.

'They're hideous is what they are. Michelle's right. Roy Orbison.'

'No,' she says. 'Actually they're more Deirdre Barlow. But in the eighties.'

'Or Dame Edna.'

Patrick smiles and it looks like a genuine, happy smile. 'I hate it when you two gang up on me.'

And there it is. The moment when it actually feels as if things will get back to the way they used to be.

Relief. That's what I feel when I wake up early the next morning. The sun is already streaming through my too-flimsy curtains. Usually – these days – this is the time when I toss and turn, beating myself up about every bad thing I have ever done. Well, just one thing, really. *The* thing. This morning it feels as if a weight has been lifted. Don't get me wrong I would still do anything if I could take it back. I will still never forgive myself. But I now believe that Michelle, Patrick and I can continue to be friends. I can imagine a time when it will all feel like a distant nightmare. Hopefully one that happened to someone else.

Famous last words.

17

I'm going to be sick.

Michelle is crying in my living room. She's trying to talk but she keeps tripping over her words, hiccupping back sobs. I have no idea what to do.

This is the moment I've been dreading for weeks. And I have no one to blame but myself.

She takes a deep, gasping breath. Blows her nose loudly on a tissue she produces from her bag. I resist the urge to go over and hug her in case she punches me in the mouth. I don't think I have ever seen Michelle cry without going to her aid.

'I think something happened,' she says obliquely, looking at me expectantly. I have no idea what to say, so I say nothing.

'I think Patrick's slept with someone.'

There's a second when all I take in is 'Patrick's slept with'. I reach for one of the denials I have been rehearsing in my head over and over – I would never do that to you, neither of us would ever treat you like that, technically does it count as sex if there's no penetration? – and then I realize that what she said was 'someone', not 'you'. Patrick slept with someone. Not 'why did you fool around with my husband, you bitch?' I am not 'someone' as far as Michelle is concerned. Could it be possible that she doesn't know it was me yet?

'What?' I say, grasping around for how best to respond. 'Why do you think that?'

'I found something,' she says, and I desperately try to imagine what evidence there might be. A stray long chest-nutty brown hair discovered down his trousers? Next she'll tell me she's just waiting for the results of the DNA test to find out who it belongs to.

'A receipt. Well, a credit card slip. Whatever you call it.'

OK. I don't think I gave Patrick a receipt. Acknow-ledgement for services rendered. I breathe out for, it seems, the first time in a while.

Michelle carries on. 'I was sorting out our receipts. Going through what needed filing and what I could throw away. And I thought I could do Pad's too, so I had a quick look through his desk in the study and I found this . . .'

For the first time I notice she has a screwed-up piece of paper in her hand. One of those small, innocent scraps we all amass by the hundred every year. She hands it to me.

It's the usual confusion of numbers. The amount at the bottom reads £393.91. At the top the words 'Park View Hotel, Knightsbridge' spring out at me.

I have never been to the Park View Hotel, with or without Patrick. The tightness in my chest eases up a little more, but then a new thought hits me.

What the fuck does this mean?

'I don't understand,' I say to Michelle, finally feeling brave enough now to move onto the sofa next to her and take her hand.

'That's the night he was supposed to be in Nottingham, remember? When he had to look at the new kind of lamps.'

I think back. I have a vague memory. I kept Michelle company while Patrick went to Nottingham for work. The night he appeared at the kitchen door in a towel. I look at the receipt again. July 16th. Four weeks ago.

'Are you sure?'

'Of course I am. I checked our calendar. July sixeenth, P to Nottingham. That's what it says.'

'Maybe you got it mixed up and the show was actually shooting in London?'

'It wasn't. And even if it was, why wouldn't he have come home after? Anyway, that's not all.'

'What?'

'This.'

She reaches into her pocket and brings out another crumpled piece of paper. This time A4. I know what it is immediately. An itemized bill from the hotel. Under name of guest, it clearly says Patrick Mitchell. The room-service breakfast charge is so high that if Patrick had eaten all that alone I'm pretty sure he would have gone straight into a coma. In small type on the top right-hand side it states, 'Number of guests: 2'.

I can hardly take this in. Is she really trying to tell me that Patrick's having an affair?

'After I found the credit-card receipt I hunted round in his stuff. This was in the bottom of his work bag.'

I wait. I can hear a woodpigeon cooing repetitively outside, in the gaps between the noise of the cars.

'You think Patrick took a woman there? To a hotel?'

She nods. 'He lied to me about where he was going. Why would he do that if it wasn't to cover something up?'

'Have you asked him?'

'No. He's at work. And I wanted to talk to you first. To be sure. He wouldn't, would he, Tam? Not Patrick?'

I'm not sure even I know the extent of what Patrick is capable of any more.

'No. God . . . no . . . I'm sure there's a perfectly innocent explanation.'

I can't help it. I'm terrified this might rebound on me. If Michelle forces a confession out of Patrick about whatever this is, then who knows what else he might tell her.

She looks at me with big, watery eyes. 'Like what?'

'I don't know. I still think maybe you got the places confused. Or he did. He wrote it on the diary as Nottingham but that was a different day or something.'

She shakes her head. 'We had a whole conversation about it when he got back. I've got an aunt and uncle who live there, remember?'

I let out an involuntary sigh. I have no idea what is going on here.

'And anyway, what about the other guest? Number of guests, two.'

'A colleague?' I say, although I can't offer up a good reason why a colleague might be sharing his room.

'Tamsin, we live in London. Why is he staying at a hotel in London? He could have been home from Knightsbridge in a cab in twenty minutes. It just doesn't make any sense.'

'No,' I say.

Michelle lets out a loud sob. 'Please let it not be true.'

I put my arms round her and pull her into a hug. 'He wouldn't do that to me, would he? Go off with someone else?'

'Of course not,' I say and I wait for someone to strike me dead. 'Of course he wouldn't.'

As soon as she leaves I pick up the phone to call Patrick – even though Michelle asked me not to say anything to him until she'd decided what to do. I have no idea what the real story is, no idea what the hell he might have done to her, but I have to make sure that whatever he decides to confess to her, whatever she finds out, it has nothing to do with me. I can't just leave it all to fate.

18

Patrick answers on the third ring. I know I can't just come out and accuse him of something. To be honest, I haven't really thought through what I'm going to say.

'Did you go up to Nottingham for a set visit a few weeks ago?' I blurt out before he can even ask me how I am.

Is it just me or does his voice sound cautious? 'Yes. Why?'

'On July the sixteenth?'

'I don't have my diary with me but that sounds about right. What are you on about, Tamsin?'

'It was definitely Nottingham, not somewhere in London?'

There's a moment's pause. 'Why are you asking me all these questions?'

There's no point in me not coming clean now. The combination of the words Nottingham and July 16th must be setting off sirens in his head.

'Just something Michelle said.'

'What did she say?'

'I . . . I don't know. Something about a credit card slip from a hotel . . .'

There's silence at the other end. It feels as if it goes on forever.

'I'm coming over.'

'No ... wait. I shouldn't have said anything. I don't want to know.'

'Then why the phone call?'

Actually, scrub that, I do want to know. 'Did you take someone there?'

'What business is this of yours exactly?' Patrick says in a cold tone of voice I have never heard him use before. I feel a rush of nausea.

'Please say you haven't been cheating on her.' In retrospect this is a stupid thing to say. Given, well, you know what.

'What, like I did with you, you mean?'

'That was different ...'

'Don't worry, I'm not about to tell her. I know that's why you called me, right? Self-preservation.'

'Why are you being so horrible?' I say. I should never have phoned. I should have stayed well out of it.

'You're the one who rang and started hurling accusations.'

'I didn't. I just asked you a question. You told me to tell you if I thought Michelle suspected you of seeing someone and now she does, OK?'

'Ah, so you're just telling me out of the goodness of your heart?'

'I'm not having this conversation,' I say, forgetting that I'm the one who started it. 'I've warned you, OK.'

'Gosh, thanks, Tamsin. Your concern for your friend is touching.'

'I'm putting the phone down.' I can't quite bring myself to do it, though.

There's a moment's silence and then he says, 'Go on

then.' I almost laugh. It reminds me of when I was a teenager and I would carry on like this for hours with whatever boy I was seeing at the time. 'Put the phone down', 'No, you', 'I'm definitely putting it down now', 'Go on then', 'No, you first'. I wasted many of my precious adolescent years having that conversation.

This time, though, there's no flirting. It's just a stand-off. I'm too old for this.

'Bye.' I press the button to end the call. Run into the bathroom and throw up.

Not knowing what is happening is killing me. I pace around the flat, trying and failing to find any distractions. Eventually I get Ron's lead, much to his delight, stuff my phone in my pocket and head out for a walk. I can't stop running scenarios in my head. Michelle showing Patrick the receipt, tearfully asking him what it means. Him denying, excuses prepared because of my phone call. All I have done is give him the weapons to get away with whatever he's getting away with. I may have saved myself, but at what cost?

Does this mean everything he said to me was a lie? Or has it just happened since me and him? *Maybe he enjoyed it so much with you he had to have another go,* some irritating voice in my brain offers up helpfully. I choose to ignore it. Deep down, though, a bit of me is wondering whether I am somehow partly to blame. Did he think, Sod it, if he was ever going to be hung at all it might as well be for a great big premeditated all-the-way sheep as for an opportunistic drunken fumbly mistake of a lamb?

I reach Primrose Hill and unclip Ron from his lead. As always, he runs round in circles while I sit on a bench staring off into space. I check my phone to see if Michelle has called. Nothing. Has she even confronted him yet? Has he told her? And, if so, what?

After a while Ron exhausts himself and flops at my feet. I lean down and stroke his wiry head and he sighs contentedly.

'Come on then,' I say, standing up. 'Home time.'

We trudge back up the hill and turn into my road, where I see a familiar figure sitting on the high steps to my front door. I feel a sharp pain in my chest and my fight-or-flight reflexes kick in, telling me to make a run for it in the opposite direction. Ron has other ideas. He's seen his beloved Uncle Patrick up ahead and he's already barking enthusiastically and straining at the leash like he's trying to pull a chariot. I have no choice but to follow. Patrick stands up when he sees us. I know that I'm scowling at him but I can't seem to help it.

'What are you doing here?'

He smiles, which unnerves me completely. It feels like Jaws asking how you are before he chomps into your leg.

'I thought we needed to talk.'

'I think you were right before. I think it's none of my business.' I don't want to have to listen to whatever he's going to say. I want to go inside and shut the door and not go out again till Monday.

'Tamsin, for God's sake. I need your help.'

I relent. What else can I do?

Inside I don't even ask him if he wants a cup of tea. I just want to hear what he has to say and then get him out of there.

'So?' I say when he doesn't offer anything up. Ron is doing loud comedy slurping from his water bowl, something that I usually find endlessly entertaining and endearing. I wish he'd stop.

Patrick exhales loudly. 'I was there with someone. At the Park View.'

I almost think I've heard incorrectly. 'What? Who?'

'It doesn't matter who.'

'I imagine it will to Michelle.'

'Just someone.'

'What the fuck were you thinking? How could you?'

'I haven't come here so you can tell me how disappointed in me you are. I've come because I need your help.'

'With what?' I say, although I have a horrible feeling I already know the answer.

'Michelle can't find out.'

'I think she already has.'

He picks up a lonely ageing apple out of the wire basket I laughingly call my fruit bowl. Puts it down again. 'No. She suspects. She knows that something isn't right, but she doesn't know what. I need you to help me convince her it's nothing.'

'Are you joking? You cheated on Michelle and now you want me to help hide the evidence. What the fuck?'

'It was a mistake. These things happen.'

'No way. I'm not going to get mixed up in this.'

'Actually, Tamsin, you already are. If she finds out about this I might as well tell her about us. I'll have lost everything anyway.'

'There is no us. There never was. We had too much to

drink and we crossed a line we never should have crossed. That was it.'

He raises an eyebrow at me. 'I'm sure she'll see it like that.'

I feel as if the floor has disappeared out from under me. I sit down on the arm of the nearest chair before my legs give way.

'Are you threatening me?'

He shrugs. 'Not threatening, just stating a fact.'

'Patrick . . . what the fuck?'

'What? You want to get all high and mighty with me about having a fling with someone but then you still want me to lie to my wife about what happened between me and you?'

'I thought we'd agreed that what happened between us was a shitty mistake when neither of us was in a fit state to know any better. That's hardly the same as booking a hotel and making up a whole story about being in an entirely different city.'

'Her best friend or someone she's never even met. Which do you think will hurt her more, whatever the circumstances?'

I know he's right. I know I don't have a leg to stand on. 'I don't understand. If you're fucking someone else then why do you care about saving your marriage anyway?'

Patrick picks up a book I've left lying on the kitchen counter. *Gourmet Meals For One* or something equally tragic. He turns it over casually, looks at the back as if it's just a normal day.

'I love Michelle. This other thing is nothing.'

'Why do it then?'

'Because I'm weak or a douchebag or something. I don't know. It'll all blow over soon . . .'

I can hardly believe what I'm hearing. I stand up, grab the book from his hands and slam it back down on the worktop. 'It's still going on?'

'I really don't think you need to know the details.'

'Oh no, hold on. If you're going to force me to be involved then I have to know what I'm involved in. Who is she?'

'You don't know her.'

'What's her name?'

'I told you, you don't know her.'

'Did you meet her through work?'

'Yes. Sort of.'

'And it's been going on for how long?'

'Six weeks or so. I'm going to end it soon. It's nothing serious.'

'Six weeks? Jesus, Pad.'

'It just happened. I didn't mean it to. You know how that goes, right?'

I choose to ignore the last part. He sweeps his hair back from his face with his right hand, one of his patented 'aren't I cool?' gestures. He has stupidly thick glossy hair. No sad pink scalp peeking through for him.

'And was she the first?'

There's a pause while – I imagine – he weighs up whether or not to lie to me.

'Yes.'

'Tell me the truth.'

'Why ask if you're not going to believe my answer?' He smirks. I edge back to put some more distance between us. I don't think it's a good idea for me to be in hitting range. I might not be able to control myself.

'Ball park. Three? Ten? Twenty? Five hundred?'

'There may have been a few over the years. None of them meant anything.'

'So all that shit about being worried she suspected you—'

'I *was* worried. I still don't know who that Cheryl woman was.'

'But the innocent act. The stuff about how you couldn't stand it if she thought that of you because you would never do anything like that.'

'Well, five minutes later you must have known that wasn't true.'

'Jesus. You were so convincing . . .'

'I don't need a lecture, OK. I'm not proud of myself. I just need to work out what to do.'

'Well, you can't do anything until Michelle brings it up. Apart from get rid of this woman, that is.'

'I don't know which would be worse. Michelle accusing me and me having to think of a cover story or her never saying anything, but I know she's thinking about it.'

'And if she does ask you?'

'I have no idea. That's why I need your help.'

I close my eyes. 'She found the itemized bill, too.'

'Shit.' He puts his head in his hands and I almost feel sorry for him. I talk myself out of that one pretty quickly, though.

'She went through my stuff?'

'Well, we're all full of surprises. I mean, why would you even keep that receipt? Were you going to try and claim it back? I don't want my wife to find out but I really want to fiddle my expenses, is that it?'

'Of course not. I just never imagined her searching through my things, I suppose. And then I just forgot it was there.'

'Brilliant. You're a master criminal.'

'There's no point being fucking sarcastic. I might be a shit husband but you're not exactly a textbook best friend either. So let's just sort this out together, OK?'

I know I don't have any choice. Not that I'm sure I have any interest in preserving Michelle and Patrick's marriage any more – in all honesty, I'm starting to think she'd be better off without him. Now I know what he's really like it's impossible to hope that they'll stay together.

'Let me think.'

I sit back down. Patrick flops into the other armchair and neither of us says anything for a few moments. I'm racking my brain but I can't make it come up with anything. The quacking of a duck that is Patrick's ring tone nearly gives me a coronary.

'Michelle,' he says, looking at the display. 'I can't answer it.'

We both wait for what seems like an eternity for it to stop. It's times like these that really bring it home why comedy ring tones are not a good idea.

Reluctantly I offer up the only solution I can think of. 'Tell her you booked it for a colleague because they'd forgotten their cards or, no, say it was someone coming for a meeting with you the next day and usually you would book those things on your business card but you couldn't find it and Verity had gone home, so you had to use your personal one. Say you think they were bringing their wife.'

'What if she asks me who?'

'I don't know. Make someone up. The blandest, most common name you can think of that isn't John Smith. Make sure you tell her the bit about the wife.'

I can't believe I'm about to say this next bit but here goes. 'I'll offer to phone your office and check it out or something.'

'What if she thinks of doing that herself?'

'I don't think she'd phone your office. She knows Verity far too well to pretend she's someone else, and I don't think she'd want to be seen to be checking up on you.' Verity is Patrick's assistant. I've never spoken to her but I know that Michelle is fond of her. I worry for a moment about whether she might be one of his conquests, but then I remember that she's in her late fifties. It seems unlikely. 'And anyway, I'll make sure she doesn't.'

'And what if Michelle doesn't report the whole thing back to you?'

'She will,' I say, sadly. 'She tells me everything. And anyway, it's all we've got.'

19

The awful thing is that it works.

Michelle tearfully tells me that Patrick vehemently denied any wrongdoing. By the sounds of it she was waiting when he got home from mine and she asked – as calmly as she could; she didn't want to sound like she was accusing him of anything – where he had stayed on the night of the 16th. He said Nottingham, obviously, so she produced the credit card slip. She didn't mention the itemized receipt because she didn't want it to look as if she had been snooping on him.

Patrick had laughed, she said, and immediately told her that he'd booked the hotel in London for the producer of one of their shows who was coming down from Scotland for a meeting at the channel the next day. He thought he'd brought his wife with him so they could go off somewhere and spend a few days together down here afterwards. Michelle had asked why Verity hadn't booked it on the company card and Patrick had told her it was a last-minute thing and she had already left for the day. He'd decided to use his own card and claim it back. He had sounded so confident, she said, that she'd felt stupid. There was no way he could have come up with that whole convoluted scenario off the top of his head. Only one thing was still nagging her – the name of the guest on the itemized receipt.

she had come clean and told him about looking through his bag. He'd looked a bit hurt – here I almost laughed, out of nervousness, not because I thought any of it was remotely funny – but then he'd said that he hadn't even noticed that, probably the hotel just got their wires crossed and assumed the room was in his name.

Michelle had paused here apparently. 'But when you booked wouldn't you have said the room was actually for Mr and Mrs so and so?'

'Probably but they wouldn't necessarily have taken it in. What I'm saying is it's not out of the question.'

'I want to believe him,' she said sadly. 'And I suppose it does make sense.'

And I – to my eternal shame – said yes, yes it did.

'Did he say who it was he booked it for?' I wanted to make sure Patrick and I had our story straight.

'Someone Robinson,' she said. 'He said he's one of the execs on some show they're making about Scottish castles.'

Thank God he'd taken my advice and picked a common name.

'I know,' I said, as if I'd just had a thunderbolt of inspiration. 'You can't do this because Verity knows you too well, but why don't I phone his office and say – I don't know – that I'm from the hotel and I've found something of his and see what they say. What's the worst that can happen?'

'I don't know. I don't want to become one of those wives who keeps checking up on her husband.'

'You won't be. I will. If not you're just going to keep on wondering whether there's something he hasn't told you.'

'What do you think?'

'Well, I wasn't there, but it sounds plausible to me.'

'You're right. Maybe I should just forget all about it, move on.'

I want this all to go away, so I push home my point. 'You could but you might still have a nagging doubt. Apart from anything else it's not fair on Pad. If I can find out for certain then why don't I?'

An hour later I called her back and told her that I'd spoken to someone else in Patrick's office because Verity wasn't around (just covering myself) and that I'd said I was from the Park View Hotel and Mr Mitchell had left something behind when he stayed that had only just come to my attention. I fudged something to cover the fact that it had taken several weeks to come to light. Something about the next guest taking it home by accident and then realizing it wasn't his (luckily Michelle didn't ask why anyone would believe that pile of implausible crap). The assistant had said that it was actually a Mr and Mrs Robinson who had stayed the night, so the item must be theirs, and had given an address in Scotland for it to be returned.

Michelle was so grateful, so happy when I told her my success. There was no reason in the world why she would ever disbelieve me. I was her best friend.

I sent Patrick a text. *'Done.'* And he sent one back in return, *'Thank you.'* And that was that.

I don't know how I'm going to work it but I have no intention of ever speaking to Patrick again – beyond the pleasantries that I'll be forced to offer up when other people are around. I'm going to refuse every invitation that has him attached. I'm done with him and his bullshit. Enough.

20

Bea is fuming when I arrive at the office in the morning. She doesn't even wait for me to put my bag down before she shuts the door of my office and launches into a tirade. I'm not really in the mood.

'I'm fucking furious,' she states, which, to be honest, I have gathered from the way she's stomping around with a face like a storm.

'Do I get a coffee first?' Bea knows I can't function without coffee first thing.

'I'll go and get you one in a minute. I just have to get this off my chest.'

'OK, that doesn't sound good.'

'Ian's just asked me to type up all his notes on the budget for *Rooms With a View* because – and I quote – "Lucy's a bit snowed under".' She sits back and looks at me, waiting for a response.

Strictly speaking, even though Bea works for me and Lucy for Ian they both work for the company, and so it's always been deemed only fair that they pick up each other's slack sometimes. This fact doesn't make either of them very happy, though.

'Well, I don't have much for you to do this morning . . .'

'That's not the point,' she jumps in before I can finish. 'If she *was* snowed under I'd happily do it . . .'

Happily, I feel, is an overstatement, but I keep quiet.

'. . . but she's got an appointment to get her colour done this afternoon. When have I ever made a hair appointment in work time? When?'

'Never,' I concede.

'I mean, surely Ian could tell her she has to go at lunchtime.'

'Maybe he needs her for something else then?'

'He doesn't. That's my point. She walks all over him and then he dumps all her work on me.'

Even though I know she's got a point, I don't want to be disloyal to Ian. It's not up to me to tell him how to work with his assistant. 'Hardly all her work, Bea.'

Bea rolls her eyes and I immediately want to backtrack. I hate it when Bea and I don't get on. It makes me panic that she'll start looking for another job. Not to mention the fact that I do think Lucy has a superiority complex and believes that we're lucky to have her in the first place.

'Do you want me to tell him you're too busy?'

Bea shakes her head. 'No. It needs to be done. I just wanted to vent, that's all.'

'I feel your pain,' I say and she laughs. 'Truthfully, though, I agree she's a bit of an entitled cow and don't think it doesn't go unnoticed.'

'Thank you.'

'Lunch on me?'

'Too busy.' She smiles ruefully.

'Tough,' I say. 'We're going to the pub.'

I've made a decision. It's been nearly killing me not telling Bea what's going on. Not being able to confide in someone. But everything that's happened, everything I've done,

137

leads back to the fact that Patrick and I did something we shouldn't have done. I wouldn't for a moment have considered lying for him, helping to cover up an infidelity, if I hadn't been afraid what might come out of his mouth otherwise. I remember all the rumours about Patrick that Bea told me, and I know now that they're all true. And if Bea hadn't messed up and dropped Michelle's name that night we might have had our proof. And everything that has happened since would have been different. Everything.

But not having anyone to talk to is eating me up. I'm distracted to say the least. And Bea notices.

'OK, what's up?' she says when we sit down with our drinks. Vodka and Diet Coke for me; red wine for her.

'Nothing. I'm fine.'

'So why did you just put a beer mat in your bag with your purse?'

I have a look. She's right. 'I collect them.'

'Ha ha. You're hilarious. There's something wrong. When did you ever drink at lunchtime, or do you always sneak off for a few, you just don't tell me?'

'You have to swear on your life not to say a word to anyone. Anyone.'

She looks suddenly serious. 'Of course.'

I trust her. She's never let me down before. That said, I am only going to tell her the edited version. My own role in this little story can stay Patrick's and my secret.

'Patrick Mitchell is having an affair.'

Bea's eyes widen. 'Hold on. Haven't we been here before?'

I nod. 'But it's true. He told me.'

'I don't know where to start. Who with? Why the fuck did he tell you?'

I look round, just checking that no one I know is lurking among the lunchtime crowds. It's one of those pubs that's reclaimed retro and most of the clientele have, too. It's all flat caps, organic ales and ironic fish-finger butties. If I had to describe its attitude I'd say it was pleased with itself. Anyway, the coast seems clear.

'You really won't say anything to anyone, will you, Bea? For Michelle's sake, if nothing else.'

'No. You know I won't. Listen, don't tell me if you're stressed about it.'

'No. I want to. I've got to tell someone or I'm going to go crazy.'

She waits for me to continue. Here goes.

'Michelle caught him out basically. Or at least she nearly did. He's asked me to help put her off the scent. Can you believe that?'

'You're kidding. I assume you told him where to get off?'

This is the tricky part to explain. Without telling her why I have a vested interest in Patrick not being found out it's difficult to make a case for going along with him.

'I didn't know what to do. Obviously Michelle would be devastated . . .'

'You're going to help him lie to her?'

'I already did. I didn't know what else to do. I know some people would think I should just go straight round there and tell her myself, but I've never seen how that was a kind thing to do. And he said he's going to dump this other woman . . .'

She snorts. 'I bet he did. They all say that.'

'I honestly think he will. I think this was a wake-up call. And who am I to step in and break up his marriage if he's just had some kind of mid-life crisis but now he's over it?'

Bea takes a sip of her wine. 'God, what a sleaze.'

'I know. The rumours were right all along. To be honest, he's always been a tosser.'

Bea raises her eyebrows. 'In what way? I thought he was one of your best mates?'

'He's my best mate's husband, there's a big difference. We're friends because we have to be. Actually, that's not fair. We get on fine, I just don't like him much. Does that make sense?'

'Totally. I'm not sure I get why, though.'

I can't really be bothered to explain and I doubt Bea wants to listen to my five-year-long list of gripes about Patrick's manners. 'It's a long story.'

'So how did he expect you to help him?'

I give her the brief lowdown. When I get to the part about me pretending to call his office, she laughs.

'At least no one had to actually do it this time. You didn't ask me to dust Morag and her Scottish accent down and phone for real.'

'Well, obviously, because they wouldn't have known what you were on about.'

'Shit,' she says. 'It's all a bit complicated.'

'Tell me about it. The awful thing is that Michelle is satisfied, though. That's what makes me feel really shitty. That she totally trusts what I say.'

'It's done now, so the best thing you can do is just forget about it.'

'I shouldn't have done it. I should have just gone straight to Michelle and told her the truth.'

'Probably. But it's too late now. You'd never be able to explain away the whole phoning-the-office story.'

'I don't want to see him again. I don't want anything to do with him.'

'I don't blame you. Although isn't that going to be hard to carry off? Given she's your friend and you spend half your free time at hers?'

'I know. I'm going to have to spend my whole life making excuses about why I can't go over there.'

'Well, I suppose that's a plan.'

I force a smile. 'What a mess.'

'I'm always here,' she says. 'If you need someone to talk to.'

'Thanks,' I say gratefully. 'I feel a lot better just having told someone.'

Later I contrive to be hanging around in the reception area when Lucy makes her escape. I'm feeling a little tipsy from the vodka.

'Hairdressers?' I say with a smile on my face.

Lucy returns the smile. 'Yes. I need to get my highlights done before I go away.'

'Things must be quiet at the moment if you're going now.'

'I'm all up to date on everything, so Ian's fine with it.'

'Great,' I say, the smile still there. 'Because Bea's snowed under so she wouldn't really be able to help you out if you weren't.'

She doesn't flinch. 'Of course not.'

When she's gone Ashley looks up from behind the reception desk. 'That was funny,' she says.

'What?' I say, turning to go back upstairs. 'I didn't mean anything by it.'

She hooks her hair behind her ear. 'I can type Ian's budget notes up if it's any help. I've got time.'

'Fine. I'll let Bea know.'

Sometimes actions speak louder than words when I want Bea to know how grateful I am for her loyalty.

PART TWO

21

Bea

Honestly, it's almost funny. If the whole frigging thing wasn't so fucked-up I'd laugh.

To be fair, Tamsin is always dumping on me about personal stuff. Her latest Tinder encounter or a date she's been on from that site she uses – Other Half I think it's called – in way too much detail. Not that she did Tinder for long. Too many close encounters with psychos. Too many questions about whether she was submissive or dominant within the first couple of exchanges. It all comes under the category of T.M.I as far as I'm concerned. Too Much Information. If she was a mate I'd be fascinated. But she's my boss. I'm sure Ian doesn't sit Lucy down and make her listen to the gory details of his sex life. Mind you, he's usually too scared to ask her to do his filing. And if he did she would probably make a formal complaint. Hold an industrial tribunal. Call her local MP and demand answers in parliament.

But when she told me about this . . . Jesus. I didn't know where to look.

She prides herself on being a good boss. Fair. If you work hard and you have her back then she'll support you. That's what she said at my interview. And I suppose it's proved to be true. What she failed to mention was that her definition of working hard is anyone else's of slave labour. She demands a lot for her buck.

I can't even remember the last time I had time at lunch to actually sit and eat. I'm used to it. Spending my precious hour picking up Tamsin's dry cleaning or shopping for whatever it is she needs but can't be arsed to go out and get herself. I'm used to stuffing in a sandwich while typing up some document or other. It's OK. It comes with the territory. I'm an assistant. I assist.

I don't mind doing all that personal stuff for my boss. I don't think it's beneath me – well, most of it anyway. I have a long-term plan. Work hard for Tamsin for three years doing anything and everything that's asked of me, however demeaning, making sure I build up a fabulous reputation and references along the way. And then move on to something better. I won't be staying at Castle. Long-running series about people buying or selling homes really don't interest me. But I'm learning everything I can while I'm there. And TV is hardly rocket science. Most of what Tamsin and Ian seem to do is give their opinion and I can certainly do that. In fact I often do, and she passes it off as hers. I never get the credit obviously. To give her her dues, Tamsin does often tell people how invaluable I am. She just doesn't go on to say that half the time I am actually doing her job for her.

Don't worry, I get my little revenges. I wore a fab jacket of hers – Stella McCartney – on a night out once, after I had picked it up from the dry cleaners on my way home. I accidentally spilled gin and tonic on it, but I told her the smell was the cleaning chemicals and she totally bought it.

And I bring her full-fat lattes instead of skinnies when she sends me out to get her coffee five times a day. She's always moaning about the fact she can't lose those stubborn couple of pounds on her thighs, however hard she tries. I just keep quiet. When I heard her telling Ashley once that she must be getting something wrong with the coffee order because when she gets it, it just doesn't taste right, I had to try really hard not to laugh.

And sometimes when I'm feeling particularly hard done by I add something for myself onto whatever shopping order she's sent me out to get. Just a bottle of aspirin or a tub of blueberries. Something small. She never checks her receipts, just chucks them on the pile of crap that is threatening to engulf her office. And even if she did I'd just say, 'Oh yes, I must give you the money for that,' and that'd be it. I don't even know why I do it. It's not as if it's stuff I couldn't afford to buy for myself. It just makes me feel a little bit less taken advantage of, I suppose.

I don't dislike Tamsin, don't get me wrong. It's just that she sometimes oversteps the mark between appropriate and inappropriate. In terms of what she asks me to do I mean. She doesn't touch me up in the stationery cupboard or anything like that.

I nearly drew the line when she sent me up to Birmingham like some kind of super spy to try to honey trap her friend's husband, though. I mean, what kind of person thinks of that, let alone gets their assistant to do it for them? It's only a little short of pimping them out. Anything could have happened.

But then, I suppose if I hadn't gone I never would have met Patrick Mitchell.

And then things might have been very different. And I wouldn't be so scared it was all going to blow up in my face.

22

Tamsin

Michelle and I are clothes shopping. That is, she is clothes shopping and I am watching and occasionally sighing with boredom. It's not that I don't enjoy buying outfits. It's that I don't enjoy buying them in high street chains that only contain what half the rest of the female population is wearing. Michelle, on the other hand, doesn't really care. She wants practical, functional, appropriate clothes. So about once a year she ropes me in and we go and she stocks up on whatever she needs and that's about it.

I find a chair to sit on while she browses. Fiddle with my phone. After what seems like an age she materializes in front of me with an armful of garments.

'Try them all on,' I say. 'Except the blue. That's a bit Princess Di.'

'How do you know that's not the look I'm going for?' She cocks her head on one side and puts on an expression I can only describe as simpering. 'Not bad, eh?'

'Very flattering.'

'Pad used to have a thing about Princess Di apparently.' She laughs fondly as she says this. 'Before my time, obviously.'

I stop myself from saying 'her and most of the rest of the female population.' I don't want to join in with an 'isn't Patrick adorable' conversation, though, so I just roll my eyes in what I hope is a non-judgemental fashion.

'That red one is very you,' I say to distract her, flapping my arm at the one red item she's holding. 'That first.'

She looks super cute in all of them. I try to feign an interest in which ones she should settle for. I even throw in a 'buy all of them' comment, which has her raising her eyebrows at me. In the end she announces she can't make up her mind – she can never make up her mind, this is one of the reasons I'm not a fan of going shopping with her – and goes round conscientiously putting them all back.

'I don't think I'm in the right mood,' she says.

Fine by me. It means we can go and settle in a café and sit and drink tea and eat cakes instead.

'Are you seeing someone?' she asks as I pour. 'Is that why you're hardly around at the moment?'

I rarely bore Michelle with the details of my love life. She's heard it all before and anyway, usually by the time I've explained who someone is I've broken up with them. I certainly didn't mention my encounter with Owen. Not that she would be shocked by the one-night stand element (more like one-and-a-half-hour stand actually if I'm being pedantic) but I would have to endure a lecture on safety and the dangers of inviting a stranger into my home.

'Not really. I've given up Tinder.'

'Thank God for that.'

'I tried Other Half again for a bit but nothing lately. I did go for a drink with a friend of Ian and Fiona's the other week actually.'

That gets her interest. 'Who? Tell me everything!'

I can't really explain the whole Adam debacle to her (she would want to know why I was so distracted and borderline rude, and I can hardly say, 'Because I was thinking about what might be happening with Patrick and Bea'), so I make up another man and the reasons I won't be seeing him again – a bit young, a daughter from an old relationship that he has every weekend – I call him Justin because it's the first name that comes into my head, and I give him a hipster beard and a flat cap. By the end I've grown quite fond of him. I could get good at this lying lark.

The following afternoon I'm half asleep on the sofa watching *Columbo* when my phone rings. When I see Patrick's name my first instinct is to throw the handset into the washing machine and set it to extra hot. Then I realize I can't not answer. Has something gone wrong? Shit. I can see why curiosity has killed so many innocent cats.

'Hi,' I say nervously.

'Hey. You good?'

Surely he's not just phoned for a chat. I can only manage monosyllabic.

'Yup.'

'Great. I need a favour.'

That wakes me up. 'You're kidding, right?'

He doesn't acknowledge that. 'If Michelle asks, could you tell her I popped over to yours for a couple of hours today? She went to a spa and I wasn't expecting her back till about five, because she had a massage booked, but when I got in just now it turned out she's been home for hours 'cos the therapist was off sick or something. She'd been trying to ring me but . . . obviously my phone was turned off. I panicked and said I'd been at yours. Sorry. First thing that came into my head.'

I can't really believe what I'm hearing. I have to ask him to say it again and then I'm still not certain if I've heard correctly. 'You want me to cover for you?'

'It's no big deal, Tamsin.'

'How can you say it's no big deal? You want me to lie to Michelle about the fact that you were with your mistress? I assume that's where you were?'

'Lie again, you mean.'

'You can't ask me to do this.'

'It's only if she asks you. Which she almost certainly won't.'

'No. This isn't fair. Tell her you were somewhere else if you want but don't involve me.'

'Too late. I already said it. Please, Tam. This is the last time, I promise.'

'Why the fuck didn't you just tell her you'd been for a walk, or shopping or something?'

'Because it just came out. It seemed like the best thing to do – to say something she could check if she wanted, given what's been happening.'

This is a nightmare. I realize then that I have to make a stand. OK so maybe he ends up getting caught one day. But do I really believe he would sell me down the river to Michelle?

Actually, yes, I think I do. I don't know this man now. He seems capable of anything.

But would she believe him? He would only tell her if she had discovered his other indiscretions. She would already know he was a practised liar. Would Michelle ever believe that I would do something so disloyal, so hurtful? His – proven to be worth nothing – word against mine?

I don't think she would.

I decide I have to call his bluff.

'I can't.'

'You can't?'

'No. I can't just keep piling deception on deception, even if you can.'

Patrick exhales loudly. 'You make it sound as if there's any other option. You know that if Michelle finds out about me and . . . her . . . it's as bad for you as it will be for me.'

OK, here goes. 'I've decided to take that risk.'

He stays silent for a second while, I imagine, he takes this in.

'Ah,' he says eventually. 'You think she won't believe me. You're probably right. Michelle's very trusting.'

'So . . .'

'I can't force you to help me out. It's just a shame you sent me that text message though.'

I feel as if I'm falling. Like the ground has shifted out from underneath me. I'm already sitting down, so I grab on to the arm of the chair for support.

'I thought you deleted that,' I say, clutching at straws.

'Really? Do you remember what it said?' I hear him pressing buttons on his phone. I don't remember it word for word. Just the gist. That's enough.

'Ah, here it is,' Patrick says, his voice more distant. "'*Still can't believe we did that last night. Too much wine, ha ha. I'm feeling horribly guilty and I'm sure you are too. Def right that we never tell Michelle. It would only upset her even though it meant nothing. T.*'"

'I thought the "ha ha" was a particularly nice touch,' he says.

23

Bea

Obviously I never intended for anything to happen. My plan was to get in there, get it over with and get out quick. I just hadn't bargained on Patrick Mitchell being so cute, that's all.

I'd clocked that he was good looking from the photos Tamsin had shown me. And his wife looked quite sweet. Michelle. Pretty but a bit drab. I remember feeling sorry for her. She clearly had no idea what her husband was capable of. I believed most of the rumours I'd heard, to be honest, no matter what I said to Tamsin. There were just too many of them for it not to be true.

I arrived at my stuffy little room at the cheap-but-close Inn at about five o'clock. It contained a TV the size of a dinner plate, a hairdryer that was fixed to the wall in case one of the guests was a kleptomaniac, and a distinct lack of a mini bar. There was soap scum round part of the sink. Something that looked suspiciously like a pubic hair in the shower. The event started at seven, so I lay around doing nothing for a bit and then, just as terminal boredom was about to set in – I can't bear doing nothing, let alone doing nothing on my own in a shit hole – it was time to get ready.

I made a real effort. I almost wanted him to make a pass

at me so that I could report back to Tamsin how well I'd done. I worried that if he didn't – if he was innocent of the charges – she might think I hadn't tried hard enough. The evidence would be inconclusive. And if I had to go through with this I might as well try and get an A plus. The more gold stars I can chalk up against my name the better.

I wore the red bodycon dress that Tamsin suggested. I'm not one to big myself up but I know what my good bits are – small waist, long legs – and that dress certainly showcases them. I spent ages doing my make-up. I am useless at making up my own face. I either finish up looking like a clown or a prostitute, or both if there is such a thing (note to self, look into whether starting a brothel full of clown prostitutes would be an astute money-making venture). At one point I wiped it all off and started again. By the end I looked pretty passable.

I arrived at the posh hotel where the event was being held at bang on seven. I was dying for a drink. Tamsin had drilled it into me, though: don't have more than three glasses of champagne. And I kept agreeing with her. I know I can be a bit of a loose cannon when I've had a few. That didn't stop her saying it five more times, though. When Tamsin makes a point she likes to hammer it home.

They were handing out glasses of something warm, fizzy and sickly sweet as you went through the door. In all the anticipation of how I was going to approach Patrick and fulfil my mission I hadn't even stopped to think how utterly miserable it would be to go to a do like this on my own. I'm not the sort of person who can strike up a conversation with a random stranger. It's not just that I don't want to – which I don't – it's that I wouldn't know how. Flirting I can do. Banal 'And what is it that you do?' conversation kills me.

I had a quick scout around but there was nobody I knew. Everyone was in groups of four or five, slapping each other's backs and clinking glasses left, right and centre. Their best night ever because they might win an award for the grading on *Tart Up Your Garden For 99p*. Later, four-fifths of them would be crying into their puddings no doubt. Their moment of glory cruelly snatched away. The mind-crushingly lame speech they'd written, thanking everyone from their partner and children to God, screwed up and chucked in the bin.

I stood about a bit, sipping my fizzy wine, and then I decided to have a look for a seating plan. I might as well at least go and sit in my allocated place. It might feel less humiliating than just standing there alone. Plus I could find out which table Patrick was on, which would make hunting him down later easier.

I was looking around for where it might be when I saw him. My prey. I recognized him immediately from the photographs, but the first thing that popped into my mind was how much better looking he was in real life. Which is saying something. The second thing was, Shit. I've really got to do this now.

He was chatting to a group of people. A man and three women. I edged a bit closer and it all seemed very businesslike. I heard words like 'bottom line' and 'contingency'. Hardly foreplay. The seating plan turned out to be right behind them so I squeezed past – making sure I took the route that meant I was closest to Patrick. He gave me a smile as I made my way through, but it didn't seem anything other than friendly. God, that man has a nice smile though.

And then that was that. They called us through to the main hall, I sat at a table full of people I had never met and had no interest in talking to, they served the prawn and avocado starter and the interminable ceremony began. But at least I had him in my sights.

24

Tamsin

So there you have it. My best friend's husband and one-time-for-a-brief-second-before-we-came-to-our-senses sexual partner is now blackmailing me. The smoking gun in question: a text I stupidly sent him in a panic after our encounter. He's kept it. He has it. There's nothing I can do about that. And what's worse is it's vague. It makes it obvious that something happened between us that I am ashamed of and want to keep secret, but it doesn't go on to say that we didn't go through with what we started. That he would have carried on but I stopped it.

Patrick seems pleased with himself, not at all like someone who has just stooped to an unprecedented low, even for him, the newly crowned king of low.

'You're fucking blackmailing me! This is unbelievable.'

'Of course I'm not. I'm just saying, that's all. Michelle might not appreciate that message.'

'What's happened to you? Have you heard yourself?'

'Tamsin, I don't want to argue with you. I'm just asking you for a favour. It's no big deal.'

'And if I don't you'll show Michelle my text?'

'God no! I don't want her to see it any more than you do. All I'm saying is that if she starts questioning where I am all the time then that's no good for either of us.'

'You really are a piece of shit.'

'It's only if it comes up.'

'That's it, Patrick. No more.'

'I owe you one.'

'I have to go,' I say and I end the call.

So now I have two choices – I can go along with Patrick, cover for him, try to make sure Michelle doesn't find out what he's up to. But when will it end? I'll do him this favour, then there'll be another one, then another. He'll still be waving that text message in my face in twenty years' time. And Michelle will still be blissfully happy, with no idea that she's spent her whole life with a cheating bastard.

Or – and bear with me, because I have no idea how I am going to achieve this – I can come up with a way to diffuse the bomb. And if Michelle finds out exactly what her husband is like, then maybe that's for the best. She can make up her own mind about whether or not she wants to be with him once she has all the facts.

I just have to try and erase that text message first.

I decide to make a list. A list always makes everything seem better.

There is only one thing I can think of to put on it:

Delete text message

I sit and stare at that for a while and nothing inspires me, so I make a sub list.

Phone
Check photos in case he's taken a screen grab
Downloaded onto his computer?
Downloaded onto his work computer?

Fuck. There's no way I'll ever know if I've erased it completely from the world. Although, in reality I can't believe he'd keep a copy on his work computer because Verity is on there all the time I assume. And Verity loves and admires him. He would never want her to discover what he's really like.

Plus, so long as he thinks he's won then it probably won't even cross his mind that I might turn into some kind of private eye. I'll just have to do what I can. Anything would be a start.

Lulling him into a false sense of security is the first step. I need to get comfortable enough round at theirs again so that I can find a way to take a good look through his phone.

A couple of days ago Michelle asked me if I wanted to do Heart Attack Saturday next weekend. I had my excuse ready. I had promised my eldest brother and his wife that I would visit for the weekend. I have to be careful what I say when it comes to my family because Michelle, as I said before, both loves and is beloved by my parents. She probably talks to them as often as I do. She doesn't know my brothers very well, though. They were too old to be interested in their little sister's friend coming over when we were at school (Rob is ten years older than me, and Sasha eight. I was 'a bit of a mistake', my mum told me once. 'In a good way, obviously,' she had added hastily when she saw the look on my face).

I call Michelle and tell her my plans have changed. Rob and his wife, Sally, have decided to go away for the weekend. My time is my own again. I'd love to come over, it's been weeks since we had a proper night in, the three of us. Michelle, of course, is delighted. Both of her favourite people in one room.

'Am I on salad duty?' I say before I ring off.

'Of course. Someone has to make the salad that we all leave in favour of the pasta.'

'I hate that my skills go unappreciated.'

'I'll tell Pad to start planning his sundae toppings. I'm bored of just chocolate and strawberry. This is 2015, where's the salted caramel or fig and balsamic?'

'Great,' I say, trying to inject some enthusiasm into my voice.

She doesn't ask me if Patrick really came over to mine. Of course she doesn't. Now that she has had her mind put at rest about Nottingham I doubt the question of Patrick's fidelity will cross Michelle's mind again. Not unless someone else asks it anyway.

Anne Marie, Ian and I are having lunch, something we always mean to do regularly as a chance to chat about how things are going, but our over-stuffed diaries mean it rarely comes about.

We're sitting outside the little Italian on the corner at our favourite table. Ian and I safely in the shade, Anne Marie, at her own insistence, in the full-on glare of the sun. She's only sixty-three but she has the lines of a seventy-five-year-old and she doesn't care. I love her for that. She's going on holiday next week. Seven days in the sun in Greece with her best friend Mary. They go every year. Anne Marie comes back looking like a raisin.

The tiny terrace is ringed with fake plastic ivy and fairy lights dripping off the trellis. Empty Chianti bottles topped with half-melted candles complete the picture. In the day it already looks like a cliché. Once it gets dark you would sack the set designer if this was anything other than the sugariest rom com. It's so naff it's perfect. We all order without even looking at the menu. Pasta with pesto for Ian and me, lasagne and salad for Anne Marie. We don't need to catch up on what's happening with our shows because that's what the development meetings are for. Lunches are so the three of us can mull over how the business is working. Iron out any glitches.

'Lucy is such a bitch,' I say out of nowhere. My feelings won't come as a surprise to either of them. In fact, I know Anne Marie feels exactly the same way I do. Ian rolls his eyes.

'She's efficient.'

'So was Hitler,' I say. Ian laughs and Anne Marie snorts into her fizzy water.

'I know she can be a pain in the arse,' Ian says, unwrapping a bread stick. 'But she does what I need her to do, so I'm not about to get rid of her.'

'Or Bea does it for her.'

Ian sighs. 'They're not still squabbling are they?'

I nod. 'But that's between them. I just think Lucy takes liberties sometimes. I mean, asking Bea to do her work because she was going to the hairdressers? What's wrong with lunchtime?'

'I'll talk to her.'

'Tell her to check with me if Bea's free before she asks her to cover next time. That'll shut her up.'

'I will if you make it clear to Bea that if there's a genuine emergency she has to muck in.'

'She always does,' I say indignantly. I always feel the need to fight Bea's corner. And actually I know Ian values her as much as I do, he just wants to be seen to be treating all the assistants equally.

'How are you finding Ashley?' Anne Marie pipes up. 'I think she's fitting in well.'

Ian shrugs, noncommittal, and I say nothing because I can't think of anything to say.

Crickets. Tumbleweed.

25

Bea

The awards ceremony was in the slightly tragically named ballroom on the ground floor. Since the hotel was clearly built in the eighties and the room had all the charm of a wholesaler's warehouse I couldn't imagine many balls having taken place here. They'd made an effort with white tablecloths and red bow-trimmed chairs, though. There were table centrepieces made from twigs with (unlit) candles – health and safety I assume – sitting in the middle. Place-name holders in silver-coloured plastic. It was all a bit budget wedding to be honest.

Thankfully Patrick was sitting at a table in my eye line. A woman in her – I would say – late forties was sitting on his left. Short hair, bad make-up and shoulders like a rugby player in her Grecian draped dress. On the other side was a bloke of about, maybe, fifty. There was no one close to him who seemed likely to catch his eye, unless of course he had a thing for bingo wings and trunky waists. Or middle-aged men in hired tuxedos.

I wasn't sure how I felt about that. Watching him chat someone else up would have been so much easier than having to make a move myself, but then I'd never really know the truth about what went on. I knew that there was nothing much I could do while the ceremony was going on, though. I made the minimum of polite conversation with the people sitting on either side of me (producer and designer from some interiors show that was up for Best Daytime Series. I forget what it was called. Anyway, God knows what they thought I was doing at their table). They spent most of the first half hour talking over me in loud whispers. I offered to swap places, but everyone else at the table seemed to be from the same production so I still would have felt like a gatecrasher.

By the time the main course arrived (and the host was announcing the third award of the night) they had given up trying to speak to each other and were happily conversing with their colleagues on the other side from me. I took one look at the anaemic lamb chop and soggy mashed potato and decided to duck out for a fag. I checked that Patrick was still safely captivated by the thrilling drama on stage and made my way into the foyer.

One of the waiters let me stand on the fire escape by the bar so that I could still keep an ear on the proceedings inside, although I had no real hope that the awards would be over soon. I knew I was in for a long evening. I smoked my cigarette and then decided, what the hell, I may as well get myself a cocktail and drink it there. The fizzy wine had long since dried up and all there was on the tables was warm Chardonnay.

I bought a Manhattan. Sat up at the counter. Wondered if I should text Tamsin again. I had sent her a jokey message when I'd first arrived – the eagle has landed, something lame like that – but I couldn't think of what else I could say. I checked my email (nothing), Facebook (168 friends. Two notifications, one from my cousin and one from Ali) and

Twitter (73 followers. Nothing). I browsed through my photos. In the other room I could hear another happy winner gush about how thrilled they were.

And then I looked up and Patrick Mitchell was walking right towards me, going in the direction of the main hall, so he must have walked past me once already on his way to – I assume – the loos. I jumped as if I'd done something wrong. Blushed. Smiled. He smiled back. I knew this was a golden opportunity, I just had to think of something witty and flirtatious to say that would properly get his attention. I took the chance that he was as bored shitless as I was.

'Do you think it's ever going to end?'

He slowed down. I could feel him checking me out. I sucked in my stomach and sat up a little straighter on my stool.

'No. We've actually died and gone to hell. This is it from now on.' He indicated my cocktail with a nod. 'That looks like a good idea, though.'

Here goes. 'I'm thinking I might have another. You should join me. It's definitely taking the edge off.'

I waited with my breath held, wanting and not wanting him to take me up on it. If he turned me down then I had no idea how I was going to get up the courage to try again later.

He held out his hand. 'Patrick Mitchell.'

I reached out and shook it. 'Cheryl Martin.'

'Another . . . what is that?'

'Manhattan.'

Patrick clicked his fingers and the barman jumped to attention. 'Two Manhattans.'

I couldn't help but be impressed.

26

Tamsin

So here we are sitting in Michelle and Patrick's kitchen, just like it's any normal Saturday evening. There's a huge bowl of pasta arrabiata in front of us, a tomato, onion, basil and mint salad made by me, and garlic bread out of a packet.

Patrick is sitting across from me and to the right. His mobile, I noticed as soon as I arrived, is clamped to him as if it's attached with Velcro. He's already been to the loo once and he slipped it into his pocket as he left the kitchen. I assume it's still there now.

I have been on operation 'Everything's fine. Nothing to see here, move along' since I got here. Before even. I practised my smile in the cab on the way over. Obviously, both Patrick and I know that everything is far from fine, that less than a week ago he was, to all intents and purposes, issuing me with some kind of blackmail threat, but apart from the necessity to fake it for Michelle's sake my plan involves lulling him into a false sense of security. I want him to feel comfortable with me again, to let his guard down. Then I can pounce.

I say 'my plan' like I am a criminal mastermind with a foolproof blueprint for the ultimate heist. So far all I have done is think about what might go wrong.

Oh, and I have a new motto. WWCD? What Would Columbo Do?

The only thing I am certain of is that I need to delete that text message and all its possible facsimiles. Objective number one: get hold of his phone. He's clearly going to be guarding it with his life, so the only thing I can do is bide my time and hope he eventually slips up. It's important that I make Patrick feel as if I am going along with his deception. So, when I arrived and he opened the front door, I greeted him like the old friend he once was, and when Michelle was out of the room for a moment and he mouthed 'We good?' to me, I smiled my practised smile and nodded 'Yes'. He's not stupid. He must know I haven't just forgotten about what's gone on. But I'm hoping he'll think I've decided on an easy life.

Watching Michelle look at Patrick with her all-out puppy adoration eyes is killing my appetite. She reaches out and puts a hand on his knee and I want to throw up. He puts his hand over hers, looks up and meets my stare as if to say, 'Well, what are you going to do about it?'

I look away. Thankfully something catches my eye.

'Did you get a new kettle?'

Oh yes, Ladies and Gentlemen, I give you some of the greatest wit of our time.

'I did! Well spotted.'

'Did you?' Patrick says, looking round.

'See,' Michelle says. 'He must have used it five times already and he hasn't even noticed. I don't know if that's the difference between men and women or if he's just a bit slow on the uptake.'

Patrick laughs indulgently and looks at her as if he loves her as much as she loves him.

There's no mention of any pressing work commitments that might take Patrick away for the night, no accidental name drops or hastily retracted references to restaurants Michelle has never set foot in. In fact, they tell me they have decided to go on a late summer holiday. Patrick has found them a bargain last-minute villa in Puglia. Their own pool.

'I hope it won't be too hot that far south,' Patrick says to me, and grimaces. He is doing a fantastic impression of a man concerned for the comfort of his fair-skinned wife.

Michelle looks at Patrick lovingly. He squeezes her hand.

'It's going to be gorgeous,' she says. 'I've got a photo on here somewhere.' She picks up her phone, scrolls through it.

'Damn, I thought I took a screen grab.'

'Oh, no, wait, that was me,' Patrick says, laughing, and produces his mobile from his pocket. And there it is, exhibit A. Taunting me. It's actually within grabbing distance.

An image pops up in my head – me ripping the phone out of his hand, him snatching it back, Michelle laughing because she assumes it's some kind of joke, then realizing neither of us is smiling. There is nothing I can do but look at it longingly. Ron when he sees a sausage.

Patrick finds the image and shows it to me, holding tight to the phone, as if he can read my thoughts. There's no denying the villa looks lovely. White stone, blue skies, olive groves.

'Gorgeous. When are you going?'

'October—'

'If I can get the time off,' Patrick interrupts.

'If Pad can get the time off. I literally can't wait.' Michelle leans into Patrick as she says this and he scoops an arm around her.

'Well, that's not strictly true,' I say and Michelle pulls a face at me. She knows I have a thing about the word 'literally'.

'I'm jealous,' I say, in an effort to be nice. They glow back at me.

To the uninformed outsider this looks like a happy couple. I imagine to one of the two of them it does, too. It could certainly fool me.

Patrick stuffs his mobile back into the front pocket of his jeans. I'm certainly not going to be digging in there to look for it.

I'm a bit stuck. I daren't even ask any leading questions because Patrick would be on to me in a second, so in the end I just think, Sod it. I might as well try and have a nice evening and hope that at some point his phone falls out of his pocket and he doesn't notice. Columbo would light a cigar. I just pour myself another glass of wine.

27

Bea

So, me and Patrick Mitchell, sitting in the bar drinking Manhattans. I was trying to concentrate on the job in hand but the truth is that flirting with him wasn't difficult. Firstly, as I've said, he was – is – hot. Plus he hardly needed any encouragement to reciprocate. And secondly, he was easy to talk to. We found we had so much in common – just stupid things like how much we both loved *The Bridge* (original Danish version only) and going to table-tennis bars.

'Is that what you'd usually be doing on a Thursday evening? If you weren't here?' he said. 'Playing table tennis and watching Scandi noir?'

'Something like that.' I laughed. 'Watching Scandinavians playing ping pong on TV would actually be preferable to this.'

'It's painful, isn't it? My face is aching from faking delighted smiles every time someone wins.'

'If I go back in there I am going to start heckling. That's the only way this evening could become bearable.'

'OK, I dare you,' he said. 'Actually, no I don't. It might make it go on even longer.'

'You should be glad you took that back so quickly. I never say no to a dare.'

'I bet you don't,' he said, which was, I admit, a little bit cringy. 'Are you here because you worked on one of these shows?'

I changed the subject quickly. Said something about having been involved in one of the nominated programmes in my old job.

'But in a very menial capacity,' I said. 'Even if we win I don't get to go onstage. They only invited me because someone dropped out at the last minute.'

'And now you work for . . . ?'

'Kismet.'

He looked blank, understandably. 'I don't think I've come across them.'

'We're new. And very small.'

After that I tried to steer away from too much 'Cheryl from Kismet' talk. I was afraid I'd give myself away for one. And it felt wrong. We were getting on so well, he was being so charming, not at all sleazy, which was what I'd imagined he would be. I liked him. Actually, I both liked and fancied him. And that put a whole other spin on things.

I'm not someone who makes a habit of going off with married men, let me make that clear. I don't have a big thing about it – it's got nothing to do with sisterhood or any of that crap, more that I've always been level-headed enough to know it will end in tears. For me at least. It just looks like a whole heap of trouble that I don't want to get into. Sometimes though, as they say, shit happens.

After about an hour or so – the awards were still droning on in the background, ignored by us – it was pretty obvious something was about to go down. At some point my brain stopped reminding me that I had to make my excuses and leave when it became absolutely apparent that Patrick was up for it, and started suggesting that there was no real harm in actually going through with what I'd started. I could never tell Tamsin, obviously, but I could let her know he really was a cheater without mentioning he had cheated with me too. She gets her proof. I have a good time. Job done.

At one point his hand grazed mine when he reached for his glass and neither of us moved for a good couple of seconds. There were a few other people around by this point, mostly losing nominees drowning their sorrows with their cronies, and weirdly it added to the excitement. Just that brief touch of hands. Nothing else could happen in so public a place. I'm not going to deny I felt more than a little turned on.

The moment was broken by someone stopping to say hi to Patrick and then boring on about some programme or other. I could tell that he was trying to get rid of them. The minute they took the hint he smiled at me and said, 'Would you like to come and have a drink in my room?'

I didn't even hesitate. By the time I called Tamsin to tell her the awards were finally over and I was going to try and strike up a conversation with Patrick, in reality I was on my way up to 639, him having gone ahead because he said people might misinterpret things if we were seen leaving together.

It felt like the worst, most exciting, most dangerous thing I had ever done.

His room was one of those suites that are like a small flat. Bedroom, living room, bathroom the size of a dance hall. Flat-screen TVs everywhere you looked and a roll-top bath. Tastefully decorated in deep reds, creams and browns. You could have fitted my hovel down the road into it at least three times, maybe four. He had opened a bottle of champagne from the mini bar by the time I got there. Two glasses lined up side by side.

'I'm glad you came,' he said, handing me one of them.

'Me too.'

And then he leaned forward and kissed me, and in all honesty I forgot everything else.

28

Tamsin

Spending the rest of my life waiting for Patrick to slip up while lying to my best friend about her husband's infidelity is not an attractive proposition. I need to do something to take my mind off it.

Since my encounter with Owen I've been a bit scared to log back on to Other Half. What if he's added a comment by my name? 'Guaranteed shag within the first hour and a half or your money back.' I consider signing up with another agency but it all feels like too much effort. And for what? A few glasses of wine and some forced chit chat before either you or he makes an excuse about needing an early night.

I flip through my contacts on my phone, looking for friends I haven't caught up with for a while. Annie, my roommate from college, is five months pregnant with her third child and threatening to make me be godmother so she's best avoided for a while; Billie (real name's Wilhelmina) won't go anywhere without her crashing bore of a husband so she's out; Carrie won't go anywhere full stop because she doesn't trust anyone to look after her kids; Caz is always so happy to have an excuse to dump her two on her husband that she insists on staying out till four in the morning and drinking her body weight in vodka. Something I have no interest in doing these days.

I go through the list on and on with more of the same. Eventually I hit on Mary, an old mate from my pre-Castle TV days. She's easy company, funny, straightforward, unencumbered. She's getting married! she tells me when I call to see if she would like to meet up for a drink. And then she proceeds to describe every aspect of the impending celebration in minute detail, right down to the colour of the petals that the bridesmaids will shower her with when the happy couple leave the church, and the font she's chosen for the menus.

'April fourth,' she says chirpily 'Save the date.'

'Gosh. Yes . . . thanks. I'll put it in my next year's diary . . .' Shit.

I wonder whether it's still worth suggesting we meet up. Maybe she's just been dying to fill me in on everything and now she has she could go back to being her normal non-bridezilla self. But then she says, 'Actually I should go through the seating plan with you, see if you spot any screaming gaffs!' and I make an excuse that I'm in a hurry and I'll call her again soon and end the call before she can object.

I chuck my mobile down on the sofa. Back to Other Half it is then.

I arrange to meet 'Paul, forty-two, divorced, two kids' for a meal at China Tang in the Dorchester. It's his suggestion. He looks pretty good in his photo – dark-haired and dark-eyed. He's pitched it just right, too. Smiling but with a closed mouth so it's not too cheesy. No collar up or comedy tie to show off what a laugh he can be. He sounds confident and friendly in the brief conversation we have on the phone. As usual, I hold out little hope, though. But at least I'll get to eat nice food.

The restaurant is dimly lit and tasteful. Paul is already at the table, I'm told when I arrive. They lead me over and a man I recognize from his picture greets me with a smile. I actually do a double take. He's even better looking than in his photo, something that is almost unheard of in the online dating world. OK, so he's definitely passed the first test. I can't imagine why he feels he has to go on the internet to meet women. Which, of course, means that I think I'm a loser along with the rest of Other Half's clientele.

'Tamsin,' he says, standing up. I'm relieved he doesn't try to come round and pull my chair out for me. That would be overkill.

'Lovely to meet you. Gorgeous dress. Vivienne Westwood?'

'It is,' I say, surprised.

'I only know because my ex-wife was a big fan of hers.'

Oh God, he's brought up the ex-wife already. This is clearly going to be his 'issue'.

'Now I sound like one of those divorced men who bang on about their exes all the time. I'm not. Just so you know we divorced seven years ago. It was awful for everyone concerned at the time but it's fine now. Civilized.'

'How old are your kids?' I ask. I might as well find out now if I'd be expected to play mummy every other weekend if we hit it off.

'Twenty and eighteen. Both at uni. I'm not looking for a nanny. Or a stepmum.'

I laugh, relieved. 'You should put that on your profile.'

'I seriously considered it. Didn't you find writing your profile excruciating?'

'Torture.'

We talk about work — he's an A and R man at a record company I have actually heard of — and he doesn't hog the conversation or big himself up. I find myself relaxing. I think I might like Paul.

It seems he might like me, too, because towards the end of the meal — which was delicious by the way, tiny dim sum parcels of gorgeousness and subtle spicy dishes of prawns and scallops — he mentions an exhibition at the V and A of rock god stage clothes from the 1980s that sounds amazing, and drops in that maybe we should see it together.

'That'd be lovely,' I say, and I find myself gazing for just a moment too long into his near-black eyes and coming over a bit lustful. Too much wine. I look away, reminding myself that I do not want a repeat of the Owen experience, or to get a reputation as the Other Half bike. I can't imagine why Paul has been single for so long.

He accepts my offer to pay my share, which I'm grateful for. I hate it when a man comes over all patriarchal and starts to insist he'd be insulted if a woman paid for her own dinner. He walks me outside, to where the taxis are waiting.

'Shall we talk in the next few days and make a plan?' he says and I say yes, let's.

I can feel a kiss on the horizon. It's as if we both know it's out there and we're trying to edge towards it without being too obvious. It's brighter out here than it was in the restaurant, and I notice that Paul's eyes have a flicker of orange amber in amongst the brown.

He's looking at me intently. I feel a bit ridiculous with the doormen hovering around and a black cab driver looking at us expectantly. I want it to happen, though. I actually think I've met someone I'm attracted to.

Paul smiles a lazy smile. I almost go wobbly at the knees, and then something jolts me back into the real world.

His teeth.

It's not that they're crooked. I like crooked teeth so long as they're clean. Paul's are . . . green. Well, dark yellow anyway, and sort of furry. I think about how long you would have to go out with someone before it would be OK to suggest they visit the dentist. And how many times you would have to kiss them in that period. I feel myself gag.

He's leaning in towards me. I make a decision, swerve to avoid his lips and give him a peck on the cheek. Hopefully he just thinks I have strict morals. I catch a whiff of the not-so-pleasant tang of his breath.

'Thanks for a lovely evening. I had a great time.'

'Me, too. Shall I ring you tomorrow?'

'Lovely,' I say, jumping into the back of the taxi before he gets any more ideas.

Great. Now I'll have to avoid his calls or make up excuses about why I can't see him again. I suppose I could just tell him. People today are always advocating the 'say it to their face' approach. Meanness dressed up as honesty. But he's a lovely bloke. He doesn't deserve to be insulted. He just has personal hygiene issues.

Does this make me shallow? Maybe. Answer me that question when you've been presented with a rancid germy pond and asked to put your tongue into it.

29

Bea

I'll leave it to your imagination what happened next. Suffice to say we didn't get any sleep. There was none of that 'sex with a new person' awkwardness, I think because we both knew that was all it was. Sex. Neither of us was looking to impress the other with our sparkling wit or deep compassionate side. We just wanted to pack as much action into eight or so hours as we could. We didn't even pause for breath. At least, not until about three in the morning. I looked over at my glass of champagne and saw that it was still full. That's how fast everything had happened.

It was during this lull – lying there wrapped up in each other, dripping with sweat – that I dropped the M bomb. It was a complete accident. In retrospect I can't believe I was so fucking stupid, but I had let my guard down so far I'd forgotten why I was there.

It was only afterwards that I realized what a stupid mistake I'd made. Patrick had uttered something romantic and Mills and Boon-esque like, 'You do know I'm married,' and I – completely unsurprised, relaxed, in a post-multi-orgasmic haze – said something along the lines of, 'Yes, don't worry, I know all about Michelle.'

The aftermath, I remember all too clearly. Patrick sat

bolt upright, looked at me and said, 'How do you know my wife's name?'

I thought about lying, thought about trying to dig myself out of the hole to protect Tamsin. Ultimately, though, I thought that I really wanted to see Patrick again, and if that was the case I needed to come clean. It was a risk. He could have got straight on the phone to Tamsin and accused her, but I took a gamble that he wouldn't want to risk her finding out what had just happened – was still happening, to be fair – with me.

I told him about the honey trap. About Tamsin's mission to find out the truth. About the rumours that were swirling around about him. It felt like an agonizing eternity before he said anything.

'So what are you going to tell her?'

'That I tried my hardest but you were irresistible to my charms. That you passed her test with flying colours.'

'Jesus,' he said, snaking his arm round my shoulders again, his hand finding my left breast. 'She is unbelievable.'

'I can steer her right off the scent,' I said.

'And none of this has come from Michelle? So far as you know?'

I actually felt a little prick of jealousy that he seemed concerned about his wife while I was lying there next to him. I knew it was irrational, though. Ridiculous even.

'No. Nothing.'

'Good. You need to know now, Bea, that if we carry on with this I would never leave my wife.'

What could I say? How many women starting relationships with married men have agreed to that clause? All of them at some point, I imagine. We'd only just met, I was hardly going to start planning how I could prise him away from the love of his life.

'Of course.'

'I really want to see you again. I'd hate to think this was just a one-night thing . . .' he said, pushing my hair back from my face. And, like an idiot I said, 'Me too.'

I really liked him – like him – I couldn't help myself M'lud.

'But it has to be a secret. It's not just Michelle, it's work – everything.'

'You have a reputation already,' I said. 'That's not good.' In all honesty I think I said this because I wanted to know I would be the only one. Goomah number 1. I thought maybe I could scare him into having me as his bit on the side and no one else, and that that would be enough. At least I could keep a bit of self-respect that way.

'I know. Shit. And there I was thinking I was always so careful.' He leaned down and kissed me and I knew I'd pretty much go along with whatever.

'I can help you diffuse it,' I said when we came up for air. 'People will forget after a while if there's nothing new to gossip about.'

'Not Tamsin,' he said.

And that's when we came up with the plan – that he would go crying to Tamsin about some woman called Cheryl and how he thought Michelle must have set her up to test him. He figured that by doing that she would be so taken aback that she would believe him. Why would he be telling her otherwise? She would be racked with guilt although, obviously, unable to admit to that to him. He

181

would lay it on thick, he said. He was pretty sure she had always had a soft spot for him.

I wasn't entirely happy with the fact that the whole thing was going to hinge on him passing on my incompetence, but the truth was that I *had* accidentally dropped Michelle's name, so I couldn't really argue. I knew that Tamsin would be pissed off with me, but I also knew that my pro-Patrick testimonial would go a long way towards placating her. Her only worry would be that her own part in the whole thing was about to be revealed, and I could put her mind at rest about that.

When we finally said goodbye at about eleven in the morning we made a plan to meet up the following week. By the time we saw each other again Patrick was satisfied he had convinced Tamsin her suspicions were wrong.

'It was hilarious,' he told me as he popped the cork on a bottle of champagne in the room he'd booked at the Mandarin Oriental. Not that we would be staying the night. Patrick's cover story only involved a bit of working late. 'She came up with this whole scenario about how "Cheryl" must have been sent over as a bet by someone at the awards to freak me out.'

'She believed you, though?'

'One hundred per cent,' he said, smiling. 'She obviously feels terrible.'

I know I should say it hasn't been easy lying to Tamsin – and at times it hasn't – but it hasn't exactly been hard either. The point is that she never should have started this. She should never have got involved. She knows that too now, I think. Sometimes you should just leave well alone.

When she told me Michelle had found proof that

Patrick was seeing someone I almost had a heart attack, though. We should have been more careful. I don't want to lose my job. I thought maybe Patrick would want to cool things down for a while, but he was surprisingly calm about it. According to Tamsin he's put pressure on her to help bail him out. According to him he pleaded with her and she agreed. I don't really understand why. I don't really care, so long as she does.

PART THREE

30

Tamsin

This is getting ridiculous. It's been weeks. Weeks of me sitting in Michelle and Patrick's kitchen laughing away, drinking and chatting like I haven't got a care in the world, all the time with my eyes fixed beadily on whichever pocket he has his mobile in, willing him to lose concentration for just a second. No chance.

One night I couldn't see where he was stashing it, so halfway through our meal I pretended I had to go to the loo and I had a quick scout around in the living room. I thought maybe he'd plugged it in to charge, so I scoured the sockets, picked up a few cushions. Nothing. When I took my seat at the table again – having flushed the toilet for authenticity – he produced it from somewhere with a flourish, supposedly to check his email, and I wondered whether he had been toying with me. It was hard to tell. Our relationship now is built on so many falsehoods and artifices that I don't really know who I'm dealing with any more. I'm beginning to think this is an impossible task.

Other things of note that have happened include: Michelle and I took Julian and Miriam out for tea and cake for their wedding anniversary and Julian told us about Petersen Media's plans for a new highbrow documentary channel that they were hoping would be the jewel in their crown, hinting – I thought – that he might be looking to Patrick to have some involvement.

'He's only ever worked on lifestyle programmes, though, hasn't he? I mean ... not that that ... um ...' I said at one point in my best innocent voice. Michelle shot me a look.

And Patrick's relationship, or however you want to label it, is still going strong in so far as I can tell. At least, I assume this is still the same woman. Funnily enough I haven't asked. He's had quite a few late nights 'working' or playing football, plus one overnight 'work trip' anyway. Thankfully he hasn't asked me to vouch for him again, although the threat is always there:

It's business as usual with a touch of fucked-upness.

'How's things with your friend Michelle?' Bea asks as we sit on our favourite coffee-drinking bench on the green eating our sandwich lunch. The summer is still going strong, even though it's now September. It's hot, dry and dusty and there has been a hosepipe ban in place for several weeks now. The flowers in the park wilted to a crisp before they had a chance to die a natural death. The grass is a stony shade of beige. We both have suntan ennui and so we are hiding in the shade.

I roll my eyes. Don't know what to say. 'It's still going on, I think. I don't really know to be honest.'

'Shit.' She takes a bite out of her tuna and avocado roll. 'I thought he said he was going to finish with her.'

'Clearly he was lying. Or maybe he tried but he couldn't bring himself to do it.'

'What? You think he really likes this woman?'

188

'God knows. Maybe.'

'He must do. I mean, if he knows you know and he's willing to risk it—'

'He's not risking anything, though, is he? He's confident I'd never want Michelle to find out that I lied for him before . . .'

'If he likes her that much then perhaps he'll end up going off with her anyway.'

I have thought about this. Recently I've even thought that it might not be a bad thing. Michelle would be devastated for a while but, with my help, she'd get over it. And she'd be happier in the long term, whether she knew it or not. I just had to erase my place in Patrick's history first.

'Who knows? Stranger things have happened.'

'You don't sound as bothered by the thought of that as you were.'

I shrug. 'Sometimes you have to accept you're fighting a losing battle.'

'Why has he stayed with Michelle for so long? That's what I don't understand. I mean, I guess he must have loved her once but . . .'

I've been thinking about this a lot lately too. Patrick clearly doesn't love Michelle. He can't. But he's decided to settle. She looks sweet on his arm and she can get on with anyone. She gives him an easy life. He'll stay with her, give her the child she so desperately wants one of these days, and do whatever he pleases on the side. I couldn't fathom out why that would be an acceptable choice until, of course, I remembered that Michelle's dad, Julian, is his boss. And Julian has big plans for expansion. One day

Patrick will inherit the earth. But not if Michelle kicks him out first.

I change the subject.

'How was your date last night by the way?' Bea met a man at a club the other week and she seems quite smitten. They've seen each other – on my reckoning – four or five times since, which is a bit of a record for her. Usually she murders her relationships before they die. Before there's even time for them to be diagnosed with anything. She's a classic self-saboteur. That's one thing we have in common. All I know about this one is that he's called Danny, he works as a web designer and he's got a flat with two mates in Ealing. Oh and he's 'funny and smart and fit' – her words when I asked her to describe him.

A look of pure bliss passes across her face. 'Lovely.'

'Where did you go?' I spent yesterday evening round at Michelle's vegged out in front of the TV while Patrick – apparently – talked shop over dinner with a couple of his deputies. I made a half-hearted search for the phone when I got the chance but I knew there was no way he wouldn't have it with him. A supposition that was proven when he rang Michelle to say he was on his way home at nine forty-five. I left before he arrived.

'That pub near mine. Where you came, remember?'

'Wow. Lucky Danny.'

She laughed. 'I didn't invite him there because of the ambience. I invited him there because it's close to my place. Ali and Sarah are away.'

'Aaah!' I already knew this wasn't the first time. They had slept together the night they met, she had told me.

But up to now they'd always gone to his flat. 'Sounds like progress.'

She shrugged. 'It's early days. It probably won't go anywhere.'

'You never know. Give it a chance. Where is it he works again?'

'Near where he lives.'

'Well, that's a result then, that he came all the way over to Islington.'

She looked at her watch. 'Shit, it's twenty to two. I'm going to pop to the shops. Need anything?'

'Oh yes. Can you go into Tesco? Ron needs Winalot. Beef flavour. Get him a couple. And pick me up a newspaper. Oh, and I've got a card needs posting but I left it on my desk. Would you mind nipping in and getting it?'

'Of course,' she said, smiling. 'Skinny latte on the way back?'

'You read my mind,' I said, standing up and leaning over to put my rubbish in the bin. 'As usual. Thanks.'

31

Bea

Jesus, the whole Danny thing is exhausting. When I started it it seemed like an easy way to be able to tell Tamsin half the truth. She's so frigging nosy. She asks me practically every day where I was the night before and how my love life is going. I sometimes wonder if she's living vicariously through me because her own dating thing seems like a bit of a non-starter. At least I get to go on dates with real-life people that I meet, not virtual men who end up looking nothing like their photos. Not that my track record is any more successful, to be fair. It's just more active.

Anyway, I was terrified she would catch me out, so I figured if I told her about what me and Patrick had been doing, more or less, but substituted Danny's name and a few other crucial details, then I might get away with it. But now, of course, she wants to find out more about 'Danny'. She's obsessed with how 'Danny' could be the answer to all my prayers.

And, actually, it was a bit of a milestone when Patrick came to the flat. Up to now we've been strictly hotels. I tend to leave it to him. He tells me where and when and I pretty much go along with it. He's the one who most needs to cover his tracks, after all. So, when I mentioned that both my flatmates were away I wasn't really expecting him to suggest we meet there. Maybe he just wanted to save a few quid. The hotel bills must be mounting up. But he made it sound as if he was actually interested in seeing where I live. And that struck me as progress.

Don't get me wrong. I'm not starting to fantasize about us becoming a proper couple or anything like that. I don't want him to come to mine so I can put a pinny on and bake him an apple pie. In all honesty I have no interest in settling down with anyone just yet, despite what Tamsin seems to think. I'm enjoying myself. But that doesn't mean there isn't something gratifying in knowing he feels this comfortable with me. That he trusts me this much.

I did a serious amount of tidying up before he came round. By which I mean I shoved a load of my stuff into Ali's room and shut the door. I only left out the things I thought projected the image of me I wanted to project. Basically I got rid of all the *Made in Chelsea* DVDs and *Twilight* books. Not that he spent a lot of time looking at the décor.

We didn't really go to the pub, of course. What would be the point in sitting there politely making chat when we only have a couple of precious hours together? I headed home straight after work, had a shower, tidied some more, put some Pinot Grigio in the freezer because I'd forgotten to put it in the fridge before I left for work, and changed clothes twice. When I opened the front door to let him in he was looking round furtively, as if he was terrified of being spotted.

'Nice place you've got here,' he said, taking in the communal hall with its peeling paint and piles of old mail addressed to people none of us has ever heard of.

'We can't all earn the big bucks,' I said. I didn't take offence. I know I live in a bit of a shit hole. But I also know it won't be forever.

'Its utilitarian ugliness just emphasizes how beautiful you are,' he said in a hammy voice and I pretended to gag.

He slid his arms round me from behind as we headed up the stairs. Traced my ear with his lips. Something – as he already knows – guaranteed to reduce me to jelly.

The outfit I had picked out so carefully didn't stay on long.

This morning I was knackered because after he left last night – at about quarter past nine – I drank another half bottle of wine and watched three episodes of *Borgen* back to back. I didn't feel like sleeping. Consequently I had a mad rush after the alarm went off and I hit snooze twice before I could face getting out of bed.

Lucy was an absolute bitch when I got to work, making a point of looking at her watch when I walked in ten minutes late. Ian was hanging around in our office trying to summon up the courage to ask her to do something for him, so it was for his benefit, I imagine.

'Tamsin said I could come in a bit late today because I had something on . . .' I said sounding, I thought, fairly convincing if a little defensive. I knew Tamsin wouldn't mind the white lie.

'Oh,' Lucy said, an annoying fake innocent look on her face, 'that's funny because she just asked me to photocopy something for her and she didn't mention it.'

'Maybe she doesn't think it's any of your business,' I snapped before I could stop myself.

'Anyway. I haven't had a chance yet because I was too

busy doing my *own* work,' Lucy said, making it sound as if she had been finding a cure for cancer. 'Here.'

She shoved a pile of papers at me.

'Yes, I'm sure you were. Thank you so much for your support.'

'For God's sake, ladies,' Ian butted in, sounding exasperated, and I wanted to kick myself for behaving so unprofessionally in front of him.

'Sorry, Ian. I obviously should have mentioned I might not be in first thing.'

'There you are, Bea! I was looking for you. It's not like you to be late,' Tamsin's voice said, and I turned to see her standing in the doorway.

Great.

32

Tamsin

It's finally happened. After two weeks and six days there it is in front of me. Unaccompanied and unguarded. Patrick's mobile.

I'm frozen in my tracks looking at it. Now I have my chance I'm not sure I can go through with it. What if one of them comes in and catches me? What if I mess it up somehow and he realizes what I've been doing?

I know I'll never get this chance again in all probability. I need to woman up and grasp this opportunity. Shit, my hands are shaking.

Here's how it happened. It's Saturday. I know that Michelle – always an early riser – gets up at the crack of dawn even at weekends, even though there's no need to, and she creeps around the house for hours because she doesn't want to disturb Patrick, who likes to sleep in on his days off. I know that they both leave their phones to charge overnight in a little cupboard in the living room that has a socket inside especially for the purpose. And now, after a couple of weeks of studying his fingers on the keys, I also know Patrick's password. Two, three, six, seven.

So, I came up with the genius plan for me to appear on their doorstep at 7 a.m. this morning, dressed in my running gear (bought years ago in another of my short-lived attempts at fitness. Worn twice. Put in a cupboard), claiming to have run all the way across the heath from Belsize Park to Highgate (something I have never even attempted before, let alone achieved. I actually got a cab to just around the corner, running the last few minutes, which was quite enough to leave me out of breath and sweaty).

I called Michelle from the doorstep and told her I was there, but that I didn't want to ring the doorbell and wake Patrick. She was delighted, as I knew she would be. Michelle hates being on her own. She never knows what to do with herself. I waited and she opened the door, still dressed in her pyjamas (as I would have been on any normal day). She took one look at me and laughed.

'I don't think I've ever seen you awake this early unless it was still part of the night before,' she said in a stage whisper. 'Let alone in workout gear. What on earth are you doing?'

I rolled my eyes. 'Fitness drive. I'm trying to turn over a new leaf. Were you up? Shall I go away again?'

She opened the door wider. 'No! I've been up for hours. I'm bored stiff. Just don't wake Pad.'

That I had absolutely no intention of doing.

We went into the kitchen and she made tea and teased me about how sweaty, red-faced and generally done in I looked, which given I had barely exerted myself for more than thirty seconds was a bit of an insult to be honest. I laughed along.

'I walked part of it. Most of it really.' I had suddenly started to worry that she might suggest we meet up to jog together sometime.

She looked up at the clock. Still only five past seven. 'God, what time did you go out then?'

I shrugged, having no idea how long it would have taken me. 'Too early.'

She set a mug of tea down on the table in front of me. 'Be careful on the heath, won't you? I'm not sure it's safe when there aren't many people around.'

'It wasn't too bad. Lots of dog walkers.'

Michelle yawned and stretched, arms above her head. 'Well, I'm happy to see you. I got up at half five and I'm bored stiff. Do you want to eat something?'

'I'll have some granola or something if you are,' I said, deliberately picking a food that wouldn't waft enticing smells to the sleeping lion upstairs.

'I've got loads of fruit. We can chop some up to put in it. Fitness drive.'

'Lovely,' I said, seeing my opportunity. I was already shaking at the thought of what I had to do. 'I'm desperate for the loo, though. I'll help you when I come back.'

I left her unloading cartons from the fridge, knowing she would be gainfully employed for a while. Heart pounding, I slipped into the living room. I listened for the sound of knife on chopping board, then crept over to the cupboard. A part of me didn't even expect to see Patrick's mobile there. Paranoid as he was, I thought he might have started sleeping with it under his pillow or slipped into the pocket of his pyjama trousers. I knew Michelle would have found that odd, though. She had always had a 'no phones in the bedroom' rule. Mind you, she also had a 'no phones at the table' rule, but neither Patrick nor I had ever taken any notice of that one.

I opened the cupboard. Saw it. Grabbed it. Tapped in the password and prayed that he hadn't changed it in the past few days. I almost dropped the thing when it worked. Was I really going to do this? Snoop through someone's phone?

Yes. Yes I was. I went into texts. Scrolled down till I found my name – which took a while. Funnily enough I hadn't been sending him any messages lately. Found it. Found the offending text. Cringed as I read it. Pressed delete. Gone.

I felt sick at the thought of what I'd done. If Patrick looked he would know exactly what had happened. That would take our conflict to a whole other level – defcon one – although hopefully he would now be unarmed.

I could still hear Michelle moving about in the kitchen. I looked for the photo icon. I had to check if he had taken a screen grab. I scrolled through countless happy pictures of Michelle, of them both, of random bits of countryside and ducks on the river. And there it was. Twice, in fact. I wiped it out.

I shoved the phone back in the cupboard, knowing I needed to get back to the kitchen before she started wondering where I was. Now I actually did need the loo but time wasn't on my side. I started to shut the cupboard door and then a thought hit me. There were bound to be messages from HER on there. From whoever Patrick was seeing. I told myself it was no longer any of my business. I had saved myself and that was all that mattered now.

Still, I was almost bursting with curiosity to know who she was. It would only take a second to look. And maybe that would give me some ammunition when he came after me.

I couldn't pass up the chance. I could probably get away with a few seconds more before Michelle sent out a search party. I picked it back up before I could talk myself out of it. Found my way to text messages again. Michelle. Verity. Mark (Patrick's best mate and once best man), Ben (no idea). Mum. Michelle. Ben. Tom (someone in his department). Clare (ditto. I checked a few of her messages just in case, but they all seemed to be work related). Aiden (Patrick's brother). Dentist. Ben. Michelle. Michelle. Ben again. Mum. Someone anonymous telling him he had won a thousand pounds' compensation if he would only go onto this website and type in all his bank details. Ben. Ben. Whoever Ben was they seemed to be in constant contact.

I glanced at one of Ben's texts as I scrolled past. It just said *'OK'* in response to a message from Patrick reading, *'Tues 6.30 Dorchester'*, which I assume was the time and venue for a business meeting. The next one of his I came across also just said *'OK'*, as did the next. One in reply to *'6.15 on Weds. Haymarket?'* and the other to *'6.15 Tues. Charlotte Street'*. His was the only name I didn't recognize. I wondered whether he was a temporary assistant in Patrick's department setting up meetings for him. I kept clicking on his name to see the whole stream. I don't know why, there was just something odd about the repetitive and terse nature of the texts.

It seemed they texted each other once or twice a week. Always the same format. Patrick would say a day, a time and a place and Ben would acknowledge. There was never any more detail. Never any embellishment. Once Patrick had sent *'Need to change to Thurs'* but that was it. A series of appointments.

My heart started to pound. I knew for a fact that Patrick wasn't having an affair with someone called Ben. He might have turned into someone I didn't recognize, but I was pretty sure he hadn't changed that much. It was hardly a plan worthy of a master criminal, but assigning whoever it was a man's name and keeping the messages short and to the businesslike point would be enough of a cover should Michelle ever glance over as he was reading his texts.

I quickly scrolled up to the top, to the more recent missives. Patrick had been out on Wednesday night. A couple of days before he had texted 'Ben' '*Weds 7. As discussed.*' Whatever that meant. I looked at the most recent exchange. An '*OK*' from 'Ben' on Friday in response to a message saying '*Mon 6.30. Soho?*'

I jabbed at the phone to get it to go back to the home screen. Shoved it back in the cupboard and closed the door. Headed back down the hallway. Remembered I hadn't flushed. Ran into the bathroom. Yanked the chain. Made a big deal of opening and shutting the door. Went back to the kitchen.

Michelle was sitting at the table, two bowls of granola, a jug of what I knew would be almond milk (unsweetened) and a bowl of diced fruit in front of her.

'You OK?'

I rubbed my belly. Grimaced. 'I don't think running agrees with my stomach.'

Nice.

'Oh God, do you need anything? I have Imodium I think.'

I sat down. 'No, I think I'm all right now. That'll teach me to be healthy.'

I tried to eat my cereal, but my stomach really was in knots now. Assuming what I already knew about Patrick's modus operandi I was pretty sure 'Soho' meant the Soho Hotel. I knew where Patrick and his bit on the side were meeting next. I just had no idea what to do with that information.

33

Tamsin

Common sense would say I should cut my losses. Tell Michelle what her husband is up to now that I have removed any evidence of my own involvement in his bad behaviour – I'd scoured his laptop for a copy of the photo, too, on a second visit to the loo, and found nothing. A much easier prospect as it wasn't password protected. Thank God he hadn't signed up for iCloud. This is what this is all about, right? Giving Michelle the whole (yes, yes I know, whole-ish) picture and then supporting her through whatever she decides to do next.

But what if I can get actual proof? A photo of Patrick and his mistress maybe. An idea of who she is so that I can try and get her to admit what's been going on? Faced with that Michelle would never believe whatever arrows Patrick tried to fire off at me as he went down. It's worth a try now that I have had this gem of information fall into my lap.

And besides, I am eaten up with curiosity. I can't deny I want to get a look at her.

I have to get there early. I need to find a vantage point where I can scout out the reception without any risk of being seen. Of course the afternoon turns out to be busy. In fact, the whole day is a treadmill. Meeting after meeting with barely enough time to go to the loo in between. Some days are just like that.

The production manager on *Rooms With a View* has called a crisis meeting with me because she's lost faith in the producer's ability to steer the ship. Ordinarily I would listen briefly to her concerns and then take it up with said producer, but Stella has been production manager on countless shows for me over the years, both at Castle and before, and despite the fact that I find her a little intimidating, I trust her absolutely.

Michael, the producer, on the other hand, is new to all of us. This is the problem when you're busy. You end up having to take a punt on people you have no prior relationship with. I even tried to promote Stella, but she wasn't having it. Some people don't want the buck to stop with them. They'd be left with no one to pin the blame on. Michael is nice enough. He's trying. But he has no experience of really long-form programming – twenty-six forty-minute episodes in this case – and things are, in Stella's opinion, getting away from him.

'He keeps wanting to reshoot everything after we've already packed up and left the location. He doesn't seem to have any idea of the cost implications, no matter how many times I try to tell him.'

'Are you going to go over?' I try to take a sneaky look at my watch. I have to leave by quarter to six to ensure I'm safely hidden away. It is now seventeen minutes to.

'Well, at the moment he's insisting we schedule an extra day on the end of this episode so, yes, probably. And I'm sure this won't be the last time.'

'Let me speak to him.'

'We need to do something soon because if I'm going to have to extend the whole schedule it'll have huge knock-on effects.'

'We can't extend.'

'That's what I keep saying . . .'

I start to gather my things together, hoping she'll take the hint. 'Like I say, I'll speak to him. Leave me the latest copy of the schedule, will you? I really have to go, sorry.'

'I don't really understand how he got the job to be honest . . .'

This is a leading question and she knows it.

'Because I hired him, Stella, OK? Sometimes chances pay off and sometimes they don't. There's no knowing until they start.'

'He doesn't seem to have any experience. I mean, what's he done before?'

Now she's overstepping the mark.

'I will speak to him, all right? He's producing the show and that's that. We just have to make it work.'

I leave her there and head for Bea and Lucy's office.

'I'm going,' I say, sticking my head round the door. Bea is all dressed up and doing her make-up while sitting at her desk. I haven't had a chance to tell her my news yet, what with the wall-to-wall meetings, and I'm not about to with Lucy sitting there.

'You got a date?'

She smiles a smile that takes over her whole face. 'Sure have.'

'Is this still Danny?'

'Yup.'

'Well have fun. I have to rush off. See you in the morning.'

'Night, Tamsin.'

It's great that she's found someone. I mean, I know it's only been a few weeks, but he seems to be making her happy. I decide that I like Danny.

The stupid tube grinds to a standstill somewhere between North Acton and Shepherd's Bush. No explanation. I sit there sweltering in the heat, watching the minutes count down. By the time we get to Oxford Circus I have no option but to run to Dean Street. I arrive at the Soho Hotel at twenty-three minutes past six.

On balance I decide that it's worth the risk to head into the hotel. Patrick is always late. There is a possibility that he's so enamoured with whoever it is he's meeting that he will make a special effort, but he's hard-wired to always arrive at least five minutes after he should. I need to find a good vantage point, where I can watch reception but not be seen myself.

The foyer contains a giant black sculpture of a cat and not much else. Certainly nothing I can safely hide behind, and besides, the reception and concierge staff might wonder what I'm up to skulking around, and call over to ask me if I need any assistance. Around the corner are a couple of small sitting rooms neither of which offers a good view of anything much. The bar is packed. And risky. I can't decide whether or not I think Patrick and his date might stop off for a drink. Unlikely given that they only have a few short hours, I assume – Michelle certainly hasn't mentioned that he is staying away all night – and there will almost certainly be a mini bar in their room. If they've booked a room, that is.

I need to act quickly. The bar is dangerous but it has great views of the entrance to the hotel. It's big enough that I should be able to find a corner to hide in. I just have to make sure I'm not near any lone women who might be HER. It's definitely possible that she has already arrived and is sinking a bit of Dutch courage.

I push my way through the crowds of after-work drinkers. Have I mentioned that I dug out the only hat I own – a kind of fedora-shaped straw sun hat – and I am now wearing it pulled low over my face, my hair mostly tucked up inside. Secret Squirrel on a mission. I keep my head down. My first cursory glances reveal no women drinking on their own. And definitely no Patrick. I relax a little. I've made it.

There are no free tables as far as I can see but I think it's best if I stay mobile anyway. In case of the need for a quick getaway. There is also, I notice, a back entrance from the bar onto what must be Wardour Street. I have to place myself somewhere where I can watch two aspects at once and still not be seen. There is no time to get a drink, but I've given up caring whether any of the punters think I'm a basket case. I find a spot near the front window, tuck myself into a corner, between tables of bemused drinkers, and wait.

Five minutes go by. Still no single women show up. Maybe her timekeeping is as bad as Patrick's. Or maybe they have somehow sneaked in through a fire exit and up the stairs before I could spot them. Of course it's entirely possible that they have changed their arrangements and either cancelled or altered the time. I decide to give it till quarter to seven before I give up.

At just before twenty to my heart practically stops. I recognize the walk first. Patrick has this way of rolling from side to side as he moves. Even his gait is cocky and thinks it's a bit better than everyone else's. It stops just short of being a swagger. I step back from the window, afraid he might see me, but he keeps his head down and his eyes on the ground. I see him enter the reception. I assume he'll go straight to check in – and it only occurs to me at that moment that he will probably call 'Ben' and let her know the room number so she can meet him up there, in which case I will never know for certain who she is – but he bypasses the desk and seems to be aiming straight for the bar.

Shit.

I edge back into a corner. Turn to face the wall like a naughty child taking its punishment. I'm sure I look perfectly normal. Middle-aged woman, straw hat, staring at a spot where they missed a bit of paint on the wall from a distance of six inches. I don't care. I just don't want to get caught.

Of course, I now have no idea what is happening behind me. Patrick might be shagging someone on the wooden floor in full view of everyone, for all I know. I have no idea how long I'm going to have to wait either, before it's safe to turn round. I know now that my plan is ridiculous. I should never have involved myself. I will it all to be over.

When a hand touches my shoulder I jump. Actually jump as if I have been shot out of a cannon. And then I hear him. Patrick.

'Tamsin! What on earth are you doing here?'

34

Bea

Jesus. That was close. A few seconds either way and fuck knows what would have happened. A live episode of *Jeremy Kyle* probably. Someone was on my side this evening, though. Or, more likely, it was just a massive stroke of luck.

I left work about ten minutes after Tamsin. She had gone off in a big hurry, apparently to meet someone. I didn't ask who. I assumed Michelle because I knew she would be on her own this evening. I had arranged to meet Patrick at the Soho Hotel. The plan was, as always, that I would hang around outside discreetly until he arrived. He would walk straight past me without acknowledging me. Once I had given him a few minutes to check in I would go to the reception desk and ask if I could call up to his room. He'd tell me the room number and I'd be on my way.

The 'Ben' rules are very strict. Days, times and venues only. No texting of room numbers because why on earth would Patrick have booked a room if he was meeting his friend? No phoning ever, except under the most dire emergency and even then, if Patrick says, 'I'll call you back in a bit, mate,' it means that he is with Michelle and I am to hang up immediately. In the unlikely event that I run into him and his lovely wife on the street I am to walk on by. Not even a glance.

I know how it goes.

I'm always a little bit cautious whenever I arrive at our chosen meeting place. You never know who you might bump into and I make sure I have an excuse at the ready. I tend to look around, checking out who is in the vicinity before I head inside. And thank God for that because that's the reason I saw Tamsin.

I didn't realize it was her at first. She was wearing this big straw hat. It wasn't a particularly sunny day so she stood out even more. She was walking just in front of me as I reached the alley where the hotel entrance is and, as she turned in, I noticed she pulled the hat down even further over her face. Large sunglasses underneath it. I spotted the bag next. Tamsin has this big bright red tote that she always carries. Full of Christ-knows-what crap. And then I realized that the pale pink pedal pushers and honey-coloured Fitflops had a very familiar ring to them.

I stopped in my tracks. A woman behind me tutted as she swerved to avoid me. I tried to fathom what Tamsin was doing here. Was this where she was meeting Michelle? It seemed unlikely just because of the coincidence alone. And if she was, then why the disguise? For a second I entertained the idea that Tamsin might be having an assignation herself. Meeting someone she shouldn't be meeting.

And then it hit me.

I scrambled for my phone. Broke protocol and called Patrick – if this didn't count as an emergency then I didn't know what did. He sounded irritated when he answered.

'What's up?'

I burbled something about Tamsin and the fact that we were in danger of getting caught.

'How the fuck did she know where we were meeting? Is she on to you, do you think?'

The thought made me shudder. 'No. Definitely not. I'd be strung up over Brook Green if she did.'

'Don't go in,' he said and I stopped myself from saying, 'No shit, Sherlock.'

'Of course not. Shall I meet you somewhere else?'

He thought for a second. 'No. Do you mind if we forget about this evening?'

I did, I was actually quite pissed off, but I stopped myself from saying it. 'OK. What are you going to do?'

'If she's there to see me then she's going to see me.'

'You are kidding?'

'No. Fuck her.'

'Patrick, don't just do this because you're angry at her. What if she tells Michelle?'

'She won't.'

'I don't know how you can be so certain of that . . .' I understood that Tamsin would never want Michelle to know the ways in which she had helped Patrick cover up his infidelity, but I wasn't confident she wouldn't decide enough was enough. After all, why was she here?

'I just am, OK.'

'Will you call me later – it'll be OK, I'll be on my own . . .'

'I'll try. If I don't, don't call me, OK.'

'I know! Patrick . . . Jesus . . .'

The temptation to hang around and try to see how it played out was overwhelming. I couldn't imagine what Patrick was intending to say to her. Or what her reaction would be to getting caught out. It was almost funny.

Almost.

35

Tamsin

I freeze.

Escape plans flash through my head. I could pretend to faint, collapsing on the floor and refusing to respond until some kind soul calls an ambulance and has me spirited away. I could claim amnesia, pretend I'm on a secret spy mission — which I am in a way — or even just the old-fashioned make a run for it. Hold on . . . why is he acting so pleased to see me . . . ?

Reluctantly I turn to face him.

'Patrick!'

He laughs. 'Why are you standing looking at the wall? And why have you got that hat on?'

'Oh . . . I just saw someone I can't stand come in . . . that bloke who works in my bank . . . actually, you wouldn't know him. But, anyway, I didn't want to have to talk to him. How about you? What are you doing here?'

He doesn't miss a beat. 'I was supposed to be meeting my mate Ben, but he just called and cancelled. Right as I walked in the door.'

'Oh. Do I know Ben?'

'I don't think so. He's from football.'

Patrick plays football once a week or so with a seemingly random group of friends, none of whom I have ever met, so that seems like as good a cover for Ben as anything.

'See him a lot do you?' I say, and I know my question sounds loaded but I can't stop myself. I'm still convinced that Ben doesn't exist. That he's her.

'I do actually. What about you, though, Tam? You haven't said what you're doing here.'

That's a good question. What am I doing here? I can hardly say I was supposed to be meeting someone but they cancelled, too.

'Oh, I just had a quick after-work drink with Bea. You know, my assistant.'

I can't tell if he believes me or not.

'Right. That's a long way for you both to come. Don't they have pubs in Brook Green?'

Fair point. 'She's going to the cinema but she wasn't meeting her friends till just before seven so I said I'd come and keep her company for a bit.'

'What's she going to see?'

'I have absolutely no idea. Why are you asking me all these questions?'

He raises an eyebrow at me. 'Annoying, isn't it?'

My heart is pounding in my chest but I don't see how he could be on to me. Not unless he's noticed that my text message has been deleted, which is possible but – I think – unlikely. Unless he'd thought to check after Michelle told him about my early morning visit on Saturday. There's no way of knowing unless he brings it up. Or I do.

'Who were you really supposed to be meeting? I assume it was your girlfriend.'

'I told you. My friend Ben. That . . . it's all over and done with.'

'Really?' Even though I know I can't trust him as far as I could throw him I can't help but grasp on to this glimmer of hope.

He nods. 'Not that it's any of your business, but yes. I came to my senses.'

'Fuck, Patrick. I wish I knew whether I could believe you.'

'It's the truth. To be honest I'm past caring about what you think. So . . . what were you really doing here?'

Oh no. He's not catching me out that easily. 'Having a drink with Bea.'

'Great,' he says, a crocodile smile on his face. 'I'm glad we've cleared that up.'

I get out of there as quickly as I can. Thankfully Patrick doesn't suggest hopping on the Northern line with me. I think he's as glad to see the back of me as I am of him. My over-excited heartbeat doesn't slow down until the tube reaches Camden. On a whim, I push my way through the crowds and out onto the platform. I head up the escalator, pull out my mobile and call Bea. I have to talk to someone.

Her number clicks straight on to answerphone. Of course. She's on a date with Danny, probably having pre-club drinks somewhere smart. I decide not to leave a message. After all, what would I say?

36

Tamsin

I know what I have to do. Scrap that. I know what I *want* to do. I want to find out who he's seeing and I want to have it all blow up in his face. I don't want to give him the chance to cover his tracks. He thinks he's so fucking untouchable.

Of course I have no idea how I am going to achieve this. That's the boring detail; I'll deal with that later. Meanwhile I have to make sure that breaking up Michelle and Patrick – or at least giving her the reason to want to break up with him – is really what I want to do. I have to make sure that I'm not just entertaining the idea for selfish reasons. And there are enough of those. I want my friend back. I want revenge.

Do I think Michelle would be happier without him? In the long term, once she knows what he's capable of, absolutely. In the short term she'd be devastated. I can't even imagine. But she'd get over it. Eventually. I think.

Three things I do know for certain, though:

- Patrick hasn't ended the relationship, however much he protests that he has.
- Michelle is never going to have the blissful nuclear family she's always dreamed about while she's with him.
- None of this is any of my business.

It can't hurt to find out who SHE is, though. Fore-warned is forearmed and all that. I can make the bomb and then decide later whether or not to detonate it.

I need help, though. There is no way I can do this on my own.

My phone buzzes into life right on cue. Bea.

'Hi.'

'Did you need me? I got a missed call.'

'Oh, shit, sorry. I'd forgotten you were on a date. I just wanted a chat. It can wait.'

It doesn't sound as if she's in a bar. I can't hear any background noise at all.

'He had some kind of family emergency. Had to rush off. I'm home already.'

'Is everything OK?'

'It's fine. He has a sister who sounds like a bit of a head case. She rang him in a state about something or other. I told him to go over and see her. No big deal. How about you? Weren't you going out?'

'Oh. Yes. I just had a quick one with Michelle. I'm home, too.'

'So . . . now we've established we're a pair of lamos who are home from our nights out at a quarter to eight, what were you calling for?'

I don't want to go into it over the phone.

'Like I said, it can wait. It's nothing.'

'Oh no,' she says, laughing. 'I know that tone of voice. Something's up. Have I done something to piss you off?'

'No! God, you and your witchy senses! Not at all! It's just . . . look maybe we could go for a quick drink after work tomorrow or something. I'll tell you then.' I know

I'm not going to be able to go through with this stone cold sober, so confiding in her in the office is out of the question.

'Tell you what. It's still early. Why don't I grab a bottle of wine, jump into a cab and come over to yours?'

I think about it. Now I know that I am going to tell her the whole story I have a kind of now or never feeling. But I don't want her to think she has to schlep halfway across London just because I've dangled the 'I need to talk to you about something' carrot in front of her.

'You don't want to do that. Honestly, it can wait. Don't worry.'

But she's adamant. 'I'm dying of suspense here. What's your address again?'

37

Bea

I'm gagging to know what happened. Patrick hasn't called and, of course, according to the Ben Rules, I can't phone him.

I'd been pacing around my flat imagining all kinds of worst-case scenarios for a good twenty minutes when I noticed that Tamsin had called. The signal in my place is so bad that nine times out of ten calls go straight to voice-mail without even ringing. Unless you happen to be up in Sarah's bedroom and hanging out of the window, that is. Which is where I went to call Tamsin back. Luckily Sarah's used to it. She just carried on watching something on her computer, giant headphones covering her ears, while I leaned precariously over the rooftops of North London and phoned my boss.

Tamsin is a terrible actress. I can always tell when some-thing's bothering her, so it must have seemed perfectly feasible to her that I had supposedly spotted an edge in her voice that made me want to run over there and keep her company. I thought it might seem odd, me offering to go to her flat. I've never been there before. She once sent me round to the place where she used to live to feed her dog. It was a bit of a tip, to be honest. But then I've never offered to go out at eight o'clock at night, when I am already happily in my PJs, to meet her before either. I was banking on her being so discombobulated that she'd accept, though.

Not that I think I'm going to glean much from her. Obviously I can't ask and I doubt she is going to spill. But it beats sitting around hoping Patrick will phone and tell me what happened. She might let something slip, however small, that'll give me a clue. And if all else fails I'll get to have a look at her new place.

She gives me a hug when I arrive, which is a bit disconcerting to say the least. I hope this doesn't mean we have to start doing it every morning. Dahling! Mwah! Mwah! From the outside her house is impressive. A big, red-brick terrace towering up over four floors. I know she only lives in part of it – Flat 3, she told me on the phone – but as there isn't a kebab shop downstairs and I know she doesn't have two annoying flatmates cluttering up the place, this already feels like a palace to me.

Inside it's smaller than I expect. That's not to say it isn't gorgeous. High ceilings and shiny real wood floors. A big bay window at the front. It smells a bit of dog, if I'm being honest. I like dogs, but I'm not a huge fan of their body odour. Ron runs over to greet me. I have no idea if he remembers that we've met before, but he's sweet and friendly so I lean down and scruff his head.

'Lovely flat,' I say, handing over the wine I picked up at the offie on the corner of my road.

'Thanks,' Tamsin says. 'Sorry it's such a mess.'

I don't contradict her. It is. It makes my place look like Kim and Aggie have been round. Mind you, I should have expected it. Her office is a toxic waste sanctuary.

She shoves a load of crap onto the floor to clear a space

on the sofa for me, pours me a big glass of wine and fills up her own. She's obviously had a glass or two already, but then so have I.

'So,' I say, 'What's up?'

I expect her to tell me some half-arsed sob story about feeling bad for having lied to Michelle to cover up for Patrick, or even, maybe, to tell me she's just had an unpleasant encounter with the man in question. Without going into too much detail, I imagine.

But nothing has prepared me for what comes out of her mouth.

'You slept with Patrick Mitchell?'

I can't believe what I'm hearing. A wave of nausea hits me. I need to know everything. When. Where. What the fuck he thought he was doing. I have to be careful not to give myself away, though. Not to let her see that this news isn't just a shock, it's like a body blow.

'No. I didn't sleep with him. Not exactly. We just . . .'

She leaves the words hanging there. I want to shake her. Just what? What the hell does 'We just . . .' mean on the scale of sexual contact?

I wait for what seems like an age. She says nothing, just looks at me. I breathe in slowly.

'You just . . . ?'

'We just fooled around a bit. A lot. Jesus, Bea, you really can't tell anyone this. Ever.'

'As if.' I need details. 'Fooled around. That doesn't sound so awful. What? You just kissed him or something?' Stop it, Bea. Stop making it so obvious.

She lets out a cross between a sigh and a moan. 'More

than that. Quite a lot more, but not everything. Shit. I'm so ashamed of myself. You've got no idea what I've been feeling like all these weeks.'

I move an imaginary cursor along an imaginary line that is labelled 'Fooled around' at one end and 'Everything' at the other. It hovers somewhere around 'Oral'. This is not comforting.

'When . . . I mean . . . ?'

Tamsin puts her head into her hands. I try to remember how I would be behaving if she hadn't just basically told me she'd had sex with my boyfriend. I would probably be trying to make her feel better.

'I'm sure it's not as bad as you think. These things happen . . .'

'It is. It is as bad as I think. It was a stupid mistake, but that doesn't make it any better. That's why . . . don't you see? That's why I've been covering up for him and everything. Because he has something over me.'

'Shit,' I say, hoping it sounds like I give a flying fuck about how she's feeling. 'Tell me everything.'

So now I know that five nights after he first slept with me Patrick had sex with Tamsin. Sanctimonious Tamsin who was so outraged by the betrayal of her best friend that she practically forced me to go and seduce that best friend's husband. Self-fucking-righteous Tamsin who couldn't bear to stand by and watch while Patrick cheated on Michelle. Holier-than-thou Tamsin who was so horrified by hearing that her best friend's husband had cheated on her that she cheated on her with him herself. The word hypocrite doesn't even come close.

Patrick told me he had put on an act to convince her of his innocence. He told me he cried. What he'd failed to add is that he sealed the deal by sticking his dick in her mouth.

'I don't know how it happened,' Tamsin tells me now, almost tearful herself. I am unmoved. 'Well, I do. We were both a bit drunk and he was so upset and then the next thing I knew he was kissing me. I should have just pushed him away.'

'Why didn't you?' I say, trying to keep the judgement out of my voice.

'I did. Eventually. I don't know. I really don't. I guess I must have wanted it too.'

'So it *was* just a kiss . . . ?' Jesus, I can't let it go.

'No . . . no.'

'But you pushed him away in the end. He would have carried on?'

'I came to my senses, yes. But way too much had happened by then.'

I have to know. 'And he would have carried on?' I say again.

She looks as if she's thinking about it for a moment. 'Yes. I don't know how long for, though. We've never actually talked about it since.'

'So . . . how far did you go? I'm guessing pretty far . . .'

She sighs. 'I can't talk about it . . . you'll have to use your imagination.'

Oh no. She is not getting away with that. 'I bet you're overreacting. You're beating yourself up but it's nowhere near as bad as you think.'

'No, it really is. You'll just have to trust me on that.'

I reach over and fill both our glasses up again. I want details, and pouring drink down her might help.

'So then what?'

'Then we both agreed it had been a horrible mistake and it would never happen again and that Michelle must never find out. I actually felt bad for him, Bea, can you believe that? He seemed as horrified by what we'd done as I was.'

'Wow! This is ... I mean, you were so outraged when you thought he was playing around ...'

'You don't have to remind me. I feel terrible. I know it doesn't make any sense.'

'So ...' I say, and this is the question I really want answered. 'Has it happened again since?'

She looks at me like I've just suggested we get down on the floor and try it ourselves. 'Of course not! Christ. Once was bad enough.'

'He hasn't tried again?'

'No. He hasn't tried again.'

That's something. She tells me she'd thought they had put it behind them. Agreed it had been a mistake of the worst order and that it could never benefit Michelle to find out.

'All I could think about was her and what I'd done to her,' she says, looking at me, watery-eyed, and I think, Yes, of course, I'm sure you weren't thinking about yourself at all.

I make sympathetic noises and try to get my emotions under control. 'So, how did it get from that to you agreeing to cover up for him?'

'I ... I sent him a text. I know, I know. It was a stupid

thing to do. But I couldn't get hold of him the next day and I just wanted to make sure we were on the same page. He kept it.'

Ah, so now I get it. Patrick didn't so much sweet talk as blackmail. I almost laugh.

'God. What a bastard,' I say and – maybe not for the reasons she thinks – I mean it. 'So, is that it forever? He has that over you so you're going to keep on bailing him out.'

If I wasn't so angry with Patrick I would probably be admiring the way he has pulled this off. It's the world's best alibi.

'Not exactly,' she says now, stopping my thought process in its tracks.

She tells me some story about wiping the text from his phone. I can tell that although tonight's events have obviously rattled her, she is feeling a bit proud of herself for this. I'm gagging to ask her what went down this evening, but I know I have to wait my time.

'Nice,' I say. 'So now you've got the upper hand?'

'I don't know.' She takes a long sip of her wine and then she tells me about finding Ben's messages and turning up at the hotel tonight to try to catch him out. I feel a shiver down my back as I realize how close I came to being discovered. Patrick, it seems, sought her out in the bar and more or less accused her of following him.

'Or at least that's what it felt like,' she says. 'I don't know if he's worked out I've deleted that text yet, but either way he knows I'm not going to lie down and let him walk all over me any more.'

A thought strikes me. 'Why were you there, though? Why do you care about who it is he's seeing?'

'Because I've decided he's not going to get away with it.'

Everything goes in and out of focus. The feeling you get when you wake up after a big night out and you know you're in for a rough day. 'I thought you wanted to protect Michelle? I thought your main priority was making sure she never found out what he was like.'

'It was. But that was when I thought he really loved her. When I thought he was having a bit of an out-of-character mid-life crisis . . .'

And before you thought he might tell her about you and him, I think, but I don't say it out loud.

'Now I know he's an irredeemable bastard, though. And it's better she finds this out now than a few years down the line.'

'Don't get me wrong, but is this really anything to do with you? I mean . . . I know she's your friend . . . what I'm saying is it could rebound on you. You could come off worse.'

Tamsin exhales loudly. 'Shit, I don't know. Am I doing the wrong thing?'

Half of me screams, 'Yes.' I don't want to be found out. I can't even imagine how it would be if Tamsin discovered it was me that Patrick was seeing. Me who was the big bad threat to her friend's happiness. But another part – a tiny but surprisingly gobby part – can't help but think that if Michelle found out what Patrick was really like then that would surely signal the death of their marriage. And I'm starting to think that I would quite like him to be single. Well, not single because, obviously, he is seeing me. But single on paper. Unencumbered by a wife. Free to make his relationship with me official.

I check myself quickly. Of course I can't hope for that to happen. It would make my relationship with Tamsin – my boss – untenable. I doubt she'd have grounds to sack me, but imagine how impossible she could make my working life. I could look for another job, but I'm sure her references would lack a certain amount of enthusiasm. 'Bea works hard – if working hard means she will try to seduce your married friends, that is.' 'Bea is a bit of a slag, so don't leave her alone with your husband whatever you do.' 'Bea is a massive skank – end of.'

On reflection I think it's best if I can help ensure Patrick and his saintly wife stay together. At least for now.

'I might need you to help me,' she says now. 'I have no idea what I'm going to do next.'

'Of course,' I say, not meaning it for a second. 'Anything.'

38

Bea

Obviously I tried to phone Patrick the second I got out of there. Fuck the Ben Rules.

I had accepted Tamsin's offer of a cab without argument. It was getting pretty late and I wasn't really in the mood for pissed-up tube-goers making their way home from fun nights out. My night out could not have been described as fun. Revealing, yes. Shocking, yes. Fun, no. Not exactly.

It clicked straight to voicemail. He obviously had it turned off. Probably tucked up in bed with Michelle by now, hand curved tenderly around her waist. The loving, considerate husband. I didn't leave a message. I'm not that stupid.

Five minutes later I was grateful he hadn't answered. If I'd blurted out exactly what was bothering me, ignoring his protestations of 'Can I call you back in a bit, mate?' then I would probably never have heard from him again. I would have overstepped the mark from something that was unthreatening to something that was decidedly dangerous. I would have made myself a liability.

I'm going to have to play this carefully. I can't storm in there all accusing and demanding. Mind you, I'm not going to let him get away with it either. At the very least I intend to tell him what I know. To see what he has to say for himself.

I tried not to think about them together. Tried to remind myself that he had only just met me when it happened. But the idea of it made me feel like throwing up.

Ali was up when I got in. She started in on some interminable story about how her ex had called her phone by mistake, but they'd ended up having a long and soul-searching conversation. Something like that. I struggled to even feign interest. I think she said they were meeting up next week. I have no doubt she'll tell me the whole story again when I see her tonight. Ali has that tendency. If she has something to tell you, once is never enough. I'll catch it on the replay.

I claimed tiredness and an early start and retreated to my room. The thought of sleep seemed like an impossibility, though, so I put in a DVD of *The Princess Bride* – a film I have watched at least seventeen times and slept through countless more, swallowed down two Nytol and somehow managed to pass out.

Tamsin has a slightly hysterical whiff about her this morning, like a kid the week before Christmas. She's a woman on a mission. I know she's gagging to talk to me about it. Now she's opened up those floodgates nothing will close them again. I get the impression she's looking forward to a brainstorming session because she's already asked me what I'm doing at lunchtime. It's laughable.

Of course I haven't heard anything from Patrick. We don't have the kind of arrangement that includes heart to hearts on the phone. All I can do is wait for him to text me about a meeting time – I'm always free, by the way.

Whenever he has sent me a date and venue I have only ever said yes. I've cancelled plans and let friends down to be at his beck and call. Suddenly this strikes me as a bit pathetic. I don't know why it's taken me so long.

I wait until Lucy finally decides to go out and get herself some lunch. As usual it doesn't even cross her mind to offer to pick something up for me, too. Mind you, I'm as bad these days. Once I realized she was never going to reciprocate my goodwill I gave up. Let her pick out her own minuscule low-fat, low-carb, low-calorie sandwich. Tamsin is out at a meeting. Across town at the offices of ITV.

I shut the door. Pick up the phone. Dial the number.

'Patrick Mitchell's office.'

'Hi,' I say in what I hope is a happy, confident tone. 'This is Bea from Castle. I have Tamsin Fordham for him.'

'Hold on, Bea. I'll see if he's available,' Verity – I assume it's Verity – says.

I wait. The door handle rattles and I jump. I hold the handset over its cradle, ready to hang up at any moment. Ashley sticks her head round the door.

'I'm just—' she starts to say and I can't help it, I practically bite her head off.

'Fuck's sake, Ashley. If the door is shut then knock.'

I hear a rustle on the other end of the line and flap my hand at her to leave. She backs out, mouthing, 'I'm so sorry.' Just in time. I hear his voice. He sounds wary, and why wouldn't he?

'Tamsin?'

I can't be bothered with the niceties. 'Anything you think you should tell me?'

'Jesus Christ. What the hell are you doing calling me at work?'

'Because I knew you wouldn't call me and I needed to talk to you.'

'I thought we'd agreed . . .'

'Yes, well, I don't feel like sticking to that agreement at the moment.'

'You want to tell me what this is all about?' He sounds angry.

'Do you want me to over the phone?'

'Stop playing games, Bea.'

'I'm not. It was a genuine question.'

He sighs noisily. 'What are you doing after work? I could meet you for an hour at six.'

He's already waiting by the little kiosk that sells teas and coffees when I get there. Not that we are planning on sharing a cuppa. It was just the only place we could agree on in the whole of Hyde Park, tucked just inside, right by Lancaster Gate tube.

I'm ten minutes late because I couldn't get away from Tamsin's manic plotting. She's like a dog with a bone now that she's decided to catch Patrick out. We already spent half the afternoon throwing out more and more laughable ideas on how to go about it. Mine were deliberately idiotic, obviously. At one point she accused me of having watched too much *Scooby Doo*. Thankfully she hasn't stumbled across any plans worthy of serious consideration yet. Nothing Patrick or I should lose any sleep over.

I feel a little flutter of excitement when I see him, as I

always do. He's looking down at his phone; he hasn't noticed me yet. Then I feel bad for having worried him and for breaking the Ben Rules so flagrantly. I'm not the only one who has things at stake.

And then, of course, I remember why we're here and I just feel angry.

He looks up when I'm still a few feet away. Neither of us smiles.

'Sorry I'm late. Tamsin kept me talking.'

Patrick starts to walk towards the ornamental pond and I follow.

'So,' he says, dispensing with the niceties, 'are you going to tell me what this is all about?'

I have already decided I'm just going to say it. I'm not going to bubble wrap it for him.

'Tamsin told me about you and her.'

That stops him in his tracks. 'She did what?'

I mean, it's actually quite incredible that his first thought is how this might impact on him. 'The fact that she told me is hardly the point. Did it happen?'

He looks at me. 'Are you jealous? We'd only known each other a couple of days.'

'That's not the point . . . I mean . . . Tamsin?'

'I didn't sleep with her.'

'So I hear. She's already given me a "blow by blow" account.'

I pause to see if he will jump in and deny what I'm implying. He doesn't. I force myself not to get sidetracked in pressing for details.

'But . . . what? It was her you really fancied all along? You've been waiting for this to happen for years? What?'

'Of course not. If you really want to know I did it to shut her up.'

Now I'm the one who is taken aback. 'What?'

'Once you told me about the honey trap I knew I had to do something. I figured if I could get her to feel guilty, too, she'd stop acting like the fidelity police.'

I flop myself down on an empty bench. I actually laugh. 'That might possibly be genius.'

He sits next to me. Close but not too close, in case some random colleague happens to saunter by with their poodle.

'I thought so. Not that it should matter, because we'd only just met and we hadn't promised each other anything, but I'm not and never have been interested in Tamsin in that way. I swear.'

OK, so now I'm going to say something really needy. Bear with me. It's going to be pitiful. 'And, otherwise, it's just been me? I mean, apart from Michelle obviously . . .'

'It's just been you. It's only going to be you. I really like you, Bea, you know that.'

I take a deep breath in. Exhale loudly. 'You're actually quite scary. To have come up with that as a plan . . .'

'It worked, didn't it?'

'I guess I have to admit it did. But that text she sent you—'

He interrupts, laughing. 'She told you about that? That was a fucking godsend.'

'She's deleted it.'

There's a comedy moment where he scrabbles for his phone, checks his messages, scrolls forward and back over and over again. Checks his photos. 'How the fuck?'

I tell him what she told me. I'll be honest, even though I've decided to forgive him I still get a certain satisfaction from seeing his confident mask slip.

'Fuck. That must be how she found out where and when we were meeting up.'

I hadn't even thought of that. 'You think?'

'How else?'

'It gets worse,' I say, and I tell him about Tamsin's new determination to unmask the real him. 'She wants me to help her.'

He thinks about this for a moment. The afternoon has turned cooler. There's the tiniest hint of autumn in the air. I dig my cardigan out of my bag and put it on.

I start to worry when he doesn't say anything, wondering if this near miss has made the whole thing seem a bit too real. 'Are you having second thoughts . . . about us I mean?'

And as I say this I realize that I desperately want him to say no, I'm not having second thoughts, I couldn't give you up now even if I wanted to.

Shit. I really don't want him to answer.

He looks at me. 'No. Of course not. But it's complicated now – you do see that?'

I nod reluctantly. I'm scared about where this is going.

'We can't get caught,' he says quietly.

'I know. But if she thinks I'm helping her then I can make sure we don't.'

This has only just occurred to me. Tamsin asking for my help might just be the thing that saves me and Patrick.

'I mean, think about it. I can send her off on completely the wrong track.'

A hint of a smile plays on his lips for the first time since we got here. That lopsided thing he does, where only one side of his mouth turns up. It's always made me go a bit weak at the knees.

'You think you can pull it off?'

I'm so relieved that my confidence knows no limits, even though I am not exactly sure what I intend to do. 'Definitely. It'll be hilarious. And after a while surely she'll give up . . .'

'That I wouldn't be so sure of. We can't get complacent. Not for a second.'

We. He said 'we'.

'No! Of course not. I know my job's nowhere near as important as your marriage' – in all honesty I've realized I couldn't give a toss about his marriage any more, but I want him to feel confident that I do, and I still very much care about my job. At least until I can find another one, then all bets are off so far as I'm concerned – 'but I don't want either to blow up in my face. We can use this to our advantage.'

His smile widens, takes over his whole face.

'So long as she never finds out it's you she's got nothing. Nothing Michelle would believe anyway.'

'It's risky,' I say, now I'm feeling secure enough to know he's not going anywhere.

Patrick laughs. 'We can really mess with her head. Get her to believe anything we want her to believe. It's actually funny.'

'I guess we can't use Ben any more.'

He thinks for a second. 'Yes we can. We have to. Just not for real meetings. Then I can make sure I leave my phone for her to find every now and then. I mean, what else is she going to do? Follow me?'

'I wouldn't put it past her.'

'I can get away next Thursday evening. You?'

I think about the night out that Ali, Sarah and I have planned. Just a pizza followed by the pub and then a club. Nothing special but we did all promise each other we'd keep it free.

'OK.'

'Six thirty at the Covent Garden?'

I nod.

'I'll send you a Ben message and you just need to say yes to whatever it is. But the plan is half six at the Covent Garden, OK?'

'Sure.'

'Oh, and get a pay-as-you-go phone before then. I will, too. I'll keep mine in the office, locked in a drawer that only I have the key to. Texts only, no calls.'

'Jesus,' I say. 'This is getting like *The Wire*.'

'We need to be extra careful,' he says, and then he looks round to check no one is watching and gives my hand a quick squeeze.

'I really do want to keep seeing you, Bea.'

I gulp, furious at myself for turning into such an idiot. I have no idea where this is going to end.

'Me, too.'

39

Tamsin

In one way it feels like a huge relief. A problem shared and all that. In another, though, telling Bea has made it real. Before it would only have been my word against his. Now I have admitted my guilt to a third party. I can't lie to myself any more because I've told the truth to someone else.

Because that someone is Bea I'm not worried though. Besides the fact that I trust her with my life, she doesn't know any of the interested parties. And having someone to brainstorm with is going to be a godsend because, to be honest, I'm struggling to come up with any more ideas myself. And I'm certainly not optimistic enough to think I will ever get access to Patrick's phone again.

Still, we don't get much further than wait outside his office and follow him, which is never going to work. On an episode of *24* maybe, when I could access all the CCTV on the underground system, and run up escalators the wrong way, pushing people aside without one of them turning round and flattening me. But this is real life.

Bea laughingly suggests I stick some kind of tracker to him when he's not looking.

'There's a Spy Shop in Portman Square,' she says. 'I bet they sell something like that!'

I almost consider it. I've got nothing else.

The other thing I do to divert myself from everything else that's going on/wrong in my life is accept an invitation from Ian and Fiona to a party that I would ordinarily chop my finger off to avoid.

Now, though, I have decided to make 'an effort'. I need to get out there and get a social life for myself that doesn't revolve around Michelle and Patrick. Spending less time with them has made me realize just how dependent I am on their company. I've become lazy. But the idea of going to a do where I won't know anyone except the hosts and Anne Marie fills me with dread.

It's Ian and Fiona's fifteenth wedding anniversary. They usually just go for dinner, but because this one has a number attached that's divisible by five that somehow makes it significant. So, party it is. And actually, to be fair, I know I'll enjoy myself once I'm there – Ian and Fiona are great hosts and lovely people – it's just that having to get myself there feels like an uphill battle.

I get lost on the way from the bus stop – the house is in tubeless Muswell Hill and consequently almost impossible to get to – which goes to show how long it is since I've been there. Consequently I arrive at their terraced Victorian villa, which screams 'nicely off young family', a sweaty mess.

I'm wearing a stylish baby pink 1960s fitted dress and painful pointy kitten heels. The bus was supposed to stop right outside their house and actually I'm pretty sure it did, it's just that I wasn't still on it. I'd panicked and jumped off early when I thought I saw a landmark I recognized. My hair is up in what was supposed to be a messy bun, but the messy half of the relationship has clearly proved to be the dominant one. I'm clutching a bottle of champagne, so I imagine I look like an upmarket tramp as I stagger along the street.

I'm about to ring the doorbell when a voice stops me in my tracks.

'Oh my God, you're a woman! I didn't realize when we met before.'

I turn round and there's Adam. Him of the failed blind date. I'd forgotten that he'd probably be here, too. Great.

'Oh, hello. I have to apologize to you,' I say. May as well get it over with. 'I was a bit distracted when we met. I might have been rude . . .'

'Ah yes, how is your mother?' he says with a bit of a smirk.

'I just had some . . . stuff . . . going on.'

'It's fine. To be honest I didn't want to be there either once I got a look at you.'

'Ha!'

His face breaks into a big, doughy smile. 'Oh thank God you laughed. That could have gone either way.'

There are about twenty of Ian and Fiona's friends and family at the party. The kids are, for once, nowhere to be seen, and when I ask Fiona where they've hidden them she tells me they've been bribed with DVDs and pizza and they're all holed up with the babysitter in one of their rooms. This seems infinitely preferable to the last time I was here, when they did some kind of *Sound of Music* choreographed performance on the stairs. I imagine the eldest, at fifteen, has reached the 'over my dead body' phase where things like that are concerned.

Their presence still makes itself known all over the house, though. There are childish works of art tacked up everywhere, toys belonging to the little ones and game consoles and sports equipment for the others. Everywhere I go I step on something I shouldn't – a plastic farmyard cow, a mess of loom bands, a sock. It's like an assault course for the Borrowers.

My plan is to huddle in a corner with Anne Marie, at least until I've had a couple of drinks, but I forgot to factor in that she is Mrs Sociable and loves nothing more than making cheerful conversation with anyone and everyone. I follow her around for a while like a lost puppy, but in the end I get a bit bored with the constant round of 'And what do you do?' type questions, so I park myself beside the buffet and pretend to be absorbed in what to put on my plate. I hate the awkwardness of the early stages of parties. They're the one time when it feels like it might actually be nice to have a boyfriend to use as ballast.

The sparkling wine is there, too, so I fill my glass, swig it back a bit too fast and fill it again surreptitiously. I've got no intention of getting drunk and disgracing myself, but I need the Dutch courage. I spot Fiona across the room, moving through the guests with a bottle, and I make a beeline for her.

'Lovely food,' I say. 'Did you spend all day cooking?'

'Why do you think I had so many kids?' she says, laughing. 'They're an instant unpaid workforce.'

'Damn. I knew there was a reason I should have had some.'

'It's the only reason. How's work?'

'Oh, you know, we're surviv—'

'Surviving. Yes, Ian said it's a bit quiet at the moment.'

'Well. You know what the summer's—'

'Exactly. That's what I said. All the commissioners are probably in Tuscany.'

'It'll be a relief when we get one more thing—'

'Off the ground. I know. Oh look, here's Adam.'

She reaches out a hand and grabs him by the arm as he walks past.

'You two have met before, obviously.'

'Is Fiona letting you get a word in?' Adam says. 'Sometimes I make up random nonsense just to see if she'll run with it.'

'Ha!' I snort before I can stop myself, and then quickly look at Fiona to check she's not offended – I would never dream of picking her up on her bad habit – but she's laughing away happily.

'Very funny. This is why I thought you'd get on,' she says, looking at Adam affectionately.

'Well, don't ever start a dating agency, will you?' I say, taking a chance that Adam will take the joke, and he obliges by chuckling. Actually what I say is, 'Don't ever start a dating—' before Fiona jumps in with 'Agency! Damn, I just did it again. Sorry. I won't do it any more. Promise.'

'Sometimes I like to talk really slowly just to watch the agony on her face while she waits for it to be her turn. Look!' Adam says. 'Look at her trying to stop herself . . . from . . . finishing . . . the . . . sentence . . . for . . . me.'

Fiona is displaying the body language of an eager dog when its owner is teasing it with a frisbee. She's like a coiled spring waiting to pounce. It actually looks as if it hurts.

'See!' she says when he grinds to a halt. 'I didn't interrupt you! I don't know what you're talking about.'

Adam grabs her in a big hug. 'You know I love you.'

Fiona pushes him off. 'I have to go and look after my other guests. The nice ones.'

'You'll be back, you can't resist me,' he says.

Left alone I wonder what Adam and I are going to talk about, and whether I should make an excuse myself and hunt down Anne Marie or Ian to hide behind. After our previous excruciating evening together that would seem a step too far in terms of rudeness, though, so I stay where I am and try to come up with something to say. But then a wonderful thing happens. Adam opens his mouth and he's hilarious. I start laughing at the first thing he says – which is, 'She really should learn to speak up for herself that woman!' – and I don't stop till we say goodnight four and a half hours later.

It's like therapy. After a few minutes we're busy chatting away like people who have known each other for years. I can't believe I didn't notice what good company he was the last time we met. We both get quite drunk and forget about even trying to interact with the other party guests. I realize that I've barely given Patrick a thought all evening. After about the fourth glass of wine I say, 'Would it be weird for us to meet up again given that we clearly don't fancy each other?'

Adam pulls a faux crestfallen face. 'How could you say

that? I just texted my mum when I went to the loo to tell her to buy a hat for the wedding.'

'Oh we can still get married. Just not . . . you know. Thousands of people do apparently.'

'OK. So long as you promise not to jump me in my sleep. I've been told I'm pretty irresistible.'

'I'll try,' I say, lunging for the nearest bottle and topping up both our glasses. 'No promises, though.'

'Actually, I need to retain my single status. It helps with the online dating.'

'I do online dating!' I say, way too loudly. I think I must be a little tipsier than I thought. 'I'm on Other Half.'

'God, me too,' he says, pulling a face. 'I was going to say it's a wonder we haven't ever seen each other on there but, you know, I put "attractive" on my list of must haves.'

'Yes, I put "must work out" on mine.' Too much? Apparently not because Adam chuckles.

For some reason – because I like him, because I don't feel as if he'll judge, because I'm drunk? – I end up telling him the whole sorry Patrick/Michelle story, and he listens to the entire sordid tale without comment. He doesn't even tell me I'm crazy for getting involved or that I should leave well alone.

'Wow!' he says when I get to the end. 'I'm thinking that if you'll sleep with your best friend's husband I'm definitely in with a chance.'

And I laugh about it for the first time since it happened.

'One, I didn't actually sleep with him. And two, I thought we agreed we had no interest in each other that way.'

'Granted I'd have to force myself, but I haven't had much action for a while so . . .'

I punch his arm. Not in a cutesy, flirty way like Meg Ryan might do to Billy Crystal, but so it hurts.

'Ow!' He rubs at the spot.

'Sorry. Couldn't help myself.'

'So, what are you going to do. About your "problem"?'

'I have no idea. Now I've told Bea I feel like we can come up with a plan. Something. God knows.'

'I will dedicate my life to thinking of something.'

'You, me and Bea should all meet up and plot,' I say, suddenly feeling as if it's important we have a plan to meet again.

'Perfect,' he says. 'I like the sound of Bea. Is she single?'

'God, you're already on to someone else. I'm devastated. But actually no, she's not. And anyway, she's picky. She wouldn't just go for any old loser.'

'I like a challenge,' Adam says, smiling, and a part of me thinks, Yes, if Danny doesn't work out I could fix Bea up with Adam. Who knows, maybe she'd go for it.

'See, I told you you'd like him,' Fiona says when she comes across me waiting to use the bathroom. 'My instincts are never wrong.'

'They are this time, I'm afraid. He's a lovely bloke, just not—'

'Your type? I never thought Ian was my type until I gave him a chance.'

'I'm off in a minute,' I say, to get her off the scent. 'It's been lovely. Thank you.'

By the time I leave it feels like Adam and I are old friends. He certainly knows more about me than my actual friends do. I throw myself in a taxi, feeling upbeat for the first time in ages.

40

Bea

Patrick and I have a scheme. It's partly to entertain ourselves and partly to fuck with Tamsin. It won't so much throw her off the scent as waste her time and energy and make us feel like we have the upper hand.

Next time Tamsin is round at theirs he is going to let me know and, out of nowhere, Ben will call him in the middle of her visit. Patrick will make a show of saying to Michelle that Ben is on the phone and then take himself next door to answer the call. His hope is that Tamsin won't be able to resist following him to listen in and will overhear him making an assignation that's miles away from our chosen meeting place of the Covent Garden Hotel. On the Thursday she'll schlep across town hoping to catch him out (encouraged by me if she confides in me, which I have no reason to believe she won't) and we can meet free from any fear that she'll be hiding behind a pillar somewhere.

Half of me thinks Patrick wants to forget our date altogether and follow Tamsin instead – the hunted stalking the hunter – to see how long she waits to catch him out. He actually calls me from his office – an unprecedented event – just for a chat, and we spend ten minutes batting back and forth more and more ludicrous scenarios about

244

where we might send her on a wild goose chase – Glasgow! Wembley Stadium when a football match is on! The top of The Shard! (Tamsin hates heights.) We're actually getting slightly hysterical, having a laugh like a normal couple, when he suddenly says, 'Shit. Verity's back,' and ends the call without saying goodbye. I deflate like a day-old birthday balloon.

When the strange ringing started in my bag and I remembered that I now had a second phone – pay as you go, number given to one person and one person only – I had headed down to the street to avoid being overheard, flapping my hand at Lucy as if to say I had bad reception. It had never rung before, so I'd forgotten there was even a possibility it might make a sound. I tucked myself round the corner, in the entrance to a block of flats, just in case some random person should overhear. Tamsin is out of the office today, trying to fix the problem that is Michael the wayward producer on *Rooms With a View*. I haven't heard from her since about eleven, so I'm hoping that for once I can take a proper lunch break. Get a sandwich. Sit on a bench.

'Lucy went out,' Ashley says as I make my way back through reception. I look at my watch. It's half twelve.

'Already?'

Ashley does a slight eye roll. Not enough to give away that she's taking sides, but I see it. 'She had to go to Westfield.'

'Probably starting her Christmas shopping early. After all, there are only about a million days left.'

Ashley snorts. Then she looks apologetic. 'She asked

me to ask you if you'd sort out Ian's lunch, though. I offered but she said you know the way he likes things, so . . .'

'For fuck's sake.' Ian's lunch order is always like a shopping list. A sandwich from one place, a drink from another, a cake from the bakery. Mayo but no butter if it's chicken. Butter but no mayo if it's tuna. Both with egg. Brie but only so long as you check how ripe they have it first. Ditto avocado. If not then cheddar. But only if they have extra mature. It's exhausting.

'Honestly, I can get it if you tell me where to go.'

'Thanks but it's OK. It'd probably take longer to explain all his stupid idiosyncrasies than for me to get it myself. Is he in?'

She shakes her head. 'Due back about quarter to.'

My dream of a full lunch hour all to myself fizzles and dies.

'Let me know as soon as he's here, will you? Meanwhile there's a pile of photocopying Tamsin needs doing on my desk. If you get the chance.'

'No problem,' Ashley says.

'Don't mention I got you to do it, will you? You know what she's like.' Just covering myself.

During our phone call Patrick warned me that Tamsin was due over at theirs this evening. He instructed me to call at half past eight. Any earlier and they'll still be eating and she might not feel she could get up and leave the table to follow him.

If the time isn't right, or if Tamsin has left already or is in the loo or whatever, he won't answer. We'll try again another evening. While he's still finding the idea of sending her miles in the wrong direction hilarious he doesn't want us to take any risks.

And neither do I. Of course I don't.

So, at twenty-five past eight I'm up in Sarah's room, leaning out of the window, waiting. She's not home thankfully. I think I'd find it difficult to pull it off with an audience. Sitting here on my own I start to think that maybe this is a stupid idea. The whole thing hinges on Tamsin not only being intrigued enough to follow Patrick and stay within earshot, but being in a position to do so, while he makes out he is trying desperately not to be overheard.

At exactly half past I punch in his number and hold my breath. After about four rings – presumably while he does his 'It's Ben, I'd better take it' performance – he answers.

'All right, mate.'

As instructed I say nothing. Can't risk Michelle hearing a woman's voice wafting from his handset.

'Hold on,' he says. 'You're breaking up. I'm taking it through to the other room.'

He's good at this. Lying. Deception. But then I knew that already.

41

Tamsin

'It's Ben,' he says, holding up his phone as if to prove what he's saying. And there it is on the screen for Michelle and me to see: Ben.

'I need to take it,' he says and he doesn't even look at me. I stare at him in disbelief. If I hadn't seen the name for myself I would almost think it was a joke. Candid Camera. A Gotcha.

'Of course,' Michelle says and smiles at him.

'All right, mate,' Patrick says into the phone. I strain my ears. I can't hear anything. Surely he's not going to have a conversation with his mistress right here in front of us?

'You're breaking up. I'm taking it through to the other room.'

He raises a hand – 'sorry'– to us as he goes. I hear him still talking as he heads for the stairs, towards the front room. 'Hold on a second. The reception's shit here.'

'His football friend,' Michelle says by way of an explanation.

'Right.'

'They have some grudge match coming up . . .' she starts to say. I'm not listening. I'm practically making my ears bleed trying to pick up the odd word of his conversation.

'Hold on. I'm dying for the loo,' I say, using my tried-and-trusted excuse. After all, who's going to argue with that? I'm a woman of a certain age. My bladder isn't what it used to be. I run upstairs before she can say anything. 'Won't be a sec.'

The door to the front room is open but pulled to. I hear Patrick's low tones coming from inside. 'OK but don't ring me again,' he's saying. 'Stick to the texts.'

I hover, fully aware that he could come out at any moment and catch me. I creep to the side of the door nearest the toilet, so that I can make a run for it if I hear him coming out.

'Where is it again?' he says quietly. And then, after a moment: 'I don't know how early I can get to Canary Wharf. I'll try for quarter to seven but it might be seven o'clock. OK ... OK ... the Radisson ... I've got to ...'

I don't hear the rest because I hotfoot it down the stairs again. Have I just heard the details of their next assignation? I have no idea what day they're talking about, but it'll be easy enough to find out from Michelle when he's likely to be home late. I congratulate myself on my quick thinking.

By the time Patrick reappears in the basement kitchen I am back sitting at the kitchen table, and I'm quizzing Michelle about how much she had to pay for a bunch of coriander in the local grocery store.

'Everything OK?' Michelle says as Patrick takes his seat again.

'Great,' he says, flashing her a big smile. 'But I'm going to be out Thursday night. They want to get in an extra training session before the "big match".' He does quote marks with his fingers as he says 'big match' to show he's being ironic.

'They're playing their main rivals next week,' Michelle offers up. 'A team from Channel 5 isn't it? They got beaten eight–nil last time so it's become very serious.'

'My old colleagues. It's got very personal,' Patrick says to me as if he really believes what he's saying. Maybe he does. Maybe there's an element of truth in there somewhere. I have no idea if he even plays football at all now. If he ever did. Or whether he made it all up as a smoke-screen. I don't know what's truth and what's lies any more.

I do know he's not training on Thursday night, though. And I know where he's going to be instead.

Canary Wharf is a hell of a long way from Brook Green, I'm not going to lie. I have to walk to Hammersmith tube station, take the Piccadilly Line to Green Park and change to the Jubilee. And it's rush hour, so I'm bound to spend most of both journeys pressed up against someone's arm-pit. It's amazing the variety there is in the aroma of perspiration coming out of Londoners after a hard day at work. You could write a book. Don't though.

I leave work early. I told Bea about my mission earlier in the day. Even tried to persuade her to keep me company.

'Oh no. You're on your own with this one,' she said, laughing. 'And besides, I promised Danny I'd cook him dinner.'

'God, he's brave.'

'I'm doing a lasagne followed by apple pie. I don't think there's much there that could kill him.'

'Still going well then?'

She smiled. I was glad to see Bea so happy. Being in love obviously suits her. 'Still going well. Are you really going to go all the way over to Canary Wharf to try to catch them out?'

'I've got nothing better to do. That's how sad my life is.'

I even thought about asking Adam if he wanted to come along. With company it would be a bit of a laugh, an adventure. On my own it really does seem a bit tragic, even to me. We've exchanged a couple of emails since the party and he's asked me how my quest is going. On balance I decide it would be weird. I hardly know him. I make a mental note to make the effort to take him up on the offer of another drink that he made as we said goodnight though.

'I'll ring you if I have anything exciting to report,' I say to Bea as I leave at five.

'Definitely,' she says. 'Although you know what my reception's like at home.'

It's raining when I leave the office, for what seems like the first time in forever. Luckily I always have an umbrella squirrelled away at the bottom of my big red tote bag, part of a survival kit that could probably keep me alive for several weeks on a desert island. I really must clean that bag out one of these days. I scrabble round underneath tissues, a thin jumper, breakfast bars, a bottle of water, packets of Nurofen and Piriton, and pull it out.

I'm sitting on the tube at Green Park when a thought hits me. How can I have been so stupid? This is too easy. What are the chances that Patrick's girlfriend would call him at half past eight at night, knowing that he must be at home with his wife? When I happened to be there. That he would make a big point of saying it was Ben, knowing full well that I know Ben is code for HER. And that I would overhear him spelling out where they were meeting up next.

It was all for my benefit.

I push my way through the crowd and onto the platform just as the doors close. I assume that the plan was to send me halfway across London – of course they wouldn't be meeting up in Canary Wharf. Why would they? – and then they could spend the evening laughing about what an idiot I was, safe in the knowledge that they weren't about to get caught out. I actually blush, I don't know if it's from embarrassment that I've been taken in so easily or anger that Patrick thinks he's getting one over on me.

I am not going to let him get away with it.

As I emerge back into the world I dig out my phone and try to call Bea. She'll know what I should do. No answer. She always leaves her mobile on silent when she's in the office, so unless she is standing looking at it she wouldn't even know it was ringing. I stand on Piccadilly with commuters swarming round me and no idea what to do.

I try Bea again. Once. Twice. Leave her a message to call me back. Pace backwards and forwards. I'm defeated. I may as well get back on the underground and head home.

My phone rings. I jump. Thank God. Finally. I answer it without checking who it is, so convinced am I that it must be Bea responding to my message. A man's voice I don't recognize greets me matily. I hesitate just for a second, giving away that I don't know who is on the other end.

'It's Adam,' he says, just as I realize. 'Have you forgotten me already?'

I'm not really in the mood.

'Adam! Hi. Listen, can I call you back in a bit . . .'

'Of course . . . any time. I should have known you'd be busy at work.'

'I'm not . . . oh God, Adam, I feel like such an idiot . . .'

I don't know what makes me say it. Desperation most probably.

'What? Are you OK? Am I still hanging up and you're calling me back later because I have to say I'm going to find it hard to concentrate now.'

I tell him the quick version. How I think Patrick deliberately fed me that information to show that he's in charge. How I was on my way to the fake meeting place when I had an epiphany.

'I'm not being flippant, but your friend sounds like a right git.'

'I stopped thinking of him as my friend some time ago. If it wasn't for Michelle I wouldn't have done in the first place, to be honest.'

'Well, I can see why you want to expose him.'

'I know, right?'

I feel incredibly buoyed up by this. It's not just that I'm being vengeful and want to get Patrick back. Normal, rational people with no vested interest in the situation feel as if I'm in the right. *One* normal, rational person anyway.

'So, what now?'

'I have no idea. There's no way he's ever going to let me near his phone again.'

'Where's his office?'

'Holborn. Why? Don't say I should follow him because even I know that's a shit idea.'

'What else have you got?'

'Nothing.'

'I'll tell you what,' Adam says. 'I was actually phoning to see if you fancied a drink tonight, but this sounds much more exciting. I'm only in Shoreditch so I'll meet you there. What's the address?'

'You're kidding?'

Adam laughs. 'This is the most excitement I've had in years. He doesn't drive in, does he? Because that would make it hard.'

'No, he gets the tube. But he might get a cab to wherever it is he's going.'

'Oh my God, I have always wanted to say "follow that cab" to a taxi driver.'

Now it's my turn to laugh. 'This is crazy.'

'What else are you going to do this evening? Cry into your frozen shepherd's pie for one?'

'I'm a pescatarian.'

'It'll be a laugh. If we miss him then so what? We'll go to the nearest bar and drown your sorrows together.'

'OK . . . I can be there by about ten to six.'

I give him the address and, at his insistence, a description of Patrick so he can watch out for him leaving if he gets there before me.

'Don't go following the wrong person, will you?'

'If I see anyone likely I'll take a photo and text it to you.'

'You really are unhinged, do you know that?' I say, but

I feel a huge wave of relief that I'm not going to have to do this on my own.

Patrick's office is in a large glass-fronted building on High Holborn that not only houses the Home Improvement Channel but also several of its sister channels, all under the umbrella of Petersen Media. All chaired by Julian Franklin. I've been here before obviously – several times, in fact – under the guise of work, so I know that Patrick's office is at the back on, I think, the fifth floor. As far as I'm aware everyone arrives and leaves through the same ground-floor foyer.

Adam has texted me to tell me he's nursing a beer outside a pub on the other side of the road. I spot him immediately. He's wearing a blue baseball cap with Miami written on it, and holding a copy of *Metro* in front of his face and peering over it. Why, I have no idea. Patrick doesn't even know he exists, let alone what he looks like.

'Subtle,' I say and he starts.

'Jesus! I have a heart condition, you know.'

I laugh, and then I think maybe he's telling the truth. I barely know him after all. 'Shit. Do you?'

'No. I might have after this, though.'

I sit next to him. Take the paper off him and hold it up in front of my own face.

'I'm the one who needs this.'

'I'd go and get you a drink but I'm scared I'll miss the action. You can have mine.' He hands me his glass and I take a long swig. I pass it back.

'Here. We can share.'

'God, I love a cheap date,' Adam says.

'So what do we do now?' I say.

'We wait,' he says and raises his eyebrows at me. 'Don't take your eyes off that door.'

42

Bea

Today's venue is the Covent Garden Hotel, a boutiquey shabby-chic place on Monmouth Street, off Seven Dials. Lots of dark wood. Very stylish. Very discreet.

I'm getting to know the smart hotels of Central London well these days. I could write a guide. Of course, it would only cover the reception areas and the bedrooms, with special emphasis on the mini bars and the comfort of the beds themselves. A small subsection on bathrooms. I never get to see the lounges or restaurants.

We know, of course, that Tamsin listened in as Patrick hoped she would. He says he heard her coming up the stairs after him, and I have been able to confirm that she picked up all the relevant information and is at this moment en route all the way over to Canary Wharf.

The funniest thing was that she wanted me to go with her. Funniest. Saddest. I'm not sure which actually.

Soon after she left I noticed that she'd called me a couple of times. One message: 'Call me.' I tried ringing her back, but she must have been on the tube because it clicked straight through to voicemail. I leave a message of my own:

'Did you need me? I have my ringer turned up now so try me again. I'm around all evening.'

I can turn it off when I'm with Patrick. Blame bad reception. She knows my flat is like the Bermuda Triangle of mobile signals.

I've come to a big decision. I'm going to have to look for another job.

There's no doubt in my mind that my position is precarious to say the least now. One slip with Patrick and I'm out. And finding employment when I'm a little inexperienced certainly beats trying to persuade someone to hire me after I've been sacked. Not that I think Tamsin would really have grounds to sack me. There are laws. But still. Why take the chance?

So, I have a plan. How can I find a job that adequately reflects my capabilities and not my experience? Who do I know who is in a position of power? Who ought to feel, in a sense, protective of me? To feel a bit responsible that I might be burning some bridges?

No prizes if you got the answer.

Because we're not meeting till half six I don't need to leave work early, but I do spend most of the last half hour getting ready. Making an effort. I'm sure he has enough of dressing gowns and saggy old M&S knickers at home. Being with me should be special. Something he looks forward to when Michelle is asking him whether he'd rather she bought cod or haddock fillets on her next trip to Tesco or if he's taken the recycling out.

I change out of my jeans and into a cute black and white Warehouse knee-length pencil skirt and skyscraper heels. I hate not being able to have a shower, but I do what I can in the little sink that is, thankfully, inside the toilet cubicle. I have a very unfashionable tan, so that means I don't have to worry too much about make-up, I just pile mascara on my lashes and slick on a bit of lip gloss and I'm done.

I collect my bag from my office. Lucy has already left for the day but the post sits on my desk waiting to be stamped and dropped into the post box. I sling it on Ashley's desk as I pass.

'Could you do this? I'm in a bit of a hurry.'

'Of course,' she says. No hint of an edge in her voice. She's too nice for her own good, that girl.

'Have a good evening,' she trills as I head down the stairs.

At the Covent Garden there's nowhere really to wait outside, so I hang about in the foyer, sitting on a bench seat that's in between the front door and the reception desk. I play with my phone, trying to look inconspicuous. Patrick will have to walk right past me to check in. He's late, of course. I know to expect this now, but I'm always afraid that this will be the time he manages to arrive at the appointed hour, so I get there early and just resign myself to waiting.

Bang on five minutes late – which by his standards means on time, I see his bordering-on-cocky walk out of the corner of my eye. I keep my eyes fixed on the screen. Even though I know Tamsin is halfway across London by now you never know who else might be around. Patrick has drilled this into me time and time again. It's one of the Ben Rules. I'm well trained.

He walks right past me and I catch a whiff of his cologne. Some kind of figgy concoction from Jo Malone. That smell will forever conjure up memories of illicit sex in hotel rooms for me. One day in ten years' time some poor unsuspecting computer repair man will pat that on his pressure points in the morning with no idea that the merest hint of it will result in me throwing myself at him, unable to resist as he tries to rid my laptop of a virus.

I hear him talking to the receptionist. Mr Charming. Patrick Mitchell, room for one night. No paper in the morning, thank you. I often wonder what they think when he leaves again at nine in the evening. What excuse does he give? Or do they just tip him a knowing wink, completely aware of the situation? Maybe hotels are full of people (or empty of people, depending on how you look at it) occupying them for only a couple of hours at a time. They should set up a rota.

She gives him the slip of plastic that passes for a key. I wait. A man sits on the seat opposite me, starts fiddling with his phone too. Probably doing the same thing I'm doing.

I wait the required three minutes. The rules state it's supposed to be five but it gets too boring. Thankfully Patrick doesn't seem to time me. Then I walk up to the reception desk, as confidently as I can, and ask to be put through to Patrick Mitchell's room.

'Hi,' is all I say when he answers.

'Hey,' he says, and then 'Four, two, four.'

'OK, see you in a bit.'

I replace the receiver. Smile at the woman behind the desk. 'Thanks.'

I know where the lift is from the last time we were here, so I make my way to the fourth storey. One last check that no one is about and I tap on his door.

Patrick opens it and smiles widely.

'Hi gorgeous,' he says, and even after a couple of months, I go weak at the knees.

I return the smile. 'Fancy seeing you here.'

He pulls me towards him, arms round me, presses his lips on mine.

'You look beautiful,' he says when we come up for air eventually.

On the coffee table are a bottle of champagne in an ice bucket and two glasses. Pre-ordered as ever. Patrick pops the cork and starts to pour.

'How long do you think Tamsin will wait?' he says with a wicked smile.

'Don't.'

'Why?' he says. 'She started it.'

'I know, I know.'

We don't say much for a while after that. We never do. Talking comes later.

43

Tamsin

Adam and I are chatting about his work, which seems to be as much about crowd control and self-defence as actually teaching anything.

'My greatest achievement is to get through the year alive,' he says, taking a small sip of our shared beer. 'Anything else is a bonus.'

'Are they scary?' I ask. My idea of hell is to be trapped in a room with a load of angry fifteen-year-olds.

'Terrifying.'

'So why do you—' I start to say, and then I see him out of the corner of my eye. Patrick. I hide behind my *Metro* again.

'That's him! Jeans. Grey jacket.'

'Brown leather computer bag?'

'Exactly. Let's go.'

We stand to leave. Patrick is heading in the direction of the tube station.

'Don't risk him seeing you,' Adam says. 'If it gets hairy you drop out and I'll phone you when he gets to where he's going. I can sit right next to him and he won't have a clue.'

'You're good at this. Do you do it all the time?' I'm slightly out of breath already. Patrick is up ahead, about to head down the escalator. I flap my Oyster card at the machine and Adam does the same. We're in danger of losing him in a sea of commuters. I catch sight of his grey jacket up ahead. 'There.'

'I'm going to get really close,' Adam says and dashes off, leaving me behind. I can just about make out Patrick moving towards the Piccadilly line, so I go in that direction and then have no idea whether to make for the south or northbound platform. I stop in my tracks, no idea what to do. People behind me bang into me, effing and blinding.

My phone rings. I fumble to answer it. Adam.

'South,' is all he says, so I hurtle towards the southbound platform just as a train rumbles in. I can't see them anywhere, which – hopefully – means Patrick can't see me either. So I just force my way into a carriage and stand up against one of the partitions, keeping my head down. I put my phone up to my ear, hopeful that Adam will still be on the other end, but the signal has gone.

Looking at the tube map I see that Covent Garden is the next stop. Followed by Leicester Square, Piccadilly Circus and Green Park. All places chocker with smart hotels. Not for the first time I think that what we are doing is ridiculous. In fact, so much so that it makes me laugh out loud.

You know that mad woman, chuckling to herself on the underground? The one that you avoid standing too close to? Apparently that's me.

As we pull into Covent Garden I edge towards the doors. When they open I peer left and right, all the while trying to stay as hidden as I can. All I see is a wave of jostling bodies. Briefcases, handbags, elbows, umbrellas. It's hopeless. The doors start to close, sealing me in. As they bump together I spot a familiar rolling walk and, hot on its heels, a somewhat less familiar but still recognizable blue baseball cap. I might have lost Patrick, but Adam still has him in his sights.

There's nothing I can do but wait till Leicester Square, run across to the platform on the other side and jump on the first train going back the way I came. I arrive at Covent Garden maybe five minutes after I left it, push my way up to the pavement – my phone beeps gratifyingly almost immediately.

'Cvt Gdn Hotel' the message says. I know where that is. I've passed it many times. Never had an excuse to go in, even though it looks so welcoming. Deep brown wood and black paintwork. I hotfoot it round to Monmouth Street. Arrive red-faced and sweating. Adam is doing his sitting-opposite trick again. I assume that Patrick has gone inside, that it's safe for me. Adam would have told me to be cautious if not. This time he's ordered a beer for me, too, and I wait for the waiter to place them in front of us, and fuss around with nuts and olives before I say anything.

I sit down with my back to the hotel, just in case Patrick has a sudden desire to look out of the window.

'Thank you.' I knock back half of it, slam the glass back down.

'Wow, should I order you another one before he goes back inside?'

'No. Tell me what happened. I assume you saw Patrick go in?'

Adam sits back, very pleased with himself. And so he should be. 'I went in after him. He checked in under his own name.'

'And did you see . . . was there any sign of her?'

'There was a woman sitting in reception. So I sat there too. A few minutes after Patrick went up to the room she went to the desk and asked if they could put her through to him. All she said was 'Hi' and 'See you in a minute', and then when she put the phone down she went to the lift. Do you know what I think?'

'What?'

'She's a hooker and they don't even know each other. Because he walked right past her when she was sitting there and they didn't even acknowledge each other.'

I think about this for a second. It doesn't make any sense to me. 'No. What about all the Ben messages?'

Adam shrugs. 'Escort agency. They send a different girl each time?'

'He told me he was seeing someone . . . Damn, I wish I'd seen her. What did she look like?'

'Brown hair. Pretty. Youngish. Compared to him any-way.'

'Clothes?'

'Yes.' He looks at me and waits for me to laugh, but I'm too impatient to hear every last detail from him.

'You know what I mean. Was she smart? Casual? Officey? Prostitutey?'

'God, I don't know. Just normal. I thought I did pretty well spotting her at all.'

'You did! I have no idea what I would have done with-out you. It's just frustrating, that's all.'

'They'll have to come out eventually,' Adam says and he waves the waiter over again. 'Want to order food?'

'We might as well, I suppose. You haven't got anything better to do?'

'Me? You met me on a blind date. Do you really think I have a rampaging social life?'

'No. Me neither. Let's eat.'

The restaurant we are sitting outside turns out to be French, so we order a blue cheese and endive salad to share, then coq au vin for him and salmon for me to follow. Every seven or eight seconds I remind him to keep watch on the hotel doors, but even so I still can't help myself asking, 'Is that her? What about her?' every time anyone of a vaguely female persuasion comes out.

'Don't forget to take a photo when she comes out. Make sure your phone's ready.'

'I think we're safe for an hour or so,' he says after the fifth or sixth time I tell him not to lose concentration.

'What if they have a row? She might cut the evening short.'

'I'm watching,' he says, taking a large bite out of his garlicky bread. 'I'm not going to miss her.'

'I know,' I say. 'Sorry. It's just that this is huge. And I don't want to blow it.'

'What are you going to do once you see her, by the way? Confront her?'

'No.' I shudder. 'I don't want Patrick to know I'm on to him. I'm going to go over and get a good look at her, you're going to take lots of pictures and then we're going to wait here till Patrick leaves and take pictures of him, too.'

'That's hardly proof.'

'It'll prove he wasn't where he said he was. It'll be something, OK. It's the best we've got.'

'Still watching,' he says, before I can ask again.

44

Bea

'I need to start looking for another job,' I say. We're lying under the duvet, away from the fierce cold of the air conditioning. Me nestled under his arm, my head on his chest.

'She's not going to find out it's you.'

I sit up and look at him. 'Just in case. It's better to jump ship now, isn't it?'

He shrugs. 'It can't hurt, I suppose.'

He looks at the clock on the bedside table. 'Time to get up.'

The way it always works after – after – is that I leave first. There's no need for me to have a shower because I'm not going home to anyone who isn't supposed to know what I've been doing. I once asked Patrick if Michelle didn't find it odd that he sometimes got in from work smelling fresh and clean – and of a different shower gel to the one they had in their own bathroom – and he told me that he makes sure that doesn't happen. He just uses water, no soap. Dries his hair thoroughly. He has it down to a fine art. He's a pro.

Once I've left, then he leaves too. Apparently he doesn't even tell the people on reception he's checking out after all. They have his card details, everything is paid for. Better that he doesn't draw attention to himself by fabricating an emergency. Especially as we'll be back again in a few weeks, no doubt. We try not to go to the same place too often.

'There's nothing going at Home Improvement is there?' I ask casually as I start to get dressed.

He laughs as if I've made a joke. 'Hardly.'

I stop tugging at the zip on my skirt and turn to look at him. 'I'm serious. That'd solve everything.'

Patrick sits up. Pours himself a glass of water. 'Where's this come from?'

'Nowhere. I was just thinking that you might have something, that's all. If I end up having to leave Castle when I've only been there a year. Forget I asked.'

'That really wouldn't be a good idea,' he says, hammering the point home.

'I said forget I asked. It was just a thought.'

'It would be madness.'

'All right. Jesus. I wasn't suggesting you make me your right-hand woman. I just thought you might know of something somewhere across the company . . .'

He's out of bed now. Covering himself with a hastily grabbed towel. It's as though a wall has gone up between us. A part of me wishes I'd never started this, but another part is furious he's reacting like this.

'. . . after all, it's not just me who's responsible for what we've been doing.'

When he speaks again it's slow and considered.

'We're pushing our luck as it is. We'll give ourselves away if we're together in front of other people.'

I respond in the same considered fashion. 'We wouldn't be together in front of other people. You'd be in your

269

office and I'd be working as the production secretary on some crappy show.'

'I don't get involved in who the producers employ at that level. I couldn't give a shit who types up their progress reports or answers the phones, so long as they do it correctly.'

'God, you're a patronizing shit.'

He ignores that. 'Imagine how it would look if I started micro-managing like that? Apparently I already have a reputation, so . . . what? They're really going to believe I was so impressed with your admin skills that I had to make sure you worked for the channel?'

'I'm not asking you to recommend me. I just meant tell me if you hear of anything, that's all. If Tamsin finds out about this I'm the one who'll be fucked at work, not you. I just thought—'

He cuts me off. 'Tamsin is not going to find out. And if she does then I'm the one who has the most to lose. So she might not give you a good reference. Big deal. I've got a wife to worry about.'

'Fuck your wife.' I shout. Followed by, 'You're the one who's done this to her, not me.'

I wish I hadn't said it immediately. Not that I don't mean it – well, not the fuck her bit. The other thing – the fact that ultimately he's the one who decided to risk it all, to betray Michelle, yes, I do believe that. Probably best not to have said it, though, because he's now looking at me like I've expressed a desire to run her over and mount her head on my living-room wall. Now there's a thought.

'I think it's time for you to leave.' His expression is cold. I know that, as far as he is concerned, I have pushed it way too far. I don't want to go with it like this. I feel as if I might never hear from him again. And that's not an option I'm willing to consider.

Before Patrick I was used to dating lads. Banter, partying and drinking. Both ducking out if things got too complicated. But my relationship with him is real. It's adult. It's special.

'Sorry. I didn't mean that. At all.'

He's immoveable. 'I'll be in touch.'

Desperation hits me. I don't want this to end. 'Can't we make a date now?'

'I'll call you.'

'Please, Patrick. I shouldn't have said it. I felt backed into a corner . . .'

'Forget it. I'll call you, OK. Now I'm going in the shower. You need to go.'

'I could join you. It's still early,' I say in a rather pathetic, flirty way. I want to find a way to erase the last five minutes. I don't want to end the evening like this when our whole relationship is only held together by a wispy piece of string in the first place.

'I have to get going. It's OK, don't worry about it.'

He puts a cursory arm around me and I try to find his mouth with my lips. He pecks my cheek and pushes me gently away.

45

Tamsin

I'm finding it hard to concentrate on my grilled salmon. Not because it isn't delicious – it is – but because my stomach is in a knot. Churned up with anticipation and fear.

About forty minutes ago my mobile rang. I jumped, gasped, looked round as if the noise might have somehow given me away to my fellow diners.

Adam laughed. I picked up the phone. Michelle. Of course, she would be calling to pass the time while Patrick was at football practice. I held it up for Adam to see who was calling. He waved his hand as if to say 'answer it'.

It was still early. There was no way Patrick and his woman would be out soon. If I didn't answer I would only have to call her back later, and who knew what might be happening then. If I had to cut the conversation short I would be able to think of an excuse. I pressed 'accept'. Tried to sound as natural as I could.

'Hi. I was just thinking about you.'

'Were you feeling my boredom? You should have come over.' Michelle needs company like most people need water.

'You need a hobby.'

I looked up at Adam just to check he was still concentrating on his mission. He was barely blinking, tongue poking up from one corner of his mouth like a five-year-old trying to remember his three times table.

'I know. There must be a reason I hate my own company so much. I'm sure it's an indicator of some terrible psychological trait.'

'I can't stay long. I'm having dinner with Adam – do you remember I told you about Adam?'

Adam looked at me at this point, surprised, no doubt, that I had thought he was worth a mention.

'Oh. New best friend Adam who you don't fancy? Looks like a potato?'

I pressed the handset closer to my ear. I would hate for him to hear the way I'd described him.

'Exactly.'

'Tell him to find his own best mate. You're all mine.'

'You could arrange a fight over me.'

Adam looked at me. 'Tell Michelle she can have you. I'm just here as back-up.'

'Ha! I heard that. Tell him I like him.'

'She likes you.'

Adam raised an eyebrow. 'Excellent. Is she single?'

I gave him a look that meant 'you know very well she's not. That's why we're here'. I heard Michelle's laugh on the other end of the line.

'God, are you sure you don't fancy him? He sounds pretty perfect.'

'OK, I heard that,' Adam said. He took the phone from my hand. 'Firstly . . . hello. Michelle . . . firstly it's me that doesn't find Tamsin attractive. She's gagging for me but I just can't bring myself—'

I snorted in protest, causing a woman at the next table

to pause, forkful of cauliflower au gratin hovering in her hand en route to her mouth.

'. . . and second, I am pretty perfect, yes. Thanks for noticing.'

Michelle said something I didn't quite catch and Adam laughed again and said, 'Not surprising really. She's dreadfully annoying.'

I grabbed the phone back from him. 'Will you two stop talking about me?'

'Who says we were talking about you?' Adam said with a smirk. 'The whole world doesn't revolve around you, you know.'

'I'll call you tomorrow Mich. When I'm on my own.' I smirked back at him as I ended the call.

'Well she sounds lovely,' Adam said.

'Told you.'

'Maybe when she's divorced . . .' he said, laughing, and I cut in, 'Don't even joke about it.'

He was suddenly serious. 'I assume that's what all this will lead to, though. I mean, if you go through with it. Once she knows she'll never be able to un-know it. You've thought about that, right?'

'Of course.'

'Well, for the record I think you're a good mate,' he said. 'It's not as if Patrick's going to have an epiphany and become a completely different person by the sound of it.'

'Exactly. The point is that he's been a different person all along. Different to what we all thought he was.'

'I'll drink to that,' Adam said and filled up my wine glass.

'I'd better not get too pissed,' I said. 'I'll end up punching her.'

He topped it up a bit more. 'God, I'm glad I didn't stay in watching *Midsomer Murders*.'

It's dark now, which makes me feel a bit less exposed to being seen. It's also started to drizzle, but we're tucked under an awning, a space heater next to us fighting off the worst of the chill. The waiter has been out twice to ask if we want to move inside, but we've said no for obvious (to us anyway. I imagine to him we just seem a bit insane) reasons. We've finished eating, polished off the bottle of wine and then, very sensibly, ordered soft drinks. We're just waiting.

I now know that Adam was married, briefly, a few years ago.

'I left that out of my Other Half profile,' he said when he told me, 'so that people didn't think I was some sad sack divorcee.'

'No, much better for them to think you're on your own because no one's ever wanted you.'

'Ah, no, that would be you,' he said. I never take offence easily. Life is way too short. But I feel there is literally – and I mean it in the true sense of the word before you pick me up on it – nothing Adam could say that would upset me. It's the way he tells them.

Apparently his separation was completely amicable. He and his ex are still matey. I must have looked at him sceptically because he said, 'Really. I think that was half the problem with us being married. We were better as friends.'

They were at teacher training college together he told

me. Met in the first month, shared a flat for a year before they decided to become a couple.

'It was a good idea on paper,' he said. 'And then I felt terrible because I knew it wasn't right. It was as if we suddenly found it hard to talk to each other. But I kept my head down. Tried to make it work.'

'So what happened?'

'One day she sat me down and told me she was worried we'd made a huge mistake, and I just burst out laughing, I was so relieved. The minute we went to see a solicitor about the divorce we went back to being how we were before.'

'I once agreed to marry an old boyfriend when I was drunk and then I had to backtrack the next day. Actually I just pretended not to remember anything about it. So did he, though, to be fair.'

Adam snorted. 'Did neither of you mention it?'

'No. We did the grown-up thing of acting like it never happened. Saved a lot of hassle.'

He waved to the waiter for another couple of Diet Cokes. 'When was the last serious relationship you had?'

I racked my brain. Couldn't remember anyone who'd lasted more than a few dates. 'You know what, my feeling is, if it isn't perfect it's better to be on your own.'

'Nothing's ever going to be perfect all the time.'

'I rest my case,' I said.

'Sometimes talking to you is like talking to my Year Tens,' Adam said, laughing.

'Are they that smart?' I said with a smirk. 'So where is she now? Mrs Best Mate Ex?'

'Australia. She got married again a couple of years ago.'

'God, she must really have wanted to get away from you.'

'Ha ha,' he said sarcastically. 'You're hilarious.'

'I know. It's an affliction.'

We've been here for nearly two and a half hours now. If I take the whole Patrick/HER element out of the equation we've had a fun evening.

I'm telling him about Ron. Showing him pictures on my phone.

'This was the day I brought him home. He wee'd all over—'

'There she is,' Adam hisses. I've momentarily forgotten why we're there, so it takes me a second to get with the programme. Adam is trying to hold his mobile up discreetly to snap pictures.

'Are you sure?' I say. My heart is pounding. I feel sick.

'Hundred per cent. Quick,' he says as I start to turn around. I feel as if this is the point from which Patrick and I can never return. Our watershed. Or is it our Waterloo? What the hell am I doing?

There's only one woman outside the Covent Garden Hotel. She's struggling to put her umbrella up. Long, thick, dark hair swinging forward over her face. Long tanned legs. For a second my brain just thinks something about her is familiar. This is my moment to storm over, find a way to make her look at me, but it's as if I'm being held back. I can't move. Something isn't right.

'Look up,' Adam urges her under his breath.

The umbrella swoops up. And that's the moment it hits me. It's not so much that I see her face, it's more the whole package.

I turn back round. I feel as if the floor has just been swept out from under me.

'You must have got it wrong.'

Adam looks at me like I've lost my mind. 'No, that's her.'

He looks over. 'She's heading for Seven Dials.'

'That can't be her.'

'It is. Listen, do you want me to follow her? See where she goes?' He jumps up.

'No. Leave it. Let's go somewhere else and get a drink.' I don't want to still be here when Patrick comes out.

He sits back down, defeated. 'I'm confused.'

'That woman,' I say. 'That's Bea.'

He looks none the wiser and why would he.

'My assistant. I've told you about her. She's great. I adore her . . .'

Adam is open mouthed. 'The one you got to try and catch him out in the first place?'

'Exactly.

'Shit. Now I'm really confused. Are you sure?'

I raise my eyebrows at him.

'Of course you are.'

'I have no idea what's going on,' I say.

'That makes two of us.'

I can't take it in. Can't begin to understand what just happened. Bea and Patrick? It makes no sense. I don't even know how it's possible.

'Actually, do you know what? I just want to go home.'

PART FOUR

46

Tamsin

Adam insisted on coming home with me. Tucking me up in bed with a hot drink like I was a sick toddler. I half expected him to read me a story. He offered to sleep in the spare room, too, but I thought that was a bridge too far. He had a classroom full of scary teenagers to face at a quarter to nine in the morning. I let him give a very confused Ron his late-night bathroom break and then I insisted he head home to Clapham.

Of course I didn't sleep at all. My mind was spinning with all the possible explanations. The question I kept coming back to was how long had Bea been lying to me for? Was it her Patrick had been seeing all along? That made no sense. She was the one who confirmed to me that the rumours were probably true when we first heard them. Why would she have done that if some of those rumours might have been about her? To steer me in the wrong direction? It seemed a bit risky.

It must have happened later, but I had no idea how their paths might have crossed again. And if she was the same woman Patrick had confessed to seeing for six weeks when I challenged him about it, then they must have got together soon after his tearful appeal to me. Soon after You Know What.

And did that mean she'd told him? About the honey trap? Had he known all along?

My head hurt. I've never been very good at problem solving. I get lost in the possibilities. Forget what it is I should be focusing on.

I turn my alarm off before it even sounds. I can't face the noise. I haul myself out of bed, bleary eyed and staggering like a drunk. I have a meeting with Living at lunchtime – one that I requested – otherwise I would just stay put. Take a sleeping pill, pull the duvet over my head and hope to pass out till Christmas.

I decide to go straight to the meeting, avoiding the office. I can't face seeing Bea yet. I wouldn't be responsible for my actions. I have to decide what to do first, how to proceed. Punching her in the face probably wouldn't help matters, although it would almost certainly make me feel better.

I make a pot of tea, take my laptop into the bedroom and get back under the covers. Then I remember Ron needs attention, so I take him downstairs still in my pyjamas, rush him through his excretions yet again and chuck some Winalot into a bowl for him. He seems thrilled by my unusual return to bed and climbs back in with me when he's scoffed the lot, panting his meaty breath in my face. I tell myself I'll take him for an extra-long walk when I feel a bit better.

Of course, I have no real intention of doing any work. I set my alarm for half eleven and lie back with my eyes closed.

I'm just drifting off – it must be no more than five

minutes later – when my phone rings. Bea. I turn off the sound and let it ring out.

When the jarring beep of the alarm blares this time I'm fast asleep. I don't want to get up, but I haven't left myself much time to get ready, so I force myself out of bed. Ron grunts and settles back down, happy to stay there till Sharon the dog walker arrives at three, no doubt. I would love Ron's life. Even though he doesn't always get what he wants – a walk, a treat, the chance to adequately sniff the most recent pee messages left by the other neighbourhood dogs – I think he has it pretty good. He seems to be in a permanent state of ecstasy anyhow.

I check my phone while I wait for the kettle to boil. A missed call from Adam. I listen to the voicemail – just checking you're OK, that kind of thing – and it almost cheers me up for half a second. Almost.

I sleepwalk through my meeting. It's obvious my heart's not in it. I leave knowing there's no chance of them picking up any of my ideas, despite us all promising to keep in touch and 'catch up when they're further down the line'. I don't care that it's a waste of time. I'm just happy it got me out of having to go into the office.

I now have three missed calls from Bea. Ignoring her is not a long-term option. Either I confront her with what I now know or I try to pretend everything is OK. For the moment at least.

Adam is the only person I can talk to. Thankfully he answers. It must still be lunchtime. Unless his class are so unruly he's just given up.

'So?' is the first thing he says.

'I haven't seen her yet. I'm on my way in now.'

'Have you been hiding?'

'Meeting.'

'Did you manage to get any sleep?' he asks, concern in his voice.

'Not so as you'd notice. I seem to have gone from being someone who can sleep standing up on the tube to someone who couldn't even manage it if they got hit over the head with a brick.'

'I've been thinking,' Adam says, and then out of nowhere he barks, 'Put him down! I said, put him down! Sorry, Tamsin. Lunch duty.'

Now he comes to mention it, I can hear the squealing and shouting of the kids on their break.

'Anyway, I was thinking. You hold all the cards now. You know everything and they have no idea that you do. Just think about that for a bit. Don't do anything rash.'

'I don't know if I can look her in the face and pretend everything's normal.'

'You've been doing it with Patrick for long enough by the sounds of it.'

'God, I'm a really bad judge of character.'

'Well, your taste in friends does leave something to be desired. Apart from me that is.'

I can't even be bothered to think of something funny to say in return. I hear a loud klaxon on the other end of the line.

'Shit, that's the bell. I'll call you this evening. Don't do anything before then. We can make a plan.'

'OK. Thanks, Adam. Really, though, I don't know who else I could talk to about this.'

'Because they'd have you sectioned,' he says cheerily. 'Which, by the way, I still might.'

By the time I get off the tube at Hammersmith I'm feeling sick with anticipation. I now have four missed calls from Bea. I should have phoned her back, just to make it seem as if everything was normal, but each time I tried I couldn't go through with it. I try to make it to the second floor without her seeing me but, of course, she's been watching out for me to arrive, so she's on me the minute I set foot in reception.

'There you are!'

I look at her. She looks like Bea. No edge, no hint that she's been up all night torturing herself about what she's been doing, no sense that pretty much every word she says to me is a lie. She's just Bea. I don't know what I was expecting – horns and a tail? – but I can't help but be impressed with her skills.

Actually, when I allow myself to look closer she does look a bit like she hasn't slept either. She has dark rings around her eyes. That slightly vacant look you get after a sleepless night.

'Sorry,' I manage to say. I tell my eyes to look up at her face, but they're insisting they're happier staring at a point just by her feet. 'I meant to phone you back when I left Living but I got stuck on another call. Everything OK?'

'All fine. I just wanted to check if you needed anything.'

'Oh. Well, I didn't, so that's fine. Is the new *Rooms With a View* edit on my desk?'

'Yes. Do you want me to watch it with you? I haven't had a chance yet.'

'No. I'll give it to you after.'

'Shall I get you some lunch then?'

I produce a salad out of my tote. 'Already got it.'

'Coffee?' Bea says hopefully, and I think I'd better give her something so I say yes, thanks. I can pretend to be on a call when she brings it so she doesn't think she can sit down and chat.

I head for the stairs and, to my horror, Bea follows me.

'So . . . ? What happened? Did you see him?'

Of course. As far as Bea is concerned I spent the best part of yesterday evening on a hunt for wild geese.

'Oh. No. Nothing.'

I have to decide quickly whether to reveal I know I was set up or not. Clearly the less information she has about anything the better.

'It's a big place. There was no way I could keep an eye on everyone coming and going. It was a stupid idea really.'

Do I imagine it? Do I see her fighting to suppress the slightest hint of a smirk?

'Not necessarily. Like you said, it's all you've got. There'll be another chance.'

I want to slap her.

'Hopefully. I can't quite believe Patrick'll be stupid enough to let something slip again, though.'

'Oh, I don't know. By the sound of it he's getting care-less and complacent. I mean, the fact that he took a call from her in front of Michelle . . .'

I've had about as much as I can stand for the moment. 'I don't have time for this . . .'

'Are you OK? You seem upset.'

'I'm fine.'

'You're not pissed off with me about something?'

Oh the irony. The arrogance. The sheer frigging nasty cockiness.

I make myself breathe slowly. I don't want to snap at her. I try not to choke on my words.

'No! Of course not. I just . . . well, you know that Adam that I mentioned to you? I saw him for a drink last night after I gave up hanging round Canary Wharf and we had a bit of a fight.' I hope Adam won't hate me for throwing him under this particular bus. I think he'll understand.

Bea's eyes – which I have finally managed to force myself to look at – are wide. 'Oh my God. You have to tell me all.'

'Later,' I say. 'There's nothing to tell really.'

And then, because it seems I can't help myself, I say, 'How's Danny, by the way?'

'Funnily enough we had our first row last night, too. There must've been a full moon or something.'

Now I'm interested although, of course, I have no idea if what she's telling me is complete fiction or the story of her and Patrick with the names changed to protect the guilty. It would explain the dark shadows, though.

'What about?'

Bea smiles and rolls her eyes. 'Something and nothing. I can hardly even remember how it started.'

'You didn't break up, though?' I say, mock concerned.

'No, no. It's all fine. I suppose that's a watershed, isn't it? Your first fight.'

'Thank goodness. I'm hoping I get to meet him soon. See what all the fuss is about.'

Does she hesitate for just a second too long? I almost

smile at the absurdity of it. 'Definitely. I've told him all about you. My bitch of a boss and all that.' She laughs.

Ha ha. How hilarious.

I force a chuckle. 'Very funny.'

'So where did you go, you and Adam?'

'I really should go and watch the edit. I promised them notes by the end of the day. And I'm desperate for that coffee.'

Bea looks disappointed. I'm sure she finds the tales of my disastrous love life very entertaining. She probably shares them with Patrick and they have a good laugh about what a saddo I am. She's always the professional, though.

'Of course. Do you want our old muck or shall I go to Caffè Nero?'

'Caffè Nero,' I say, thinking that'll get rid of her for a few minutes. 'Large skinny wet latte.'

'I know!'

She turns and heads down the stairs, long hair swinging. I go into my office and shut the door. OK, that wasn't so bad. In fact it was quite empowering. Her thinking she had one over on me when, in fact, I'm the one with the big guns. In fact, I have the whole artillery now. Adam was right.

I write him a text. 'I haven't given anything away. You'd be proud of me.' I send it knowing I won't get a reply for a while. He'll be cowering in a corner trying to quote Chaucer while form 11B throw screwed-up bits of paper at him, I imagine.

47

Bea

I hardly slept at all last night. It's been years since I cried over a boy. I can't even remember when. But the thought of losing Patrick – of him just cutting me out of his life altogether – absolutely floored me. I know I'm always skating on thin ice a bit, but I really didn't expect him to take my suggestion of a job so badly. I miscalculated that one wildly.

I spent hours trying to think of ways I could contact him without making things worse. I thought about going through the official channels again – calling Verity and making it sound as if I was phoning on Tamsin's behalf – but he might see that as some kind of implied threat. I can get to you if I want, that kind of thing. A bit bunny boiler. I don't really have any choice but to wait it out. I hate not being able to do anything to influence the outcome. Waiting has never been my forte.

The day has been interminable. I'm sure I was put on this earth to do more than pick up dry cleaning and get coffee. Tamsin actually needs a wife, not an assistant. The compliant, demure kind who lives to serve her husband. Quietly taking Quaaludes when his back is turned. I am acutely aware of the way Lucy smirks every time I am given another menial task to do. She would never get coffee for Ian. He would never ask her, preferring the easier option of Ashley instead.

In between cups of coffee Tamsin has me clearing out her old production files and shredding whatever is no longer of any use.

Ashley is supposed to be in charge of shredding. Tamsin worries that she won't do it properly and that all the deep dark secrets of the *Home For Two* budget will be there for the binmen to see. Ashley offers – she always does – but Tamsin practically bites her head off. When Tamsin's not around, though, I leave a stack of papers on Ashley's desk with a note on: 'For shredding'.

I'm on my way home when Patrick finally calls. I remember, now, to turn the volume on my second phone up when I leave for the day and off again in the morning. I live in hope of it bursting into life. I almost press ignore by mistake in my overeagerness to answer.

'Hi.'

'Is it OK to talk?' he says, and I have to stop myself from saying, Obviously or I wouldn't have answered.

'Yes.'

'Sorry for snapping at you,' he says, and I almost cry with gratitude.

'No. It's me who should be sorry. It was a stupid suggestion. I was just in a panic about what to do. I should never have brought it up.' I always do this. I always over apologize. I'm about to tell myself to shut up when he does it for me.

'OK, stop now. Can you do Monday?'

I don't even pretend to have to think about it. We make

a plan. Half past six at The Langham. He tells me he'll send a fake Ben text.

'Tamsin waited at Canary Wharf for two hours, by the way,' I tell him and he laughs. 'She didn't even suspect anything. She just thinks she missed you.'

'Serves her right. Although I don't think we can pull that off twice.'

'I'm going to work on her to give it up as hopeless,' I say.

'Good luck with that.'

He's nearly at his destination, he tells me, and he rings off. I practically skip down the street. Everything's OK.

I sail through the evening in a haze of happiness. I don't even care that Sarah blasts out Katy Perry at a volume that would usually make me feel murderous (which is pretty much any volume really), or that Ali comes in pissed at midnight and falls over the hall table, waking me up. Patrick and I are OK. I have a clean slate.

And you know what they say. It isn't over till it's over.

48

Tamsin

Michelle and I are staring into our drinks. We've been sitting like this for at least two minutes. The noise of the bar goes on around us. It's one of those places where they encourage shouting. The music's too loud, the staff too familiar. There's a foosball table right in the middle of the room, where rival teams get ironically excited as they compete. It's my idea of hell, really, but today we need the distraction.

Next to us is a boisterous after-office party who think they're hilarious, except that all they seem to do is repeat what one of the others has just said, but in a high-pitched voice. That passes for humour in these parts apparently. Ordinarily they'd irritate me so much I'd probably suggest moving somewhere else. Tonight I'm just glad something is filling the silence.

I can't think of anything to say. Nothing. I've been finding this more and more with Michelle lately. There are so many subjects I have to avoid. So much shit that I have running round in my brain that she is blissfully unaware of. I'm terrified of giving something away. Both terrified and tempted, an explosive combination. I still think she needs to know exactly what her husband is capable of, I'm just not sure I can begin to explain to her how the person he ended up having an affair with is the woman I've been telling her is a saint for the past year. I've thought about nothing else all weekend.

I take a too long swig of my wine. Make myself cough.

'Are you OK?' Michelle is looking at me with concern.

'Fine. It just went down the wrong way.'

'No, I mean generally. Is something up? You don't seem like yourself.'

If only she knew. I know I can't get away with out and out denial. She knows me too well. 'Just a bit knackered is all. Stressed at work. We need to get something else commissioned quickly. The usual.'

'It's not something I've done? You seem a bit . . . distant.'

'No! God, no. It's nothing. Those people are doing my head in.' One of the lary office crowd brays a laugh that could break glass.

Michelle pushes a loose strand of hair behind her ear. Sizes me up. 'There's something you're not telling me.'

'There really isn't. Let's change the subject. What's Pad up to tonight?'

'Working. I forget what. I feel as if I hardly see him at the moment.'

My ears prick up. Is there the tiniest crack appearing? 'Really?'

'I'm exaggerating. But he does seem to work late a lot these days.'

I have to play devil's advocate, much as it pains me. That's what I would usually do in a situation like this. 'It comes with the job.'

'But late late. Not just a meeting at seven or whatever. He gets home at, like, ten. Later even.'

'And you're worried about . . . ?' I can't put words into her mouth, but I can't deny I feel a flicker of excitement that Michelle might be starting to question Patrick's behaviour.

'It can't be good for him. He's exhausted half the time. His moods are up and down. I wish I could get him away on holiday.'

Of course. In typical Michelle form she isn't worried that Patrick is up to something, just that he's working too hard. The hotel receipt she found is a long forgotten MacGuffin, thanks to me.

'It's probably just a busy period. I'm sure it won't last.'

'I should have just told him it was too late to cancel the week in Italy. Then he would have had no choice.'

'He cancelled?'

She nods. 'We got our deposit back, it's OK.'

I stop myself from saying that I assume he felt he could no longer afford it with all the money he's been spending lately.

'Try telling him he has to slow down a bit. When he says, "Do you mind if I work on such and such an evening," say yes.'

'He'll just think I'm a nag. Part of me wonders if he's making a special effort to impress Dad. I think he quite fancies taking over the new documentary channel they're talking about setting up.'

Ah yes. The big jewel in Peterson Media's still evolving crown. Of course Patrick would like that job. It would have way more kudos than running a channel about decorating.

The barman catches my eye. Gestures to ask if we'd like another.

'I think I might call it a night if you don't mind,' I say to Michelle, even though it's still only ten to seven. 'I've got an early start.'

'I'm giving her all the jobs I know she hates doing. That's my pathetic little revenge.'

Adam chuckles into his beer. Luckily for me he was at a loose end when I called from the toilet of the bar, and happy to meet up. He even agreed to come up to Belsize Park so that I could share a cab home with Michelle as I usually do. It dropped me off on Haverstock Hill – I made the excuse that I needed to pop into Budgens – and Michelle hugged me goodbye.

'Get some sleep,' she said. 'And ring me tomorrow and tell me you're OK.'

I watched as the taxi pulled away and then headed up the road to the Roebuck. Adam hadn't arrived yet so I bought us two lagers and found a table in the corner.

'It's the small things that count,' Adam says now. 'You might as well amuse yourself while you work out what to do. What *are* you going to do by the way?'

'I have to make sure the time is right. Get all my ducks in a row.'

'Do you have any ducks?'

'Not really. I just like the expression. To be honest I think part of me is hoping Michelle will find out on her own. That I won't have to be the one responsible.'

'Well, that's a plan. To be honest, it's going to get ugly either way,' he says, and I know he's right. And the longer I wait the more Michelle and I are going to drift apart. It's inevitable.

My phone makes it's tinkly 'you have a text' noise. I dig around in my bag and find it. Michelle. What I see makes me smile. I read it aloud for Adam's benefit.

'Pad is meant to be playing football on Friday but I've put my foot down. We're going for dinner instead xx.'

I don't doubt that playing football really means an assignation with Bea. Now he'll have to cancel. It's almost too perfect.

'Good for you,' I text back, saying it for Adam's benefit as I type. 'Make sure you book it before he can change his mind xx.'

'And I always tell my pupils that revenge never makes you happy.' Adam laughs.

I drain the last of my beer. 'You must be a crap teacher then.'

'Oh, I am. I didn't say it was a valuable lesson I was teaching them.'

'It would be a sickener if Patrick managed to get the big job, wouldn't it?' I say as we walk down Haverstock Hill; Adam to the tube station, me on my way home. It's turned cold. I pull my jacket in tighter. 'And Julian'll give it to him too.'

'Unless Michelle finds out what he's up to first.'

'Exactly.'

'I wish I had a father-in-law who could nepotize me into a great job.'

I laugh. 'So do I. Although Julian did give me a foot in the door when I was first starting out.'

'Different,' he says as we stop at the corner of my road. 'Do you want me to walk you to the door? I don't mind.'

'No, it's fine. It's still early.'

'I'd feel awful if you got mugged on my watch.'

'But then I'd have to walk you back here again in case you did. It could go on all night.'

'Good point.' He kisses my cheek. 'Call you tomorrow.'

49

Tamsin

Of course this is the night that one of the local muggers decides to do his thing down Belsize Avenue. Despite the fact that there are people around and it's still only ten o'clock, my big red tote acts as a beacon he is powerless to resist. I'm making light of it. Actually it was the scariest, most shocking thing that has ever happened to me.

It must have only been two minutes since I said good-bye to Adam. I could still see the main road behind me if I turned around. I hear footsteps but I take no notice because there's a couple up ahead, a woman beyond them. A pair of cars pass me. People on their way home for an early night.

The rest is a bit of a blur. The footsteps break into a run. My tote – which is over one shoulder and tucked under my arm – suddenly moves as if it has a life of its own. I go flying in the other direction. It's over in a second and I'm left lying on the pavement with my face in a bit of stray grass, surrounded by miscellaneous items that have escaped the bag as it arced through the air, attached to a strange man's hand.

I think I scream as it's happening. I hear some kind of noise that sounds like a hysterical pig anyway, and I assume that's me and not him. I doubt 'shouting to draw attention to yourself' is in his MO. I don't even think about running after him. He's way off in the distance and I am too busy lying on the ground.

I haul myself up into a sitting position. The couple have turned around and are now scrabbling about to pick up my stray possessions.

'Are you OK?' he says as he hands me a screwed-up reusable shopping bag that I'm not even sure is mine. His girlfriend – young, maybe early twenties and teetering on huge platforms – sits down next to me and rubs my arm.

'Fine, I think.'

'You didn't hurt yourself?' Girlfriend says.

'Not so as I can tell,' I say, and then I burst into tears.

'Oh God, you poor thing,' she says and she rubs my arm a bit harder. 'You've got a cut on the side of your face.' She points it out and I feel its raspy edges.

'We could probably give the police a description,' Boyfriend – also early twenties, off-the-peg suit – says. 'A bit of one, anyway. Young bloke. White.'

That'll nail him, I think. 'It's probably not worth it, but thanks.'

I scrabble to my feet as Boyfriend hands me a roll of Mentos and my Oyster card.

'Do you live near here?' Girlfriend says. She's having as much difficulty getting to her feet as I did, platform shoes sliding out from underneath her like a fawn on ice.

'Right there,' I say, pointing up ahead. 'Thanks for your help. I'll be fine.'

'Oh no, we'll walk you,' she says. 'Won't we, Ryan?'

'Of course. Oh wait, did he take your keys?'

Thankfully my keys and phone are in the pocket of my coat, a habit I've had for years since I left a previous handbag on a train once. I try to do a mental inventory of what swag the robber must now be salivating over. My wallet. Only about fifteen pounds thankfully, but my bank cards. I'll have to cancel them when I get in. Umbrella, jumper, used tissues, lip gloss. I think there may be a clean pair of knickers in there somewhere, so that'll be nice for him. Marks & Spencer. Size 12. A notebook I've never used.

'No, I have them.'

'Do you want us to call anyone?' Girlfriend says as we stumble up the road.

'No, thank you. You've been really kind.'

They take me right to the door. Wait while I go inside. I feel like giving them both a hug they've been so sweet, but I restrain myself. Once I have shut the door, waving to them as they doggedly stand there until they know I'm safely inside, I run up to my flat, fling my arms round Ron and sob into his fur.

I'm feeling horribly alone. It's not that I'm scared the mugger is going to somehow find out where I live and come and have a look to see if I have anything else worth having (hold on . . . I mentally scan through my missing possessions again for anything that might have my address on it. Nothing). It's more that I feel vulnerable and stupid and like I never want to go outside again.

I don't want to phone Michelle. She'll be with Patrick. Bea, of course, is out of the question. The only other person is Adam. He's probably on the tube, wending his way back to Clapham, but I try him anyway.

He answers almost immediately. 'I'm still sitting on the

platform. Are you sure you really have trains this far north?'

'I got mugged,' I stammer and, of course, he laughs because he assumes I'm joking.

When I don't join in he says, 'Not really?'

'Yes.'

'I'm coming round.'

'No! It's fine. I'm not hurt. It was more of a bag snatch really, but he pushed me over . . .'

'I'll be there in five minutes.'

'Be careful,' I say as he ends the call, as if Belsize Park is now teeming with people who want to knock you about and steal your stuff.

Four minutes later the doorbell rings. I check that it really is Adam before I buzz him in.

'Oh my God, you poor love,' he says as soon as he sees me. 'Are you really OK. Did you hit your head? Do you want me to clean that cut up?'

I shake my head. 'I'm fine. I'm just a bit wobbly. I didn't expect you to come round, honestly.'

'Have you got any brandy?' he says, looking round my messy living room. 'If you did have, would you know where to find it?'

'No. I mean, no I don't have any. I think there's some vodka somewhere.'

I move a few things out of the way and find a nearly full bottle of vodka and an unopened whisky I bought once when I thought I should try to drink like a grown-up. Adam pours two glasses and hands me one.

'Knock it back,' he tells me authoritatively, and I suddenly feel like one of his pupils. I bet he's a well-liked teacher. 'It'll be good for the shock.'

I do as I'm told. I still can't stop shaking, though. Adam leads me over to the sofa and sits me down. He plonks himself next to me and puts his arms round me.

'It'll take a few minutes to work its magic,' he says, so we sit there. Ron licks one of my hands helpfully.

After a few moments I calm down. And then I realize that I like this feeling, sitting here with Adam holding me. I feel safe.

God knows where that came from.

Adam insists on staying in the spare room. To be honest I'm grateful. I don't want to be in the flat on my own. I feel uneasy there for the first time ever. Afraid of I don't know what, but afraid nonetheless.

We sit there on the sofa for what seems like a long time. There's no awkwardness. No subtext-loaded fingers rubbing my arm or stroking my hair. It's like being held by a giant teddy bear, that's the best way I can describe it.

When he finally lets me go and offers to help me find the phone numbers to cancel my bank cards I feel a bit self-conscious. This isn't how our friendship is supposed to develop. We tease each other and joke around. He's light relief. Although the truth is that I already don't know what I'd do without him in my life.

While I explain what happened to three different people on the phone ('Have you informed the police?' 'No, I don't think there's any point.' 'You need to inform the police.') Adam makes up the spare bed.

'Or would you rather I slept on the sofa so I'm right outside your door?' he says when I end the third call and start googling the police non-emergency number.

'No. Spare room is fine. I really appreciate it. Just know-ing someone's here . . .' At that point I start to cry again. I haven't cried this much since my childhood cat, Tilly, went missing. He turned up three days later, by the way, suspi-ciously fatter than when he'd left and wearing a pink collar with someone else's phone number on it. He became an indoor cat after that.

'Shit, sorry.'

'Stop apologizing. If you didn't break down a bit after someone basically attacked you in the street there would definitely be something wrong with you. I knew I should have walked you to the door.'

'Don't be stupid.'

'I'll have to leave pretty early,' he says as he steers me towards my room. 'I need to go home and change. I can't have my class thinking I'm doing the walk of shame.'

'God, of course. I didn't expect you to stay over at all.'

Later I lie in bed replaying the mugging in my head over and over again. I think about how Adam went out of his way to come back and look after me. That's what friends are meant to do. Go the extra mile for each other. Wasn't that why I had a duty to Michelle not to let her be taken in by a serial cheater?

When I get up after a fitful night's sleep, there's a note on the coffee table. 'First time I've ever slept with a dog burping Winalot in my face all night. I like it. Hope you're feeling better. Call you later xx.'

Ron pushes his nose against my leg. I lean down and rub his head. 'You like him too then?'

Jesus! Do I like Adam? Is that what's happening? With his potatoey face and his stupid jokes? No chance. I like my men with cheekbones and angles. I'm just feeling vul-nerable is all. It's a knee-jerk reaction. I'm Whitney Houston falling for her bodyguard – it's all about needing to feel protected.

50

Bea

My euphoria doesn't last long. I'm walking from Hammersmith tube, heading for Brook Green. Coffee for Tamsin in one hand, tea for me in the other. I hear my second phone buzz. I plonk the drinks down on a bench and root around in my bag. I know it's Patrick, although I've had a few false alarms, even with this phone that no one knows exists. Vodafone. Someone telling me I could claim for an accident I didn't know I'd had. A wrong number. Still, every time it beeps my heart skips a bit, I am so convinced it's him.

This time it is. It's a text. I press to read the message impatiently.

'Sorry, have to cancel Friday. Family emergency.'

I read it again just to make sure I haven't missed something. What the fuck? What does family emergency mean? It had better be that someone's at death's door. Michelle hopefully. There's no mention of when else we might meet up.

I sling the phone back into my bag. My good mood has evaporated. So maybe he hasn't forgiven me for our little fight the other night after all. I feel sick. My heart is pounding. I grab the drinks, not caring that some of the coffee spills over the top.

Tamsin is arriving just as I get there. I spot her from halfway down the road – auburn hair, pink jacket, minus her red tote for once. I keep my head down so we don't have to do that waving hello thing all the way along the street. I actually consider ducking into one of the shops to avoid meeting her on the doorstep, but it would only postpone the inevitable for a few minutes and, besides, I'm not sure how I could justify the sudden urge to buy a bathroom fitting or a table lamp to her if she saw me.

'Morning.' I look up and she's waiting for me at the door. She does that thing where she looks at me expectantly, waiting for me to notice – what? And then I see it. There's a raw red scrape down the side of her face.

'What on earth? What have you done?'

She was mugged, she tells me. Practically on her doorstep. It sounds scary – I'm a bit of a coward when it comes to stuff like that. Whenever someone tells me about something bad that has happened to them I have a tendency to re-imagine the whole scenario with me in their place to frighten myself. It works too.

For once I genuinely feel bad for her. 'Did you go to A & E? Do you think you should get yourself checked out?'

'I'm fine,' she says. 'Do I have anything this morning?'

I try to remember. Usually I'm good at this, but today my focus is off.

'I don't think so. I'll double check when I get upstairs.'

Turns out she has a general meeting with a producer scouting for work at half past nine. I just have time to hand her his CV and the coffee before he arrives. I'll leave it up to Ashley to offer him a drink when he gets here.

'Could you get this for me?' Tamsin says, holding out a

306

dry-cleaning ticket. 'And get me a Red Bull? I didn't sleep much last night. And you might as well pick up a *Marie Claire* while you're there. And pop into Boots on the way past and get some Savlon. And some Vitamin E cream.'

Anything else? I want to say. Would you like me to give you a massage or trim your nose hairs? I keep my mouth shut, of course.

'Oh, and I have a load of filing needs doing. It's on that little table in the corner of my office.'

'I'll ask Ashley to do it.' Filing is the most brain dead of all brain-dead jobs. Apart from shredding. The fact that Tamsin always insists on giving it to me to do is, frankly, insulting.

'Could you do it? I don't want her away from the phones for too long.'

I try to keep the irritation out of my voice. 'Fine.'

'No rush,' she says. 'Just before lunch.'

Lucy, it turns out, is off sick. So she says. I imagine she's having a Brazilian blow dry or a Brazilian wax. Something South American anyway. I spot a pile of her work on my desk – she must have asked Ashley to put it there. I pick it up and dump the whole lot on the reception desk.

'I have to go out and do errands for Tamsin.'

Ashley doesn't even flinch. 'OK. I'll try and work my way through some of this. She was adamant I give it to you, though, otherwise—'

'She doesn't even have to know,' I say, already heading down the stairs.

Being out of the office gives me more time to check my second phone. Nothing. I turn the ringer on just in case. I know Tamsin will be in with the producing hopeful for at least forty-five minutes, so I dawdle along, in no rush. Get it out of my bag at least ten times and check it. Dial his number twice and then chicken out of pressing call.

Not for the first time I realize how helpless I am in this relationship. The balance of power is – and always has been – in Patrick's favour. When I allow myself to think about it I feel a flush of shame. Did women really throw themselves under horses so I could mope around and wait for a married man to phone me when it suits him?

Who am I kidding? I'm someone's bit on the side. And maybe, in so far as Patrick is concerned, I am never going to be anything more. I'm a walking cliché.

When I get back Tamsin is just showing her visitor out. I can tell she wasn't that impressed because she's edging him towards the door without introducing him to any-one or making any 'Welcome to the family' type comments. She beckons me into her office. It's actually looking less like a tip for once, because I threw a load of stuff into a bin bag last night, knowing she had someone coming in first thing. The cleaners have been in, too, and there's a vague hint of furniture polish rising up from the odd naked bit of desk. They should wear hazmat suits, those cleaners. I can see a law suit one day where one of them sues for some tropical disease they've picked up from a weeks-old bit of cheese sandwich they've found under her chair.

I hand over the dry cleaning, the copy of *Marie Claire*, the drink and the toiletries. She opens the Red Bull and necks half of it back in one.

'Feeling any better?'

She wipes her mouth with the back of her hand. 'I'm OK.'

I flop down on the sofa. 'So, tell me exactly what happened. How late was it?'

Tamsin grimaces. 'Actually, Bea, I need you to help Ashley out with Ian's stuff. It's not right to leave it all to her.'

I wonder if she hit her head as well as grazed her cheek. 'Oh. OK. You do know Lucy's skiving, right? She was fine yesterday.'

'Even if she is. It's not Ashley's job . . .'

Well, that told me. 'Sure.'

There's an awkward pause where I realize she means go and do it now. I stand up again. 'Right . . . I'll just . . . let me know if you need anything.'

51

Bea

Finally – after endless agonizing days – there's another message. A date. '*Tonight. 6.30. Claridges?*'

I consider replying with some genius witticism like 'Are you sure your family are all OK?' or even 'Sorry, I'm meeting someone else', but of course, I don't. I text '*OK*' back within nanoseconds.

Friday evening was agony. Sarah was meeting a few friends in Covent Garden. Including some bloke from her work that she'd been banging on about for ages, and she was trying to impress. I invited myself to tag along. Drank way too much way too quickly. Flirted with him outrageously. There's a blurry memory of crying at one point. Me, not him. Threw up on the way to the tube. Sarah hasn't spoken to me since. Not that I care much. She can be very annoying.

I spent the rest of the weekend nursing my throbbing head and rehearsing what I was going to say to Patrick. I still believed he would be in touch to explain more. I couldn't think he would just leave me hanging. I kept on checking my new phone every two minutes, even though there was no way he would have taken his home with him at the weekend. He wouldn't risk Saint Michelle coming across it.

Yesterday afternoon, I'm ashamed to say, I got the tube up to Highgate and wandered along North Hill as if I had every legitimate reason to be there. I don't even know what number he lives at – not that I had any intention of knocking on the door. I haven't lost the plot that much. Not yet – I don't know what I wanted, to be honest. Actually, I do. I just wanted to stop feeling like it was all out of my control. I wanted to feel as if I had the power for once.

As soon as I got there I realized what a waste of time it was. I walked for about ten minutes and still hadn't come to the end of the street. It goes on forever. And then I started to panic that I might bump into him and Saint Michelle, out for a cosy Sunday stroll, so I jumped onto the first bus that came along and seemed to be heading vaguely in the right direction and got out of there.

But then at lunchtime today I check and there it is. The clouds part, the sun comes out. I breathe a sigh of relief.

Tamsin stands up. Stretches. Yawns. 'Will you go through that filing cabinet in reception and chuck anything we don't need any more? It's way too full.'

'Couldn't Ashley do that?' For fuck's sake. I'm supposed to be her personal assistant not the general dogsbody.

'Are you busy?' She knows, of course, that she hasn't really given me anything to do this morning. I've been hanging around hoping to get some insight into what might be happening chez Patrick, but she's refusing to indulge in small talk.

'A bit. I'd just planned to catch up on a few things, that's all.'

'Well, maybe start this afternoon then.' She turns on her heels to go. 'Oh, and could you get me a Caffè Nero? And some Mentos? Thanks.'

She's gone before I can even say OK.

Lucy is back. She's doing that thing where every now and then she remembers she was supposedly off sick last week and lets out a little cough. Ian is all concern.

'Do you think you came back too soon?'

She gives him a martyred look. 'I didn't want to leave you in the lurch.'

'I appreciate it,' Ian says. 'But don't stay unless you feel a hundred per cent.'

I hear myself sigh loudly and keep my head down in case he decides to try and offload some of his stuff onto me because Lucy's not feeling up to it.

'Maybe I will leave a bit early,' she says. 'Just a little.'

'I have to go at half three today,' I say. It has suddenly occurred to me that I need to go home and shower and change before this evening. I didn't come prepared. 'Tamsin said it's fine. So, if you do leave early, Lucy, I can't cover for you. Sorry.'

Lucy gives me a look like I've just shat in her coffee. Something I've considered once or twice.

'Well, I suppose I'll have to stay till the end of the day then,' she says in a pained voice. 'I hope that doesn't mean I feel worse tomorrow.'

Tamsin is behaving a bit oddly. I don't know if it's down to her still feeling a bit wobbly after the mugging or she's pissed off with me about something, but she's keeping her door shut and not beckoning me in for little chats. I knock lightly. Go straight in. She's sitting at her desk staring off into space.

'You need anything?'

She jumps back to life. 'No. Thanks.'

'Is it OK if I leave a bit early today? Our boiler's on the blink and the only slot I could get is four till eight, so I'll have to go by half three latest. Ali's got some meeting last thing that's life or death apparently, and Sarah's away . . .'

'No, not really,' she says. I feel as if she hasn't even listened to what I've asked.

'It's just the plumber's going to be there.'

'Really sorry, Bea, I need you.'

I can't help myself. 'For what?'

Tamsin smiles an apologetic smile. 'You have to watch the latest *Rooms With a View* edit. I just can't decide what I think of the middle section. I mean, it might be OK, but it drags a bit and I'm not sure what else they could put there. It needs a fresh pair of eyes.'

Unbelievable. 'Couldn't Lucy have a look? I wouldn't normally ask but this was the only time we could get and we've got no hot water.'

'I wish you'd asked me this morning,' she says. 'I would have got you to watch it earlier.'

I think quickly. I'll be home by ten, I could have a look at it then, 'Tell you what,' I say. 'I'll take it home with me and watch it while the plumber's doing his thing.'

'No, that's no good. I promised them I'd get back to them by the end of the day. Sorry.'

I can't help my irritation showing. Now I'm going to

have to meet Patrick with unwashed hair and wearing my most unflattering jeans.

'Fine,' I say huffily. 'I'll just call and let them know we'll have to cancel. They'll probably charge me a cancellation fee this late in the day.'

'Like I said, I wish you'd asked earlier . . . Oh, and can you get me another coffee,' she says as I go to leave.

'Of course,' I say. 'Anything else?'

She gives a vague shake of her head, so I take that as a no. I go to Caffè Nero and buy her a full-fat latte. It's the least I can do.

52

Tamsin

Michelle and I are meeting in Pizza Express. I couldn't face the intensity of sitting round at hers. I need people around us. Distractions. I thought about telling her I was busy again. Even that I had a date. But I've used that excuse so often recently I'm worried she either thinks I'm avoiding her or she'll be expecting me to introduce her to some new boyfriend soon. Invite her to the engagement party.

'Let's go out,' I said when she invited me over to keep her company. She screwed her face up.

'I don't know if I can be bothered.'

'I don't mean to a night club, I just mean to grab something to eat. Just for a change.'

We arranged that she would come over my way because she had a meeting just up the road last thing. Pizza Express was the only restaurant we could think of that we both knew where it was, so it seemed like as good a place to meet up as any. I'm flapping a bit of powdered foundation over my face in a haphazard fashion when my phone buzzes.

'Michelle is in reception for you,' Ashley says when I answer.

'She's here? Why?'

'Um,' Ashley says. 'I'm not sure.'

'She's not expecting me,' I hear Michelle say. 'Just tell her I was early. I can wait if she's busy.'

'No, it's fine,' I say. 'I'll come down.'

The thought of Michelle in my office makes me feel distinctly uncomfortable. I haven't seen Bea since she shared her thoughts on the *Rooms With a View* edit with me, but I'm pretty sure she wouldn't leave without telling me she was going, even if she's still in a bad mood. I'm hoping she's hidden away in the toilets preparing for the date that I have no question she has this evening.

I can hear Michelle's voice as I head down the stairs.

'Whistles. But it was a couple of years ago.'

'It's a great colour.' Bea says. I feel a wave of nausea. Not that I think there's the slightest chance that Bea would give herself away. It's just not right. The two of them making friendly conversation when Bea knows exactly who Michelle is but Michelle has no clue.

'Hi,' I say before I hit the bottom step. 'I thought we were meeting in Pizza Express.'

I give her a hug.

'I was early.' She rolls her eyes as she says this. 'I can wait, though, if you're still busy.'

'No, it's fine, let's go.' I just want to get her out of there.

'Plus I got the chance to finally meet the infamous Bea,' Michelle says, smiling widely at her rival. 'She's been banging on for the past year about how amazing you are.'

Bea laughs. 'Ha ha ha. I do my best.'

'To hear Tamsin talk you'd think you were the second coming!'

'And this is Ashley,' I say, trying to change the subject.

316

Michelle waves. 'Hi, Ashley.'

'I was just admiring Michelle's dress,' Bea says, a smile I know must be insincere on her face. 'It's so . . . cute.'

I pick up the condescending edge in her voice. Will Michelle not to take the bait. Of course she does, though. She's Michelle, she can't help being nice to everyone.

'It would look fantastic on you with your figure.'

Do I imagine it or does Bea give a hint of a smirk. 'Maybe I'll have a look, see if they have anything similar. Although no one's really doing that A-line thing this year.'

How mature. Have a love rival who's a few years older than you? Have a dig at their fashion sense.

'I can't keep up.' Michelle laughs with no hint of having been slighted.

'Only idiots stick slavishly to fashion trends,' I say with a bit too much vehemence. 'It's all just a ruse to make you spend more money.'

'Oh I didn't mean to—' Bea says. 'I just meant I probably wouldn't be able to find it anywhere . . .'

I'm sure you did, I want to say. I'm sure you were just being friendly.

'Where are you off to? Anywhere nice?' Bea says with a smile.

'Just for a pizza. Hardly a big night out.'

'It's fun just to hang out with your girlfriends sometimes, though, isn't it? Leave the men to their own devices,' Bea says and I want to slap her.

'Shall we go?' I say to Michelle. I just want to get out of there.

'Sure. Nice to meet you both.' Michelle picks up her bag and tucks her hair behind her ear. 'Especially you,

Bea, it's good to put a face to the name after all this time.'

'You, too. I've heard so much about you. Have a nice evening.'

'Are you off out, too?' Michelle says, ever polite. I want to physically push her out of the door.

Bea is all innocence. 'Just meeting my boyfriend.'

'Well have fun.'

'Oh I will.'

Actually what I really want is to push Bea down the stairs.

'See you tomorrow, Tamsin.'

'Night,' I manage to say. 'Night, Ashley.'

'She seems lovely,' Michelle says as we step out onto the pavement. I pretend I don't hear her.

Michelle looks happy. Like she's got a secret. I feel as if she's bursting to tell me something.

'Come on,' I say. 'Confess.' We've ordered. An American Hot for me and a Salad Niçoise for Michelle. I try to argue that there's no point coming to a pizza place if you're just going to have a salad, but she's not having it. A big glass of white wine sits in front of each of us.

'What do you mean?'

'You're up to something. Don't even try and pretend you're not.'

She gives me a big smile. 'OK. I have totally not told you this. If Pad asks, that is. He thinks we shouldn't say anything until it happens.'

I get a sinking feeling in my stomach. 'Of course. Go on.'

'We're trying for a baby. Actually trying!'

Shit.

'Wow! Mich that's fantastic.'

'Actually, I shouldn't be drinking this,' she says, putting her wine glass to one side.

'What's made him change his mind?'

'I have no idea. I suppose he just realized that it's now or never.'

'When? I mean . . . when did he tell you?' I'm trying to keep an enthusiastic tone in my voice. Oh my God. How exciting.

'Friday evening. You know I made him cancel football? I don't know . . . we had a takeaway and some fizzy wine, and then he just said he'd changed his mind.'

I lean over and hug her. 'That's fantastic.'

Michelle brings me up to date with the baby-making progress (in toe-curling detail, I might add. There are charts involved and sperm-enhancing super-food drinks and post-coital legs up walls, that much I know. Anything that might increase the chances). I try to listen, but all I'm thinking about is what does this mean? If Michelle gets pregnant can I really step in and destroy her relationship with the baby's father? Shit.

'He's really into it now,' she says.

'I'm not surprised. It sounds like a shag-a-thon. You should get sponsored.'

She rolls her eyes at me. 'You know what I mean. The whole idea of a baby.'

'I'm glad. I really am.'

'Probably because at the moment I pounce on him and start ripping off his clothes the minute he walks through the door.'

'Too much information. Way, way too much.'

'It's not as exciting as it sounds. It's sex-with-a-purpose as opposed to sex-for-fun. There's a big difference.'

A fleeting image pops into my head. Patrick looking at me intently, hand between my legs. I've become so adept at blocking out what happened between us that it takes me by surprise.

'Don't tell me any more or I won't be able to look him in the face.'

Michelle laughs. 'He'd be the first to tell you it's all business.'

'Enough,' I say, holding up a hand. 'Really.'

'Just think, any day now I could be pregnant.'

I should just say it now. Tell her. Put her out of her misery. I can't do it.

Her face is shining, glowing even. I hope to God that doesn't mean she's conceived already. How long does it take before women start to glow? I wish I'd paid more attention in biology.

This, ladies and gentlemen, is what is known as a ticking-clock motive. Any minute now Michelle might find out she's pregnant by her cheating psycho husband. Once she does, all bets are off. However I feel about him I don't think I have it in me to deny a future baby its father. Even if Michelle saw sense and left him he would still be in her life forever. It would change everything.

I have to act quickly. Speak now or forever keep it to myself. Watch them bring up their kids from a distance, trying not to blurt out what I know whenever he 'works late'.

Somehow I need to present Michelle with incontrovertible evidence that Patrick is having an affair. The latest of many, although there will be no way of proving that. In an ideal world I would be able to get this across to her without her ever finding out that the woman he's having it with is Bea. The brilliant assistant I have raved on about to her for the past year. The woman she just met and declared to be lovely. She would want to know how their paths crossed and I don't think I'm ready for that to come out.

I could just tell Michelle what I know – leaving out some of the more incriminating aspects, obviously, but I worry she'd shoot the messenger. That she'd go straight to Patrick and he'd managed to convince her it was all a lie again. I need evidence.

I haven't spoken to Adam since the night of the mugging. I mean, I have – we've texted and he's left me a couple of messages. Something has shifted between us – at least from my point of view – and I'm not entirely comfortable with it. You know that thing when you're a teenager and you like a boy, and you suddenly can't look at him? That.

I think I like Adam. Adam who happily agreed with me that we could never possibly be attracted to each other. Mr Potato Head. Great.

He's my only option, though. I have to suck it up and call him. Try to act as if everything is normal. I need his help.

53

Bea

Saint Michelle. Right there in front of me. Just as chocolate-box pretty as she is in her pictures, annoyingly, although in that slightly neglectful way that starts to tarnish as you get older. Hair that could do with a bit of conditioner. Skin that's seen better days. Ageing is all about grooming as far as I'm concerned. You need to keep on top of it or the cracks start to show. OK figure. Dressed like a Sunday school teacher.

This is self-preservation by the way, this meanness. I have to comfort myself with her faults. I have to look for the flaws that help me believe he will look at me and prefer what he sees.

She was friendly. Sweet. Unchallenging, I imagine. A wife for an easy life. I can imagine they look good together. Mr and Mrs Perfect.

I wonder if she'll go home later and say, 'I met Tamsin's assistant Bea today?' What he'll say if she does. Will his face give him away? I have decided not to mention her visit. I want to have a drama-free evening. I don't want him going into a spin about whether it's all got too close to home and the risks are starting to outweigh the rewards.

This is our first time at Claridge's and I'm a bit lost as to where to wait to spot Patrick when he comes in. I'm excited. I've always wanted to come here. Although in my fantasies I was being wined and dined in the restaurant, not skulking about like a criminal.

In the end I settle on a chair that's not in the reception area, but has a good view of it. Ten minutes later he strides in. He's looking good (as am I, despite the two-day-old hair and jeans, I think. Don't get me wrong. I have never believed I'm punching above my weight as far as Patrick is concerned). He's wearing a tweedy jacket. But cool tweed, not Jeremy Clarkson going shooting. A kind of stripy tank top thing over a soft-collared shirt. Black trousers. Hipster, but without the face fur and stupid hat. His brown leather computer bag is slung across his chest. He looks like he belongs here. Confident. Like he owns the place.

I notice him give me a quick once over as he passes on his way from reception to the lifts.

He opens the door to room 1206 almost before I knock. Gives me a big grin.

'Come here.'

He pulls me towards him, pushes me up against the now closed door. Both his hands are on my face, scraping my hair back. He puts his lips on my lips, pressing the length of his body up against mine.

I think about his sweet pretty wife sitting in her frumpy dress, eating pizza with Tamsin. Oblivious. Unaware.

Fuck her.

I head into work in a better mood than I've been in for a few days. Five minutes with Tamsin and that soon dissipates, though. By quarter to ten I'm fuming, although I'm trying my hardest to act like an impartial observer.

'Oh,' I say. And then I manage. 'How nice.'

I feel as if I'm gasping for air. A fish flapping helpless on the beach.

Tamsin is smiling. 'She's been wanting this forever, but he's finally agreed now's the right time.'

'Right.'

'I'm glad you got to meet her. She's lovely, isn't she?'

'Mmmm. So, you think Patrick's really into having a baby? I mean, I thought he was still playing away.'

'I actually think this might turn things round. He's trying to make it up to her.'

'When did having a kid ever save a marriage.' I'm struggling to keep the bitterness out of my voice.

'I don't mean like that. I mean he's so up for the idea that I reckon he'll dump the woman – that's if he's still seeing her at all. He's rushing home from work every night and straight up to the bedroom if you get what I mean. I've had way too much detail. Anyway, she says their sex life's never been so good.'

I actually think I might be sick. Of course, I'm not stupid enough to think they never do it. But he's hardly made it sound as if he finds her irresistible. As if, on the nights he doesn't see me, he's acting out the *Kama Sutra* with his wife.

And what if she does get pregnant? Where does that leave me?

'It sounds like a last-ditch ploy to try to save a dying marriage to me.' Desperate, I know.

'No,' Tamsin says. 'I honestly think he's changed.'

'I don't believe anyone changes that much.'

'Do me a favour.' She props her feet up on her desk. 'I'm dying for a latte and a KitKat.'

54

Tamsin

OK, so I exaggerated a bit. Just for my own amusement.
What do you want me to say?

55

Tamsin

'The way I see it you only have a couple of options,' Adam says as we sip pints of lager in a mock-Tudor pub on the South Bank. It's a bit like sitting in a theme park. I half expect a fat out-of-work actor dressed as Henry VIII to appear and start singing 'Greensleeves'. I suggested the venue. It's on neutral ground. I'm trying to act as if everything is normal between us. Which it is, in so far as he is concerned. Business as usual.

As for me, I have been struggling for things to say. Suddenly tongue-tied with the person I found it so easy to reveal my whole life story to. The only person in the world, now, who knows everything about me. Except, of course, for the fact that I may have succumbed to an arbitrary crush on him.

'Should I get you a whiteboard?'

He gives me a 'very funny' look. The one I imagine he gives his Year 7s when they start playing up. It works, too. I shut up and listen.

'You could try and find out where they're meeting up next – although God knows how you're going to do that. Patrick is never going to let you have access to his phone again . . .'

'Bea's phone?' I chip in.

'Do you know her password?'

I shake my head.

'And anyway, my guess is they won't be leaving each other incriminating messages any more. Not since the last time. Anyway, my point is that even assuming you could find out that information, what are you going to do? Take Michelle along to catch them in the act? Imagine how humiliating that would be for her. OK, so you get your big shocker revelation, but I think it would be cruel.'

'I know. You're right,' I have been thinking about this a lot. If I'm going to do anything I need to do it in the least painful way for Michelle.

'So that's out of the window. You could do something anonymous. Send her a letter or something, but that seems pretty heartless, too.'

'Plus she wouldn't believe it. Why would she?'

'You could tell Bea and Patrick that you know all about them but that you won't tell Michelle if they break it off.'

'He'd just get someone else. He's never going to change.'

'Agreed. Or – and this is my preferred, grown-up, best-friend option – you just tell her. You cushion it as much as you can. Then deal with the fallout.'

I let out a sigh so loud the couple at the next table look round.

'The first thing Patrick will do is tell her about me and him.'

'Well, you always knew that. You just have to decide whether you're going to come clean or not.'

'God no! If I tell her, this'll all have been for nothing. Why do you think I went to such lengths to delete the text message?'

327

'Then you front it out.'

'I'm scared,' I say. 'It's all going to get so nasty.'

'Well,' Adam says, 'there's no way there can be a happy ending for everyone. And that's not your fault. That's Patrick's fault.'

'Fuck, I wish I'd never started this.'

'You didn't. He did.'

'Thank you,' I say. 'For making me feel better. Or, should I say, helping to stop me feeling so shit.'

'To be honest it's only because I can't bear to see you moping around any more. It's like having a drink with Eeyore.'

I manage a laugh. 'Well, thanks anyway. Even if it was for purely selfish reasons.'

'Anyway,' he says with a smug look on his face, 'enough about you. I have a date tomorrow night.'

'Oh . . .' A little knot forms in my stomach. 'Someone from Other Half?'

'No. A real live human woman. She's the mother of one of my Year Eights. I got to know her when I had to give him detention. She came to the school to complain.'

'Nice,' I say and then I realize it sounds sarcastic. 'I mean, that she cared enough to find out what was going on.'

'I was a bit frightened of her at the beginning, to be honest. She's very feisty. I can see where he gets it from.'

'Isn't it against the rules? Teachers and pupils' parents?' I'm clutching at straws here, as you can tell, but I don't want Adam to find himself a girlfriend just when I'm starting to think I might like him myself.

He snorts. 'Hardly. At least I don't think so. It's never come up before.'

'So how did it get from "Your son's a psycho" to
"Fancy a drink"?'

'Actually, she asked me. I was scared to say no in case
she hit me.'

'Isn't it going to be a bit odd, having to face little Johnny
across the classroom when he's seen you in your pyjamas?'

'Steady on. We're only going for a drink. And his name's
Jordan.'

'Isn't that a girl's name?'

He gives me a look.

'So, at least you know what you're in for. You don't
have to worry about whether or not she looks like her
photo.'

Can you see what I'm doing here? I'm trying to elicit
details about how good looking or not Adam's date is. I
know it's pathetic, needy and all round unacceptable, but
I'm all out of dignity. I need to know.

'Exactly. No nasty surprises like with you.'

I laugh like I'm meant to but, actually, that hurt.

'She's a looker, then?' I keep my tone light, like I'm
making a joke of it.

He thinks about it for a second. This gives me hope.
Although hope for what, I don't know. Me and Adam
would be ridiculous as a couple, even if he was interested
in me.

'She is. Actually, she looks a little bit like you, which is
just weird.'

'Well, that must mean you don't fancy her then.'

'Not necessarily. With you it was a combination of
the way you look and your God-awful personality that
put me off.'

329

I know he's joking and I know I'm not meant to take anything he says seriously, but I feel a bit wounded, and it must show because Adam's smile drops.

'You know I'm joking, right? Have I upset you?'

'No. Of course not. I'm fine,' I say as a pair of large tears plop onto the table. What the hell is happening to me?

Adam looks horrified. Puts his hand on my arm. 'God, Tamsin, I'm so sorry. I was just being stupid. I thought you'd laugh.'

'I know. It was funny. I'm just in an odd mood, that's all.'

'Is this still about the mugging? I can see you home tonight by the way.'

'Don't be daft. It's the other side of London. And I'm not worried about that. I'll get a cab and ask the driver to wait till I'm inside.'

'What then?'

'Nothing. Just ignore me. I feel really stupid.'

'I should have censored myself. It didn't even occur to me you might not find it funny.'

'I did! I do. Please don't start thinking you have to edit what you say to me.'

'It's the Michelle thing, isn't it? It's all got too much?'

'Yes,' I say, deciding on the path of least resistance. Although, to be fair, if I dwelt too much on the Michelle/Patrick situation it probably would bring me to tears.

'You don't have to speak to her at all, you know. You could decide to just forget you know anything. Let them all sort it out themselves.'

'You know I can't do that. I'd still lose Michelle anyway

because I can't bear to go round there any more. At least this way she might not waste her whole life married to someone who doesn't even care about her.'

'Just get it over with. The stress is going to finish you off.' He puts his hand on my arm when he says this. I look down at his stupid sausagey fingers with their stubby nails and another tear edges its way out of the corner of my eye.

'I know.'

56

Tamsin

This is it.

I have chosen to do it at Michelle's house on a night when I know Patrick is away. I agonized about the venue. Ultimately I came down on the side that dropping this particular bombshell in public wouldn't be the kindest thing to do. It's not going to be pretty.

I deliberately picked an evening when Patrick would be gone for the whole night. I have no idea where he is going, obviously. The official story is Manchester. But I know he'll be holed up in a London hotel somewhere with Bea. At her flat even. Safely out of the way. And I even thought maybe it would give her a chance to check up on him. To do some detective work before he started to cover his tracks.

I just have to hope she trusts me enough to believe what I'm telling her. Oh the irony.

I call Adam while I'm in the cab on my way to Highgate. I need someone to reassure me I'm doing the right thing. Plus I need a diversion to stop the cabbie droning on at me about his family. There are lots of them, that's all I can tell you. I tuned out early on, but even the effort of grunting in a non-committal way every time he leaves a pause is exhausting. It takes him a moment to cotton on to the fact that I am making a call so, at the point I say, "Hi, it's me," he is saying:

'. . . with some geezer lives on the Old Kent Road . . .'

'Are you at a Chas and Dave concert?' Adam says.

'I wish. I'm on my way.'

'Like I told you last night, just get it out there. Once you've told her, the rest is up to her.'

Adam had called me on the way home from his date with Jordan's mum who, it turns out, is called Mel. I don't know if he knew that I'd be hunched over my mobile waiting for a debrief like a crack addict over a pipe. I hope I haven't given myself away that much.

I had spent most of the evening trying to imagine how it was going between my unlikely crush and my doppelganger. I poked myself with images to see if it really did hurt. And it did. Not majorly. Just a little. Just enough to confirm that my feelings for Adam have morphed from friendly to something entirely different. I pictured him making her laugh, teasing her in the same way he does me. Asking her about herself, because he's genuinely interested in other people. Seeing her home, because he'd learned his lesson on that one.

Her inviting him in.

When he phoned at quarter past ten I breathed a sigh of relief that nothing too newsworthy must have happened. Unless he'd given her a quick one up against the pub car-park wall. Adam didn't strike me as the up-against-the-wall type, though. Unless she'd insisted. Then he might have been too polite to say no.

'So, how did it go?' I said as soon as I answered.

'Good,' he said. 'She's nice.'

'Wow! Don't get a job as a reviewer, will you? Don't you teach English?'

Adam laughed. 'OK, it was an enjoyable evening. She's edifying company.'

'Better. OK, I need a step-by-step account.'

'Not now. Now we need to go over what you're going to say tomorrow.'

'Are you seeing her again, though?'

'Yes. Probably. Right . . . hold on, I'm just getting off the bus . . .'

I heard the doors open and the whoosh of the wind through his phone. Back in Clapham already? I did a quick mental calculation. His date must have ended by quarter to ten at the latest. Surely not an auspicious sign?

'So . . .' Adam said. 'It is still on for tomorrow, right?'

'It is. Apparently Patrick is in Manchester for the night.'

'Tell me what you're going to say.'

Adam and I had worked this out in detail. I had even written notes so that I could revise. The whole story is a minefield that requires careful negotiation. Firstly I had to make up the reason I knew any of this in the first place. We had decided on a combination of industry rumours that were hard to ignore followed by Adam and I spotting Patrick and a woman coming out of the Covent Garden Hotel together on the night when I knew he was supposed to be playing football. It wasn't too much of a stretch of the truth. A bit of a glitch in the timeline that had Patrick and Bea leaving together rather than separately.

The big issue was, did I tell her it was Bea? I had been there when she met Bea just the other day. I had watched them chat (and Bea patronize Michelle) and said nothing.

Plus I didn't even want to skirt near the question of how Patrick and Bea might have met in the first place. On balance we decided I should say nothing. Maybe make the point that while Adam had seen her I had only caught a glimpse. Like I said, fudge it.

I was banking on her being too distraught about the big picture to focus too much on the details.

Then I would just wait. Be there for my friend and duck when Patrick threw the big grenade. By then I hoped she would be so convinced of his guilt that she wouldn't believe a word that came out of his mouth.

As plans went it was hardly the Hatton Garden robbery.

'OK, good,' Adam said when I had run through the whole thing again. 'The secret is to stick to your guns. Don't deviate.'

'I feel sick,' I said. 'I don't know if I can do it.'

'I'll call you tomorrow. Try and get some sleep.'

'I'll try. So . . . you're definitely going to see her again . . . Mel?'

'I think so. Yes.'

'Great. Where are you going to go next time?'

'Stop trying to avoid going to bed. I'll speak to you tomorrow. Night, Tamsin.'

Today he phoned me again on his lunch break. I was in Anne Marie's office going through a budget, but I knew that if I missed him the chances of me getting hold of him later were slim to none. He would be on lunch duty or overseeing detention or in the middle of asking someone if they'd do whatever they were currently doing in their own

335

home. So I told her it was important and I ducked out and into my own office, shutting the door behind me.

'Ring me the second you get out of there. The second. I don't care how late it is.'

'I was thinking I might even stay the night. If the dog walker can have Ron.'

'If you do, let me know. I'm going to be sat there all evening by the phone like a saddo.'

'I will. I promise. Wish me luck.'

'It'll be fine. Well, it won't, but it'll be over.'

I had been avoiding Bea all morning. I couldn't look her in the eye. I knew she thought I was behaving oddly, but I couldn't seem to do anything about it. Once Adam had given me another pep talk I handed a pile of filing to Ashley on my way out to get myself a salad.

'Do you mind?' I said, chucking the whole stack on her desk, where it teetered ominously. 'It's not urgent.'

'Of course not.'

'Thanks,' I called over my shoulder as I headed down the stairs, keen to get out before my assistant caught me giving her work to someone else.

'I'm staying over at Danny's,' Bea said when she saw me clock her overnight bag as she was leaving for the day. I'd exhausted myself trying to avoid talking to her for the past eight hours.

'Wow! That's a big step, isn't it?' I said, trying to disguise the fact that I knew she was lying through her straight white teeth.

'Epic,' she said with a cat-that-got-the-cream smile.

'Well, have fun.'

'Are you OK?' she asked, and if I hadn't known better I would have thought her concern was genuine.

'Sure. Just . . . PMT. I'll be fine tomorrow.'

Now I'm sitting at Michelle and Patrick's kitchen table. Somewhere I have sat countless times before over the years. My home from home. I suddenly wonder who'll get to keep the house. I remember when Michelle first saw it. She took me along with her for a second opinion before she even told Patrick about it. We both fell in love with it on sight. A cosy two-storey, plus a basement kitchen terrace with a tiny walled garden out the back. A 'real' gas fire burning in the original Victorian fireplace. A full wall of fold-back patio doors. The perfect blend of period meets modern. Two bedrooms. I could read what Michelle was thinking – this is the perfect place to start a family.

By the time she took Patrick round to see it it was a done deal. I remember thinking how touching it was that he would go along with whatever would make her happy. It made me think that maybe it wouldn't be so terrible if she married him after all.

She plonks a mug of Salted Caramel Green Tea down in front of me. She is still on her conception health kick and I don't want to risk the effects of alcohol. She sits on the chair opposite.

'Everything OK?'

I breathe in slowly. Throw myself off the cliff.

'Actually no. Mich . . . there's something I've got to tell you.'

57

Bea

A whole night away. This is only the fourth time this has happened. To say it's a big deal, a milestone, would be an understatement on a par with announcing Kim Kardashian's back end is a little on the full side.

A whole night means ten times the intimacy. By which I don't mean sex, I mean teeth brushing and morning breath and waking up with no make-up on. Grown-up stuff. The meat and potatoes of relationships.

It was me who pushed for it. It wasn't a big romantic gesture on Patrick's part. I have been feeling a tad insecure since our fight about me wanting a job, I'm not going to lie. It brought it home to me that I am never going to be the number one priority in his life. So I whined a bit. Stamped my foot and said I felt I was being used. For a while I thought I'd pushed him too far and that he was going to decide it was all too much hassle. That what he had with me was meant to be fun, not hard work. So I backed off a bit and the next thing I knew he'd booked a room – an executive suite, no less – at The Langham.

It was a victory. One I could only share with Ali, who I had finally confided in because, despite Patrick's insistence that no one must ever know, I was desperate to let someone into the secret to make it seem real. I thought she would be disapproving – she has a tendency to lecture on about the way women treat women, but she has a new boyfriend, so she's mellowed out a bit lately. Until it all goes wrong again, that is. And she actually laughed and said good for me if it was making me happy.

Which it was until Tamsin told me about him and Michelle trying for a baby.

I mean . . . listen, I'm not thick. I know he has to carry on as if everything is normal and that, I suppose, includes sleeping with his wife every now and again. But there's a world of difference between that and 'they're trying to get pregnant'. Trying to get pregnant means envisioning the future together. It means happy families and let's be mummy and daddy. It means commitment.

And, according to Tamsin it means they're at it like a pair of virgins in their first week at university. Now they've started they can't stop. And the thought of that literally makes me feel sick.

So now I'm on my way up to the fourth floor of The Langham, not fizzing with anticipation, not with the rush I usually get as I approach his room that's a combination of anticipation and fear of being spotted. I'm feeling pissed off, used and taken for granted. I want to know where I stand. I want answers.

'Hey,' he says, when he opens the door a couple of milli-metres to check it's really me.

'Hi.'

He lets me in. I've noticed that a few times lately we haven't spent the whole evening in bed. We've talked. I'd put it down to the fact that our relationship was evolving into something more serious. We cared about each other. It wasn't just the sex, we had a connection. Yeah, right. Or maybe he's just been so knackered from his marathon sessions with Michelle that he hasn't got the energy. Perhaps I should suggest we skip the bedroom altogether and just have a nice cup of tea and a catch-up.

It's as if he picks up on the atmosphere. I'm not surprised, it's oozing out of me like ectoplasm from a ghost. 'You good?' he says, and for the first time it irritates me that he has a tendency to use a kind of cod American way of speaking sometimes. I used to find it sexy. Now it's grating. Same with the hipster clothes. Suddenly they seem too self-conscious, too studied. I want to shout, 'You're not from Brooklyn, you know. You're an over-privileged English grammar school boy from Epsom.'

'I'm fine,' I say, clearly not fine.

He rolls his eyes. He's got with the programme. We are on the same page. 'For fuck's sake, Bea, what's up now?'

'Nothing,' I say huffily, thus giving away that there most definitely is something.

'Oh no. I am not going to play this game. If you're upset about something say so, but don't do the whole "everything's fine" martyr act.'

He sits down on the edge of the bed. The champagne cork remains unpopped. I'm dying for a drink actually. I think about opening it myself but it doesn't seem appropriate at the moment. This is not going well. I have two choices: cave in as usual and accept my second-class status, or have it out with him. It's about time.

'OK.' I sit on a chair opposite him. 'Tamsin told me you and Michelle are trying for a baby.'

340

I lean back, let him take in the full weight of what I'm saying – which he does pretty quickly, it seems, because he laughs. Not the reaction I was anticipating.

'That's it? That's the reason you're in such a shit mood?'

'Well, are you?'

'What if we are? I've told you before she's always wanted kids.'

'What do you mean "What if we are?" You're going home every night for shag-a-thons and I'm supposed to think that's OK?'

He laughs again and it has a hollow, mean sound.

'Hardly. And even if I was, she's my wife. What do you want me to say to her? "Sorry, I hope you don't mind, but my girlfriend will be upset if I have sex with you?"'

'You know what I mean.'

'Do you know what, Bea? I don't.'

'You're really going to have a baby?'

'Ah, so, are you upset about the fact that you think Michelle and I are at it like rabbits, or are you upset about the fact that we might have a baby? I'm confused.'

I try to ignore the sarcastic tone. I can't bear it when people try to win arguments on technicalities.

'If you have a baby, what happens then? For us, I mean.'

'Nothing happens. We carry on as normal.'

I don't know how I feel about this. I do know, however, how I feel about the other half of the picture. And even though I know I should probably keep my mouth shut, I can't.

'So, is it . . . I mean . . . Tamsin basically said Michelle told her you can't keep your hands off each other . . .'

'And Tamsin is so trustworthy.'

'Why would she make that up, though? Michelle must have said something to her.'

'I really don't want to talk about this, funnily enough.'

'But what if I do? It's not fair that I'm kept in the dark about everything . . .'

'You want me to tell you all about mine and Michelle's sex life?'

That stings. They don't just have occasional sex, they have a sex life.

'No. You know what I mean.'

'Fine. Yes, Michelle and I are trying for a baby. Yes, it means we need to have intercourse in order to achieve that. Happy?'

'But why are you trying for a baby? Why now?'

'Because she has wanted one forever and I've run out of reasons why we shouldn't get on with it and do it. Besides, d'you know what? I've decided I want a kid. Sue me.'

This is not the admission of a man who's thinking he might leave his wife one of these days and set up home with his girlfriend.

'I thought . . .' I stumble, I can't say it.

'You thought what? You've always known I was never going to leave Michelle. Apart from anything else, her dad is my boss.'

'So you're going to stay with a woman who makes you unhappy because it might affect your career prospects if you don't?'

He looks at me levelly. My stomach turns over. 'When have I ever said she makes me unhappy?'

He's right, he hasn't. I just assumed, what with all the

affairs on the side. He hardly acts like a man who values his marriage.

And then I do the thing I always swore I would never do. I get personal.

'How can she? I mean, look at her. She's such a ... frump.'

I know the minute it's out of my mouth that I shouldn't have said it. Lesson number one: never criticize the wife. He gives me a look that could freeze mercury.

'How do you know what she looks like?'

Ah, yes, there's that, too. I didn't tell him about my encounter with Michelle at the office. I worried it might make him panic that things were getting too close to home.

'She came into work to meet Tamsin.'

'You've met her?'

'Only for a second. Don't worry, I didn't give you away.'

'Jesus. Why didn't you tell me?'

'I don't know. It wasn't that big a deal.'

If he believes that he'll believe anything.

'Michelle is one of the sweetest, nicest people I've ever met. Probably *the* nicest. I would never want her to get hurt, that's all.'

'But if I do that's just collateral damage?'

'Don't be stupid. This isn't about you. I just want to be sure Michelle's protected. None of this is her fault.'

'So that's why you're fucking me?' I can't help myself, it just comes out. In a rather loud, shouty way.

He stays calm. I'd rather he yelled back at me if I'm being honest. It would show passion. Show that he cares.

'What we have is irrelevant. It's separate from my marriage.'

'How convenient. I wonder if Michelle would see it that way.'

'Don't. You. Dare.' He spells it out, emphasizing each word.

'I'm not . . . that's not what I was saying.'

He stands up. 'You know what, Bea, I don't really feel like being here now.'

Shit. This wasn't what I expected to happen. Although what I did expect to happen I don't really know.

I stand, too.

'No. I'm sorry . . . I just . . . I need to think before I open my mouth.'

'You can stay here if you want, but I'm going home.'

'No, Patrick—'

'Maybe we just need a bit of space, I don't know.'

'I'm sorry about what I said . . .'

He's picking up his jacket. 'I'll call you, OK. The champagne's paid for. You might as well drink it.'

'No, please don't . . .'

Now I'm begging. Very attractive, I'm sure. But I don't even have time to wonder what happened to the strong independent woman I once was, because I'm using all my energy to try to stop him going out of the door.

58

Tamsin

I've rehearsed this so many times in my head (and out loud to Adam) that I should be word perfect, but seeing the worried look on Michelle's face gives me stage fright. I have forgotten my lines.

'What? What's wrong?'

I know that her immediate assumption will be that I'm going to tell her I'm seriously ill or that I'm emigrating to New Zealand. I know I have to put her out of that misery quickly and into a worse one. Shit. Here goes.

'You know when you thought Patrick was having an affair? Well he is.' I say it all in a rush to get it out there before I bottle out. I watch as her expression goes from confusion to heartbreak via disbelief. She knows I wouldn't lie to her. Ironic, isn't it?

'I'm so sorry, Mich. I wish I didn't have to be the one to tell you.'

Her first reaction is to laugh nervously. It must be obvious from my face, though, that this is no joke. 'I don't understand . . .'

She looks so vulnerable I reach a hand over the table and take one of hers.

'I saw him . . . them. He was meant to be at football practice – that time I was with Adam and you called me, do you remember? We were sitting opposite the Covent Garden Hotel and Patrick came out with a woman.'

'That was weeks ago . . .'

'I know. I've been agonizing about how to tell you. And I wanted to make sure it was true first. That I wasn't imagining things. It seems like it's an open secret in the industry . . .'

She crumples. 'No, Tam . . .'

'I'm sorry.'

Michelle looks up. 'Who is she?'

I try to keep my composure. 'I don't know. I didn't really see her, Adam did—'

Michelle dives on this lifeline. 'So he might have misinterpreted. Or it could have been Vic . . .'

Vic is Patrick's older sister. She couldn't look less like Bea if she tried, with her red curly hair.

'It wasn't Vic. This one had long dark hair, I saw that much.'

'How does Adam even know what Patrick looks like anyway?'

'He doesn't. I saw Patrick come out, and I knew he wasn't meant to be there so I guessed something was up. I turned away so he didn't spot me and told Adam to see if he could make out what he was doing. He saw a woman come out and, well, apparently it was obvious they weren't just colleagues. He told me when it was safe to look, so I just saw the back of her. They were holding hands.'

Please God don't let anyone be taping my testimony for use in court. It would never stand up to cross-examination.

Michelle lets out a sob. 'And all these people who apparently know all about it, they have no idea who she is either?'

'It doesn't seem so. I think it's true, Mich. I wouldn't have told you otherwise.'

'So all the evenings he's working late . . . ?'

I nod. 'I think so.'

'Do you think he's with her tonight? All night?'

'I don't know. It looks like it. Where's he meant to be?'

'Manchester.'

'Do you know what hotel he's supposed to be staying in?'

She shakes her head. 'I can't believe he'd do this. There must be an innocent explanation.'

'He came home that night, right? The night you called me when I was with Adam?'

'Yes.'

'So we could ring the hotel and see if he had a room booked. I mean, why would you book a room if you were only going to be there for a couple of hours?'

'Oh my God,' Michelle says, as if it's just starting to sink in. 'Do you think that's what they do?'

'God knows. But it's worth a try.'

'They're not just going to tell me something like that.'

'We can make something up – say we think he left something there . . .'

'Hold on – what about when I was worried before and you called his office. It turned out we were wrong. How do you explain that?'

How indeed?

'That must have been genuine. Same as some of his nights away probably are, I guess.'

347

'We were going to have a baby.' Big plump tears run down her face. I squeeze her hand.

'I know. Awful as it is, it would have been worse to find this out after you were pregnant.'

Please agree with me. Please say yes, thank goodness for that lucky escape. No such luck.

'Maybe it's a one-off thing. Maybe it's the idea of having kids. He just had a bit of a mid-life crisis or something. That might be it, mightn't it?'

Shit. She's going to try to find a way to forgive him.

'I think it's been going on for a while. And . . . I wasn't going to tell you this bit, but I don't think she's the first.'

'Why agree to the baby then? It doesn't make any sense.'

'No it doesn't. I don't know.'

'I'm going to call him,' Michelle says and she reaches for her phone. I need her to believe what I am saying is unequivocally true before he starts poisoning her with stories about me.

'Hold on. Let's try and find some proof first. What about his credit card bills?'

She sniffs. Thankfully sets her mobile back down. 'He gets them online, I think. I don't know his password. I never thought there was reason to ask.'

'So phone the hotel it is, then. What's the worst that can happen? That they won't tell us anything? It's worth a try.'

'OK. You do it, though. I can't.'

I google the number and then dial with the phone on speaker. I already know what I'm going to say, obviously, because this was all part of the plan. After a couple of rings a woman answers.

'Covent Garden Hotel.'

I hesitate, not sure if I can carry this off.

'Hi. My husband stayed with you a few weeks ago and he thinks he left something behind in the room. Is there any way you can check?'

'Of course. What date was it?'

'September the twenty-fourth.' I have this date embossed on my brain.

I hear her clicking away on a computer.

'And your husband's name is?'

'Patrick Mitchell.'

'Ah yes, Mr Mitchell,' she says, as if she only saw him yesterday. I hear Michelle gasp. She looks as if she's about to be sick.

Click click click.

'He was in room four two four, and there's no record of anything having been handed in to us after he left. What is it he's lost?'

'His watch. To be honest he didn't realize until a couple of days later so he could have mislaid it anywhere really . . .'

Now I just want to get off the phone and look after my friend.

'Thanks for your help.'

The helpful receptionist isn't having it, though. 'I'll certainly ask housekeeping if anyone remembers seeing anything. Is there a number I can reach you on if I have any luck?'

'Oh . . . I'm going away for a few days . . . to a health spa where I won't have my phone with me . . . don't worry . . .' Shut up, Tamsin.

'Well, we have Mr Mitchell's number on file, so I could

always call him. Oh, I see he's booked in again on Sunday. I'll make a note for someone to let him know then if we find anything.'

I look at Michelle and she's staring at me wide-eyed. I can't get off the phone quickly enough.

'Perfect. Thank you.'

I end the call without waiting for her response. Michelle breaks down in noisy tears. I get up and head round to her side of the table, leaning down to hug her. She sobs into my jumper.

'He's taking her there on Sunday,' she says when she emerges. 'He told me he had football again. I don't think I can bear it.'

'He's a bastard. I'm sorry, but he is.'

'What am I going to do?'

'I've got an idea,' I say. I can already see a plan forming. 'Just bear with me.'

59

Bea

If you've never experienced the sensation of chasing a man down a hotel corridor while crying and begging at the same time, I can't say I'd recommend it. It does very little for your self-esteem.

He's already by the lift when I reach him.

'Please come back.'

He looks round. Nervous.

'For fuck's sake, Bea. What are you doing?'

'Don't let's leave it like this.'

'There's no point. I'm going home,' he says in a low voice. 'I'll call you tomorrow.'

'No. This isn't fair.'

'Ssshh! Jesus! I'm not going to have this conversation in a public place.'

The lift bell dings. I have no doubt that if he heads off now, home to his frumpy wife and his soon-to-be-a-family home, that'll be the last I see of him. He's angry with me. He's irritated by me. He's worried that his whole world is going to come crashing down because of me.

'That's why you need to come back to the room. Just for a minute. Please.'

He huffs. 'Fine. But I'm not staying.'

He follows me back along the corridor. Thankfully I

remembered to bring the key with me so I wave it at the sensor and we're in.

'We might as well open this,' I say, picking up the champagne. Having a drink might chill him out a bit.

'There's no point to this if we keep fighting,' Patrick says as I hand him a glass.

'I know. I'm sorry. It was just . . . it was a shock to hear, that's all. I shouldn't have said anything.'

'This was meant to be fun. I don't need any more stress in my life.'

Well, that put me in my place. I am still just a bit of fun. Nothing more than a diversion. I don't want to get into another row, but I can't let it go completely.

'It was. It is. But I suppose it was inevitable I'd start to want a bit more after a while.'

'It can't be more, though. You know that.'

'More doesn't have to mean leave your wife and set up home with me. I would never ask you to do that.' Who am I kidding, of course I would, but now is clearly not the time. 'But surely what we have has gone beyond a quick convenient shag in a hotel room? Or am I deluded?'

He puts his hand on my arm. That feels like a good sign. 'No. I care about you, of course I do. I'd hate not to have you in my life.'

'Honestly, that's all I wanted to hear. It's just sometimes I feel a bit cheap, you know. Like I could be anyone . . .'

'You really think I would have carried on seeing you and risked starting to care about you if you were just anyone? It would have been much easier to keep things casual.'

'I know. I'm sorry.'

He smiles. Hallelujah. 'Stop apologizing.'

'Sorry,' I say. 'Ha ha.'

He puts down his glass. 'Come here.'

I practically pass out with relief. Nothing is really resolved. He still might be a father-to-be any time now and want to start playing happy families. But I'm hanging in there. I'm still in the race. I just have to work out how to win it.

60

Tamsin

'I don't think I can,' Michelle says.

We are still sitting at the kitchen table, me now on the same side as her, chair pulled close, arm round her shoulders. She's cried out for a while, although I imagine she'll get her second wind soon.

'It's only for a couple of days.'

Of course, I completely understand that every fibre of her being wants to run straight to Patrick and accuse him. I'd be the same. She wants answers.

'He'll just keep lying to you. This way he won't be able to. Think of it – how's he going to explain the fact that he's leaving a hotel with a woman when he was meant to be wherever he told you he was meant to be? And even if he does try to make out he was having a meeting or she's a colleague, we can ask reception about the room. In front of him.'

I know, of course, that it's unlikely Patrick and Bea will leave together. They are far too careful for that. If last time is anything to go by – and I can imagine they have a well worked out and rehearsed plan – she will leave first, followed by him a few minutes later.

Even though I've been nervous about Michelle finding out it's Bea who Patrick has been seeing, I now see that this is a way to let her know without implicating myself at all. Bea will spot Michelle and I waiting in reception. She'll be forced to stop and say hello. I'll keep her talking – I'll think of something – so that she has no opportunity to warn Patrick. He'll emerge a few minutes later and bingo. One of their faces will give them away, I have no doubt. And then I can act as shocked as Michelle by the realization that my assistant is her husband's mistress.

Of course they will try to throw me straight under a very big bus, but I can bluff it out. Unless they both announce in perfect unison that they met when I sent Bea to try to trap Patrick, or that I have a history with him myself, then I will be able to persuade Michelle they're clutching at dust.

'There's no way I can act as if everything's normal. I just can't.'

'Is he likely to call you tonight?'

She shakes her head. 'He always says he gets back to the hotel too late, he doesn't want to disturb me. He texts at some point in the evening usually. When he can sneak off to the loo or . . .'

She trails off, remembering that everything Patrick has told her about his nights away, including this, is a lie.

'. . . anyway . . .'

She wipes away another tear. Blows her nose on the tissue I find somewhere in my pocket.

'What are you doing at the weekend?'

Michelle shrugs. 'I'm going to see my mum and dad on Saturday morning . . .'

'Just you?'

She nods.

'Perfect. Make an excuse to stay the night. Tell Patrick your mum's not feeling well or something. That way it'll only be tomorrow night and Sunday afternoon. I'm assuming you don't talk much during work time?'

She shakes her head.

'If we do this you'll know for sure. Then it's up to you what you decide to do. Otherwise you'll always have doubts. Either way.'

'You're right. I'll try. But I don't know if I can pull it off. How could he do this? I just don't understand. Am I a running joke at his work then? Poor old Michelle. She has no idea we're all laughing at her behind her back.'

'No one's laughing at you.'

'Do you think Verity knows? Oh God, this is so humiliating.'

'I don't know. She might suspect . . . maybe. You can't start worrying about that.'

'I feel so stupid.'

'If anyone thinks anything it'll be that Patrick is a huge bastard and he doesn't deserve you.'

'Poor stupid little wifey at home while her husband runs round with some young thing. Is she young?'

'I don't know. I told you I didn't really see her.'

'What did Adam say, though? He must have described her to you. Is she pretty?'

'He didn't. I didn't ask. I was in too much shock, I think.'

'Look at the cliché I've turned into already. It matters, though. If she's younger . . . if she's gorgeous . . . it makes it so much worse somehow.'

I think about Bea's model looks. 'Or maybe it would be better. He's just gone for the superficial. It makes it more mid-life crisis and less about how he really feels about you.'

'How am I going to tell my mum and dad?'

'Worry about that later. Let's just get through the next few days first.'

Eventually I persuade her to go to bed and I sit next to her, stroking her hair away from her face while she cries.

'I don't know what I'd do without you,' she says at one point and I try to ignore the knot that forms in my stomach.

'Get some sleep,' I say, and I feel like the worst person in the world. 'I'll be here if you need me.'

61

Tamsin

So here we are. Me, Michelle and Adam, sitting in the restaurant at the Covent Garden Hotel like it's the last supper. This is not how I ever imagined my two best friends would meet.

Adam organized it. He asked for the table with the best view of the reception, and luckily that seemed to be a perfectly valid request. Now Adam and I sit facing the door, just in case either Patrick or Bea decide to make an early exit. Michelle has her back to it. She can hardly bear to look.

She's exhausted. Big dark rings under her eyes. She's made an effort, though. Her blonde hair looks shinier and she's got a bit of colour with the help of some bronzer. She doesn't want to meet her rival without feeling like she's looking her best, she said.

The morning after I broke the news, I woke up still on her and Patrick's bed, lying on top of the covers. Michelle was nowhere to be seen. I dragged myself downstairs and found her sitting at the kitchen table, still in her pyjamas, nursing a cup of tea. She looked wretched.

'How long have you been up?'

She shrugged. 'I didn't really sleep. I finally gave up and came down here about an hour ago.'

I looked at the clock on the wall. Ten to six. 'You should have woken me.'

She gave a sad smile. 'You looked so peaceful. I couldn't bring myself to.'

Then her face crumpled and she started to cry again. I noticed several balled-up tissues on the table in front of her.

'Please tell me it's not true,' she said into my T-shirt.

'I can't.'

Thank God Patrick wasn't due home until the evening. It was obvious now that there is no way Michelle could have got through this without giving away that something was seriously up if he'd come home the night before.

'Why don't you go back to bed for a couple of hours? I'll make sure you get up for work.'

'No. I'll feel worse, I think. I'm not sure I can face the office . . .'

I didn't think it would be helpful for her to spend all day on her own, brooding about what was happening. She had to try to suppress it somehow. She had a whole evening with him to get through.

'I think you should. You need a distraction . . .'

'I won't be able to do anything . . . look at the state of me.'

'Tell them you're a bit under the weather when you get in. No one'll question it. You just need to get through today, Mich.'

'I can't.'

'Tell you what. We'll both call in sick. I'll stay here with you.'

She reached over and squeezed my hand. 'That's so

sweet of you. I can't ask you to do that. I know how anal you are about never having sick days.'

I manage a smile. 'I'll make this an exception.'

'No,' she said, sitting up straight. 'You're right, I should go in.

'I'll get us some breakfast.' The early hour had made me feel nauseous but it seemed important we keep our strength up.

'I'm going to go for a quick run, clear my head,' she said. 'Coming?'

'I don't have any stuff with me and your feet are way smaller than mine, otherwise . . .'

She managed a laugh. 'I was kidding. I'm going to, though. It helps me think sometimes.'

By the time she got back I'd made the bed, had a shower, put the same clothes back on, resisted the urge to poke through Patrick's things in the study in the hope of finding proof, and I was making scrambled eggs.

'You are sure this is the right thing to do?' she said when we were eating – or, at least, I was eating and Michelle was pushing her food around the plate.

'I hope so. I think so. I mean . . . it'll be awful but it'll probably save months of him trying to wriggle out of it.'

'OK,' she said, finally swallowing a forkful of eggs. My scrambled eggs are pretty irresistible, by the way. Just saying.

We travelled as far as Euston together on the tube. 'Phone me any time,' I said. 'I'll keep my ringer on. And if Patrick should happen to call don't answer.'

'I won't.'

360

I gave her a big hug as we got near her stop, and then I wished I hadn't because I saw tears pooling in the corners of her eyes again.

'Thanks again.' I wished she'd stop thanking me. It was making me feel worse than I already did, if that was possible.

'Knock 'em dead.'

I was so early for work I stopped in a café near Hammersmith tube, ordered a large coffee and called Adam. I'd been expecting to have to leave a message but he answered on the first ring.

'So?'

'Grim,' I said.

'God, I've been pacing up and down half the night like an expectant father.'

I had sent Adam a brief text just to let him know that I'd told her and that – hopefully – there was a plan in place, but I hadn't felt I could call him and elaborate more. It didn't seem right to be discussing Michelle's marriage in front of her with someone she'd never even met.

I filled him in on the call to the hotel.

'Result!' he said, and I wondered if he spent too much time with twelve-year-olds. 'I mean . . . not . . . that made it sound as if I thought it was a good thing . . . it was just excitement . . .'

'It's fine. Hopefully it'll solve everything. They won't have time to get their stories straight and they'll look like a pair of desperate liars when they point their fingers at me.'

'Poor Michelle,' he said and I remembered why I liked him so much.

'I know. She's devastated. Obviously.'

'Obviously.'

'You are free Sunday night, aren't you. I think I need you for moral support.'

'Are you kidding? I wouldn't miss it for the world.'

'No hot date with Mel?'

'Mel and I are having dinner tomorrow.'

'Oh. Lovely.'

'A little bistro near the school.'

I didn't know what to say, so I just said, 'Great.'

I wondered, briefly, if Adam would have cancelled his date if it had clashed with my plans.

The timeline for this evening goes like this. Michelle and I are meeting Adam at the Covent Garden Hotel at quarter past seven. We don't want to risk either Patrick or Bea spotting us on their way in.

Once at the hotel Adam, Michelle and I are going to eat dinner – or at least pretend to, I'm not sure any of us will have an appetite – while keeping an eye on the hall in case of an early exit. Patrick has told Michelle to expect him home about nine thirty, which would mean him leaving here at about ten to at the earliest. Our plan is to decamp to the foyer by about eight thirty – assuming nothing has happened by then – and then just wait it out. If asked, our excuse will be that we are waiting for some friends.

Michelle was a bit unsure about me asking Adam to come along. She feels embarrassed, I think. The scorned wife trying to catch her errant husband out. I persuaded her, though. We need him for moral support, for advice, for ballast. To keep us entertained and occupied while we wait, because the two of us will be nervous wrecks. In the end she agreed reluctantly. I don't think she's feeling up to fighting. Not with me at least.

So now we are sitting here. Trying to drink just enough to give us courage but not so much that we turn the evening into a scene from *Shameless*. Looking at our food rather than eating it.

'So you got a good look at her?' Michelle says eventually, turning to Adam. She's starting to relax around him a little. It's impossible not to. It would be like ignoring the advances of a puppy who was nuzzling your arm for a bit of attention. Adam looks cornered momentarily. He's terrified he's going to give away something he shouldn't.

'It was dark but, yes, pretty good.'

'And?'

He gulps. I hope she doesn't notice. 'Um . . . she's got long dark hair. She's quite tall.'

'How old?' Michelle says quietly.

'Oh, well, I'm not very good at this kind of thing, but I'd say thirties. Mid thirties . . .'

'Pretty?'

He flushes red. I want to tell him he's doing great. 'I suppose so.'

'I guess he'd hardly be sneaking off to meet a gargoyle.' Michelle attempts a laugh but it comes out like a cross between a cough and a cackle. A cat chucking up a hairball.

'Sorry,' Adam says sweetly.

'No. Don't be. I want you to be honest with me. I need to face the truth.'

'There's no point in torturing yourself with the details, though,' I say, reaching a hand over the table and rubbing her arm.

'I'm fine. And . . . what did you see that made you so sure they were a couple? I mean apart from the fact he was somewhere he shouldn't have been.'

We've been over this. He knows what to say. 'They held hands, just for a moment when they thought no one could see them. And then they looked round, like they were making sure they hadn't been caught.'

Michelle nods.

'It's hard to explain. It was just . . . obvious.'

'If you hadn't seen that I'd never have known,' she says. 'I mean, what are the chances of that?'

Thousands to one probably. Millions.

'It still would have been happening, though,' I say. 'Even though it's awful, it's probably better you found out.'

'I know. It just doesn't feel like that at the moment.'

We sit there in silence for a minute. There's no point any of us making small talk because no one's interested. At one point Michelle tries, though: 'So, you're a teacher? What age?'

'Secondary,' Adam says, and that's that.

By half past eight we've answered the waitress's concerned enquiry about whether there was something wrong with the food (No. Delicious. Just not hungry.) Ordered another round of drinks to sip on in the foyer while we wait, and paid the bill.

'You're welcome to sit here and drink those,' the waitress says helpfully. 'At least till someone else wants the table.'

'It's OK,' I say, trying to think of an excuse that doesn't make the three of us sound insane. In the end I don't bother. 'Thank you, though.'

We arrange ourselves on the chairs in the foyer, me and Michelle on one side, Adam on the other. The lift is in full view. There's no way either of them will get by us unnoticed. It occurs to me that I probably should have checked that Mr Mitchell had actually arrived as planned and hadn't cancelled at the last minute. It hardly seems worth it now.

I hold on to Michelle's hand. She's shaking.

'It'll all be over soon,' I say, although I'm not sure how appropriate that sounds.

I look at my watch. Time is moving unimaginably slowly. It reminds me of being a kid and waiting for church to be over. It always felt as if the hands on my Timex were moving backwards rather than forwards. The only way to stop it was not to look.

After what seems like an age the lift pings. The three of us jump up like we're a circus act shot from a cannon. An elderly couple get out. I actually feel annoyed with them for the false alarm. I feel myself glaring at them as they pass.

We settle back down. Wait.

Ping.

This time we remain seated, eyes glued to the lift doors. And then there she is. My assistant. Patrick's mistress. Bea.

There's a split second before she sees me. She steps out of the lift, flicking her hair back from her face. Confident.

And then our eyes meet. She's a rabbit caught in the headlights. She looks round as if she might just evaporate back into the lift but the doors have closed behind her.

Trapped.

Here goes.

'Bea!' I say in my best 'how lovely to see you' voice. I

have to remember that I'm not supposed to suspect her yet.

'Tamsin?'

'What on earth . . . ? Michelle, you know Bea, don't you?'

Bea's eyes flick to Michelle. What's left of the colour in her cheeks drains away. She tries to rearrange her face into a smile. Fails.

'Oh, and this is Adam. I've told you about him.'

Adam steps forward, arm outstretched. Big smile on his face.

'Bea! Finally! I'm sick and tired of Tamsin banging on about how brilliant you are!'

We've been over this. Adam is the only one of us who can recognize Bea as the woman who was with Patrick. It's his job to force her to stay without letting her realize what he's doing. If I do too much Michelle will wonder – in retrospect – what my motive was. He shakes her hand and I find myself thinking again that he's missed his calling. He should be playing Macbeth at the National.

There's a tiny moment where Bea relaxes. They're not on to me yet.

'Actually,' she says, 'I'm in a bit of a rush. Lovely to see you all.'

'Oh no,' Adam says, still hanging onto her hand. 'You're not getting away that easily. I've been dying to meet you and now I insist you have a drink with us.'

'I can't, really.' The panic is back.

'Just a quickie.'

'I'll be late.'

She snatches her hand away. I can see we're in danger

of losing her. She needs to get somewhere where she can phone Patrick and warn him.

'Of course. Where's Danny, by the way? I thought you were meeting him.'

She's trying to edge towards the door. 'I was. He cancelled so I've just . . .' She flaps her hand. She's got nothing. I change tack. Pull out the boss card.

'Actually, I just need a quick word about Ashley.'

She looks at me incredulously. 'Now?'

Adam, I notice, has casually moved between Bea and the door, as if he thinks she might make a run for it. Michelle is just looking a bit confused. Looking round as if to say, Shouldn't we be keeping our eye on the prize.

'It'll take two minutes. It won't make any difference to . . . who is it you're meeting again?'

'Ali. We're going to the cinema and it starts at ten past nine so I really should go.'

'Let the poor girl leave,' Michelle says, being nice. 'Sorry, Bea. You know what she's like when she's got a bee in her bonnet. No pun intended.'

'I won't get a chance in the morning,' I say, desperately flailing around for what it is that's so urgent I'd apparently be prepared to rugby tackle Bea to the ground rather than let her leave before we've discussed it.

'Walk with me then,' Bea says. 'You can tell me on the way.'

I have nothing to say in response to this. I can't say yes and abandon the objective. And if I say no she's gone.

'No. It's fine. It'll keep.'

'Right, well, see you tomorrow,' she says, turning towards the door again. I have no idea what to do. Without surprising Bea and Patrick in one place I have nothing. But if I'm any more unsubtle Michelle will never believe I didn't know it was Bea all along. I need Adam to step up.

He's still lurking in the doorway. The doorman, thankfully, is outside. Probably hailing a cab for someone, unaware that his abandoned post is in chaos. Bea strides towards Adam.

'Night everyone,' she says as she goes. I can see she is already reaching into her bag for her phone.

'Night, Bea. So lovely to meet you finally. I wish you could have stayed longer.' He throws his arms out theatrically, going for a hug. Manages to knock the mobile that she's holding in her left hand out of her grip. There's a scrabble of 'Oh Gods' and 'Shit, sorrys'. It's almost comical watching him get in her way while she tries to pick it up. Pretending to help. I'm sure I see him 'accidentally' kick it further away at one point.

'God, I'm such a klutz,' I hear him say. He picks up her bag, which she's dumped on the ground, as if to search under it. Holds on tight.

Bea can no longer keep the hint of irritation and – I imagine – pure terror out of her voice. 'Leave it. Just let me pick it up.'

She practically pushes him out of the way, grabs her mobile from a dusty corner, snatches her bag away.

'See you tomorrow,' she says to me, trying to reclaim some dignity. I have no idea what to do, how to stop her leaving and the whole plan falling apart.

'Night,' is all I can manage. I give Adam a pleading look. Do something.

He steps between Bea and the door again. Puts his arm

out to block her way. Oh God. I look at Michelle, and she's just looking confused, flicking her eyes between the lift and the front door.

'I know who you are,' Adam says in a tone that wouldn't go amiss in *Midsomer Murders*. You're bang to rights.

Bea looks panicked. Pushes his arm. I have a moment when I'm impressed that he is capable of resisting.

'Will you get out of the way. Tamsin, I don't mean to be rude but your mate is weird.'

I see her looking over Adam's shoulder, trying to catch the eye of the doorman.

'What's going on? I don't understand,' Michelle says quietly.

'I saw you together,' Adam is saying. 'Here. A couple of weeks ago.'

Bea ignores him. Makes another rush at the exit.

'Excuse me!' she shouts at the doorman, who is thankfully occupied helping a family into a cab. It's a bit like an am dram farce. The timing's a bit off and we could all do with some more rehearsal.

'This is her,' Adam says, eyebrows raised, to me. Help me out here.

'Bea?' I say for lack of any other inspiration. 'You're kidding, right?'

'I've got no idea what he's on about,' Bea says. 'But if he doesn't let me pass I'm going to punch him in the face and then call the police.'

'Go ahead,' Adam says and I almost laugh because he actually looks terrified.

'Tamsin . . . ?' Michelle says. 'What's happening?'

I open my mouth to say something, I have no idea

what. Bea has one last shove at Adam and manages to dislodge him. Before we can do anything about it she is off down the road. We all stand there, unsure what to do next.

'Bea is Patrick's mistress?' Michelle says eventually.

'Adam?' I say. I have to keep up the pretence of being in the dark.

'That's the woman I saw him with, so if that's Bea . . . I'm sorry, Michelle.'

'How do they even know each other?' she says, and then I'm dimly aware of the ping of the lift.

All our heads whip round again like hungry owls and then I hear, 'Michelle?'

We all stop what we're doing. Patrick is standing white-faced, confronted with the sight of his wife in front of him. He spots me and there's a moment when I almost lose my nerve.

'What are you doing here? Michelle's voice is shaky. She knows what she is supposed to say, but the revelation about Bea has thrown her. 'Weren't you supposed to be at football?'

There's a buzz from his pocket as his phone starts to ring. Bea, no doubt. Patrick looks thrown for a second. Decides he needs to deal with the problem standing in front of him.

'It got cancelled. I just popped in for a quick drink,' he says evenly. 'More to the point, why are you all here?'

'Upstairs?' I say, and he looks at me with irritation.

'What?'

'Were you having a drink upstairs in one of the rooms? Only you just got out of the lift.'

'What is this? A fucking inquisition. Don't listen to anything she has to say to you, Mich.'

'Why not? She's our friend.'

'I really don't think she is any more.'

Michelle ignores this. 'So why were you upstairs?'

'Michelle, Tamsin has some kind of a vendetta against me. She's basically been accusing me of all sorts of stuff—'

'So why is there a room booked in your name?' Adam pipes up.

Patrick looks at him for the first time. 'Who the fuck are you?'

'This is Adam,' I say. 'My friend.'

'Is it Bea?' Michelle is still staring blank-faced at Patrick. I see him gulp.

'Who? I've got no idea what you're on about.'

'It's Bea,' Adam says, triumphant. Poirot in his big denouement. 'Only, of course, I didn't realize she was Bea before. But that was the woman I saw him with the other night.'

'I don't understand,' I say, giving it my best.

Patrick looks at Michelle intently. 'Don't listen. I don't know what the fuck is going on, but this is some kind of bullshit. This bloke doesn't even know me, so how can he claim he saw me with anyone?'

'Bea is your mistress?' Michelle says.

I need to express my shock. 'What the fuck? You've been seeing my assistant?' OK, so I never said I was a scriptwriter.

'Just tell me the truth?' Michelle says. The only truly confused person in the room.

'Of course not. I don't even know Bea,' Patrick says.

'So how come you were leaving here together the other night?' Adam asks.

Patrick casts a furious glance at me. 'Really, who is this bloke? Because I'm going to fucking flatten him in a minute.'

People are starting to look now. One of the receptionists is casting slightly wary glances over in our direction and a couple of diners in the restaurant are openly gawping.

'Is everything OK, Mr Mitchell?' The curious receptionist is now on her way over, heels clicking on the wooden floor.

'Fine. Thank you,' Patrick says tersely.

'OK.' She smiles. 'Oh, by the way, your watch wasn't handed in.'

'What?' he says, confused and bordering on rude. I imagine he just wants her to go away. Fast. I look at Michelle. She's watching him intently.

'There was a note on the computer that you thought you might have left your watch in the room last time you stayed, but nothing's been found.'

'Last time?' Michelle says, looking at Patrick.

'Let's talk about this at home,' he says, ignoring the receptionist and taking Michelle's arm. She shrugs him off.

'No. Let's not. Let's talk about it here. You've stayed here before?'

Patrick looks round. The receptionist has slunk back behind the desk, aware that she has put her foot firmly in it. She's making sure she stays in earshot, though. This must be too good to miss.

'I come here all the time for meetings or drinks with colleagues in the bar. She's obviously got me confused with someone else.'

'Is that why she called you Mr Mitchell?' Adam says.

'Can we at least lose Inspector Fucking Clouseau? This has nothing at all to do with him. Or her for that matter.' He indicates me with his thumb as he says this.

'Actually, Pad, it does. If it wasn't for them I wouldn't even know about it. I'd still be the stupid little cheated-on wife. The butt of everyone's joke.'

Patrick's face crumples. Acting 101. 'No . . . Mich . . . You have to believe me. I'd never cheat on you.'

'You just book a room and sit in there on your own watching TV, do you?'

'I love you. I've never been interested in anyone else.'

'If you love me then you'll explain. Do you have any idea how humiliating this is?'

He breathes in deeply. Wipes away his crocodile tears. Or maybe they're real. He can see his career prospects ebbing away after all.

'Tamsin has some kind of vendetta against me. I told you. She's been making up all kinds of stuff . . .'

'Why would she do that?'

'I don't know. She's decided she hates me for some reason. Or that you could do better. She's always been way too protective of you.'

'She's my best friend.'

'How can she be if she's been filling your head with all this shit?'

'She's the only person I can trust to tell me the truth.'

Patrick snorts. 'You think so?'

'You're going to have to keep your voice down a bit, Mr Mitchell.' The doorman places a hand on his back. 'Why don't you take this conversation up to your room.'

Patrick flinches.

'Of course,' Michelle says. 'You have a room. Let's go up there. I'm dying to see it.'

There's no point in him denying it. He knows she knows.

'Just us,' he says quietly.

'No,' Michelle says, and even though I'm terrified of what's going to happen next, I'm proud of how strong she's being. 'We all go. If you really want to explain yourself then you do it in front of all of us.'

'Not him.'

'All of us. Or I'm leaving.'

'Then let's go home.'

'I want to see it, Patrick.'

'Michelle . . . no.'

'Stop patronizing me. I want to see the room you booked.'

'Fine,' he says, turning on his heel.

I have to fight the urge to run away. I know what he's going to tell her and I know that I have to be there to make sure she doesn't believe him. The dying man throwing grenades to take everyone else down with him. But I don't know whether I can go through with it. Whether I can pull it off.

Adam takes my hand and squeezes it.

OK. Here goes.

62

Bea

Shit. Fuck. Jesus. I have no idea what the fuck to do. Where to go. I'm just glad I'm out of there. But they know. Somehow that podgy twat Adam has worked it out. All I can hope is that Patrick does what he has always said he would do if cornered. Deny. Deny. Deny.

I have no way of finding out what is going on. All I can do is wait for him to call me. Try his second phone tomorrow if I hear nothing.

In the meantime I have to decide whether or not to go to work in the morning.

Fuck.

63

Tamsin

It's impossible not to look at the unmade bed. The covers
thrown aside by people who weren't the slightest bit worried about covering themselves up. The room practically
smells of sex. On either side of the bed a champagne
flute sits on the night stand. The empty bottle is on the
coffee table. It looks like the set for a bawdy bedroom
farce.

Michelle gasps and I put my arm around her shoulders.

'OK, so now you know,' Patrick says. 'But it means
nothing, OK? It was a mistake that got out of hand. I'm
so sorry. I never meant for it to happen.'

'How long?' Michelle says.

'Why not ask Tamsin. She's the one who introduced us
in the first place.'

Michelle looks at me. This is my big moment.

'What?'

'I didn't think you'd want to own up to your part in
it.'

OK, here goes. I try to blank out the fact that it's
Michelle I am really lying to.

'If I had any idea what you were on about I would.'

He turns to Michelle. 'Tamsin sent Bea to try and
honey trap me. Supposedly she'd heard rumours that I

was sleeping around and she decided that somehow it was any of her business.'

I let out a cross between a snort and a scoff. A snoff. 'What? Michelle, I have absolutely no idea what he's talking about. Why would I ever do something like that?'

'She's obviously going to try and deny it. Anyway, it all went wrong because Bea told me what was going on.'

'He's delusional,' I say. 'He'll say anything.'

'I've got nothing to lose now,' he says, indicating the state of the room. 'Why would I need to lie?'

He's got a point. 'Because you think you can divert Michelle's attention from what's been going on by pulling me under the bus with you, I don't know?'

Michelle looks at me. 'Is anything he says true?'

I force myself to hold her gaze. 'No. Of course not. Why would you believe anything that came out of his mouth now you know what he's capable of?'

'How long?' she says to Patrick again. 'Just tell me the truth.'

'Not long. And what I said to you about the way we met is true.'

'I don't believe you. And even if I did, who cares? Even if Tam did do that, she was only trying to protect me.'

'As if,' I say, doing my best incredulous voice.

'I know you didn't. I'm just saying how they met isn't the point.'

'You're a fucking bitch,' Patrick spits at me.

'And you're a cheating bastard.'

'Actually Tamsin always stood up for you. When I found that hotel receipt she was the one who said there must be an innocent explanation.'

'There's a reason for that,' he says and my heart lurches. Is this it? Adam – who has been keeping a dignified silence – presses a hand into my back for support.

I speak quickly. 'Because there *was* an innocent explanation that time. I phoned his office pretending to be from the hotel about a bit of lost property, and whoever I spoke to said it hadn't actually been him who'd stayed there, remember?'

I have to blurt this out now because this is one piece of the puzzle Patrick shouldn't know about, unless what he is trying to say was true. If he'd brought it up without my first having put it out there Michelle would eventually work out that something was off.

'You didn't really, though, did you?' he says now. 'You just told Michelle you did because I asked you to cover for me.'

'Ha! Now you're really clutching at straws.'

'You can ask Verity,' he says to Michelle.

'It wasn't Verity she spoke to,' Michelle says now and I want to hug her for remembering my lie so perfectly. 'She told me at the time it was someone else.'

'Who?' he says accusingly.

'I didn't ask their name, funnily enough. Why would I?'

'How convenient.'

'You really think I'm going to believe Tamsin agreed to cover up for you? That she'd find out you were having an affair and she wouldn't come straight and tell me?'

'She couldn't.'

'Why are you doing this, Pad?' Michelle says, tearful. 'It's not bad enough that I find out you're having an . . . affair . . . but you want to try to destroy my friendship with

Tam as well? How can you be so sadistic? You must really hate me.'

'No! Mich, listen. I'm not saying this to be cruel. I just think you should know what kind of person she is.'

'You think I should believe you like I believed you were really working late or playing football all those evenings you were out?'

'I was for most of them, I swear. This thing with Bea has only been a few times. Which I know is still unforgivable. But don't let Tamsin convince you I was having some big love affair.'

'She's not trying to convince me of anything. She just told me what Adam saw, that's all.'

Patrick turns a vitriolic gaze on Adam. 'And what exactly did Adam – who doesn't know either me or Bea – see?'

'I saw you together,' Adam says calmly. 'Tamsin was with me, that's how I knew it was you.'

'Stroke of luck in a city of nine million people, wasn't it?'

'Not really,' I pipe up. 'I'd rather never have known.'

'You're a much better actress than I thought you'd be.'

'Keep talking, Patrick. No one is listening. You're a drowning man clutching at a life raft.'

'I think we should go,' Michelle says to Adam and me. 'I think I've heard enough.'

She turns to Patrick. 'Please don't come back to the house tonight. You can go in tomorrow when I'm at work and collect some stuff. I need to be on my own for a while.'

He reaches out a hand to her. 'Mich . . . don't . . . please.'

'I'll be in touch. I just need to take it all in.'

379

She walks out and Adam and I follow. Patrick mutters something to me as I go but I don't catch what he says.

I wonder if I've got away with it, but I know it's just a rain check. I can only assume that Patrick isn't blurting out what happened between me and him now because he's still hoping he might be able to win her round. Once she knows the whole truth there would be no chance. But he will. When it becomes clear Michelle has no intention of taking him back – and I don't think she will. The lying as much as the affair will leave her unable to trust him again – then he'll throw it in her face. If he can't have her, then neither can I.

I don't think she'll believe him now, though. Whatever he says.

64

Tamsin

Adam and I travel up to Highgate with Michelle. I tell her I'll stay the night and he says he will, too, even though I try to persuade him he doesn't need to. She's quiet on the journey home. Overwhelmed by the reality of what's just happened.

We sit up in the living room long after Michelle has gone to bed. I doubt she'll sleep but I think she wants some time on her own to process everything.

'Do you think I've done the right thing?' I ask, once I hear her shut the bedroom door.

'No idea. I don't see what else you could have done really. She needed to know.'

'I wish I was blameless in all this, though. I feel like a shit. And a hypocrite.'

He leans over and pats my knee. 'You can't change any of it. You're still going to have Michelle. The rest'll be ancient history soon.'

'I don't think I've ever lied to her before about anything. Now I can't stop.'

He reaches for the bottle of wine we've pilfered from Michelle's fridge, and I hold out my glass.

'You need to stop beating yourself up.'

I look at Adam. He's so kind. Such a good person. He's been attentive to Michelle all evening, anxious to make sure the whole experience was as painfree as it could be. I feel a lump in my throat.

'Thank you for being here. I'm not sure either of us could have got through it without you.'

'Oh no. Let's not start getting maudlin or I'm taking your glass away.'

'I mean it, though.'

He holds up his hand. 'Stop it.'

For a split second I wonder what he'd do if I kissed him. I want to. In fact, I suddenly realize I want to do more than just kiss him. I want to launch myself at him and give him a good seeing to on Michelle's sofa. Mind you, the last time I got into a clinch with someone on a sofa it didn't turn out so well. And what if I did and he was horrified? What if he said we couldn't be friends any more because it would be too awkward now I'd made my true feelings clear?

Or what if I did and he went for it, and then I woke up tomorrow morning and thought, What the hell have I done? After Patrick I swore I would never have drunk sex again. With anyone.

I force myself to stand up. 'OK, bed.'

'I thought you'd never ask,' he says with a wry smile on his face.

'Ha ha.'

I head towards the door. Wave one hand as I go. 'Night.'

'Night night,' he calls after me. 'And, Tamsin, don't lie awake worrying about it.'

In the morning at breakfast – made by Adam at his insistence – Michelle says, 'I want to speak to Bea. I want to hear her side of it.'

'They will have got their stories straight by now. Whatever she said to you would be whatever they've agreed to say.' I need to keep reinforcing the fact that neither of them can be trusted to tell the truth.

'Do you think they met up after we left last night?' she asks sadly. Adam puts a rack of toast on the table.

'I don't know. But they definitely will have spoken.'

'That stuff he said last night about the honey trap. Did he just make that up? I mean, why would you even think of something like that?'

I pause, just long enough to compose myself, not so long that it looks as if I don't know what to say.

'God knows. I think he blames me for you finding out and he just wanted to try to hurt me, too.'

She shakes her head. 'I feel as if I don't know him at all.'

'Are you sure you should be going in to work today?' Adam says, sitting down at the table with us.

'Oh God, yes. I'll go crazy if I just sit here.'

'Well eat then.' He passes her the toast, then the butter. I half expect him to cut it up into soldiers and feed it to her. 'You need to keep your strength up.'

'You can tell he's a teacher,' I say and he pulls a face at me.

'Thank you both,' Michelle says and a tear drops onto the piece of toast she's halfway through buttering.

'You'll be OK,' I say. 'I promise.'

65

Bea

Obviously I will be phoning in sick today, hiding in my flat, head down, tail between my legs. Trying to think about damage control.

As I walked home from Angel tube last night – having hung around discreetly outside the hotel for about fifteen minutes in the rain, I then lost my bottle and headed to the tube station before anyone caught me – I got a call from Patrick. An almost unprecedented actual real-life phone call. When I heard my secret mobile ring this time, though, there was no flurry of excitement. Only dread. I knew he wasn't calling me to indulge in a bit of phone sex.

'Fuck!' he said when I answered. 'She's gone home with Tamsin. She's told me to stay away. What am I going to do?'

'Do you want to come over?'

'No! I need to stay here in case she decides to come back. I couldn't have her think I was with you.'

Ah. Right. 'Do you think she might?'

'I don't know. I doubt Tamsin would let her. How did they know, that's what I don't understand.'

There's a tiny hint of accusation in his voice, as if he thinks I might have told someone our secret.

c

'No idea. Adam says he saw us together, but we never are together outside of hotel rooms, so that can't be true.'

'Fucking Tamsin,' Patrick spits. 'We should have been more careful.'

'Why don't I come back down to the hotel? We can try and work out what to do.'

'Are you crazy? What if Michelle does decide to come back here?'

I have no desire to bump into Michelle again. Ever. But it's getting on my nerves that his only concern seems to be where he stands with her.

'I can't go in to work tomorrow,' I say. I've stopped on the corner of my road. Any closer to home and my signal will disappear before I can make it up to Sarah's room.

'If she tells her dad, then I'm done for,' Patrick says, ignoring what I've just said. 'He'll never give me the Truth Channel job. And he'll find a reason to oust me from Home Improvement. Shit!'

'At least you've got the experience to get something else.'

He laughs. It's more of a snort actually. Dismissive. 'Yes, if my own father-in-law – the man who promoted me years prematurely according to half the industry – thinks I'm not capable, then I'm sure they'll be forming a queue to employ me.'

'So set up on your own.' His self-pity is starting to get on my nerves.

'It's not that easy, Bea.'

'Well, let's hope Michelle sees sense and takes you back then, eh? After all, we couldn't have you actually needing to make your own way in the world.'

He ignores the sarcasm.

'Don't tell her about me and Tamsin. She might contact you . . .'

So this is the reason he's called me.

'Why not? I thought that was the whole point, you wanted to pull her under the moving train with you.'

'Not yet. Not until I know it's definitely over with Michelle. If she finds out about that she'll never change her mind.'

Enough.

'I have to go. I'll talk to you soon, OK.'

'Promise me,' he says.

'Funnily enough I'm not likely to be speaking to her. But if I do I'll be sure to protect your best interests.'

'Are you pissed at me or something?'

'Night, Patrick,' I say and end the call. Let him sweat.

66

Tamsin

'Any word from Bea?' I say to Ashley once it gets to twenty to ten and she's still not in. Of course I never thought she would be, but I need to keep up appearances.

'No. Shall I try her?'

'Give it ten minutes. She might just be stuck on the tube.'

'Is there anything I can do for you in the meantime?' Ashley says, smiling.

I hesitate. 'I'd love a coffee.'

'Of course,' she stands up. 'Skinny wet latte, no sugar?'

'Perfect.'

I am still in a state of shock. Last night seems surreal. A bad dream. There's no turning back now. I have made a lifelong enemy of Patrick Mitchell, Bea's and my relationship is doomed. My friendship with Michelle could be about to take a serious blow to the stern. It's all a bit frightening, to be honest. A bit too much.

Concentration is out of the question, so I shut the door to my office and sit there staring into space, waiting for the shit storm to arrive.

There's a tap on my door and Ashley pokes her head round nervously.

'I just spoke to her,' she says. 'She's not feeling well so she's staying at home. She's been at the doctor's, that's why she didn't call. Apparently he's told her she needs a couple of days off.'

I almost laugh. So that's how Bea is going to handle being found out. She's going to hide.

'Oh dear. Well . . . thanks . . .'

'I can cover anything you need.'

'Thank you. I'm sure Lucy will manage.'

Ashley stands there. Clears her throat. 'Actually, Tamsin, I really would like the chance to do more if that were possible. I have time while I'm on reception and it seems mad for you not to utilize me when you need the help.'

It's probably the longest sentence I've ever heard her say. I think about it for a moment. What's the worst that can happen? She'll mess up and I'll ask Lucy to take over.

'OK. Let me have a think about what needs doing.'

'Thank you,' she says, and I notice that her eyes light up when she smiles.

Ian, Anne Marie and I are sitting in Ian's office. On a plate on the low table in front of us are a selection of lethal-looking brownies. Packed full of chilli and sea salt, Ann Marie tells us.

'You have to experiment with bold flavours,' she says with conviction, like it's one of the ten commandments.

After a lot of thought I've decided that I need to tell them what's going on – that I have just found out Bea is having an affair with Patrick Mitchell and, given that he's my best mate's husband, our working relationship is going to be a little challenged from now on.

'Bea?' Ann Marie looks incredulous, and well she might. All I have done for the past year is sing Bea's praises.

Ian just looks uncomfortable. He's the kind of person who likes to believe everything is all right with the world and he never wants to hear anything to the contrary.

'I know. Shocker.'

'I don't think it's grounds to sack her, though.'

'I'm hoping she'll have the decency to resign. It's going to be pretty impossible otherwise.'

'We can't have an atmosphere,' Ian pipes up.

'I'll do my best,' I say. 'Maybe she won't even come back.'

'If she does, perhaps she could work for Ian and Lucy could work for you?' Anne Marie, ever the diplomat, offers up.

'No,' Ian and I say in unison. I'd actually rather take my chances with Bea than try to negotiate Lucy's self-importance. I imagine Ian is thinking he wants to stay as far away from the drama as possible.

'How's your friend taking it?' Anne Marie says.

'She's devastated. Obviously. She had absolutely no idea.'

She dunks a brownie in her coffee, losing a chunk in the process. 'I have to be honest, I'd always heard he was a bit of a womanizer.'

Unbelievable. 'Why did everybody apparently know this except me?'

Anne Marie shrugs. 'Would you tell me if you thought Ian was cheating?'

'Yes!'

'Hang on a minute, leave me out of this,' Ian says.

'OK, well, not Ian then. Someone you knew I was friends with?'

She has a point. 'I know, I know. It just makes me feel like an idiot.'

'Well, it looks like we're all idiots where Bea's concerned.'

I sigh. 'Are you sure I can't sack her, because it would make me really really happy.'

'Definitely not.' Anne Marie is a stickler for the rules. Personally, I hardly think Bea would take me to a tribunal if I slung her out but promised her a reference. Actually, that's not a bad idea. Surely it's OK to put this to her: leave now = good reference; stay = bad reference. But what if she then just decides to stay forever? Maybe not.

'Let's see if she even comes back,' I say. 'I can't believe she's going to want to be anywhere near me.'

The next couple of days go by in a haze. Bea stays away, telling Ashley – who I ask to call her again – that the doctor has told her to stay in bed till the weekend. Ashley keeps on top of my filing and alphabetizes the DVDs on my shelves.

In the evenings I go straight round to Michelle's after work. The first afternoon I find her in tears because Patrick has been in – as she requested – while she was out and has taken some of his clothes. He's been bombarding her with calls, she tells me, none of which she has answered. He's left messages saying that he's staying in a hotel, that it's all over between him and Bea, that he'll do anything it takes to get Michelle back.

'Do you really think there were others before her?' she asks me as we share a bottle of wine.

'I do. And I think it had been going on with Bea for far longer than he's admitting.'

'How do you know?'

'I don't. But that's what the grapevine is saying.'

'I should at least talk to him. Give him the chance to tell me the whole truth.'

'I don't think that's going to happen. I mean, talk to him, obviously, but don't believe everything he says.'

'Oh God,' she says, tearing up. 'I don't think I can stand it.'

I reach out and rub her arm. 'It'll be OK in the end. You'll feel better.'

'I'm never going to have a baby now,' she says. I've been wondering whether Patrick might use the baby thing as leverage. I know Michelle will be calculating in her head. Working out that by the time she's met someone new – assuming she eventually does – and they decide to settle down and have kids it might be too late for her.

'Thank goodness you're not already pregnant, though. I mean, imagine being tied to him forever now you know what he's capable of.'

'I don't know. Maybe a baby would make him change—'

I cut her off. 'No! No, no, no. You know that's not the way it works. You'd be left looking after a kid while he ran round and did whatever he wanted.'

I think I take her by surprise with the forcefulness of my reply. I can't stop there, though.

'Think what it would be like for the baby. Would you really want to bring a child into an unhappy marriage?'

'We weren't unhappy, though, that's the thing. Or at least I didn't think we were.'

'But now you know . . .'

'You're right. I know you are. Shit.'

Her phones jumps into life. Patrick again.

'I'm going to ignore it,' she says, turning the ringer off.

I head back to my own place at about ten, asking the cab driver to stop by the dog walker's so we can retrieve Ron on the way. He greets me as if it's been fourteen weeks not fourteen hours since he saw me last, and my guilt ramps up a notch. I pay Sharon the extra, check she's OK to do the same the following night and head home.

I know that Adam is on date number three with Mel this evening. I've been checking the time nervously ever since I left Michelle's. It's already later than it was when they said goodnight last week. I don't know why I assume he'll automatically phone me the second it's over, but the fact that I haven't heard makes me fear the worst. I'm tempted to phone him. Do a bit of 'Oh, sorry! Are you with Mel? I forgot!' and then casually ask how it's going, but I know I'm being ridiculous. He says she's nice. I should just be happy for him. I'm not, though.

The following evening when I get to Highgate, Patrick is there. Standing in their living room glowering at me as Michelle lets me in. My first instinct is to turn and run. My second is to call Adam – who is meant to be joining us later with a takeaway curry – to tell him to hide outside until the coast is clear. I know Patrick hates me, but he'd never physically harm me. Adam, on the other hand, might be fair game. Not that I've ever known Patrick to be violent. But then a couple of months ago there were all sorts of things I didn't know about him that I've found out since.

'What are you doing here?' he says.

'I could ask you the same thing.'

'Yes, but then you'd sound like an idiot because this is my house.'

'Michelle asked me to come round. I doubt you can say the same thing.'

He turns to Michelle. 'Mich, we need to talk. Can we just have a bit of time without her around?'

'I'm not sure there's anything to talk about any more,' she says. 'Unless you want to tell me why you've apparently had a reputation at work for years.'

He looks stung. 'I suppose she told you that?'

'It's not true then?'

'Of course not! This ... Bea ... is the first time, I promise.'

I make a scoffing noise.

'Pad, just stop lying to me,' Michelle says. And while I know what she means, there's still obviously one lie – or at least one omission – I wouldn't mind him making.

'I'm not.' He can't even look at me now. Or won't.

'There's no point in you being here,' Michelle says, her voice wobbling. 'I think you should go.'

Patrick reaches out a hand towards her and she steps back to avoid his touch. 'Michelle, please . . .'

'If you don't want to talk in front of Tam then I don't want to talk at all. You'll only try to bamboozle me.'

He glares in my direction. 'Is that what she's told you? You do know she's only concerned about herself, right?'

'I can think for myself, you know.'

'Don't listen to her. Don't believe anything she says.'

Michelle steadies herself on the little side table where,

for as long as they've lived here, they have both kept their keys. 'Why would Tamsin lie to me? She's my best friend. I've known her a lot longer than I've known you . . .'

'You think you know her? You've got no idea.' He flashes me another filthy look and I will myself to stare back defiantly.

'How did you manage to make this about Tamsin?' Michelle says, with a strength in her voice that makes me feel both proud and even more ashamed at the same time. 'Is that all you care about? Some stupid little vendetta? You think Tam's responsible for our marriage failing because she told me what you're really like? You don't think it's about what you've done, not the fact that you've got caught?'

'You want to tell her or shall I?' Patrick spits at me. I feel my stomach turn over. Here goes.

I fake a disbelieving laugh. 'Tell her what?'

'You know what. Do you really want me to go there or do you want to leave so I can talk to my wife in private?'

I level my gaze at him. Will myself to stop shaking. 'I have no idea what you're on about.'

'Fine. Michelle, when I tell you this you're going to know I'm being truthful because you'll never take me back once you know. But I need you to see Tamsin for who she really is.'

Michelle looks confused. Looks from Patrick to me.

'I can't wait to hear this,' I say. My heart is pounding through my ears. Remember to act surprised by what he says, I tell myself. Remember to find it laughable.

'Tamsin and I had sex.'

He looks at Michelle as if to say, What do you think of that?

394

I guffaw loudly. 'OK, that is brilliant.'

'She's obviously going to deny it, but it's true.'

'And when exactly is this supposed to have happened?' I say. 'Did we have a threesome with Bea?'

'Your flat. About four months ago.'

'Don't be ridiculous,' Michelle says.

'It's true,' Patrick says. 'She even sent me a text saying we should keep quiet about it afterwards, but she deleted it that morning she turned up really early. Remember?'

'How convenient,' I say.

'Ask Bea. She even told Bea about it.'

'That's enough,' Michelle says in a strident tone I have never heard her use before. 'You can leave now.'

'She knew about me and Bea for ages, but she covered up for me because she was scared of what I'd tell you if she didn't.'

'Don't even mention that woman's name to me. You think I give a damn about what lies you and . . . she . . . have concocted?'

'How could I have known about it for ages?' I say. 'You keep saying you've only seen her a couple of times. And did this supposedly happen before or after I sent Bea to honey trap you? Get your story straight.'

'How long has it been going on? You and Bea?' Michelle looks at him intently.

Patrick looks at the floor. 'About four months.'

'So you were still lying to me even after I found out? How do you expect me to believe anything that comes out of your mouth?'

'It's true,' he says. 'I swear.'

'If you slept with me,' I butt in, 'how come you were so

adamant that Bea was the only one. Or was that another lie?'

He ignores me. Looks at Michelle.

'Do you really think there's any chance for us?' she says. 'Either you cheated on me with my best friend—'

'It's a total lie,' I say quickly.

'I know that. Or you made up a story about cheating on me with my best friend just to try and destroy our friendship? Either way, you're sick.'

He says nothing, turns on his heels to leave. He's played his full hand and it's failed.

'Don't come round again,' Michelle calls after him. 'Don't call me. Nothing.'

I hear him open the door and then, 'What the fuck are you doing here?'

'Bringing takeaway,' Adam's voice says. Nervous.

The door slams. Adam appears in the doorway, plastic bags in hand. 'God, what have I missed?'

I unpack the curry in the kitchen, although I'm not sure either Michelle or myself feel much like eating. I can hardly hold the plastic containers, my hands are shaking so much. I can hear Michelle telling Adam about Patrick's claims and Adam doing a great job of finding them ridiculous.

'I imagine he'll say anything at this point. He's pretty desperate.'

'That's decided me,' I hear her say. 'It's over. There's no point even thinking about giving him another chance. That he would make up something like that . . . no, I could never trust him again.'

'I'm so sorry, Michelle. I wish it could have worked out differently.'

I hover in the doorway.

'Food's ready if either of you wants any.'

'I never refuse food,' Adam says. 'And you need to eat something, Michelle, otherwise I'll be offended.'

'I'll come in and sit with you. I'm not sure I can eat, though.'

In the end she does, because Adam keeps offering her tasty titbits and she hasn't got the strength to keep refusing.

'Have you never wanted children, Adam?' she says when he's practically doing a version of 'here comes the train, open wide' at her with an onion bhaji.

'God, yes. Been desperate for years.'

'Are you?' I say, incredulous. 'You've never mentioned that.'

'You've never asked.'

Michelle persists. 'Did your wife not want them?'

'It just didn't happen, and then we realized we'd made a bit of a mistake getting married in the first place.'

'So if it worked out with Mel you'd have a ready-made family.'

'God. Please don't let me have to take responsibility for that little shit. He's a monster.'

'Oh,' I say, as if I've only just remembered. 'How was your date last night?'

He pulls a face. 'We went to the cinema. I let her choose.'

He raises his eyebrows expectantly and I laugh. 'And . . . ?'

'*Dumb and Dumber To.*'

'Ha!'

'I fear we may not be a match made in heaven.'

'You can't just dump her because she chose a rubbish film!' Michelle says, and she laughs for what seems like the first time in ages. I think how glad I am to have Adam there. It's like having a walking, talking comfort blanket in the room. He's such easy company.

'It's indicative of more fundamental things. A crap sense of humour. No understanding of narrative. A lack of empathy. Plus I decided I didn't really fancy her. And I don't think she fancied me either, to be fair. It wasn't so much me dumping her as us both finding excuses not to have to meet up again.'

I struggle to keep the smile off my face.

'He's such a nice bloke,' Michelle says later when he's in the loo. 'It's a shame you don't like him that way.'

I roll my eyes. As if.

'I've made a decision.' We're a couple of glasses of wine down. Michelle has been bearing up remarkably well. Buoyed up, no doubt, by Adam's attempts at cheering her up. I wonder if hearing Patrick say what he said about me was actually a relief. It made it black and white. The grey area of 'maybe we could try again if he promised to behave' was gone. The irony of the fact that the one truth he told was the one thing that made her believe he was a liar does not pass me by unnoticed. I don't feel good about it. How could I? But the end result is what counts.

'I'm going to move out,' she says. 'Let him have the house.'

'What? No, Michelle, you love this house.'

'I don't think I do any more. And this way we won't have to have a long, tortuous battle. I'll just take my stuff and rent somewhere. He can take over the mortgage on his own.'

'This place must be worth twice as much as when you moved in. You can't just hand all that profit over to him.'

'I don't care. If he wants to do the decent thing and buy me out he can, but I'm not going to fight him for it. It's money I never had in the first place and property prices could plummet again next week and wipe it all out anyway. Will you help me pack my stuff up?'

'Of course,' I say. 'If you're really sure. Think about it for a couple of days, though.'

'I will. But I don't think I'll change my mind.'

'You know you can stay with me for as long as you like.'

She reaches over and puts her hand over mine. 'Thank you.'

'Good for you,' Adam says. 'Move on and don't look back.'

'Who said that? Was it S Club 7?' I say and he rewards me with a smirk.

'Oh God, I'm going to have to tell my parents.'

'For God's sake do it quick, before Julian offers him the Truth Channel. I don't think I could bear it.'

'Will you come with me at the weekend?' she says and I say yes, of course. Whatever she needs me to do.

67

Bea

When the doorbell rings at about half seven I assume it's someone for one of the others. I'm not expecting anyone. Sad little Cinderella sitting at home on her own, nursing her wounds. So when Ali appears at the door of my room with Patrick in tow, it's a shock to put it mildly.

My first thought is, Shit, I'm in my PJs, which I've been wearing for forty-eight hours straight, with no make-up on and a large comfort sandwich on the go. Cheese and mayo with butter a centimetre thick. I almost certainly have lettuce in my teeth.

I've fantasized about him showing up here unexpectedly so many times. Telling me he's left her. That he can't live without me. I wait for the high, the nervous euphoria to kick in, but I feel nothing.

'Sorry, I should have called first,' he says when he sees the state of me. Ali is hovering in the hallway. Hoping to see some drama.

'That's OK,' I say, shoving the sandwich away.

'Can I come in?'

'Sure.'

He shuts the door in Ali's face. I'm sure the room must stink of old food, stale air and God knows what else, so I open the window a little and flinch when the cold breeze floods in.

Patrick comes up behind me, snakes his arms round my waist, nuzzles into my neck. I'm torn for a second and then I move away, out of his reach.

'So, what's happening?' I say.

'What do you mean?'

'You know what I mean. Last time we spoke you were desperate to get your wife back. I assume the fact that you're here means it hasn't worked.'

He does that thing where he puts his head on one side and narrows his eyes. I used to find it sexy. Still do if I'm being honest. But I will myself to resist. Time to get some self-respect back.

'I was just panicking. The thought of losing all that familiarity, I suppose. Heading into the unknown.'

'So you're saying it was your decision? I thought she'd kicked you out.'

'She did at first. But then she invited me over this evening and it was obvious she was coming round. That's when I realized it wasn't what I wanted.'

God, this man can lie.

'Does she know about you and Tamsin?'

He nods. 'I told her. Once I knew I had to end it I thought I should come clean. And give Tamsin what she deserves, obviously.'

'And does she believe you?'

'Tamsin will convince her it's not true. I don't care any more.'

Right.

'So, just like that, your marriage is over? And it's what you want?'

'We could move in together,' he says.

'What about your father-in-law? What about your job?' There's no way in a thousand millennia that Patrick would voluntarily throw away the chance to run the new flagship channel. No way.

He shrugs. 'Like you said, I could set up on my own.'

He reaches an arm out, pulls me towards him.

I look right into his eyes.

'Do you swear this is your decision? This isn't just a rebound thing because you know it's definitely over with Michelle?'

'Of course not. I love you, Bea. That's it, I've said it.'

'You are such a fucking liar,' I say and push him away. 'You can't treat me like some kind of booby prize. You were desperate to mend your marriage and you couldn't give a shit about me until Michelle clearly wasn't having it.'

'I was confused . . .'

'No. I'm done with being second best.'

'You won't be second best. I'm trying to tell you . . . God, Bea, why are you making this so hard?'

'Sorry. I know it would be much easier for you if I just went along with everything you're saying, but that's not going to happen.'

'For fuck's sake, I've lost my wife because of you.'

'And I've lost my job because of you. I can hardly go back now. Plus, for the record, you've lost your wife because of *you*. You're the one who made promises to her, not me.'

'This is stupid,' he says with all the maturity of a toddler who's been denied a chocolate. 'If I leave now, that's it. There'll be no second chances.'

'I don't want a second chance. I don't want to be someone whose boyfriend is only with her because his wife wouldn't take him back. It's humiliating, can't you see that?'

'What can I do to convince you that's not how it is?'

'Nothing,' I say. 'It's too late for that.'

'So what am I meant to do now?'

'I don't know. Go back to wherever you're staying. Try being single for a while. Look for another job. Join the priesthood. I don't care.'

'I should never have got into this,' he says, angry.

'No, you probably shouldn't. Me neither.'

He stands there for a second, as if he doesn't know what to do, and then he walks out, slamming the door behind him.

I'd like to say I feel relieved, proud of myself for the stand I've taken. I don't. I get back into bed and I cry into my pillow until Ali brings up two huge glasses of wine and we decide we might as well get drunk.

I'm sitting in my office. No one else is in yet and I've had to stop myself from grabbing my stuff and making a run for it several times already. I have no idea what to expect. None.

At first I wasn't intending to come back at all. It's clearly not an option for me to carry on working for Tamsin. But then I thought about it for a couple of days and I changed my mind. Why should I be the one to lose everything? She can't sack me on the spot, I know that much. So my intention is to hand in my notice today (which is one month), book any remaining holiday I have in hand (eight days) and just spend the rest of the time keeping my head down and looking for another job. If Tamsin won't give me a reference I'm sure I can ask Ian or Anne Marie. It might look a bit odd to a potential employer, given it's Tamsin I am assistant to, but it'll be better than nothing. Four weeks. That's twenty working days. Minus eight. Twelve days to put up with whatever shit she throws at me.

I hear the door bang and then footsteps on the stairs. My heart starts pounding. Ashley jumps when she sees me, which makes me jump in return. We both squeal like we're on a rollercoaster.

'You gave me a fright,' she says laughing. 'Are you feeling better?'

Clearly she doesn't know anything. I relax a little. 'Yes, much thanks. I hope you don't all come down with it.' I'd told Ashley on the phone that I had a stomach bug. Some kind of norovirus.

'Well, you didn't miss anything. Everything's up to date.'

'Great. Thank you.'

Lucy's next. Her concern is all for herself, of course. She makes that clear by opening the window wide and wafting her hand in front of her face whenever I speak.

By the time I hear the door again I'm calmer. However much Tamsin might want me dead, she's not going to cause a ruckus in front of these two. Maybe she hasn't even told Ian or Anne Marie, I think, but I dismiss that idea pretty quickly when I see Ian appear in reception, take one look at me and flee upstairs. I suppose it was too much to hope for.

Anne Marie manages a stiff hello and then Tamsin rolls in. I hear Ashley cheerily saying, 'Bea's back,' and I keep my eyes on my computer screen, seemingly engrossed.

'Great,' Tamsin says. From what I can see out of the corner of my eye she doesn't even look at me. 'Would you mind phoning that director who's meant to be coming in today and asking him if he can make it half an hour later, Ashley? I'm sure Bea has things to catch up with.'

There's a turn-up for the books. Tamsin asking Ashley to make a call for her. That's how desperate she must be not to have to deal with me. Fine. The more she keeps her distance the better.

And then she's standing in the doorway.

'Bea, could I see you in my office for a minute?'

68

Tamsin

I hadn't expected to see her sitting there. Over the weekend I'd convinced myself that she was never going to come back. We could just post her final payslip to her – with some considerable deductions because of the way she'd let us down with no notice – and I could start the arduous task of finding a new assistant. An older, married one this time, with a face like a worn-out boxing glove.

I was actually feeling good. Lighter, as if a huge fat weight had been taken off my shoulders. Michelle had spent the weekend at mine. On Saturday morning we had spent hours removing everything she wanted to keep from her house. It was precious little for a thirty-eight-year-old, but it still filled both our cars. Michelle had decided to leave only with the personal things. The rest – the 'stuff' that a couple accumulate – was replaceable. Thankfully I had talked her out of just signing the place over. Patrick could buy out her share or he could sell up and they'd split the money, those were the options she was going to present him with.

All her worldly goods were now stashed in my spare room and she had already started looking at adverts for flats to rent. Adam – who had tactfully declined to help with the move when I put it to him, because he thought it might be insensitive for someone Michelle had only known for such a short time to be rampaging through the dying embers of her marital home – had offered to help her move in whenever she found somewhere new.

'I'm very handy,' he said. For some reason that made me laugh. It was such an unimpressive boast.

'Great. Let's hope the place she finds is falling down.'

On Sunday afternoon Michelle and I had gone to see Julian and Miriam in Maidenhead. Of course they were thrilled when they opened the door. An unexpected visit from their daughter and surrogate daughter was their idea of the perfect surprise. They took one look at Michelle, though, and with their parents' witchy sixth sense knew something was up.

'What's happened, love?' Miriam said before we'd even taken our coats off.

Michelle had sighed and then burst into tears, reduced to being a child again at the sight of her mum.

'Patrick's having an affair,' she sobbed.

Needless to say Julian and Miriam were shocked, upset and ultimately angry. In fact Julian was practically incandescent with rage that his protégé could have repaid the family in this way. I saw the promise of the Truth Channel job escape from Patrick's grasp and flutter to the ground.

'You can move back in here,' Miriam said when Michelle had finished telling them everything.

'Don't let him keep the house,' Julian butted in. He had already threatened to go round and punch Patrick in the face, and even Michelle had tried not to laugh.

'I won't. And I'm staying with Tam for a bit, just till I find a flat.'

'Well, your bed's always here if you want it.' It was, too. Michelle's room was still almost the same as it had been when the two of us left aged eighteen. Our twin beds still facing each other on opposite walls. The same white throws and pale green sprigged curtains. Only the clutter had gone. And my poster of The Backstreet Boys.

'Look after her,' Miriam whispered in my ear as we left, after being force fed sandwiches and cakes. I had a chunk of a Victoria sponge wrapped up in my bag 'for later'. What is it with me and cakes? Julian was busy telling Michelle he would dig out the name of a good solicitor for her.

'I will.'

She hugged me. 'Thank goodness she has you.'

'Of course,' I said, hoping she couldn't sense the guilt that I could feel coming off me like heat from a radiator. She didn't have to worry. Making Michelle happy was going to be my main priority from now on.

'Close the door and sit down.' Bea looks white faced. I actually have no idea what I am going to say to her. I just know I can't pretend nothing has happened.

'I'm a bit surprised you're here, to be honest.'

'You can't sack me,' she says, and I wonder if this is going to be more tricky than I'd hoped.

'I know. I just thought you might stay away for a while longer, that's all.'

'Don't worry. I'm handing in my notice. And I have holiday to use up. You won't have to see much of me.'

'Are you not even going to say sorry?'

'Why do I need to apologize to you? You've behaved as badly as me after all.'

I ignore that. Now I have to put what I did to the back of my mind. Pretend it never happened.

'I confided in you. You knew how worried I was for Michelle. God, Bea, you knew how much I thought of you.'

She looks a little chastised at that. Takes a long drink from her bottle of water. 'It wasn't meant to happen. It just did and then it spiralled out of control. I could hardly tell you. And let's not forget it was you sent me up there to seduce him in the first place.'

'To pretend to. Jesus Christ, how did you go from "please don't make me do this" to shagging him?'

'Same as you did, I suppose.'

'We didn't . . . anyway . . . it happened that night? That's when it started?'

She nods.

'If it makes you feel better I'm not seeing him any more.'

'You can marry him now, for all I care. The damage is done.'

'Listen, I feel awful for Michelle, I really do. But if it hadn't been me it would have been someone else.'

She's right, of course.

'Probably.'

I feel as if there's nothing more to say. I'm not going to ask her to stay because I couldn't ever trust her again. But I can't find it in me to hate her, either. The bottom line is that Patrick is the one to blame. And Bea and I probably tie for second.

'I'll give you an OK reference.'

I see tears well up in her eyes and I look away. Her

leaving is still the only possible outcome. 'Thank you.'

'You'd better go and tell Anne Marie you're leaving. Make it official.'

'Right. Yes.' She stands up, sniffs. 'Coffee?'

'Lovely, thanks.'

And just like that I need to start looking for a new assistant.

PART FIVE

69

Tamsin

I'm sitting in the bedroom of Michelle's flat in Maida Vale, watching while she gets ready for her first post-Patrick date. She looks gorgeous. The drawn, wan look has gone and been replaced by something more like her old self. The past week or so she's actually started to look happy. Happier at least. On the road to happiness.

Next week she'll complete on her new place – a one bedroom, one and a half bath, flat near St John's Wood High Street. She – with me and/or Adam in tow most of the time – looked at about thirty apartments, from the big and beautiful in a scary area to postage-stamp-sized studios in chi chi postcodes. This one is a compromise. It's on one of the not-so-desirable streets mere metres from high-end loveliness. The block is well cared for and safe, but with none of the added extras, like concierges and twenty-four-hour gyms, that would push the price over the edge. With the help of her share of the profit from the house – which sold in a matter of days to a cash buyer once Patrick got it into his head that there really was no happy ending on the horizon and buying Michelle out was out of the question given how dodgy his career prospects had suddenly started looking – and a large mortgage, she managed to charm the elderly home owner into accepting her offer.

Meanwhile she has been staying here since the week after it all blew up. Somehow she's managed to make it feel like home, despite the dodgy décor and utilitarian furniture.

'Too much?' she says now, blotting her pale pink lipstick with a tissue.

'You look gorgeous. And besides, it's not like he doesn't know what you look like.'

'I'm actually nervous, how dumb is that?'

'Just forget it's meant to be a date. Don't get all self-conscious.'

'Is this a really stupid thing to be doing?' She turns to face me.

'Not at all. I think it's great.'

The last couple of weeks working with Bea were what you might call interesting. Even though I knew she was feeling guilty, it was too little too late. I couldn't shake the thought that she would still have been with Patrick if she'd thought he was really interested. But I couldn't be bothered to punish her either. After all the hysteria and excitement, all I wanted was a peaceful life.

To be fair, she kept her head down and got on with her work. I'm not entirely sure what it was she was doing, because it seemed far preferable now to ask Ashley when I needed something, or to do it myself, than to have more contact with Bea than was necessary.

She went for several interviews while she was still with us, and I happily gave her the time off. I'm not even sure what they were for. I didn't ask.

On her last day Ian and Anne Marie made a fuss of her,

as indeed they should have. She'd done nothing wrong professionally, only personally. I hovered in reception as they toasted her with fizzy wine and cake, and handed her a gift voucher and a card. She came into my office just as I was putting my coat on. I'd been hoping to avoid any kind of a goodbye. I didn't know what to say.

She shut the door behind her, which immediately made me nervous.

'I just wanted to say,' she said before I could ask her what she wanted. It all came out in a rush, as if she'd been rehearsing and wanted to get it out there before she forgot her lines. 'I don't want you to think I would ever go round spreading gossip, or telling anyone anything about what happened. I didn't want you to think I'd go to a new job and be bad mouthing you or talking about . . . you know what . . .'

She paused. I have to be honest, it was a bit of a weight off my mind. Even though Bea wasn't prone to bitching, I had wondered whether she might not be able to resist smearing my name a bit. Not that I thought people would believe her – they would most probably just assume it was sour grapes – but since when did people have to believe gossip to spread it?

'Thank you. And the same goes for me. I'll give you your reference and that'll be the end of it.'

'I'm sorry I fucked up. It's not something I'm proud of.'

'I know. You'll be fine. Someone will snap you up.'

She stood there awkwardly for a moment, as if she didn't know what to do or say next. I felt a lump in my throat. Willed myself not to cry.

'Right. Well . . . I should go . . . Thanks, Tamsin. I mean it . . .'

I felt a ridiculous urge to hug her. I stopped myself, though. It was a positive thing that we were moving on like two adults, but I didn't want her to think all was forgiven, because it wasn't.

'Good luck with finding something,' I said. 'If I hear of anything . . .'

She flashed me a wary smile. 'Thank you.'

Two weeks later I had a request for a reference from one of the big independents, who were looking for a production secretary for one of their shows that was about to be re-commissioned. A long-form home-makeover programme. One of those ones where it's all about the big personalitied builders. It's been running for years. Probably on its last legs, but they wanted to offer her a nine-month contract, which is about as good as it gets in the freelance world. I recommended her highly, said she would be a great asset to their team.

A few days later I received a card from Bea telling me she had got the job. I gave it to Ashley to put up in reception.

Meanwhile we advertised for a new assistant.

'What are you looking for?' Anne Marie said to me as we sat shivering outside a local café, cups of coffee in front of us. She had a notebook out. Pen poised.

'Someone who's not going to run round shagging the commissioners,' I said and she gave me a look. Very funny.

I had been thinking hard about this. Did I value efficiency over loyalty? Would I forgive someone a few typos if I knew there was no chance of them sleeping with my friend's husband? Not that she had one any more, but you know what I mean. Did it matter if we weren't friends, if we didn't have a laugh and an occasional drink together? No. Not at all.

'Assuming I can't have it all? Someone I can trust.'

'Well, let's not assume you can't have it all yet. There must be hundreds of good candidates out there.'

'Oh God,' I groaned. 'The thought of having to train someone up.'

'I know you won't be interested, but Ashley wants to apply.'

My first instinct was to scoff. A few months before and I would probably have said, 'Ashley who?' I thought about it for a second, though. For weeks now Ashley had been more or less doing the job anyway. Keeping her head down, getting on with it quietly, manning reception at the same time. She hadn't fucked up anything yet as far as I had noticed. She hadn't done anything to piss me off either.

'Actually, that's a genius idea.'

Anne Marie looked surprised, as well she might. 'You're not just saying that because she's the devil you know? I've never thought you were that keen on her.'

'I just never really noticed she was there. Which I now realize might be a good thing.'

'We'll still have to advertise, so you don't have to decide now.'

'Shit, really?'

She nodded. 'That's good, though, because then if you went for her you'd know you hadn't just done so because she's the easy option.'

'OK. But unless someone brilliant walks through the door I'm thinking she's the right choice.'

'Well, that would make me very happy,' Anne Marie said, smiling. 'Now, what do you want to put in the ad?'

Of course you know what I'm going to say. After two days of mind-numbingly dull interviews we gave Ashley the job. She's an efficient, willing and supportive assistant. I like having her around. We don't shut ourselves in my office and put the world to rights, but I think that's a good thing. I don't tell her about my love life or ask her to go and buy me control underwear. We have proper boss/assistant boundaries. It's working.

At the beginning I put in the effort to make sure she knew the way I liked things done.

'Sort them by experience first, but then separate the piles into where they're based,' I said, handing her a pile of crew CVs.

'I know,' she said, with no edge in her voice. 'I used to do it for Bea.'

Turns out she used to do a lot of things for Bea. All the time I thought my assistant was the only person I could trust to get things right, it seems she was delegating half of it to an assistant of her own.

When Ashley gets me coffee it still doesn't taste as good as it did when Bea got it, though, but as flaws go, it's one I can live with.

Patrick and Michelle have severed all ties now that the house has been sold. To be fair to him he left her alone once he realized there was no hope. And, of course, once he found out she had told her father he probably thought there would be no reason to attempt a reconciliation anyway. I think he did love her, but not that much. She suited him – she was sweet and trusting and uncomplaining – but if she didn't come with a hefty job title attached she wasn't worth fighting for.

He's still clinging on to his position at the Home Improvement Channel, by the way, although I know that Julian has made it clear he would like him to leave. He's ordered the finance department to go through Patrick's expenses with a fine-tooth comb. Particularly to double-check the details where any claims for hotel rooms are concerned. There is no promise of a good reference for him. In fact, Julian now seems to relish bad-mouthing him to whoever will listen. So his chances of being snapped up elsewhere are growing slim. I imagine he'll grasp on where he is until it becomes untenable. And then he'll probably have to take a step down. Do it the hard way.

He phoned me a few times after it all blew up. The first time I accidentally answered and then quickly cut him off again when he started hurling insults and accusations at me. Since then I've been more cautious. There have been messages, too. Always alluding to what happened between us. I've ignored them all. I feel as if they're a trap he's setting, trying to get me to incriminate myself with my reply.

Lately I haven't heard anything from him, and I don't want to. For the time being Castle will not be pitching any new shows to Home Improvement. We'll live.

70

Bea

Production Secretary on series 8 of *DIY Heroes*. It's more exciting than it sounds. Actually, it's not really, unless you thought you might never get a job in the TV industry again, in which case it's the Holy Grail. I'm grateful. It's more than I deserve.

It films in Manchester and they have told me I have to be 'Manchester based' (which means that they don't care where I really live, they won't pay for my accommodation) so I decided to give up my flat with Ali and Sarah and rent a room in a shared place up there. There's nothing to keep me in London, and it's good to be flexible in this business. Now I'm living in a room in a terraced house near Salford, with Katya and Lindsay for flatmates. I haven't really got to know them yet, I haven't had time.

My new ethos is work, work, work. Get noticed. Get promoted. Don't get involved in anything that will fuck it up. The hours are long but I'm grateful. I don't want to spend too much time staring at the walls of my new place.

Patrick has finally stopped calling. The second phone is long gone, obviously, but for weeks my proper mobile buzzed with missed (for which read 'ignored') calls from 'Ben'. I didn't answer any of them. Deleted the texts. He's a part of my history I have no desire to revisit.

Men in any shape or form are off the agenda for a while. I need to focus on me and my career. Everything else can wait.

I never thought I'd say it but I miss Tamsin. I've finally realized that as bosses go she was pretty good. Up there with the best probably.

71

Tamsin

In the immediate aftermath I relied heavily on Adam. Michelle stayed with me for a couple of weeks while she looked for a place of her own to rent. It was almost like being in our early twenties again, but with added crying.

Adam traipsed over from the other side of London every night, bringing bottles of wine and more takeaway. Having him around was like switching on one of those plug-in air fresheners that are supposed to calm your mood. Or does that only work for cats?

Because I was feeling edgy and Michelle was – understandably – a bit of a basket case, there was a danger we might rub each other up the wrong way. We came close to arguing a couple of times when we were on our own, something that was unheard of for the two of us. Nothing significant, just snipey irritations, as if we couldn't work out how to communicate with each other in such close quarters. I think we both started to look forward to Adam's visits for a bit of light relief. It was as if we needed permission to laugh and relax and pretend that everything was OK.

I won't lie, my crush racked up a notch every day. Who needs cheekbones when you could have a relationship based on being friends first? Suddenly the idea of being with someone so kind, caring, so uncomplicated seemed like the sexiest thing ever. I had even come round to the fact that he wanted a horde of kids. I'd grown to love the ones I had conjured up in my head. Happy, chubby, mischievous mini-Adams with a wicked sense of humour and a kind streak a mile thick.

I tried to rein it in, but I started to feel awkward around him. Self-conscious. I would find myself daydreaming at inappropriate moments, and then I would blush the next time I saw him, as if he could read my thoughts.

He, meanwhile, continued to be exactly as he had always been. Funny, insulting, teasing, thoughtful. Nothing in his behaviour said that he reciprocated my feelings. I knew I was going to have to confront it sometime, but I was so scared of frightening him off, so worried at the prospect of losing his friendship, that I kept backing out at the last minute.

I didn't even tell Michelle how I felt. I'd spent so much time telling her – truthfully at the time – all the ways in which I didn't fancy Adam that now that I did, I couldn't quite admit it. Besides, he was so wrong for me, so unlikely, that I thought she might laugh. Not that that would have been a bad thing. She needed things to laugh at.

Something else happened around this time that took my mind off it, too. Guilt kicked in. Not that I hadn't already been feeling guilty. I was bursting with it. But suddenly it became my major preoccupation. Not the guilt about what had happened, so much – although obviously that was there – but about the fact that I was still deceiving Michelle. She had no idea what I'd done to her, what her best friend was capable of. It wasn't fair to let her trust me and rely on me when I wasn't trustworthy or reliable. I became overwhelmed with the urge to tell her the truth. It was like a nagging voice in my head every time Patrick's name came up in conversation. I knew it would be a horrible mistake. I knew it would mean she and I could no longer be friends. But I didn't see how we could be friends if I didn't tell her, either. Friends don't treat each other like that.

'Where has this come from?' Adam said as we sipped beers in The George before collecting our Chinese from Weng Wah House on Haverstock Hill.

'I don't know. It's just so wrong for me not to have told her and now I can't shake the thought. I'm scared I'm going to blurt it out one day.'

'She'd be devastated.'

'I know. But is that a reason not to tell her?'

He fiddled with a beer mat on the table in front of him. 'I thought everything we did was to make sure she never found out about you and Patrick.'

'It was. But now I think that was selfish. It was about protecting myself as much as her.'

'What's the difference?'

'I don't think it's right. She's my best mate. I shouldn't have lied to her.'

'But if you tell her, not only do you lose her but you'll break her heart.'

I know he's right but it doesn't seem that simple any more. 'I don't think I can stop myself. I keep getting this overwhelming urge to confess.'

He looked me directly in the eye and I went slightly weak at the knees. I think I even blushed. Great.

'Here's what I think. Telling her would be selfish. In some weird masochistic way it would make you feel better. Your conscience would be clear. But Michelle would feel worse. Much worse.'

'But she deserves to know the truth.'

'What she definitely doesn't deserve is to lose her husband and then lose her best friend in the space of a few weeks. The kind thing to do would be to keep it to yourself.'

'Really? Do you think so?'

'I know so.'

'What if I can't?'

'You have to. So you feel shit, so what? This isn't about you. It's about putting things right.'

'How did you get to be so fucking clever?'

He raised his eyebrows. 'I'm a teacher, I know everything.'

He looked at his watch. 'We should go. Our prawn balls will be getting cold. It'll get easier once she moves into her own place, trust me. You're spending too much time together, so it's impossible to act normally.'

'I wish you'd been my teacher. I might have listened more.'

'OK,' he said, standing up. 'That is quite a weird thing to say.'

'I bet your kids love you, though.'

'They call me Pillsbury. After the Pillsbury Dough Boy. I'm sure that must be a sign of affection and respect, yes.'

I snorted. 'They don't!'

'Oh but they do. Not to my face, obviously. Behind my back, but very loudly so I can hear. It's dreadfully wounding. Bullying, really. I should sue the local authority.'

'Ha! Can I call you that?'

He pulled a wounded expression. 'Definitely not. I'm already scarred for life.'

On the way home I thought about how nice it would be to slip my hand into his. How safe.

I almost did it too.

72

Tamsin

'I've got to tell you something.'

This was last weekend, a couple of months after Michelle's split from Patrick.

Michelle had been up and down, but gradually the ups had started to win out. It finally felt as if she had put Patrick and her failed marriage behind her. I was still eaten up by guilt, but I had taken Adam's advice. Nothing could be gained by Michelle finding out the truth. However much I felt I wanted to exorcise that particular ghost, I had to learn to live with it. It had got easier with time. I was almost able to forget it had ever even happened for days at a stretch.

We were back at the spa. This time it was her treat – no doubt because that way she knew I wouldn't be able to say no. We were in the sauna, red-faced and sweating. She had waited until the two other women who were in there with us left.

'What?'

'I feel stupid.'

I can't stand when people tease me with a trailer instead of cutting straight to the main event.

'About what? Just tell me.'

'OK. You have to promise not to laugh. Or to say anything.'

'Mich, I am going to kill you if you don't just tell me what you're on about.'

She sat up and looked at me. 'I think I like Adam.'

For a second I didn't quite take in what she was saying. Of course she liked Adam. Adam was great. Then it hit me. She LIKED him. The same way I LIKED him. This was my chance to own up that I did, too. Stake my claim.

'Say something,' she said. I looked at her and her eyes were shining. She looked animated in a way she hadn't done for months.'

'Wow!' I said. 'When did this happen?'

'I don't know. Is it ridiculous? It's ridiculous, isn't it?'

Yes. I thought. Please don't let her be serious.

'No. I mean . . . it's a surprise. I had no idea you even thought of him like that.'

'Neither did I. It's been creeping up on me, I think. He's just so . . . lovely.'

And kind. And sweet. And thoughtful. And funny.

'You fancy him?'

She actually flushed red. 'Yes. Like crazy.'

'Does he know?'

'No! God, no. Don't say anything.'

'I won't.' I wouldn't know what to say.

'I know you probably think I'm stupid. I mean, I know you think he's completely unfanciable . . .'

'I didn't say that.'

'You pretty much did after that first date you went on.'

That's because he's a grower, I thought. He's not going to knock anyone off their feet at first sight, but gradually he'll get under your skin by sheer force of personality. It's a much more insidious, much deeper kind of attraction.

'I think I just said he wasn't my type . . .'

'Anyway. What I'm saying is, I know he's not obviously drop dead gorgeous, but I happen to think he is. There. Now you can laugh at me.'

I didn't want to. I wanted to cry.

'No. I . . . I don't know what to say . . .'

'I know he's your friend really, so I wouldn't want you to think I was trying to muscle in . . .'

Every part of me wanted to scream, Please don't, I'm still only just coming to terms with how I feel about him myself. I had been building myself up to coming clean with him. Fantasizing about him reciprocating and us having a future. Why couldn't I have done it a week ago? The day before? Why couldn't I have confided in Michelle about how I was feeling?

Not that I had any evidence he would be anything other than horrified. I knew this was the main reason I had been so hesitant. Adam had never done anything to make me believe he had fallen in love with me as I had with him. Or even that he found me even halfway attractive.

And then it hit me. Michelle would be a much better match for Adam than me. Both of them deserved someone who would value what was so special about them. Who would treat them well and never cheat on them or lie to them.

And when I thought about it, I realized he probably liked her, too. He had been so attentive and supportive. He was always telling me how lovely she is and what a shit Patrick must be. I just didn't put the pieces together.

I took a long breath. Tried to stem the feeling of panic. Smiled. 'No. Go for it. I think you could be great together.'

73

Tamsin

Michelle was incapable of making the first move. Just the idea of it made her start to sweat.

'What if he laughs in my face? Or, worse, he's horrified.'

'He won't be. Just contrive to be on your own with him and go for it.'

My stomach turned over at the thought of it. I had thought about nothing else since she first confided in me. Adam taken by surprise, unable to believe his luck, touching her face, moving in for a kiss. My Adam.

I couldn't deny her this, though. Somehow if I gave up my hopes for me and Adam, stepped aside and gave Michelle my blessing, I would feel as if I'd paid my penance for what I'd done. I should have been brought up a Catholic really because I have an impressive capacity for guilt. Not that there's anything wrong with that. I deserve to feel guilty. But maybe if I could make things right in another way I could allow myself to ease up a little. Let myself off.

'Can't you sound him out a bit? Just get a sense of whether he thinks I'm a complete horror?'

'No. Please don't ask me to do that.'

'You don't have to make it obvious. Just get a sense . . . in theory . . .'

I remember when Michelle asked me to do this once

before. We were about fifteen. I couldn't think of what else to say so I just marched up to the boy and said, 'Do you fancy Michelle or not?'

Luckily he said yes. They ended up going out for a couple of months after that. This time it was more complicated. There were friendships to be compromised. Proper grown-up hearts to be broken. But there was also a chance that two people I loved could end up really happy.

I owed her.

'OK. I'll try. I'm not promising anything, though.'

'Don't give me away, will you?'

'Of course not. I'll be the height of subtlety.'

'I feel sick,' she said, and I thought, Me too.

Before I had a chance to put him on the spot, the three of us spent an evening together eating and drinking too much at Michelle's place. It was like Heart Attack Saturdays all over again, just with a change of personnel and venue. Somehow Michelle had managed to make her rented home feel like the place we all still wanted to congregate in. Cosy, warm, homey.

Adam was already there when I arrived, and I was relieved because I didn't want to have to fill Michelle in on my progress – which was none by the way. I hadn't seen Adam for a couple of days and it didn't seem like the kind of thing I could bring up on the phone. And besides, I was still trying to process the implications. To let go and give up the dream that had been quietly fermenting away inside me for weeks.

They were both beavering away in the kitchen when I let myself in. Radio turned up. Adam, wearing a Santa hat, doing a stupid little dance as he sliced tomatoes. Singing along to a Christmas carol. Michelle – who never sings – joining in with tuneless harmonies. I say kitchen, it's a corner of the living area given over to a couple of units, an oven, a fridge and a hob. It's smartly done but basic. Compared to Michelle's well-loved, lived-in space in Highgate anyway.

The first thing that struck me when I saw them side by side, both chopping something or other, was that they looked like a couple. A couple where he was punching well above his weight, but a couple nonetheless. They looked so comfortable together. He was saying something to make her laugh and she was looking at him with what I can only describe as adoration, warbling away. The knot in my stomach tightened.

'Evening,' I said and they both jumped. We all dissolved into fits. Me out of nerves, them from the shock of seeing me standing there, I imagine.

'OK. So I'm just going to walk out again and pretend I didn't see that.'

'He's teaching me the descant,' Michelle said, laughing.

'Oh! I thought you'd hurt yourself.'

She gave me a look. 'Very funny.'

'Here,' Adam said, ladling some evil-looking red stuff from a saucepan into a glass. 'We've made mulled wine.'

'It's only the second of December,' I said, accepting the warm glass.

'Exactly. It's December. That means it's Christmas.'

'Oh no. You're not one of those people, are you?'

'What people?'

I pulled a face. 'The month-of-forced-jollity brigade?'

'What can I say? I'm full of the joys of the season.'

'Don't mind Tam,' Michelle chipped in. 'She goes a bit Scrooge when it comes to Christmas.'

'That is so not true. I love Christmas. I just love it *at* Christmas. Not for weeks before.'

'Well, I warn you,' Adam butted in, 'I am going to be unbearable, then, because I can't get enough of·it.'

'That's what comes of spending all your time with teenagers,' I said, reaching over and picking up a cucumber to slice. 'You have arrested development.'

'Adam's helping teach the school choir for their carol concert,' Michelle said, like a proud parent.

'Jesus Christ. I thought most of the kids you taught were basically feral.'

'They are. But they get to miss maths for a week to come and rehearse. You'd be surprised how many of them have discovered a love of singing. You're welcome to come, by the way.'

'I think I'm busy that night.'

He laughed. 'I haven't told you when it is yet.'

'I know. Just assume I'm busy every night. Very, very busy.'

'Well I'd love to come,' Michelle said and Adam flashed her a smile that spoke volumes.

'Great,' he said. 'I can show you my chair in the staff room. It's very exciting.'

'God, I need to sit down.'

Adam was on a fitness drive. This involved him joining me and Ron on walks to Primrose Hill, and occasionally running round in a big circle while I sat on a bench and watched. A delighted Ron trotted after him, tail wagging, tongue hanging out. Both of them panting. It was a bit like having two dogs.

It was paying off, too. He looked a little firmer round the jaw. I wanted to tell him not to go too far. He was perfect as he was. But it was nothing to do with me any more. Not that it ever had been, except in my fantasies.

I had been trying to find an in to the Michelle conversation for a few days. I didn't know if I kept putting it off because I was scared of fucking it up or because I was scared of what might happen next.

'You're trying to do too much too soon. You have to build up to it.'

'Says the expert.' He flopped down beside me, Ron at his feet.

'Actually, I have lost a couple of pounds lately. No idea why, though. Really I was just trying to give you an excuse to stop.'

'Ah. In which case you're an authority and I need to do what you say.'

'I have a date tomorrow night,' I said as we sat staring off into the distance. I didn't. I was using this as a segue into the talk I really wanted to have, but also because I thought it might be an idea to put a full stop on it if – and I really didn't think this was the case – Adam was harbouring any of the same clandestine thoughts about us as me.

Since Michelle's revelation I had been trying to wean myself off my crush. I had been pointing out all of Adam's faults to myself. Reminding myself that physically I would not have looked at him twice before I got to know him. I couldn't tell if it was working. I still felt the urge to reach out and grab his fingerless gloved hand, but maybe it didn't feel as overwhelming as it had done. I wasn't sure.

What was stupid was I didn't even know if he liked Michelle. If I found out he wasn't interested maybe I could still hold out hope for myself. Eventually. So it wouldn't feel like I was stepping in and stealing him from under her nose. I knew he should like her, though. If he knew what was good for him.

'Other Half?'

'Yup.'

'Excellent,' he said. 'Tell me all about him. Good sense of humour? Must love dogs?'

'God knows. He looks OK in his picture. Works in the theatre. That's about it.'

'What's his name?'

'Um . . . Tim. Or Tom. Something like that. I don't know why I'm going, really.'

'Find out first, won't you? Because calling him by the wrong name really isn't the way to a man's heart.'

'How about you? Any action?'

He shook his head. 'No.'

I felt a rush of relief, and then I remembered why I was there. Here goes. 'I was wondering whether to suggest Michelle try it.'

He laughed. 'Because of how successful we've been?'

'Exactly. Do you think it's too soon for her to be dating again?'

'God, no. Although she might think so.'

'I wouldn't think she'd need to go online, though. I mean, she's so attractive . . .'

I waited. Tried to gauge his reaction.

'Mmm.'

Great. Very conclusive.

I tried again. 'Maybe we should try and think of someone for her. Do you know any nice men?'

'That's always a disaster, don't you think? Our idea of who's nice might be her worst nightmare.'

'She needs someone kind. Someone who'll be good to her. She doesn't care about looks,' I added hastily. Did I imagine it? Did his ears prick up a bit at that last remark?

'I'd say Patrick was up there in the looks department. Isn't he? Although I'm not an expert on men's sex appeal. I always thought John Stapleton was sexy.'

'What? Anyway – exactly. And look at what a shit he turned out to be. Patrick that is. Not John Stapleton. Besides, Michelle's never really cared about any of that. Patrick was just an aberration.'

He pulled the sleeve of his hoody down over his hand. It had turned cold. 'I think Michelle's too good for Other Half.'

'Unlike us, you mean?

He laughed. 'Right. I can't imagine her dealing with all the bullshit.'

'You're on there. You turned out to be who you said you were. Apart from the very amicable divorce bit.'

He raised an eyebrow. 'How do you know? I could have a wife and six children squirrelled away somewhere. Or be a serial killer. Just one who likes to get to know his victims very, very well first.'

'Oh I always assumed both those things about you. You're right about Michelle, though. She's way too trusting. She needs to meet someone the old-fashioned way.'

'Maybe you should encourage her to . . . I don't know . . . join a salsa class or something.'

Oh, for God's sake. 'What about you? You're single. And normal. Ish.'

He snorted. 'She's not going to want to go on a date with me.'

'Would you want to, though? I mean, if she did?'

'She wouldn't.'

'Hypothetically.'

'I'd have thought Michelle could pretty much have her pick of—'

'For Christ's sake, Adam! Do you fancy her or not, because she does you . . .'

That shut him up.

'And if you don't that's obviously fine, but please don't tell her I just out and out told you, because I was supposed to be subtle.'

'Well, that went well.' He had a little smile on his face and I knew that any ideas I'd been harbouring about me and him together were over.

'And if you do think you like her and you end up getting together, just know that if you do anything to hurt her I will kill you.'

'Trust me, I've seen what you're like when someone crosses you . . .'

'When someone crosses Mich. There's a difference.'

'Does she really . . . ? I mean . . .'

I nodded. 'God knows why.'

'Desperation?' he said, and that made me laugh.

'Probably. You're interested then?'

'God, yes. She's lovely. I just never thought . . .'

'I mean it, Adam. Don't ask her out unless you really think there's something there. Beyond the obvious.'

'I think she's pretty perfect.'

'And you have to let me hang out with the two of you and not feel like some kind of spare part saddo.'

'Oh God. It won't make any difference to us, will it? You're my best mate.'

Was I? I took in what he said and tried it on for size. Discovered I liked it.

'Not if we don't let it.'

'Never. I mean, I can imagine a beautiful life with Michelle and babies and happiness, but I'd still need someone to sit in the pub and moan about the wife to every now and then.'

'I look forward to it.'

He looked at me. He had finally stopped sweating. 'This isn't some kind of elaborate wind-up is it?'

I rolled my eyes.

'Wow. So what do I do? Ask her on a date?'

'I think that's how it works.'

'As my Year Eights would say, "Shit just got real."'

'That's because they're thirteen-year-old halfwits. You, on the other hand, are an articulate forty-two-year-old man, so please don't.'

'True dat.'

I snorted. 'OK. I'm leaving now. Call me when you hit puberty.'

I stood up, clipped Ron's lead onto his collar.

'I'm heading home for a shower,' Adam said. 'I'll call you later.'

He gave me a hug. Slapped me on the back. I did the same in return.

74

Tamsin

Both Michelle and Adam have insisted that I join them later, even though I tried to protest that crashing their first date was a bit extreme, even for me. In response, Michelle announced they were intending to have a meal at the tapas place on Haverstock Hill that is in walking distance of my flat, and that they were planning on dropping round afterwards whether I liked it or not.

I've spent the evening watching TV, wrapping the odd Christmas present (some chocolate-scented body butter for Anne Marie, a scarf from Ted Baker for Ian) and both thinking about and trying not to think about what's happening down the road.

My inappropriate crush on Adam is receding, but it's not fully gone yet. I can't quite let go of the picture I'd created of future us laughing our way into old age. I just have to adjust it. Tweak the dial. Because have no doubt, if he and Michelle decide to go for it there is no chance I will ever be found half naked rolling round on my sofa with him. Even if he wanted to, which he doesn't and never would. Do I think I'd ever have to worry about Adam being loyal to her? Not for a moment. That man is made out of principles.

I can't ever take back what I did with Patrick, but now

I feel as though I can make amends. I can bring together the two people I love most in the world and watch them forge a happy future. The thought of it makes me cry, but it makes me feel good, too. I'm doing the right thing.

And let's face it, in the long run Michelle will be ten times happier with Adam than she ever could have been with Patrick, so maybe I did her a favour. Not that I imagine she would ever see it like that.

Do I worry that Adam will ever reveal my secret to her? Not for a second. It would hurt her too much and there's no way he would let that happen.

The doorbell rings and Ron jumps up and starts to run round in circles. I buzz them in and I know as soon as I see their faces that it's gone well. They look like two excited children on Christmas Eve. Knowing without a doubt that there are treats on the horizon.

I wait for a pang of envy. Instead I feel a warm glow. A proud parent.

'So?' I say before they've even taken their coats off.

'Awful,' Adam says. 'I forgot that I've only ever seen Michelle when you've been there, too. When you're not she's like a completely different person. Racist. Homophobic. She called one of the waiters a snivelling little pleb because he dropped her napkin . . .'

Michelle squeals her disapproval. 'Obviously none of that is true.'

I join in. 'Well you did once tell a taxi driver he was a lowlife piece of dog shit because he went up Fitzjohns Avenue instead of through Primrose Hill.'

'I did not!' She turns to Adam laughing. 'That never happened.'

Adam tuts theatrically, shakes his head. 'It's always the ones you least expect.'

Michelle ignores him. 'I'm having a glass of wine. Anyone else?'

She pours for all of us and we flop down – me on the armchair, Adam and Michelle next to each other on the sofa. At one point one of them – I don't see which – slips their hand into the other's. I feel happy, sad, envious and relieved all at once. A cocktail of conflicting emotions.

Ron hauls himself up onto the chair next to me, huffing and puffing with the effort. He snuggles in the space between me and the arm, head on my lap, and starts snoring almost immediately. I ruffle his wiry ears.

'Oh, Adam and I are going to go Christmas shopping at Selfridges after work tomorrow, do you want to come?' Michelle says. 'We could eat in St Christopher's Place somewhere.'

'Oh . . . I'm not sure . . .' I know they want to be inclusive, to show me that them getting together doesn't mean I'm out in the cold, but I don't want to get in the way of their blossoming romance.

'You have to,' Adam says. 'That way Mich can shop and we can moan.'

Michelle pulls a face at him. 'And you have to be there to help me choose something for Mum and Dad.'

'OK. But don't start thinking you have to invite me along on all of your dates because that would be weird.'

'Just the really intimate ones,' Adam says.

Before they leave – Adam is taking her home before heading off himself as he has school in the morning. And I don't imagine either of them are sex-on-the-first-date people – Michelle and I are on our own for a couple of minutes while he's in the loo.

'You had a good time then?'

She looks at me. Eyes shining. 'It was lovely. I felt so comfortable. There was none of that first-date awkwardness.'

'Because you know him so well already.'

'Exactly. I feel so happy. Really properly happy for the first time in ages.'

'Well, you deserve to be.'

'It's funny how things work out, isn't it?'

'Sometimes you have to go through all the shit to get to the gravy.'

'Descartes?' She laughs.

'One of Adam's pupils, I think.'

'Very profound.'

They leave in a flurry of coats and scarves and promises to meet up tomorrow. I pour myself another glass of wine, settle on the sofa with Ron. I feel relaxed in a way I haven't done for months. The nagging, self-loathing voice in my head seems finally to have stopped. I sit down at my computer. Log on to Other Half.

I look down at Ron, scratch his head and he sighs with ecstasy.

I feel OK.

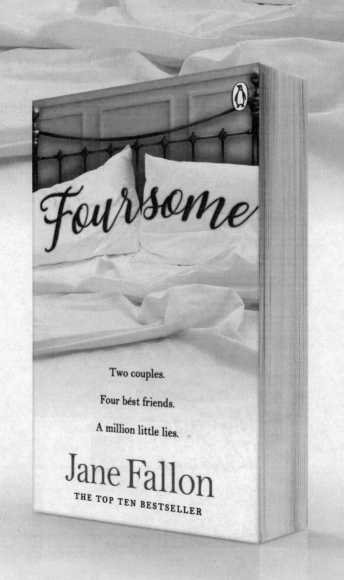

Rebecca, Daniel, Alex and Isabel have been
best friends since university. Rebecca married
Daniel, Alex married Isabel and, for twenty
years, they have been inseparable.

But all that is about to change . . .

Sometimes there's a good reason for behaving badly.

Discover the biting new novel from Jane Fallon.